WINTER'S WRATH

DIMINISHED

BIANCA SOMMERLAND

Acknowledgements

Another year has gone by and I still can't believe how lucky I am to be living the life I've always dreamed of. It might not be as glamorous as I'd imagined it would be as a little girl, but I wouldn't trade it for anything. I am here because of not only my hard work, but the love and support of some of the best people I've ever known.

Cherise, we've got to stop meeting like this! Lol! Seriously, though, your guidance never fails to strengthen the stories a push me to reach deeper, reveal more, and truly let the character's voices be heard.

To Heather, thank you for encouraging me every step of the way. Your friendship means so much to me and I can't wait to see you again.

Stacey, you are family. The kind of family who has your back through the most difficult times, who celebrates your accomplishments. Who always makes you feel as though you're enough. One that's chosen because we have a bond that's stronger than blood.

In other words, I love you and I'm keeping you forever! <3

As always, I will end this with a note to my girls. I want to tell you to stop growing so fast, but, at the same time, I'm eager to see all you will accomplish. You're both strong, beautiful young women with big hearts and an inner strength I'm so proud of. Some days will be hard, but don't forget who you are. Intelligent, loving, and unstoppable. The world belongs to people like you. Don't let anything stand in your way.

Also by Bianca Sommerland

"There is a crack in everything, that's how the light gets in."

~Leonard Cohen

THAT WHICH WE CALL

Snow falling as you drift,
Farther and Farther away.
Pulse slows
But did your heart ever beat at all?

Come closer,
Please don't fall
Fall farther and farther away.
I need you now.
Need you more every day.

What's in a name?
A promise never kept,
Deceit so high.
The pedestal where we buried you,
With flowers in the snow.

Come closer,
Please don't fall
Fall farther and farther away.
I need you now.
Need you more every day.

Let me pretend,
Make it a new game.
You were the man I looked up to,
So alone.
Never found,
But I'll never stop searching.
For you in my reflection.

Chapter One

The bitter cold of the morning seeped into the room, chilling and refreshing all at once. Shiori Ayase pulled on the black leather duster jacket she'd found at a vintage store earlier that week, long enough to cover her simple, snug black dress and keep her warm. Black stiletto boots and her outfit was complete.

And would get her out of the house for her interview without an interrogation. If she could reach the bus stop, she could handle whatever the world threw at her.

She slipped out of her bedroom and walked the twenty-two steps along the carpeted hall, holding tight to her purse strap so the metal chains wouldn't jingle. A flash from the living room doorway, followed by the theme song for Sesame Street told her Hiro was awake. He'd be fine with his cartoons while she was gone, but she didn't want him to hear her leaving. If he fussed and woke her stepfather, the man would demand to know where she was going.

She managed to get the front door open without so much as a click before soft, padded footsteps sounded behind her.

"Where are you off to?"

Shiori planted a calm smile on her lips and turned to face her stepfather's girlfriend, Elizabeth. "Just a job interview."

The tall, slender brunette looked her over, her brows lifting as though she was ready to question Shiori's words. Then she smirked. "Good. You're too old to still be living off Brian. Are you thinking of moving out?"

That was a tricky question to answer. Shiori would have moved out a long time ago if it wasn't for Hiro, but Elizabeth was convinced that she stayed because she was too lazy to get a job. Nothing Shiori said would change her mind, so she didn't bother explaining herself anymore.

And if she wanted to get out of the house before her stepfather woke up, she needed to keep the conversation short.

So she simply shrugged. "If I get the job, I might. Wish me luck?"

"Good luck." Elizabeth rolled her eyes. "Not to be a bitch, but it's about damn time."

Not bothering to answer, Shiori stepped out onto the front walkway, closing the door softly behind her. She hurried through the fresh white snow covering the sidewalk, reaching the bus stop with a few minutes to spare.

Only once she'd taken a seat on the bus heading to downtown Detroit did she let herself relax. She plugged her earbuds into her phone and slipped them in her ears, closing her eyes as the music pulled her in.

She'd listened to this album over and over since it came out. Her best friend, since high school, Wendy, had pre-ordered the album with a whole fan pack—T-shirts, guitar pick, phone cover—last month for Shiori's twentieth birthday. They both loved the music, but Wendy follow the band almost religiously. She'd been over the moon about the interview, convinced that Shiori would definitely get the contract and would soon have backstage passes to hand out.

If Shiori got the job and had access to passes, she would get Wendy one. But she didn't consider anything in life a sure thing. And even if she got the contract, could she take it? Wendy knew all her plans, and most of the reasons behind them, but she didn't understand why Shiori was afraid to leave her nephew for any length of time.

Elizabeth might hate Shiori, but she was good with Hiro. He loved her and he'd be taken care of if Shiori was gone for a few weeks.

But her stepfather was a different story. Elizabeth thought he was an amazing man, taking care of his stepdaughter on his own for so long, as well as the child of the other stepdaughter who'd lost her life so young. In her eyes, the man was a saint.

Just thinking of her big sister brought tears to Shiori's eyes. Kyoko had Hiro when she was only sixteen, but while she was pregnant, she'd still had so many plans for their future. She wanted to get a place somewhere. Take Shiori with her. And leave the life they'd been trapped in since their mother's death.

She gotten to hold her son only once as her small, delicate body lost the last of the strength she'd retained during the difficult pregnancy.

"Promise me you'll take care of him, Shiori. That he'll never...that what happened to us will never happen to him."

"I promise." Shiori had taken Hiro into her arms as the doctors and nurses rushed around her, one drawing her aside as they tried to save her sister.

The doctor had warned Kyoko that she might not survive bringing the baby to term. Shiori watched them, helpless, knowing her sister was already gone.

Kyoko hadn't cared about the risk. She loved Hiro's father and used all her strength to cling to the only part of him she had left. Asking Shiori to care for their child had meant more than her own survival. Once Shiori said the words, Kyoko let go.

I would have taken care of him no matter what.

Keeping her promise to her sister hadn't been hard, but Hiro was getting older. Almost six now. Another year or so and she might not be able to protect him. The casting call had come at the perfect time. Her stepfather was going to Taiwan for a couple months to negotiate a business merger. There was nothing holding her back.

Wendy had called her, freaking out when she saw the post involving their favorite band.

"*Diverse Faces, Shiori! You'd be perfect for this!*" *Wendy laughed, happy even though she had to be a little jealous.* "*Too bad they're not looking for a cute, short, pudgy redhead. I'd so try out!*"

"*Oh stop it, you're beautiful.*" *Shiori read the article on the heavy metal site, which speculated on why the band would need another model on such short notice. Her pulse quickened as she clicked on the link to the agency and filled out the application. She'd left the link open until the next day, bringing her laptop to Wendy's house so her best friend could read over all she'd written and take a few pictures to upload.* "*There's gonna be girls all over the country applying. I'll try, but there's no guarantee I'll get in.*"

"*But you deserve it! Shiori, listen to me. None of them are you and you have an advantage.*" *Wendy bit her bottom lip.* "*Maybe if you tell them everything, they'll—*"

"*No.*" *Shiori clicked send on what she'd put together and set her laptop aside.* "*What if they say something? I won't risk it. If this doesn't work, I'll find another way.*"

"*What if you can't?*" *Wendy frowned, her smooth, freckled forehead creasing with concern.* "*This isn't only your chance to get away, Shiori. It's his.*"

Shiori's throat tightened. "*I know. And I…I'll think about it, okay? But if I'm not a good fit, any story I might tell them won't change that.*"

Wendy had let it go at that. She imagined a much better future for Shiori than she'd ever considered for herself, but her enthusiasm helped Shiori get a little wrapped up in the dream. Maybe tomorrow would be better. Maybe she could actually change her life.

Hope could be painful, so she didn't lean on it too much. Tonight, she'd be coming home to the same life she'd been living since she was a little girl. Being ignored was usually the best scenario. Being noticed was bad.

But today, she *needed* to be noticed. To stand apart.

The bus pulled up to her stop and she quickly made her way onto the curb. Double checked the address, then headed into the office building. Getting past the first stage, where she'd actually been invited for an interview, was a big deal. Even if she didn't get the job she wanted, she might have other opportunities.

Could she take them, though? A chance to give Hiro a better life—even if she had to leave him for a short while—was worth just about anything. But money alone didn't guarantee that.

The receptionist smiled at her and waved her on, instructing her to go to the waiting room on the eighth floor. Shiori took the elevator up, slipped her jacket off, and folded it over her arm. She stepped out, looking around at the clean, crisp white and glass room, with photos of models on every wall. Her eyes went wide as she took them in.

Every picture portrayed a woman that defied the typical standards of beauty. Many magazines still had blue eyed, blond women on the cover, but these images made them seem plain. There was a black woman in several pictures whose fierce gaze alone made her impossible to forget. Another prominent picture was of an older Chinese woman whose smile lit up the whole room. A picture of an Indian woman, with a *bindi* mark on her forehead, hung on the wall behind the desk in the center of the room. As stunning as every woman on display.

Did Shiori really belonged here? Sure, she was pretty. Being pretty hadn't worked in her favor since she was little. She wasn't as smart as people assumed she would be. Even well-meaning teachers asked if her parents expected better than the grades she managed.

Her stepfather didn't care about grades. So long as she didn't do bad enough for teachers to annoy him, he was satisfied. She'd learned how to make his coffee in the morning, to be sweet and quiet. He considered that traditional enough. She was his good little girl. Pretty and submissive. What more could a man want from a daughter?

Her own father would have expected more. She told herself so all the time, even though he'd died before she was born. Maybe he would have been one of those fathers who went to violin recitals and smiled when his child played perfectly. Or showed up at teacher/parent interviews, asking how his child could improve in math or science.

She had Japanese friends who complained that their parents always wanted them to do better. And she'd give anything to be one of them. Her grandparents had been like that with her mother, and she'd always spoken fondly of them. Even after they disowned her for marrying Shiori's stepfather.

They'd hated the man. Had wanted better for their daughter. And, in some way, even her mother had believed them cutting her off had been out of love. But she'd chosen a man over her family.

And refused to admit she'd made a mistake until her very last breath.

"Shiori?" A tall, black woman, in a charcoal-colored suit, came into the waiting room, pulling Shiori from her thoughts. She smiled when Shiori looked up, holding out her hand as Shiori approached her. "A pleasure to meet you. Please come with me."

She led Shiori to an office down a long hall, lined with various pictures of the agencies models. Shiori spotted a portrait of the model who worked with the band and inhaled roughly. After just a few months in the music scene, the model's face could be recognized anywhere. She'd done perfume ads with a member of the band. Several magazine spreads. A music video that was already considered one of the most impressive in the business in recent years.

If Shiori got the job, she'd be working with her. And despite all her other reasons for wanting the contract with the band, one of the most personal was that she really wanted to meet the woman. Ever since she'd first heard of Danica Tallien, she'd admired her. There were rumors of Danica dating one of the members of the band, but none shadowed the impression she'd made with her presence in the music scene. She wasn't the first model to step on stage during a heavy metal performance, but few had made as big of an impact as she had.

Her beginning as a child star, then her return as a fierce performer, set her apart.

The office Shiori stepped into had walls of glass. She shut the door carefully, intimidated by the knowledge any who walked by could see her. Maybe one of those famous models? She focused on the room. A modern office, with a sharply defined black desk and two art deco, red padded metal chairs sitting in front of it. Suitable for the CEO of one of the leading agencies in the fashion world.

"Shiori, please have a seat and make yourself comfortable. My name is Sophie." The woman motioned Shiori to one of the chairs. "I'll assume you read the email and know your profile will be done here once we've spoken, since you don't have one already. I don't want you to feel overwhelmed, but things move fast here. I called you in because I think you have the look my agency needs. You applied specifically for this casting call, but are you interested in other work if we find something for you?"

Well, at least she wasn't beating around the bush. Not that Shiori had the first idea how to answer that question. She wasn't aiming for another job, but would she turn one down?

She smiled her practiced smile and met Sophie's level gaze. "To be honest, I came into this hoping to fill the spot you'd made the casting call for, but I think I'd be willing to consider other options."

"You *think* you'd be willing to consider them?" Sophie took a seat behind her desk, her eyes fixed on Shiori's face. "Why do you want to work with Winter's Wrath, Shiori? Very few models would even consider getting on stage with a band as a way to start their career."

"But Danica Tallien did and you represent her. From what I've read she signed on with them to change her image."

"She did, but she already had an impressive portfolio. Only, she was seen as a child star and that wasn't helping her move forward. You don't have that issue." Sophie placed her hands on her desk, her eyes narrowing. "You're a beautiful young woman, Shiori. I could find you work. But you implied being on stage with the band was what you wanted, more than anything."

"It is."

"Why?"

Not easy to answer, without revealing too much. Or looking like a desperate fan. Shiori clasped her hands on her lap and took a deep breath. "There are…personal reasons, but I don't want them to matter. I want the job because you think I'm the best for it. The rest? I…I don't know. I didn't plan that far ahead."

"But you did plan something?" Sophie's frown drew lines in her forehead. She shook her head. "Shiori, I will tell you this. I need to see you dance. See you with the band before I make my decision. That said, they've had more than their share of drama. I'm not ready to sign up for more."

Drama? Shiori hadn't considered that. And maybe she should have. The headlines about the band had been nasty for a while before the press got bored. Drugs, sex and violence sells. They could have used the tawdry gossip to their advantage.

Instead, they ignored the speculation and focused on their new album. On creating cutting edge music videos that reached their core audience and kept fans begging for more.

They were known for their talent and worked hard to keep it that way.

Shiori's presence could change all that. Sophie deserved the whole story. And a promise it wouldn't be the next headline.

Media attention wouldn't save Shiori. Or Hiro.

But the job just might.

"I don't want the spotlight…" Shiori ducked her head as Sophie arched a brow. "Okay, on stage, yes. I want to be *seen*. But I want people to love the band. And I'm good with being a pretty prop."

"Oh, sweetie. You'll be so much more." Sophie reached across the desk and took Shiori's hands in hers. "If it helps, there is a non-disclosure clause in your contract. Which works both ways. Anything you tell me remains between us."

Saying she didn't need a clause in her contract to trust Sophie would be easy, the woman was a wonderful mix of professional and approachable, something she hadn't expected.

Shiori had read so much about different models, how they got into the industry, horror stories of being manipulated by their agents. Danica's Instagram posts covered some of her journey, showing her on tour with the band, her trips around the world to different fashion events whose coordinators competed for a chance to have her make an appearance. And scattered among those posts were pictures of her and Sophie, with captions that showed how close they were.

Danica spoke of Sophie as though she was family. Something between a maternal figure and a close friend.

What must it be like to have someone like that in your life? Shiori couldn't even imagine. And didn't dare to. Not yet.

But she could have someone who'd work hard to give her a successful career. Who'd have her best interest at heart. It was no secret Sophie did that for all her models, giving that personal touch which made her one of the best in the industry.

Her future would be in Sophie's capable hands.

After she gave the woman a glimpse of her past.

"I hope this doesn't change your opinion of me. Or ruin my chances to work with the band." Shiori took a deep breath. "I'm not sure where to begin. Or…or maybe I am. I should tell you about my sister. Because as much the opportunity to work with the band means to me…I need to do this for her."

Chapter Two

Another crumpled paper filled with lame attempts at lyrics. Five new songs to write and this one had become an obsession. Brave Trousseau slumped on the leather sofa spanning the front lounge of the tour bus. The noise from the other bands hustling around the parking lot outside wasn't helping him brainstorm. He tossed his notepad on the cushion beside him.

I fucking hate that bastard. Why write a song about him?

Worst thing was, no one had asked him to. Well, no one besides Winter's Wrath's ex-manager who was stuck in prison for the next three-to-five. That son-of-a-bitch had insisted a song about the 'tragic' death of the eldest Trousseau brother, Valor, would bring a spike in sales.

His other ideas for publicity almost ended the life of Brave's younger brother, Alder, so fuck what he thought.

Still, Brave couldn't shake the urge to write the song. And nothing else seemed to inspire him. With a studio deadline looming he didn't have time for writer's block, but there was no way around it.

The front door to the bus opened, bringing in more noise. He looked over to see Jesse Vaughn, their new tour manager and longtime roadie, climb up the steps with a clipboard in one hand and a cigarette in the other.

"No fucking smoking on the bus." Brave scowled at the slight quirk of Jesse's lips, but at least the man tossed his cigarette out on the curb. "And I'm good on time, so don't get on my ass."

"Wouldn't dream of it." Jesse chuckled as Brave ground his teeth, making the innuendo even more obvious. He stepped up to the dinette across from Brave, setting down the clipboard before turning to face him. "You asked for an update on the security detail. Their van's still stuck on the side of the highway—they gotta wait for Triple A. Your bodyguards won't be here in time."

"Cancel the show." Brave took a deep breath, rising slowly as Jesse shook his head. "This isn't up for discussion."

"No. It isn't."

I'm about to knock this asshole's teeth in. They were in Detroit for the first time since Alder had been stabbed. No fucking way in hell was the band getting on stage without bodyguards. Jesse claimed to love his brother, but he had a fucked up way of showing it.

"Brave, listen to me. I get it. Every goddamn time you guys hit the stage I'm watching the crowd, wondering..." Jesse rubbed a hand over his face. "It's been seven months. There are no new threats."

"You need one?" Brave fisted his hands by his sides, leaning heavily on his newfound restraint. "Not that we'd know if there's another psycho out there since Reese has all our mail screened."

"She does that so you don't have to stress about it." As usual, Jesse acted like Winter's Wrath's new manager walked on fucking water. Sure, she was great for the band, but she hadn't been there while Alder almost bled out on stage with a 'fan' holding a knife to his throat.

Seven months and everyone treated Alder's brush with death like old news. Everyone except Brave.

Recording the first few songs for their new album rather than going on the road had given Alder time to heal, and releasing a new single, along with a kickass music video, had kept the band relevant. Brave had delayed the tour as long as he could, but then Reese called a meeting to cement the importance of building off fan excitement. Avoid hitting a plateau.

The band took a vote.

And he'd surrendered to the overwhelming majority. Not that he'd had a choice, but the team of military trained bodyguards shadowing them seemed like a reasonable compromise.

Now they wanted him to give that up too?

Not happening.

He had one card to play. And he didn't think twice before tossing it on the table. "The band can't go perform without me."

"True... Alder could probably sing a few songs on his own, but the fans will be disappointed." Jesse glanced around, a thoughtful expression on his face. "You never mentioned how much the bus cost you. I know you're all making good money now, but I suspect our new house was cheaper."

'Our' was Jesse, Alder, and Danica Tallien—the band's stage performer. The happy trio had bought a nice little bungalow in upstate Michigan. Which they'd be renting out now that they were back on tour, because they were all about the purchase making good business sense.

Brave was fine with his old apartment. Investing in the band meant more to him. His first big paycheck on signing with their new label went to buying the bus, a slick 2014 Prevost XLII. A few of the guys had wanted to pitch in, but he needed to do this for them.

He'd almost destroyed the band once in a spectacular meltdown. Winter's Wrath was his whole world. And there was nothing he wouldn't do to prove it.

"Get to the point, Jesse." He folded his arms over his chest and held Jesse's level gaze. One that once would have been filled with lust. Lust Brave could have used to get anything he wanted.

The game had been fun while it lasted. The big, muscular man had a mouth meant to suck cock. And a hard body, with sleek muscles and an ass Brave could—

He belongs to your brother. His ass is off limits.

Right. They had a professional relationship now. One that grated in moments like this. Jesse had been an excellent choice for tour manager because his extensive knowledge of the band members' strengths and weaknesses left them all at a disadvantage.

He knew where to find Tate Maddox, their drummer, when he went AWOL. He effortlessly kept heated arguments from coming to blows, making it easy to forget how volatile he himself had been less than a year ago. The man had become calm and collected, slipping into his new role like it had been made for him.

And he'd probably figure out exactly how to get Brave up on that stage no matter what he said.

Let him fucking try.

"You are aware you signed a contract with the label? You'll be fined if you don't perform barring medical reasons. And that's not in the fine print, so no way you could have missed it." Jesse shook his head when Brave glared at him again. He went to the fridge to grab a beer. "Unless I'm wrong, you can't afford the fine. Which will create all kinds of issues for the band. Possibly screw up the recording schedule, the promotion, pretty much everything the label supplies."

"For missing one show?" Brave snorted, but his confidence faltered. Reese had been clear that the label was taking a chance with them. She wasn't tough on them for the fun of it. They had a lot to prove. "Security concerns are a good reason to postpone."

"If there were any, I'd agree." Jesse opened the fridge again, grabbing another beer and holding it out to Brave like a peace offering. "Do you think I'd put any of you in danger? Seriously, Brave. You know I love your brother. The venue has its own security and I've met their guys. They don't fuck around."

"They're not *our* guys. They don't know—"

"They *do* know. Damn it, haven't I earned your trust?" Jesse set the bottle aside when Brave didn't take it. "Look, business aside, I get it. I was with you on postponing the tour, but the band needs this. *Alder* needs this. He's been going nuts with everyone trying to put him in a fucking bubble. He can't let that night cripple him forever. He needs to get past—"

"Can you? Can you get past seeing him up there, bleeding out? Am I the only one not willing to put him at risk again for the almighty dollar?" Damn it, Brave felt like he was losing his damn mind. Part of him wanted what was best for the band. Another part was fucking scared to death, because success wasn't worth losing another brother. Not Alder. Alder was better than them all.

"No one is risking him—or *any* of you—for money! No one's risking you at all!" Jesse slammed his fist on the table, losing his annoying as fuck composure. "I thought you were done pulling this diva shit!"

Diva shit? Brave let out a cold laugh. "You wanna go there, Jesse? Maybe I wouldn't need to pull 'this shit' if you'd been doing your job that night."

Jesse's fist cracked into his jaw. He stumbled, then threw himself forward, slamming his shoulder into Jesse's gut. Jesse fell over the dinette table. Beer bottles hit the floor. Latching onto his arm from the floor, Jesse jerked Brave down. He flipped Brave on his back, pinning him with a forearm on his throat.

"Enough! Get off him, Jesse. *Now.*" The cold snap of a familiar voice had Brave and Jesse scrambling to their feet. Reese Griffith, their new manager, regarded him, then Jesse, like a teacher would a couple of kids in the schoolyard acting like fools. And she had no time for their shit. "Sound check is in ten minutes. The rest of the band is setting up. Why are you still here?"

"He's decided not to sing tonight because our security detail was held up." Jesse straightened his black shirt, then ran a hand through his neatly trimmed, dirty blond hair. "We were...discussing his options."

"Clearly." Reese's lips thinned. She was a Korean woman with sharp, angular features and wide, dark brown eyes that narrowed with annoyance when she caught them being childish. She also had a brilliant smile the whole band craved, though she hadn't graced Brave with it yet. She didn't seem to like him very much.

And what she'd just walked in on wouldn't help.

He cleared his throat, going for his most calm and reasonable tone. "I'm sorry. Maybe I didn't handle this well, but—" He cut himself off and dropped his gaze. If Jesse thought venue security was good enough, so would she. "This is our first show in Detroit since Alder was attacked."

"Very true. And while I don't believe the city itself has any bearing on what happened, there's been some concern expressed on social media. People will be watching this show to see how we address those concerns." Her tone softened slightly. "Brave, I can see how this would be difficult for you. If I believed the venue security was lacking I'd postpone the performance myself. The band's safety is my top priority."

"So a few bouncers are supposed to be good enough?"

"No. But this venue has a capacity of five hundred, limited specifically for the most hardcore events. They're known for handling unruly crowds. Which is one of the many reasons I booked you here." She moved to the sofa and took a seat, smoothing her crisp gray skirt over her knees. "Please sit." She waited until he joined her before continuing. "Your own security being delayed was unexpected. However, this venue has full screening. Metal detectors, bag-check, rules against crowd surfing, and a wide barrier from the stage. No one will get anywhere near you." She stared at him until he met her eyes. "Or Alder."

He took a deep breath and nodded. "You probably think I'm being paranoid."

"You have reason. But your safety and security is my highest priority. And Jesse's." She shot Jesse a look he couldn't read. "For future notice, please don't hesitate to contact me with your concerns. I need you focused on singing and writing music. I am here to make sure you don't have to worry about anything else."

"I'll do my best." He rubbed his throat, wondering if he could use it being sore as another excuse to reschedule the show.

Reese let out a soft laugh. "Don't bother. Your voice sounds fine. You will perform tonight." She pushed off the sofa and smiled at him. "I must say, you've proven to be a much different man than I thought I was dealing with."

"Thank you."

"Don't thank me yet. That was an observation, not a compliment." Her slight smile softened her words. "I hope this will be a mutually beneficial partnership. You have reservations because of your former management. I have my own, to be perfectly honest, because your track record is shit."

He wet his lips, nodding slowly. "But things have improved."

"Slightly, yes. But not enough. You've agreed to three of the ten stops on the tour so far which is unacceptable. There are fifteen planned in North America before you begin your European tour. I will give Jesse a list of places Winter's Wrath will perform before I leave." She looked around the bus, her lips thinning slightly at the pile of dirty dishes by the sink. But she didn't comment on them. Instead, she jutted her chin toward the door leading to the bunks. "How many spare beds are there?"

"Technically three, but one's used for storage." His whole body tensed as she continued to give the bus a critical once over. The dishes were only there because he refused to clean up after Connor Phelan, their bass player. The muscle-head had been off with their opening bands all morning. Soon as he came in tonight, they were gonna have a chat.

"Good." Reese started for the door. "You have two interviews with bloggers scheduled tonight."

"Yeah. Jesse told us."

"I'm happy to hear he's fulfilling his role." She paused and glanced back at Jesse. "Let me know if that changes."

She left the bus to a heavy silence. Brave retrieved the still intact beer from the floor. He took a few swigs, arching a brow as Jesse pulled a cigarette from his shirt pocket.

Jesse rolled his eyes and started off the bus.

"Wait." Brave followed him to the door, tension building between his eyes as he met the other man's hard gaze. They'd gotten along better when they'd been fucking. Now, he had no idea how to talk to the guy. "I wasn't trying to mess with your job."

"I know." Jesse sighed and rubbed the back of his neck. "But you should be in there, working this shit out with the band. And with your brother. He convinced me and Danica he was ready. Maybe he'll convince you too."

The man had a point. Brave stared at the door after Jesse shut it behind him, wishing it was that simple. Writing music—or attempting to—was all he knew how to do anymore. His relationship with the band was still strained. And it was up to him to fix that, but old habits died hard. For years he got the final say, no matter what they wanted. The shift in dynamics gave him whiplash.

Running the band like a democracy meant more than discussing their plans for the future. If he suggested so much as a restaurant to stop for lunch, one of the guys would come up with a 'better' option. And the rest would agree while watching Brave to see if he'd get pissed.

He kept his damn mouth shut. Every fucking time. He got it. He wasn't in charge anymore. He'd abused his power and to make up for it, he was left with none.

But he hadn't felt that extreme lack of control so fiercely until now. His one redeeming quality, one that had been a surprise to everyone, was that he'd do anything to protect Alder. Reasonable for a big brother, right?

Apparently not.

Finishing off his beer, Brave eyed the time. He should have been inside a few minutes ago. Shoving his long black hair back he pulled a leather tie from his snug black jean pocket and tied his hair at the nape of his neck. A glance in the mirror on the far wall showed a smudge of gray—probably from his left hand rubbing over the pencil-scrawled pages for so long. He rubbed it off. Not a huge improvement. There were dark shadows under his eyes and his clothes were rumpled. He looked like shit.

At least one thing he could control. The fans wouldn't care, but his bandmates would be annoyed after having spent time primping for the show. He glanced at his nails, covered in chipped black polish and smirked.

Too fucking bad.

Leaving the bus, he hustled across the lot, lifting his hand to wave at the people in line who noticed him and started screaming his name. The metal barriers held them at bay and in seconds he was inside, taking the back entrance and striding along the dark hall toward the greenroom.

One of the doors along the hall opened and Danica stepped out. She blinked when she saw him, her blood red lips tipping at the edges.

"You're a mess." She grabbed his wrist and tugged him into the dressing room she'd just left. Her makeup lady straightened from where she'd been cleaning up all her tools from the vanity. "Lucky for you, Gloria can fix you up in no time."

"Ah…yeah." He gently pried his wrist free. "Unfortunately, we have *no* time."

"We have plenty. Lighting blew a breaker. Sound check's been delayed, so you've got nothing to worry about." She patted his cheek. "I'll let the guys know you're getting prettied up. See you in a few."

"Awesome." Brave frowned at Danica's back as she skipped off, but flashed a smile at Gloria when she spun the chair—which looked like it belonged in a barber shop—around and motioned for him to sit. Wasn't her fault his one last attempt to exert some control had been foiled.

So this is the life of the rich and famous.

Only, he wasn't rich anymore. And none of them would be famous for long if they didn't work this shit out.

For the moment, the distance between them was only felt by the band.

But it wouldn't be long before it poisoned the music as well.

Shiori hugged herself tightly as the lights went out and the curtain at the very back of the stage parted, revealing the huge Winter's Wrath logo, a skull in a snowflake, which had been hidden while the opening bands played. Beneath it was a drum kit, which seemed to have twice as many drums as any band she'd seen before.

One bass drum had the logo, while the other had the band's name in realistic blood splatter. The drummer, Tate Maddox, made his way behind it, drawing excited screams from the crowd.

From the side stage, Shiori could see his little smirk as he took his seat. He was too freakin' cute—even cuter than she'd expected from his pictures. His golden-brown hair was shaved all around, except for a long part on top that fell over one eye when he bowed his head. The black eyeliner around his eyes made his pink-toned, white skin even starker in contrast, and he almost glowed under the neon lights.

Next came Malakai Noble, the bassist, who strode on stage and gave the crowd a cold smile. His darkly tanned skin, broad jaw, and the way he moved made her think of a powerful beast with a wild edge tightly leashed by his own hand. If he loosened his grip, he'd be dangerous. Having him so close gave her a strange thrill, like the temptation to play a risky game, exciting and scary all at once.

She shivered as he glanced her way and crept further into the shadows, bumping into Sophie who steadied her with a hand on her shoulder.

"He plays the part well, but he's not as mean as he looks." Sophie whispered to her. "Reese, and I have spoken about ways to work on the band's image, but he's one we've agreed doesn't need to change. On stage, he's dark and mysterious. All tight muscles, military style, and out of reach. His fans have all kinds of theories about his dark past, which puts him just below Brave as the favorite."

"Does he *have* a dark past?" Shiori bit her bottom lip, not sure she should have asked. She was here to see the band in person, meet with them after, and get the stamp of approval from Reese to start her trial run.

For two weeks, she'd gone through a crash course in modeling. Her audition and training were rolled together, everything from proving that she looked good on camera, to becoming comfortable with interviews—all pretend ones with Sophie, but she'd been assured that was enough. Over and over she'd been tested on her ability to mimic Danica's dance moves, but the work had paid off. She'd been offered a temporary contract with the band as Danica's understudy. Sophie and Reese had gone back and forth for another few days and finally come to some kind of agreement.

Shiori didn't know all the details. Only that she'd be on tour with them for at least a week to see if she was a good fit. Starting tonight.

She hadn't met any of the guys yet. Or Danica, who she'd been taking over for if all went well. Reese insisted Shiori needed to see the band perform first. When Shiori admitted she'd only been to the concerts of a few small local bands, Reese hadn't been pleased.

Seeing that huge crowd out there, she understood Reese's reluctance. As much as Sophie tried to sell her as a perfect fit, she couldn't hide her lack of experience. Sure, Shiori would get to rehearse before she actually got on stage with the band, but that didn't change the fact that a high school play was the biggest performance in her portfolio.

Strangely enough, one three-way phone call with Shiori and Sophie was all it took for Reese to give her a chance.

"I'll be honest with you. Danica set the bar high. This may not be PC, but I refused to consider replacing her with the standard pretty white girl most agencies would have offered. Her presence made an impact because she's different and talented. She has a special quality that can't be matched." Reese went silent for what seemed like a long time. *"I'm not asking you to go up there as a token, Shiori. I'm asking you to become a presence. To earn your own fanbase. To give the crowd something they'll never forget."*

Sophie jumped right in. *"A new talent could do that. We won't know until—"*

"I need to hear it from her." Reese had a no-nonsense tone that intimidated Shiori, but she respected the woman for knowing exactly what she wanted.

So she took a deep breath and did her best to assure she could fulfill her role with the band while Danica was gone. *"Danica is…everything I want to be. Her confidence on stage inspires me. I wasn't sure what I wanted until I saw her up there. I want to be able to do that. To know that some other girl, somewhere, will look at me and know she can do anything."*

"You could do that in many professions. Become a journalist. An actress. You're a beautiful young woman with a lot of potential." Reese sounded kind and supportive, but Shiori knew this was another test.

She cleared her throat. *"I could. And maybe I will one day. But when will I get another chance like this? I want to be on that stage. I want people* to see me, to feel how much I love the music so they can share their own passion with me."

Reese let out a soft laugh. "Damn. That was perfect. If nothing else, I want to see if she can be this convincing when all those bloggers start grilling her."

"She can. She has something Danica didn't and I think the fans will love it." Sophie's tone was light, as if she'd known all along Reese would agree that Shiori was the best choice. "She loves the music just as much as they do."

"I don't need a fangirl." Reese's voice sharpened. "Or a groupie."

"You're not getting one. Shiori is well aware of who your boys are. She has no illusions about them."

"Perfect." Reese's smile was clear in her tone. "That's all I needed to know."

Sophie squeezed her shoulder. "You're not even listening to me, girl. Please tell me you're not star struck already. I'd hate for you to prove me a liar."

Shiori blinked as she realized she'd been staring at Malakai while lost in thought. Good thing she'd drifted away too, because as she focused on him again, her belly got all fluttery. He looked over and her mouth went dry. His expression never changed, but something in his eyes told her he was well aware of her presence.

His playful wink heated her cheeks.

"No, I'm not… This is all just…" *Trial run, Shiori. Pull it together.* She wet her lips with her tongue. "I'm excited. And yes, he's incredible to see in person, but he's not the one I'll be looking at."

"Good." Sophie straightened as two guitarists strode onto the stage. "Keep that in mind and you'll do fine."

Smiling with relief, Shiori focused on Alder Trousseau, her chest squeezing slightly as she caught the familiar features. His long, sleek black hair sliding down to cover most of his face helped, but for a split second, she could imagine how Kyoko had felt, six years ago in the crowd, looking up to see that face.

The Trousseau brothers all had that smooth, irresistible appeal. They were so different in attitude, but even the worst of them could charm a woman with a smile. Make her forget that they had so many girls like her lusting after them.

A few sweet words, a bit of attention, and Kyoko had been a goner. Back then Shiori had thought it was so romantic that her sister had fallen in love with a rock star. Sure, the band played metalcore, but it was all the same. The dark hero, the sweet virgin, a forbidden love that ended in happily-ever-after.

They'd both been silly little girls, ready to latch on to whatever dream they could find.

Only, Kyoko had paid the price for hers.

And Shiori had learned from it.

Connor Phelan, the rhythm guitarist, didn't mess with her senses like the others, so she observed him as the band began the opening of their latest big hit, *Subsist*. He had bigger muscles than the rest, mussed up blond hair, and a ruddiness to his skin that told her he spent a lot of time outside. He flashed a charming smile at the girls leaning over the metal barrier set a yard back from the stage.

A deafening scream rose from the girls and spread through the crowd as Brave Trousseau sauntered up to the mic, his head down, his wavy, long black hair covering his face completely.

The beat quickened. Rose to a fever pitch. Goosebumps spread over her skin as she anticipated the sound of his voice.

He latched onto the mic and tipped his head back enough to reveal his lips. "Red gifts, teeth, and candy. So many innocent lies. Let me believe… Let me always believe."

The whispered lyrics sent a chill down her spine. She'd listened to this song over and over, it affected her every time, but never like this. He growled and her pulse skipped a beat as he threw his head back, the power of his voice vibrating through her bones with each word. In seconds the music had a hold on her soul, clearing her mind of all but the aggressive beat as Brave's passion wrapped around her.

Like thunder fading into the distance, the first song ended and Brave raked his hair back to grin at the rowdy throng. "Fuck, it's great to be home! Let's hear it for the best city in the world! Detroit, you ready to tear this place apart?"

Screams and howls. Devil horns in the air in a wild salute. Fans pressed against the barrier.

Shiori held her breath as she watched them reach toward the stage, crushing one another in their excitement. Being up here was incredible. Down there? She'd be freaking out.

Brave laughed. "Let's hear it for the opening bands! Atlas, Spider-Spawn, and Gear-Core!"

More cheers and some clapping. A group in the back started chanting 'Gear-Core!' and pumping their fist in the air. Shiori hadn't come out until just before Winter's Wrath hit the stage, but she knew a few songs from the other bands. Unlike some shows, this line-up fit Winter's Wrath's style perfectly. She wouldn't be surprised if the opening bands earned themselves some new fans.

"Now, I know you're all waiting for something, but I can't quite put my finger on it…" Brave cocked his head to one side. "Wanna give me a hint?"

Silence. Then a low hum, growing louder and louder as everyone in the crowd seemed to catch on. Voices rose, singing lyrics of another song Shiori knew well.

Journey's *'Don't Stop Believing'*. She'd almost forgotten Winter's Wrath did a cover of the song every time they played in Detroit. A few bands did, but she might be a little biased because none of them came close to this intensity. This wasn't an offhand tribute. The way Brave sang, the way every member of the band played, truly expressed the feeling that they'd come home.

Before the song finished the beat changed, shifting effortlessly into the opening of 'Center Mass'. Shiori shook with excitement as Danica ran onto the stage, sliding on her knees to the edge in front of Brave, forming a gun with her hands and 'firing' over the crowd.

Oh god, she's gorgeous! Shiori bit her bottom lip as Danica leapt to her feet, punching her fist in the air at the chorus. She was wearing a camo skirt, tight little vest, and a green beret. Her incredibly long legs were covered with strategically ripped fishnet stockings and she had platform combat boots on her feet.

Boots Shiori would probably break her neck trying to walk in, and here Danica was, dancing in them. As confident as she'd been about her ability to take this job, actually *seeing* the woman out there gave her serious doubts. Would the fans even accept her as a temporary replacement?

"I know that look!" Sophie practically screamed in her ear to be heard over the music. "Don't do that!"

The uber professional Sophie shouting while making faces at the music was too funny. Shiori stifled a giggle, her mood instantly lighter, and went back to watching the show.

Two more songs, then Brave worked the crowd a bit, flirting and making risqué comments about a local politician everyone seemed to hate. Most of the fans seemed to enjoy his jabs, but a group of guys near the barrier started grumbling.

"Hey, who fucking cares?" One man, whose words were slightly slurred, leaned over, giving Brave a one fingered salute. "Didn't you learn anything from your brother? We want to hear about pussy!"

For the first time that night, Alder spoke into his mic. "Yeah, I tried to teach Brave about pussy, but the two girls with him told me he's got it covered."

The attention got the man even more riled up. He burst out laughing. "Not *you*, loser! Valor!"

Oh no. Shiori brought her hand to her lips as Brave stepped forward and Alder grabbed his arm. After losing a sibling herself she could imagine how painful it was to have their dead brother thrown in their face so heartlessly.

At least Alder remained calm. A good sign.

"Whatever, pal." Alder gave the man a cold smile. "You need material to whack off too, try PornHub."

"You wanna entertain us? Play something by LOST!" The man looked around for support, but even his friends were trying to get him to calm down. He ignored them and pointed at Alder. "I say the wrong brother died! Go home and fuck your nasty bitch! Get us some real talent!"

The second Alder jumped off the stage, Shiori covered her eyes and groaned. The night was about to go to hell. And even though she understood Alder snapping, she couldn't ignore the impact of his actions.

If this went on his permanent record, she might as well go home now.

Sophie tugged her away from the stage, nudging her to keep going. "Wait for me outside. And don't worry. Reese will have a plan."

Will she? Shiori retreated from the chaos, her throat tight as she felt all her hopes slip away. She'd known meeting Alder and Brave wouldn't fix all her problems. Might not solve anything at all. Their hardcore lifestyles weren't ideal. Still, she respected all they'd accomplished.

But those accomplishments wouldn't do her any good if they didn't come off as stable on paper. She didn't judge them, but her opinion didn't matter.

She wouldn't be the one who decided Hiro's future.

Chapter Three

Alder leaped over the metal barrier, crunching his fist into the face of the asshole who'd insulted Danica. He'd been worried about Brave losing it when Valor was mentioned, but now all he cared about was shutting this fucker up. He'd gone too far. Then further.

Enough was enough.

A punch caught him in the mouth as his wrists were restrained. A shoulder hit his gut. He was lifted over the barrier. Another fist caught him in the eye before he was jerked out of reach.

Growling, he struggled against the grip on his arms.

"Alder!" Jesse pinned him against the stage. His big hand framed Alder's jaw. "Cool it!"

"You heard what he said!"

"Words! Nothing but the words of one drunk fucker who's getting dragged out as we speak." Jesse leaned against him, breathing hard. "Don't you *ever* fucking do that again." His eyes widened as he brought a hand to Alder's lips. "Damn it, you're bleeding."

"I'm fine." The lights glared on. Alder ground his teeth. Shit, were they shutting everything down? "We have to keep going! Jesse—"

"I know." Jesse fisted his hand in Alder's hair, fixing him with a hard stare. "They haven't told anyone to leave yet. Get on stage. Talk to Brave."

"What about Danica?" She'd heard what the man said. Sure, she was tough, but that didn't make it okay.

"Malakai kept her from jumping in the crowd after you. She's fine." Jesse gave his hair another tug. "Are you?"

"Why wouldn't I be?"

Jesse put a hand on his chest, over the scar where he'd been stabbed. The wound had healed well, though there was some nerve damage. His doctors weren't worried.

But Jesse still was.

"Jesse, I love you, but you have to stop. I'm good. An ugly scar is all I have left of that night." He cupped Jesse's cheek when his man didn't look convinced. "Trust me. I'm *fine!*"

"Are you?" Jesse's brow creased. "Prove it. Sleep with me tonight."

"And leave Danica alone?" Alder bit into his cheek at Jesse's confused frown. The three of them had a strong relationship—anything less wouldn't survive the crazy schedule or the long tours—but in bunks that were a tight fit for two people, someone always ended up alone.

Since Danica didn't take up much space, sharing with her made the most sense. And Jesse liked snuggling more than he'd admit. Alder used to tease them that he wanted his turn, but not lately. Even at home, he didn't spend much time in the bed they'd bought to accommodate them all.

He didn't sleep much and he didn't sleep well.

Maybe that was the issue Jesse was trying to tackle.

"What's the right answer?" Jesse pulled away and sighed. "Sure, me and her still have our weird moments, but at night we cuddle like it's the most natural thing in the world. Am I supposed to focus on that? Am I a bad boyfriend if I'm not thinking about her right now?"

A 'Yes' would shut down the conversation, because Danica was Jesse's first girlfriend and he still wasn't sure he knew what he was doing. He was bisexual, like Alder, but leaned toward men. His relationship with Danica meant exploring something new. Lust was easy. Jesse was a passionate man and there was no doubt he desired Danica.

But romance was a different ball game. Jesse was still learning and acted like Alder was some kind of authority on the subject.

Using that against him would be a dick move.

"You're not a bad boyfriend." Alder glanced up at the stage where Brave was speaking to the venue's head of security. The crowd was grumbling, making conversation difficult. He turned back to Jesse and gave him a quick smile. "We'll talk later. Let me see if I can help Brave salvage the show."

"Good luck." Jesse stepped back, and Alder could feel him watching as he climbed back on stage.

Brave glanced over, his eyes hard. "You look like shit."

My loving brother. Alder swiped his hand over his bottom lip, biting back a wince at the dull throb of pain. "It's nothing. What's the verdict?"

"We can finish the set." Brave nodded to the security guard. "Tell him you won't jump offstage again."

The beefy guy smirked and shook his head. "Don't bother. I know your type. Do what the fuck you want, but the owner will clear this place out if there's any more trouble."

"Works for me." Alder stood by Brave as the guard left the stage. Rolling his shoulders, he eyed his brother to gauge his mood. "Sorry about that."

"Don't be." Brave's jaw ticked. "I didn't want you out here at all, but you can handle yourself, right?"

"Yeah."

"Good." Brave inhaled roughly. "Guess that's it then. You wanna tell the fans the good news?"

"Sure." Alder reached for the mic as the overhead lights went out, leaving only the spotlights to see by. He pressed his tongue into his bottom lip. "You ain't pissed?"

"Does it matter?" Brave's tone was cold. Which Alder was used to, so he simply shrugged.

Things were better between them since he'd been attacked on stage, but they still weren't close. The difference was, Brave wasn't to blame.

He'd been protective. Asked Alder all the time how he was doing, if he wanted to hang out or even just talk. And every time, Alder brushed him off.

Not intentionally. Part of him wanted to accept the effort his brother made, but the concern reminded him of what had happened and he wanted to fucking forget it. He needed people to stop treating him like he was fucking fragile. Like there was something wrong with him.

How messed up was it that he knew exactly what was off between him and Brave, but he couldn't fix it?

The words were on the tip of his tongue. His lips parted, but Brave had already retreated, leaving him to the crowd.

Rubbing his chin, he forced a smile and spoke into the mic. "So...that was fucked up, huh?"

Nervous laughter spread through the crowd. They watched him expectantly.

Brave would probably know exactly how to get them back on track. He worked the mic like a fucking master. Alder was perfectly happy in the background, but he was the one who'd screwed up.

He cleared his throat. "Will you all forgive me if I promise not to punch anyone else?"

More laughter, like a massive exhale this time, relieving all the tension from the room.

"We love you, Alder!" A girl screamed.

"I'd pay to see you punch someone else!" A guy shouted.

Then there were more voices, coming all at once, some praising him for attacking the guy, others requesting different songs.

He focused on the later.

"You want more?" He let his tone drop and reached out, confidence building as his guitar was placed in his hand. "Tell me how much you want it!"

Howls, whistles, cheers and more screams. Behind him, Malakai and Connor began the chords to *S.L.U.T.*

Which drove the fans wild.

Tate pounded out the beat and Danica skipped up to Alder, licking the side of his face before snatching the mic.

"He's been a bad, bad boy." She nudged him back to his own spot on stage. "Should I punish him?"

The crowd loved that idea. Danica handed Brave the mic, grinding against him and shooting Alder a saucy look as Brave began to sing. Playing along, Brave tangled a hand in her hair, thrusting his hips at her suggestively.

As the song continued, Danica moved from Brave to Malakai, slinking close to Alder seconds later, only to slip out of reach and dance over to Connor. While she only flirted lightly with Alder, the rest of the guys got her full attention. Which drove him nuts, but got the crowd engaged.

They finished the next two songs, along with an encore, without issue. Heading to the bus, he looped his arm around Tate's neck, ready to celebrate a damn good performance.

Ducking his head to slip out of reach, Tate glared at him. "Fuck off."

Alder stopped short, staring after the drummer as the kid sprinted for the bus. Malakai followed him in without a word. Connor took off with one of the opening bands.

Footsteps approached him and he stiffened as his brother stopped to his side.

"Give them time, they'll get over it." Brave's tone was stiff. Detached. Almost as though he expected any comfort he offered to be rejected.

All Alder wanted was to know what the hell was going on. "This isn't the first time one of us has gotten into it with a fan."

"True. But this is different."

"Because they don't think I'm ready? Because they think—"

"No." Brave put a hand on his shoulder. "They believe you're ready."

So what's the fucking problem? "I don't get it."

"*They're* not ready, Alder." Brave sighed and let his hand fall to his side. "You scared them."

Shit. Hunching his shoulders, he brought one hand up to rub the tense spot between his brows. Brave having to remind him he wasn't the only one scarred by that night was pretty messed up. Alder hadn't given a thought to what the others must be going through. He needed to prove to himself, to everyone, that he was back to normal.

Only he wasn't. And neither was anyone else.

"How do I fix this?"

Brave chuckled. "You seriously asking me?"

"I don't see anyone else here." Alder ground his teeth. A few words and he'd left himself vulnerable to his brother. Let the man know that he still cared about his opinion when he shouldn't. "Never mind."

"All right, stop." Brave grabbed his arm before he could walk away and towed him toward the front of the bus, away from the watchful eyes of the roadies who'd begun carting out all their equipment. "I can't tell you how to make things better with the guys. Maybe talk to them. Surprise them with beer and bacon. Who fucking knows?" Releasing his arm, Brave took a step back and leaned against the hood of the bus. "This is our band. Our family. We started this together, Alder."

"I know that."

"Do you?" Brave shook his head. "We're going places, which is fucking awesome. But we've got to be solid."

"Is it my fault we aren't?"

Lips parted, Brave stared at him. Then dropped his gaze. "No."

This was getting them nowhere. Things had been so easy when he almost died. Now it was like they were rebuilding everything from scratch. The band. His relationship with his brother.

And maybe that's what Brave was getting at. *Their* relationship had always put a strain on the band. Maybe, if the guys saw they were doing better, the rest would fall into place.

If only he could figure out how to take that first step.

"Brave, I..." He swallowed hard. Tipped his head back to stare up at the black sky, patchy with gray clouds and a few dim stars. "You laugh at me and I'm gonna hit you."

"I won't laugh."

Alder nodded. "I want my brother back."

Sighing, Brave scuffed his boots in the dirt. "You hardly knew him, kid. He might have eventually straightened up and been a good man, but—"

"I'm not talking about Valor." Alder looked at Brave. Really looked at him for the first time in a while. The man was worn down. Fucking tired.

Brave had watched one brother die, almost lost another, and had been ditched by their parents. He'd assumed Valor was the one Alder wanted because that's how fucked up their family was.

"Remember when I was little and you used to pack my lunch for me?" Alder smiled at the memory. If he closed his eyes he could still picture Brave tossing him an apple before he left the house every morning. And he'd done so much more. "I was really young, but I think I remember you tucking me in at night too. Reading to me until I fell asleep."

Lips curving at the edges, Brave inclined his head. "I read you Lord of The Rings and The Circle of Time. You got so bored you passed out."

"I loved it, though. I tried to stay awake."

"They weren't the best books for a little kid." Brave lifted his shoulders, staring off into the distance. "But I loved them. I wanted to share them with you."

"I'd like to read them sometime. You got a bunch of books—you still got those?"

"I've got them all on my kindle. You can read them on your phone… I'll hook you up on my account." Brave shoved his hands in his pockets. "Uh…this is good, right? Progress?"

"Definitely progress." Also kinda weird. Alder snorted. "Not sure this will cut it with the guys. You said bacon and beer?"

Brave chuckled. "Yeah. Though Tate will go for a blowjob if you're up for it."

"I'll leave that to you."

"Malakai would kill me."

"And you like to live dangerously." Not that he should encourage Brave to mess with their drummer, or piss off Malakai who guarded the kid like a momma bear, but for the first time in forever, he didn't feel like his brother's keeper. He didn't have to make excuses for him. Didn't have to watch his every word to keep the lead singer happy.

"Yeah, I do." Brave let out a soft laugh. "And it's my turn to stick my neck out. I owe you."

"Not that again." Alder groaned, wondering if it was fucked up to wish Brave could save *his* life so they'd be even. "I like you alive, big brother. I did what I did. Just drop it."

Putting a hand on his shoulder, Brave inclined his head. "I'll try." He gave Alder's shoulder a little squeeze. "But I love you, you stupid fucker. So I get to worry."

Alder took a deep breath as his throat tightened. "Fine… We good?"

"Do I get a hug?"

Blinking at the other man, Alder tried to figure out if he was joking. Brave didn't *do* hugs. "Who *are* you?"

With another stiff smile, Brave drew away and shrugged. "Forget it. You ready?"

Nodding, Alder turned to head into the bus. He stopped when he saw a young woman he didn't know standing by the door with Reese and Sophie. While their manager and Danica's agent were deep in conversation, the girl seemed to have her full attention on him and his brother.

He wasn't sure how much she'd heard. Or why she'd care about any of it.

But she did.

And for some reason, she looked disappointed.

Which bothered him more than it should.

Chapter Four

Malakai slammed the cupboard and looked around the bus for someone to kill. Connor would be a good target, since he was probably the one who'd polished off Tate's cookies.

Unfortunately, Connor had skipped out after the show. And the only one on the bus was Tate. Twitchy as fuck and shaking. Malakai could hear Reese outside. She couldn't see the kid like this.

"I'm fine, man. Just need a minute." Tate brought a trembling hand to his face. Inhaled roughly. "And some air. Some air would be good."

"No." Malakai opened the freezer, grinding his teeth when he found it empty. Damn it, this night just kept getting better and better. The kid needed something with sugar. Sugar curbed the edge of his addiction enough to keep him calm. To keep him from hunting down a fix that would erase all the emotions he couldn't handle.

'Some air' meant going out around the others bands. Other bands whose members would give Tate anything he asked for because they didn't give a shit.

The click of heels on the steps brought Malakai's head up. His brow furrowed as a girl he didn't recognize met his eyes from across the lounge.

"Hi." She bit her red glossed bottom lip, her sleek black hair falling forward to cover one eye. She brushed it back and he couldn't look away. Her eyes were a startling shade of gray, mesmerizing in their beauty. Almost white around the pupil, gradually darkening to a black ring.

Dragging his gaze from her hypnotic eyes was difficult, but he finally managed. He focused on her lips. Not much better. The way she tugged her bottom lip between her teeth was distracting. Chicks used that to tease him all the time and he thought he'd grown completely immune, but she wasn't doing it to tempt him.

Actually, her nervousness, the way she stood there like she was forcing herself not to make a run for it, tugged at his protective instincts. He had no idea *why* she was on the bus, but she wasn't acting like a crazy groupie who'd slipped by security.

"Hey." He shut the freezer and smiled at her. "Are you looking for someone?"

"Umm...no. Reese told me to come in and wait for her."

Interesting. If Reese had sent her she was probably part of some media gig. Maybe she was a blogger? She was cute. He could see people logging on to watch her talk about pretty much anything. He'd never met a music blogger this freakin' adorable and shy, but there was a new one every damn day.

She seemed...different, though. People who made it big on YouTube had big personalities. They were loud and funny or sarcastic and mean. This girl didn't strike him as either.

But if she wasn't a blogger, why had Reese brought her?

"Malakai, I'm out. Seriously, if I don't move I'm gonna be sick." Tate stumbled into his side. He noticed the girl and flashed a weak smile. "Hey, sexy. Don't mind me. I'll be out of your way in a minute."

The kid was a fucking wreck. Malakai let out a low growl as he latched onto Tate's arm and maneuvered him onto the bench by the kitchenette.

"You're not in the way." Malakai tried to focus on Tate. Which was harder than it should be. He couldn't seem to dismiss the girl. But he did his best. "Tell me what I can do to help, drummer boy. Hell, you want a cigarette? A drink? Name it."

The girl crossed the room and crouched in front of Tate. "Are you all right?"

Tate moaned and dropped his head to his hands. "Yeah. It's stupid. I need a fix. I'd be good if I had cookies."

Frowning, the girl glanced up at Malakai. "Is he diabetic?"

"Not that I know of." Would be good to look into, but he couldn't see beyond the issues he knew of. Tate had replaced a drug addiction with a sugar addiction. Getting the 'reward' from eating sweets kept him from seeking out the satisfaction he'd once gotten from hard drugs.

There might be a better way, but getting Tate to see a doctor was beyond Malakai's abilities. Keeping him clean was all he could do.

Reaching into her little black purse, the girl pulled out a small package of fruit gummies. She smiled as she pressed the package into Tate's hand. "Not cookies, but just as sweet. Maybe they'll help."

Giving her a big grin, Tate opened the package and poured all the treats in his mouth. He let out a soft sigh the second they hit his tongue. "I don't know who you are, but I think I'm in love."

Rolling his eyes, Malakai sat on the edge of the sofa and rubbed Tate's back. "Reese sent her, so behave yourself."

Snickering, the girl straightened. "Don't worry, I'm not that easy."

Her cheeks reddened and Malakai bit back a smile. Damn, she was a breath of fresh air. After dealing with screaming fans, handsy groupies, and strung out starter bands, this young woman was a nice reminder of the real world. A world not blinded by the neon lights. One that kept spinning with nothing but a curious glance at the money and fame.

"Thank you." Malakai held out his hand as the girl took a seat on the bench at the other side of the small shelf table. "My name is Malakai. And this is Tate."

"I know." She shook his hand, looking dazed. Then she jerked away and slapped both hands over her face. "Oh god, not at all what I meant to say. I'm sorry. I love your music. You're both awesome, but I don't care. That's not why I'm here."

"Oh-kay..." He cocked his head, taking in the words that had come out in a breathless whisper. Her being a fan didn't change much. Put his guard up a little, but he could forgive almost anything after her helping Tate. "Did you win a contest or something? I should be the one apologizing if you did. I don't know what we're supposed to be doing with you."

"I didn't win anything. Well, maybe I kinda did, but—" She snapped her mouth shut as Reese and Sophie climbed onto the bus. Hopping to her feet, she faced the two women. "I should go."

"Already?" Reese frowned at Malakai. "I assumed she'd be safe with you. Was I wrong?"

"*What?*" Malakai shoved off the bench, almost knocking his head on the edge of the cupboards.

The girl reached for him. Froze halfway. Placed her hand over her mouth and groaned. "It's not his fault. Tonight was just—"

"Not the best first impression." Danica appeared behind Sophie, her tone light, but her level gaze speaking volumes. She was a woman on a mission. "But that's understandable." She turned all her attention to the girl. "And like me, I'm sure you want to give the guys time to work out the drama." Danica shimmied past her agent and the band's manager, hand out. "Sophie told me all about you and I'm looking forward to working together. I got us a room—if you don't mind sharing. The bus doesn't leave until tomorrow. Which means we can sleep in real beds tonight."

Reese's brow furrowed as she glanced over. "I didn't approve the—"

"Expense? I know." Danica's chin lifted stubbornly. "Per my contract, so long as I'm available for performances, I'm free to stay wherever I choose."

"True." Reese's brow lifted. "But hotels are only covered when you're on location for a minimum of three days."

"Oh, we don't need the room covered. It's a quick girl retreat. On me." Danica hooked her arm to the girl's and guided her toward the exit. "We'll meet for breakfast in the morning to discuss business. Goodnight, Malakai. Tate, honey, I hid some cookies in my bunk for you. Go grab them before Connor gets back."

"I love you, Danica!" Tate scrambled over to the bunks as the girls left. A box being torn open was followed by a crunch and a happy sigh.

Malakai shook his head, then rose to face the agent and the manager. "I didn't know we'd scheduled a meeting. Do you want a drink or something? Make yourselves comfortable. I'll round up the guys."

"They're on their way." Brave strode onto the bus, his expression hard. Following him, Alder had his head down, looking guilty as fuck.

Good. Malakai glared at him, wishing they had a few minutes alone so he could find out what had come over the idiot. Sure, someone had said mean things about Danica, but so fucking what? Wasn't worth putting himself in danger.

"I'll have a tea if you don't mind." Sophie took a seat at the kitchen table, turning her attention to Alder. "Come sit down and let me take a look at you."

Alder's lips parted. He glanced from his brother, to Reese, then cleared his throat. "I appreciate your concern, Sophie, but—"

"It's not concern, you silly boy." Sophie's lips slanted with amusement. "You have a photo shoot with Danica next week. I need to see the damage."

"Oh." Alder eased onto the seat across from her. He hissed in a breath as she prodded his bottom lip, but stayed put.

For some reason, seeing Alder suffering a little cooled Malakai's rage. He and the guys giving Alder shit wouldn't get them very far, but Sophie would make the guitarist pay in her own special way.

"Brave, get your brother an icepack. And stop scowling, those lines around your mouth aren't very attractive." Sophie touched the dark purple bruise under Alder's eye. "This should fade enough to cover by then. The cut stopped bleeding, so it isn't deep. We can make it work."

Returning from the fridge with an icepack wrapped in a dishtowel, Brave stared at Sophie like she'd lost her mind.

Chuckling under his breath, Malakai finished making her tea. He knew better than to annoy the woman.

The lead singer was a slow learner.

"Sorry, but who the fuck cares how he looks?" Brave looked over at Reese, who'd finally taken a seat on the leather sofa on the other side of the bus. When she simply arched a brow at him his jaw ticked. "Security should be—"

"Keeping you on a shorter leash?" Sophie held the icepack against Alder's lips, motioning for him to take it as she regarded Brave with interest. "That's something you can discuss with your manager. Alder is my client. Fighting can negate our contract, but since he hasn't damaged the product, I'll let it slide. This time."

"The *product*?" Brave's eyes, deep brown with molten gold glowing at the center, darkened as he stepped to his brother's side. "He's not a fucking product."

"No, *he* isn't. But I'm not his mother and my priority is making sure he can still do his job. The band, the music, may be more than a product to *you*, but as far as the label is concerned, the results are all that count." She took a sip of her tea. Inclined her head at Malakai. "This is very good. Thank you."

"No problem" He regarded Reese, hoping to distract her long enough for Brave to pull himself together. "Are you sure you don't want anything?"

"I'll have a tea as well." Reese relaxed back into the sofa, her hands folded on her knee. "Brave, please sit down. Like Sophie, my focus is on the results of what transpired tonight. People are posting videos on YouTube. There's already been a spike in sales. The fans enjoyed the show."

"So that's it? The results are good, so the label will be happy." Brave rubbed his lips as he perched on the loveseat on the other side of the kitchenette. "Alder's not in trouble?"

"I didn't say that." Reese's lips thinned. "When I became your manager I asked you all individually what the biggest issue with the band was. Not a single member wanted to discuss your internal problems, which I assumed meant you will handle those obstacles yourselves. If that's changed, let me know."

"It hasn't."

"Good." She thanked Malakai softly when he brought her tea, easing back again as though getting comfortable to stay awhile. "We talked about safety concerns earlier." She paused as Connor and Jesse joined them on the bus, standing at the entrance like they weren't sure they should be there. "Take a seat, gentlemen. You all need to hear this."

Connor plunked down next to Brave while Jesse slipped onto the bench beside Alder, eyeing him with concern. Seconds later Tate came out of the bunk area. He hopped up on the closest counter, looking much better than he had before.

Reese observed them all for a moment, sipping her tea, her gaze thoughtful. "As I was saying, the security concerns were expressed by Brave, but no one else. I can set tighter guidelines for your regular detail, but those are useless if you don't all respect them."

"This is my fault. I'm the one who jumped offstage." Alder moved the icepack from his mouth to his eye. "I didn't think."

"And last week in Memphis, when Connor bodysurfed across the crowd, was that 'your fault' as well?" Reese turned to Connor, who seemed to find the black carpet fucking fascinating. She smirked and jutted her chin at Brave. "Or when your brother had fans hold him above their heads while he sang in San Diego? I could come up with more examples. Will you claim responsibility for them all?"

Alder ducked his head. "No."

"Very well. Then as a band, you will decide how to proceed. If you're all happy with the status quo, this matter is closed." She fixed a level gaze on Brave as she said the last.

He didn't look happy, but kept his mouth shut.

Malakai almost felt bad for him. The guy was trying to watch out for his brother. Too little, too late, but protecting Alder was the one thing they could agree on.

Not that they needed Reese to get involved to set Alder straight. He had a feeling the whole band wanted words with their lead guitarist.

Alone.

Reese inclined her head as though satisfied and set her mug on a side table. "Now that that's out of the way I'd like to address the reason both Sophie and I came to speak to you. A performer will be joining you starting tomorrow. As you know, the band will begin their European tour next month. This is a huge step for you all and I'm excited to see how it will extend your international reach with fans."

Nods all around. They were looking forward to the trip.

"Unfortunately, Danica will not be joining you."

Oh fuck.

Jesse blinked at Reese like he'd been slapped. Alder dropped the icepack on the table and stood.

He glared at Sophie. "You said she could come. She would have told me if she couldn't."

"Are you saying she didn't? I recall her mentioning the possibility of several opportunities conflicting with your schedule." Sophie's eyes narrowed when Alder shook his head. "I'd be very careful if I were you, Alder. Danica is dedicated to her career. She loves you, but if you force her to choose between her career and you I don't think you'll like the answer."

"I wouldn't do that to her. I just…" Alder rubbed the back of his neck. "Why didn't she talk to me?"

"She did." Jesse inhaled roughly. "She told us both, but it was like something that might happen. In the future. There were three fashion shows she mentioned. And a magazine spread. And something else... She was afraid she wouldn't get them, so we kept talking about Europe. About all the things we'd do there."

"She was asked to do all three shows and several magazine shoots. The last was confirmed this morning." Sophie straightened. "Once she signs the contracts she can continue to focus on her work with the band until she leaves."

"Once she signs..." Alder's brow furrowed. "So she hasn't yet?"

"She will." But Sophie didn't sound so sure.

I have a bad feeling about this. Malakai studied the other members of the band as each slowly came to grips with what was going down. Sophie wasn't an underhanded woman. She'd done a lot for them, given them exposure they couldn't have gotten without her.

But Danica had always been her priority.

Reese and Sophie were talking about Danica not coming as though it was a done deal. It wasn't. She might have been leaning in the direction they wanted, but Alder getting in a fight would weaken her resolve. Since she'd left with Shiori, Sophie couldn't do damage control.

She was hoping the band could help her.

Malakai couldn't imagine touring without Danica, but her career had never been limited to performing for Winter's Wrath. Sure, she managed to balance her schedule with the band's more often than not, but this opportunity would be her time to shine.

So long as she wasn't held back because he and the guys would miss her.

Brave remained silent, watching Alder. Connor wasn't going to step up, he was totally out of his element. And Tate... Well, Tate was Tate. If anything, he'd come up with a dozen reasons why they needed Danica because she'd become like a big sister to him.

Which left Malakai.

He folded his arms over his chest and met Sophie's eyes. "If this is what Danica wants, she has our support."

"Thank you." Sophie's expression didn't change much, but some of the lines around her eyes smoothed. "She'll still be connected with the band. Will still bring you good exposure since Winter's Wrath will be mentioned wherever she goes."

"She won't see it that way." Alder spoke so softly Malakai wasn't sure anyone else heard him.

But Brave had. And decided to be fucking helpful, as always. "Danica joined this band on the road as a way to improve her image, but it's more than that now. She loves being on stage. She won't want to leave the band, and her boyfriends, for whatever fucking money she can make doing a damn fashion show."

"No, if she feels pressured, she probably won't." Sophie slid off the bench, rising and glaring down at Brave. "I hope you care about her enough to understand this is about more than money. About more than how good she makes *you* look fawning over you for the crowds."

Brave's eyes went cold. "Didn't you say we'd regret making her choose? Seems you're not so sure what she'll do if *you* try to force her hand. Which is exactly what you're doing here. And we're not about to help you."

"Very well. Have a good night then, boys." Sophie inclined her head to Reese. "I'll see you in the morning."

Reese nodded, waiting until Sophie was gone to let out a sharp laugh. "Well, this was fun. And probably a waste of time. Danica's potential replacement will be joining you on tour. That is if seeing the shitshow tonight didn't scare her away."

And this was exactly why Reese was a perfect manager for them. She could be all prim and proper if she had to be, but when it came to dealing with them alone, she had no problem stooping to their level.

"I'm going to put this to you straight, guys." Reese rose from her seat on the couch and went to the fridge. She grabbed a beer, twisted off the top, and took a swig. "You're fucking lucky to have Danica. She's dynamite on stage. The fans love her. I'm not sure your show will be even half as impressive if she's not up there."

Dead silence. Reese had just given the whole band a swift uppercut. Told them, in her usual no-holds-barred way, that they might not be good enough.

Which should have pissed Malakai off, but he got it. If they were gonna hang on to Danica, no matter what was best for her career, they'd prove they didn't believe they could be successful without her.

He wanted to spell out, very clearly, that they weren't dependent on her, but what did he fucking know? Maybe Reese was right.

Tate cleared his throat and hopped off the counter. "You said something about a replacement? How does that change anything?"

Smiling, Reese turned to the young drummer. "The way I see it, having another girl on stage gives you a chance at a real success story. With Danica, she already had a career. Sure, she needed your grit, but in the end, it's all about her. I like the girl, you know I do, but her getting all kinds of deals does nothing for Winter's Wrath."

"But this new girl is different?" Brave's tone was hard. Unconvinced. "If we agree the band needs to make a statement without Danica, why have a dancer up there at all?"

"Because it works. Not many metal bands bother with eye candy. Pop artists have their flashy dancers, their fireworks, their whole spectacle. I'm not asking you to go to that extreme, but I am asking you to consider what works. What draws the short attention span of the masses." Reese sounded like she was handing them the golden key to all they'd ever wanted. All they had to do was take it. "Don't cut yourselves short. Be different!"

"Isn't this supposed to be about the music?" Connor frowned at Reese's exasperated sigh. "What? We can't rely on Danica. I get that. But we're *not* a pop band."

"No, you're not. But that old-school pride won't get you new blood." Reese shrugged. "Maybe I'm wrong, but honestly, I think you need to get in people's faces. Do some crazy shit. Give them a show they'll never forget."

"And you think this girl can help do that? Like Danica did?" Malakai got a few dirty looks, but the guys clearly weren't using their brains. Reese wasn't playing games. She had a vision and they weren't seeing it.

"I do." Reese gave him a sly smile. "Maybe you could let them know what you think of her. You and Tate have met her already."

We have?

Oh.

Oh!

The girl. The one he'd had trouble looking away from.

Who'd helped Tate.

Who was a fan of the band.

And who'd looked nervous as fuck.

"She's…" Beautiful. Sweet. Tempting. *I want to see her again.* But none of those reasons would convince the band. And he didn't have enough to go on yet. But he had enough to want more. "I think she's worth a shot."

"Good. Now to convince her you are." Reese chuckled. "I wanted her to see you completely in the raw. Your wonderful fucked up selves. A little test, let's say."

"Did she pass?" Tate sounded like he really hoped she had. Malakai could relate.

Reese shrugged. "We'll see. If she comes back tomorrow for rehearsal, then she's off to a good start."

The meeting ended shortly after, with Reese pulling Jesse aside to discuss a few things. Strangely enough, neither Malakai or anyone else seemed to be in the mood to tear into Alder anymore.

Finding out his girlfriend would be in another country for at least a month had hit him hard. Between the busted lip, the bruises, and not having her with him now...

Hell, the guy was suffering enough. Malakai couldn't add to that.

Neither could anyone else.

They all decided to turn in. About an hour later Jesse crept quietly onto the bus, checking on Alder and climbing into his bunk. They spoke quietly for a bit, then Jesse slipped down to his own bed.

Laying on his thin mattress, staring at the ceiling only a few feet above him, Malakai tried to lose himself to sleep. He recognized Tate's steady breathing, telling him the kid was out for the night. Usually all he needed to let go.

But his brain wasn't ready to shut down. Every time he closed his eyes he saw the girl. Damn it, he didn't even know her name yet. All that talk and she was simply 'the replacement'.

To everyone else. But not to him.

She didn't know Tate, but she'd immediately wanted to help him. And had. Even if she wasn't so alluring, that simple act of kindness would have made her impossible to forget.

The rest of the guys were being loyal to Danica. Hadn't even accepted that she could—or *should*—be replaced.

Did that mean Malakai didn't care about her as much? Did the fact that he couldn't see beyond the opportunity for her and the band make him heartless?

He didn't think so. But he also knew he didn't think like the other guys.

Life was fucked up. Shit happened. He'd had to find a way to keep moving forward after failing people he loved. After realizing he hadn't done enough. Tate was his second chance. A kid who needed a protector. Who needed to be saved from himself.

Looking out for Tate wasn't easy, but Malakai had to do it. Wanted to.

The drummer was too fragile for the world he'd been dragged into.

And maybe that's why he couldn't stop thinking about the girl.

He had a feeling she'd need him too.

Chapter Five

The night had been weird. Shiori stretched and rolled on her side, glancing over at the empty bed. Which had been empty all night.

Coming to the hotel with Danica had been awesome. They'd talked a little about performing together, about the new choreographer, about big crowds, and crazy stuff that happened on tour.

But they hadn't talked much about Shiori replacing Danica. About when that would happen. Or if it would happen at all.

The one time Shiori brought it up, Danica pointed out that Shiori's contract wasn't dependent on Danica leaving for an extended period. Technically, her presence could help free up Danica for any side projects.

Then Danica changed the subject. She wanted to know more about Shiori, but there was only so much she could say.

A little while after Shiori pretended to be asleep there was a soft knock at the door. Then a man in the front room, keeping his voice too low for Shiori to make out a single word.

Since then things had been quiet, so maybe Danica had fallen asleep on the sofa with him. Going out there to check shouldn't be a big deal, right? Shiori was supposed to sleep on the bus last night. With a bunch of men she didn't know.

Putting that off had been easy. After seeing the fight she'd been about ready to call this whole thing off. Her reason for wanting to know Brave and Alder was scrapped. She might as well go home.

Seeing the brothers talking had given her some hope, but they were...broken. There wasn't a better word for it. She'd been so close to her sister. Missed her so much. If she had the chance to be with her every day, like Brave and Alder were, she'd be so damn happy.

It wasn't like they didn't know what it was like to lose someone. They'd both lost their older brother, Valor. They had every reason to fix whatever was wrong between them. From what she'd read about them, about Alder saving Brave's life, they came off as closer than ever.

Reality wasn't so pretty.

But maybe she was wrong. She was desperate to be wrong about them, and that was the only reason she hadn't taken the next bus home.

Climbing from the bed, she glanced out the window, watching thick snowflakes fall as the sun began to rise. She shivered as she opened her suitcase, dressing quickly in simple black jeans and a band t-shirt. A Winter's Wrath T-shirt actually. One she'd gotten a year ago for her birthday. She wore it so often it was a little faded, but the soft material felt good on her skin.

And would be perfect for the rehearsal. A rehearsal she'd decided she had to follow through with.

Seeing Brave and Alder talking once after a fight wasn't enough. She had to give them another chance. This was too important to make any rash decisions. If she had to give up on them, who else did she have?

She'd be alone in a fight she wasn't sure she could win.

But she'd do her best. In the end, there was only one goal.

Hiro being with her. Where she could protect him.

There was still time to see if she didn't have to fight alone. She refused to waste it.

Pulling her hair into a high ponytail she headed into the main room, hesitating when she spotted a shirtless man standing in the middle of the room with a tray of coffee and fruit.

He shot her a big smile as he carried the tray to the round table by the picture window. "Good morning."

"Good morning." She could hear the faint sound of the shower. Must be where Danica had disappeared to. "I don't think we've met."

"We haven't. I'm Jesse. Do you want some coffee?"

"Sure?"

"And this is the part where you introduce yourself." He let out a light laugh when she stared at him. "Tate does the same thing. You could talk to him for an hour before he tells you who he is. Since you're a fan, I'm guessing he wouldn't have to tell you."

"No, but…" She shook her head and grinned. "That's a good point. I met both him and Malakai and didn't introduce myself."

"And you still haven't introduced yourself to me."

"Oh. Umm…Shiori." She stuck out her hand. He gave it a light shake.

"A pleasure to meet you." He poured coffee into two mugs. "How do you like yours?"

"Lots of cream and four sugar."

His eyes widened. "Really?"

Why did it feel like a test every time she talked to these people? "Yes. Is that bad?"

"No, just surprising for a model. Danica takes some fake sugar shit and got Alder on it too. She talked me down to three sugars, so don't tell her I'm taking extra this morning so you don't feel left out." He tore open eight packs, dumping them into the cups. "So what do you think of the band?"

His question caught her off guard. She grabbed the offered mug and took a gulp. With so much cream it was the perfect temperature. And braced her enough for an honest answer.

"I'm not sure."

"Fair enough." He took a few swigs of his own coffee and dragged out a chair by the table. Once he was settled, he eyed her curiously. "You don't strike me as a metal chick."

"Well, I am." She pulled out another chair and faced him. "What's your favorite band?"

"I should say Winter's Wrath, but I'll have to go with Limp Bizkit."

Just the name of the band had her wanting to throw something at him. "Lame."

"Really?"

"Yes. I think you should be fired. They aren't even close to being metal. Or music. Or worthy."

The bathroom door opened and Danica came out, glistening from her shower, wrapped in nothing but a towel.

She grinned at Shiori. "Girl, you just gained yourself a fan. Jesse, you're such a jerk. Some people *do* like Limp Bizkit. Like *me*."

"But they aren't metal fans. You have an excuse, babe." Jesse's tone became all sweet. "I love you, anyway."

Danica rolled her eyes. "Uh huh. Nice try. For that, we're listening to them on the way to the bus."

"Please, no." Shiori shuddered at the thought. When she was little, her sister used to rant about how they'd ruined Woodstock '99. Neither had been old enough to know anything about the chaos that had ended the epic event, but her sister preached the metal blogs like gospel.

"You so owe her now." Danica laughed and came over to the table as Jesse fixed her another coffee. "By the way, I'm sorry I didn't warn you about him. He's not supposed to be here. I was hoping you'd sleep a bit longer so I could introduce you."

"I always get up early, but it's all right. I need to get used to this." Shiori wrapped her hands around her mug and looked down at the light brown coffee. "I thought I was ready, but I'm happy you had me sleep here last night. It's…a lot to take in."

"I know. But you'll be fine. They're good guys." Danica gave Jesse a pointed look. He grabbed his coffee and disappeared into the bedroom. "Sophie didn't give me details, but she implied you have some connection with Alder and Brave. Do you want to talk about it?"

Shiori bit down hard on her bottom lip. Sophie had said she needed to tell Danica *something*, but sharing details would be up to her.

And she wasn't ready.

Soon, hopefully, she would be, but she still wanted the option to back out if she needed it. Back out without Brave and Alder knowing anything about her. About her sister and Hiro.

"Will you be mad if I say no?"

"Not at all. I know you have your reasons. And you're more than a fan or you wouldn't be here." Danica finished off her coffee and stood. She made a 'get up' motion with her hand and Shiori stood. "Baby, this rehearsal is another audition. You can't show up like that."

"I can't?" She smoothed her hands over her jeans. They were well worn and she knew she could move in them. She could dance in heels, but why bother for rehearsal? Danica always wore boots. Shiori didn't have boots. Her black Chucks had seemed perfect.

"No. You can't." Danica motioned her to follow to the bedroom. "You're close to my size. Let's find you something that will make an impression. I hear one more person refer to you as 'the replacement' after this and I'll lay them out."

Being 'the replacement' for Danica didn't seem like a bad thing. But she wouldn't argue with her. Having someone like Danica to give her pointers was a once in a lifetime thing. No way she was passing it up.

A wardrobe change, hair and makeup overhaul, and Shiori was given the stamp of approval. For their breakfast meeting.

Which would take place right before they headed to rehearsal, but Shiori still felt weird going to a small diner with thick black eyeliner and a revealing outfit.

Thankfully, neither Sophie or Reese even blinked at her wardrobe. Or Danica's, which matched hers. They looked like they'd both walked out of some anime. Danica could pass as a goth Sailor Moon.

And with all the red, Shiori would be Sailor Mars.

Only that chick was tough.

One look from Reese and Shiori wasn't sure she belonged on Danica's team. Or even standing in her shadow. She sat back as Sophie ordered for her and Danica, watching them silently.

Shiori hadn't paid any attention to the order, but she was expecting yogurt. Or eggs whites.

Instead, the waitress set a blueberry muffin, waffles with syrup and whipped cream, and a bowl of fruit salad in front of her.

Prepared for another test, Shiori looked at Danica.

Who slathered butter on her own muffin as she spoke curtly to Sophie. "I'll look at the contracts."

"When?"

Danica tightened her grip on her knife at Reese's curt question. "Excuse me?"

"I know I'm not *your* manager, but Sophie and I work together when it comes to your involvement with Winter's Wrath. This delay is unprofessional. Shiori has been brought in to take your place. I need to know how much time she has to prepare."

Ignoring Reese, Danica looked at Sophie, her eyes darkening with anger. "Is that why you went to the guys without me? I haven't agreed to anything."

"And you wouldn't have. I've seen you discussing this with Alder. He doesn't want you to go, but he pretends to encourage you. Danica, time's up. Those contracts need to be signed today. I needed him to understand—"

"Not like this. After last night—"

"*Because* of last night. I knew seeing Alder lose control would make this so much harder for you!"

Through the window, Shiori could see Jesse standing by the band's van. She wished she could be out there too. The back and forth between Danica and Sophie was hard to listen to. Why was she here? If Danica refused to leave they didn't need her.

Of all people, it was Reese who spoke her very thoughts. "Sophie, I get why you wanted to give the band a nudge, but it's not fair to drag Shiori into this."

"Whether or not Danica leaves, having someone else on stage will draw the attention you're looking for. Shiori has a place in your vision for the band. We need to clarify what that is." Sophie glanced over at Shiori. "I can find you other work. I've told you that before. Do you still want this?"

Do I? It was humiliating, having people talk around her like she wasn't there. Like she didn't matter. Any other model would be seriously considering her options.

If she wanted to see more of the men, if last night wasn't enough, then she had to accept nothing was guaranteed. But every moment mattered. Unless she was ready to tell them all exactly why she was here, she'd have to accept being the understudy. An understudy no one seemed to want.

"I want to dance for the band." She met Sophie's eyes and gave a short nod. She'd come this far. She wasn't turning back now. But she didn't like the position they'd put Danica in. "We have a month, right? Let the band decide what they want to do. Danica is one of them. I get that my performance might make her feel better about leaving, but it's clear there's more involved."

Sophie inclined her head. "There is. But you don't need to worry about that. Go on stage and focus on what *you* need to prove. This has become much more complicated than it needs to be."

"No. This is my life you're messing with. If you find that complicated, too fucking bad." Danica shoved her plate away and stood. "Shiori, I'm sorry. Please know this isn't your fault. But I have to go talk to Alder before this goes any further."

Without Danica there, things got really uncomfortable. For the rest of the meal, Reese and Sophie talked business, trying to include Shiori now and then, though she had nothing to add.

Finally, it was rehearsal time and Sophie drove her to the rented space. They walked up to the second floor of a building on the edge of town, which looked like it had once been a ballet studio.

The stage was set. Speakers were placed in every corner, one end of the room crammed with the drum kit, amps, mic stands. At the other end roadies and bodyguards stood around chatting, but silence fell as she crossed the threshold. All eyes were on her, watching her through the mirrors lining the walls.

They knew why she was here.

And they hated her for it.

They hate that Danica might leave. They don't *hate you.*

Sure felt like it, though.

Jesse approached her, an apologetic smile on his lips. "The sound won't be great, but there's plenty of space to move." He gave her hand a little squeeze. "You've got this."

She returned his smile, guilt weighing heavy on her chest. He shouldn't be encouraging her. She'd been brought here as more than a performer. Her whole purpose was to prove the band didn't need Danica. That they'd be fine with a replacement.

But if Shiori wanted to stay, she had to prove all that and more. Because convincing the band and the fans was one thing.

Convincing herself? A whole different story.

Chapter Six

Brave was not a nice person without sleep. Standing behind the studio they'd rented, he watched Skull, their oldest roadie, take a long, very satisfying drag on his cigarette.

Maybe secondhand smoke would kill the cravings. Coffee definitely wasn't cutting it. And he'd had three cups. Black and hot enough to burn his tongue because he wanted it to hurt.

Things that hurt made sense. Physical pain he could handle. Emotional shit? Not so much.

He'd been better off completely numb. Worrying about his brother, telling anyone how fucking scared he'd been...shit, at this point, no one cared what he thought.

But he'd done that. He'd pushed them all away.

Job well fucking done.

"What's eating at you, boy?" Skull let out the smoke slowly, his lips curving slightly as Brave stared at his mouth. He chuckled and held out the cigarette. "Go ahead. A few puffs won't kill you."

Brave took the cigarette even as he shook his head. "The guys might if they catch me."

"Bunch of hypocrites, the lot of them." Skull folded his arms over his chest, not speaking until Brave inhaled deeply. "Life was simpler when they all hated you."

Snorting, Brave opened his mouth to reply, but the smoke caught in his throat, sending him into a coughing fit. He bent over. Gasped in air.

As Skull laughed his ass off and pounded on his back. "You were saying?"

"They—" Another ragged cough. "—still hate me."

"Then why would they care if you slowly kill yourself with this shit?" Skull had retrieved his cigarette at some point and went back to smoking like the damn thing hadn't nearly suffocated Brave. "And before you call *me* a hypocrite, remember I've been doing this for almost forty years."

"I smoked for fifteen."

"Then you quit." Skull's lifted his shoulders like he couldn't care less. "I won't get on your case, Brave. You're a grown man and lectures didn't work when you were a cocky little shit, never mind now."

"How about some advice?"

Skull's lips slanted up slightly. "Might be able to manage that."

Dropping his gaze to his knee length, worn leather boots, Brave swallowed hard. "I suck as a brother."

"Yes, you do."

"Thanks," Brave said, dryly. "What am I doing wrong?"

"You're trying to make years of damage disappear. Alder needs you, but he also needs to heal." Skull dropped his cigarette and crushed it under his boot heel. "And that won't happen if he's still trying to hold everything together for you. Fix yourself. The rest will come."

With that Brave was dismissed. He headed inside as Skull ambled off to the roadie van.

Fix myself? Brave tugged the length of suede binding his hair, letting it flow loose as he reached the rehearsal room. He had no clue what Skull meant, but he didn't have time to figure it out. The band was all he and Alder really had anymore. Maybe they could build on that.

Stepping into the room he spotted Alder with Jesse and Danica. On the makeshift stage, Connor was tuning his guitar, laughing at something Tate said to him from behind the drum set.

Off to the side, Malakai stood holding his guitar by the neck, his eyes on Sophie. The man rubbed one hand over his closely shaved hair, then let it fall in a fist at his side.

Had Sophie done something to piss him off? He'd been all onboard with her plan to replace Danica. Had the agent changed her mind?

That would make Alder happy. Brave had no idea what Malakai had against their dancer, but fuck him. He'd get over it.

Striding up to the stage, Brave grabbed his mic and let out a low growl, smirking when almost everyone in the room jumped. He cleared his throat. "Sorry, just warming up."

"Asshole." Malakai muttered before pulling his guitar strap over his shoulder. He glanced at Sophie one last time, then came over to take his place on 'stage'.

With everyone in place, Brave began their set, starting with their new cover of Ed Sheeran's *Sing*. He hadn't been a huge fan until he'd heard his brother singing the song all slow and seductive to Danica.

After that, he must have listened to the song a hundred times, trying to figure out how to put an edge to it. Brave usually stuck to lyrics, then told Alder and Malakai what sound he was going for. They worked their magic and music was born.

With the cover, he'd *heard* the melody so clearly in his head, cut down, deepened to a twisted, seductive tone. He sang it once for them with no music, asking Alder to take the chorus because he had the smooth quality they needed.

A week later they recorded the song. The day it came out it was playing everywhere. Topping charts like crazy.

For the first time, the band truly came together. Everyone was happy. Danica had a new routine that had her gliding across the stage and grinding low in a way that made the fans drool. Watching her prompted Brave to create a silent new mantra.

'Off limits. So fucking off limits. Damn hot, but stay far, far away.'

He'd noticed Malakai and Connor adjusting themselves after the first performance, so he didn't feel too bad.

Halfway to the chorus, he braced himself for Danica's entrance. Movement caught the corner of his eye even as she slinked up to his side. He glanced over and his mouth went dry.

Mirroring Danica's moves, dipping low with one hand barely brushing his thigh, was a vision of exquisite beauty so pure he wondered for a minute if he was dreaming. A sleek spill of black hair with a hint of moonlit ocean blue. Pale flesh with a touch of gold. And her eyes...he could write amazing lyrics about her eyes. Which had to be the sappiest thing he'd ever considered, but he couldn't shake the dizzying high that had him staring into them.

Like a star sapphire with true light trapped in the core, slowly fading to darkness before spilling out around it. And that light drew him in. Came from something deeper, beyond anything he could see. Her brief touch simmered through him and the whole world tilted on its axis. She locked her beautiful eyes on him for a split second, letting out a sharp breath as though she felt the shift too.

Fuck, this was crazy. He tried to focus on the song as Alder finished the chorus. Drawing away from Brave in a sharp spin, the girl lost her balance on her spiked heels. He dropped the mic to catch her.

The loud feedback *SCREECH!* of the mic hitting the floor snapped his brain back into reality. Where he was wide awake and everyone was holding their hands over their ears, glaring at him.

He looked down at the young woman in his arms, the way she trembled, face hidden against his chest, like ice water thrown in his face. She was fucking terrified, and at first, he couldn't figure out why. All he'd done was keep her from falling.

Then his brain decided to function again. She was 'the replacement'. The girl who'd take over for Danica.

But only if she proved herself here. Now.

And because of him, she'd failed.

Which he should want. Her failure gave Danica another reason to stay. To reject all the offers and be where Alder needed her.

Checking that the girl was steady on her feet, Brave eased back. She wrapped her arms around her stomach and swallowed hard.

He looked over to Reese, who'd approached the 'stage', lips thin.

"Is there a problem with the routine, Shiori?"

Shiori shook her head. "No. I just—"

"I tripped her." Brave cursed internally as all eyes turned to him. Damn it, what kind of excuse was that? He rolled his shoulders, scrambling for something that made more sense. "I'm used to one chick all over me. Two takes some adjustment, but I've managed before."

"*Charming.*" Reese frowned at him. "I didn't see you anywhere near her feet."

"I kicked her heel. Fuck, we doing this or what? I messed up. I'm a singer, not a dancer." He glanced over at Shiori. "Sorry about that."

Shiori's lips parted. Then closed. She gave him a little smile that warmed his heart. "It's okay. I'm not used to dancing around so many people. I should have stepped farther away."

"No harm." Brave met Reese's eyes, brows lifted. "Should we start again?"

"Do *S.L.U.T.*" Reese sounded pissed, but she simply returned to her place against the wall by Danica's agent, Sophie.

S.L.U.T was even worse than the routine for *Sing*. Most of the moves involved Danica dancing close to all the guys, and she put a different spin on it for almost every show now that she knew how to work the crowd. Shiori stuck with the original choreography, and he struggled to keep his eyes off her as she danced around the stage. The first time she came to him, grinding against him, careful not to actually *touch* him, he fucked up his breathing and went off-key.

No one seemed to notice. He took a few deep breaths during the guitar solo, pulse pounding in his ears as Shiori and Danica shimmied up against his brother. Alder divided his attention between them well, performing with ease and smiling like he enjoyed their touch.

The next growl Brave let out was a bit too low. A bit too real. Alder shouldn't be messing with the girl. He'd fuck this up for her. Or make Danica jealous. Danica didn't look jealous, but the chick was weird. She shared Alder with Jesse. Maybe adding Shiori to the mix was the next step in their twisted relationship.

Not my problem. Finish the damn song.

That he could do. He needed it to end.

But he'd forgotten what came next. Danica didn't kiss him during this song anymore. Her coming close then dancing away was enough.

Pressing against him, Shiori pulled his arm around her, smoothly guiding him into his part of the routine. But the next move was his. He ground his teeth, not sure if he should follow through. Her touching him had fucked him up once already. Which made things harder for her. And for some reason he wanted her to pass this test. To impress Reese. Impress the band.

Could she continue if he finished as he was supposed to? If he kissed her?

"Please?" Leaning back, forcing him to hold her, Shiori gazed up at him, whispering. "Please finish it."

Bending down he brushed his lips over hers, kissing her as the final chords faded away. The heat, the soft pressure, her little gasp, called to him. A taste wasn't enough. She was so damn sweet. So tempting.

Giving in would be easy. Taking everything he wanted nothing more than he'd always done. He tightened his grip, flicking his tongue over her bottom lip. Her lips parted and he knew he could have it all. Taste her, pull her close until she could feel everything he wanted from her.

But they weren't alone. And this was as much of a test for him as it was for her. Not that anyone expected any better from him, but he needed to prove he'd changed. That the man they thought they knew was gone.

The man he was trying to be wouldn't screw things up for her. Not for the pleasure. Not even for his brother. Alder wouldn't want to force Danica's hand. Not like this.

Smiling against Shiori's lips, Brave spoke softly, hoping he hadn't already gone too far. "I'm impressed."

Shiori frowned as he helped her straighten and drew away. "Why?"

"Danica slapped me the first time we did that move."

"Oh. I didn't think of that." She blushed and smoothed her little red pleated skirt. "Was it okay?"

"Very okay." Lucky for him, she didn't seem very experienced. If she'd been trying to mess with him, he'd be done for. As it was, her innocence was tearing him to shreds. That outfit shouldn't be legal.

Aside from the tiny skirt, she wore a tight, white corset with a big, blue bow between her breasts that made him think of a show he'd seen, but couldn't remember. Either way, her long legs and her pale breasts swelling above the neckline of her shirt were spoiling all his good intentions.

Also, they both seemed to have forgotten they had an audience.

"Danica wasn't a fan. And she clearly knows how to handle you." Reese sounded even more pissed off than before. "Sophie, this isn't going to work."

"Why? Because she has good chemistry with him? Reese, I've never known you to be this short sighted." Sophie walked up to the stage, and Brave tensed at the excitement in her eyes. "So far Danica and Alder are the only two I've been able to truly shop out for ads. We've both been trying to find a way to use Brave more, but his reputation has made him unsuitable for most brands. For a moment he looked almost...sweet."

"*Sweet?*" Reese wrinkled her nose. "Metal and sweet don't mix. With Alder it works. He can play the dark hero with his beautiful lover. If it sells perfume and brings income to the band, fine. But Brave being the cold, unapproachable lead keeps them hardcore."

"The music keeps them hardcore." Sophie faced Reese, hand on her hips. "I thought you were willing to explore any possible exposure."

"I am. But I also have to consider their image. We don't want to alienate fans by coming across as sellouts." Reese shook her head. "Brave, I know *S.L.U.T* is about ditching negativity toward female sexuality, but it's not a love song. I'd almost prefer her slapping you."

"I'm sure she can slap me if that's what you need." Brave latched onto Shiori's wrist. "Here, sweetie. Slap me now so we can continue."

Shiori's eyes went wide. "Now?"

"Yes. Now." Reese's tone sharpened. "Because at this point all I see is a star-struck little girl who won't make it a week in the metal scene. I'm not willing to sign on a child who will run crying the second things get rough. And believe me, they will get rough. And violent. The crowd won't be *sweet*."

"Kiss her again, Brave." Malakai came to his side, voice hard, grip tight on his guitar. "Kiss her like you kissed Danica. Like you don't care what she wants."

What the actual fuck? Brave stared at Malakai. The man who'd wanted to kill him for doing shit like that. For using people. People like Tate, who'd been ready and willing.

But still someone Malakai needed to protect from all of Brave's fucked up shit. From his self-destructive attitude, when he did whatever he wanted without considering the consequences. Without a thought of who he'd hurt.

Brave knew he'd been an asshole. He'd almost destroyed the band. For months he'd been fighting to leave all that behind him.

And now the man wanted him to go back there?

"Don't look at me like that." Malakai glared at him. "This isn't about you."

Malakai was right. And while the rest of the band had checked out, ignoring the whole exchange, Malakai was the only one willing to tell him what he needed to do.

Because for some reason Malakai wanted Shiori to succeed

And whether or not Brave *should*, he did too.

Reese had a point. If Shiori couldn't take him being his old self, the metal scene would bury her alive. He couldn't protect her from it. And pretending he could wouldn't do her any favors.

Letting the cold, detached emotions that had once been so familiar settle over him, he lifted his hand and wrapped it around the back of Shiori's neck, dragging her close.

And just to make sure she had plenty of motivation, he whispered softly against her lips. "Whatever they think, I don't care. The way you touched me told me everything I need to know. You're desperate to be fucked. And when this is over, I'm all yours."

He claimed her lips in a rough kiss, closing himself off from any feelings. From how careful he wanted to be. From how she whimpered at the brutal pressure. From how she struggled to twist free.

Her hand slammed into his chest. She threw her head back.

But instead of slapping him she nailed him with a swift punch.

Letting her go, he brought one hand to his eye. Blood slicked his fingers.

Chicks and their damn rings.

Her lips formed a wide O, but before she could say a word Danica grabbed her by the shoulder. Whispered something in her ear.

Shiori squared her shoulders and turned her back on him.

Good girl.

"I stand corrected." A huge smile spread across Reese's lips. "That was… Damn, imagine that live?"

How about no? Brave pressed his palm over his eye as the blood continued to flow and everyone kept talking. Reese called for a short break and took off with Sophie. Alder followed Danica and Jesse as they led Shiori out.

A heavy hand settled on his shoulder. "Come on, let me take a look."

Brave let Malakai lead him to a chair, not sure what to say. Of all the guys Malakai was the last person he'd expect to give a fuck that he was bleeding. The man was honest about how he felt about Brave.

They weren't friends. Hadn't been in a long time.

"Shit, that was so fucked up!" Tate crouched in front of Brave, glancing at his eye with a wince when Brave lowered his hand. "She got you good."

"Yeah." Brave tipped his head back, ignoring the dull throb and the warm spill forcing him to keep one eye closed. "I guess being a complete dick pays off."

Coming to his side, suddenly shirtless, Malakai held something against the cut. "Sorry. I thought we'd have a towel or something. Tate, go get the med kit from the van."

"On it!" Tate scampered off.

Malakai's darkly tanned, bare chest filled Brave's vision. Fuck, the man was ripped. Not bulky like Connor, but every inch of him was carved with sharp definition. He folded his shirt over to look at the cut. "Damn. What did you say to her?"

"That I could tell she was desperate to be fucked." Brave bit into his tongue as Malakai pressed down hard. "Ease up, man. I didn't mean it."

With a deep breath, Malakai eased the pressure over his eye. "I know."

"Good." Brave exhaled slowly. "I like her. She's…she seems nice."

"I think so too." Malakai's lips thinned. The sleek muscles of his shoulders hardened. "But you have to be careful with her. She's walking on thin ice. Reese wants *someone* to take Danica's place, but I think she's looking for someone who will just look pretty up there. She talks a good game, but she doesn't want another performer with other options."

"Then why go to Sophie? Danica's agent doesn't hire shallow cookie cutter chicks."

"Yeah, but Reese wants to keep Danica. Think of it. Even if Danica has other things going on, every time she comes back will be a big deal. While she's gone we put on a great show with a decent backup." Malakai checked the cut again. Took a knee at Brave's side while still applying pressure. "The backup can't overshadow the band's 'image'. She can't be important enough to get too much attention."

"I'm missing something. I thought Reese wanted another success story to play on."

"Maybe she does, but she also doesn't want to pay for another well-established model. She can't have Danica and another star." Malakai shrugged. "I could be wrong, but I think she sees something in Shiori. Something special. She'd rather lose her now than pay for her later."

"But you want her to stay."

"I do."

Brave considered Malakai, not sure what to make of them being on speaking terms. He hardly knew the man anymore. To him, the bassist was the guy who wrote the music and acted like Tate's guard dog. He had a fucking temper and when the band started had spent the night in jail a few times for fighting in bars.

They'd been cool back then. Hell, Brave had jumped into the fights a few times, even the ones Malakai started over stupid shit. They drank and smoked together. Picked up girls and ran a little wild.

But when Brave drew away from Alder, Malakai became distant. No huge surprise there. He wasn't just protective of

Tate. He had this thing for stepping up for anyone he thought needed him in their corner.

Brave never had.

The girl, however, would easily fit into the bassist's hero complex. His concern could be all noble and pure. But what if he had alternative motives to get Brave out of the way?

"She's about Tate's age I think." Brave kept his tone light, like they were discussing the weather or the pit stops along their route. "This has to be overwhelming for her."

"Ya think?" Malakai shook his head. "I saw her on the bus yesterday. She gave Tate some candy while he was craving a high bad. She's gonna have trouble fitting in, but she's got a good heart. If she stays I'll keep an eye on her."

So far so good, but not enough. Time to stop beating around the bush. "So you don't want to fuck her?"

Malakai dropped the bloody shirt and straightened, his eyes narrowing as he stared down at Brave. "What the actual fuck, man?"

"It's an honest question."

Letting out a cold laugh, Malakai inclined his head. "From you? Guess it is. Tate should be back soon. He can patch you up."

"You're not gonna warn me to keep my hands off him?" Brave knew he was pushing, but he couldn't help it. Malakai hadn't answered. The fucker had forced Brave to do something that would make Shiori hate him, while keeping his own hands clean.

And now he was gonna play like Brave was the asshole?

Fuck that noise.

The look Malakai gave him chilled him to the bone. Leaning close, one hand on the back the chair, his lips brushed Brave's ear as he spoke. "Keep testing me. I dare you."

Pulse quickening, Brave eased forward, letting his tone drop to the deep growl that filled his bed almost every night. "You're hot all scary. Tell me what you're gonna do. I'm already hard."

"You would be." Malakai shoved away, clenching his fist and staring at Brave like he was very tempted to knock him the fuck out. "We both know Tate will do what he wants. Hurt him and I'll bury you."

"I make no promises." Brave smirked, arching a brow. Which wasn't smart because, without the compress, it started bleeding again. He sighed and grabbed the shirt as blood trailed hot over his eye. "And the girl?"

"That you're even asking proves you haven't changed at all." Malakai's expression changed and Brave wanted to take it all back. Rather than anger, regret flashed in the man's eyes before he walked away. Maybe he'd felt the shift in their relationship too and hoped things would get better.

With a few words, Brave had ruined any chance that they could be friends again.

But at least he knew exactly where things stood between them. Friendship with Malakai came with many perks, but Brave didn't meet his standards in any sense of the word. And he didn't need protection.

Keep your enemies close and all that. When Malakai saw him as a rival, as a threat, Brave could just be himself. He'd tried to change and it hadn't done any good.

So maybe he should stop.

Hell, even Reese wanted the old him. Being wicked and reckless worked with the fans. Fit the music. Who he was on stage was all anyone cared about.

Who was he trying to impress anyway? He'd wanted to be better when he'd almost lost Alder, but his brother didn't need him. Not when he had Danica and Jesse.

If that changed he'd do what he could, but he was done turning himself inside out for people who'd paint him with the same brush no matter what he did.

Even now he could hear Valor laughing at him for trying.

"This lifestyle doesn't last, bro. And everything you put into it means fuck all. Today they love you. Tomorrow you might as well be dead." Valor's bloodshot eyes met Brave's. Brave had just read a review about one

of their songs and he needed his big brother to tell him they had something to offer the world.

The review had cut deep. He knew better than to read them but he couldn't help it. He cared what people thought about the music he'd worked so hard to put out there.

"Why bother then? People hate *us!"* Brave dropped the magazine on the table and slumped in the seat next to his brother, looking around at the dirty motel room where they were spending the night. He hadn't slept in days. Couldn't remember the last time he'd eaten a decent meal. Probably last Friday, on his nineteenth birthday. Only the guys got him so wasted he hadn't kept much down.

Brave sacrificed everything for the band. His relationship with his parents, his chance at a normal life. And hadn't thought twice about putting his faith in his brother.

But that was back when Valor's drive went beyond satisfying his addictions. The band's earnings on the road barely covered gas money, but their sole album sold enough to cover travel and merchandise for another month. Brave had carefully worked out the budget, but Valor had trashed it in a day. He refused to let Brave's plans cut into their drug money.

Feeding Valor's vices limited the band's opportunities.

Still, Brave struggled to find ways for them to succeed. His cut had gone to pay for their last recording. He'd scrimped on meals to save up for more studio time. They were putting out one song every six months. Not enough to keep them relevant. He wasn't as strung out as the rest of the guys, but a few pills kept him from getting hungry. Valor didn't mind sharing his drugs.

But if Brave passed out on stage again, would they leave him behind? He dropped his head to his hands. "Valor, what are we doing? We almost got signed last week, but you showed up late and—"

"And what? Dude, don't start with me." Valor snorted another line, then straightened. "You want to be a good boy? Go home. You want to be part of this band, how about some fucking gratitude? That pussy you nailed last night gave it up because you're one of us. The drugs, the reputation, the fucking sweet ass lifestyle we get to enjoy? That's why we're doing this."

"We can do more. Our music can—"

"Can what? Make an impact? Become classic shit?" Blood trickled from Valor's nose. He swiped it away with a laugh. "You can't pay the bills with those dreams, kid. Wake up. That legacy you want won't happen. But getting that next high, that hot mouth on your dick? That's today. And tomorrow. Enjoy it before you get old and regret not living it up."

Brave stared at his brother, who already looked old. 'Living it up' had his eyes sunken in, his skin a sickly yellow and his long hair thin and greasy. Only twenty-four, but their father could pass as younger than him.

He used to admire his big brother, but there wasn't much to look up to anymore.

The band meant too much for Brave to give up now, though. Jaw clenched, he met Valor's unfocused eyes. "I'm grateful, but you're not gonna have the money for all the shit you love so much if this keeps up."

"So what do you suggest? I'm all ears."

"We double our shows. Get a few new songs out." Brave's excitement grew as Valor nodded and motioned for him to go on. The man was actually listening. "If we practice more our sound will improve and we'll get new fans. I could work out a schedule and—"

"Fucking ambitious, aren't you?" Valor looked down at the white streaked mirror on the table. His eyes suddenly went wild. "What the fuck? Did you take my dust, man?"

"No, you finished it. You know I wouldn't—" Brave's blood ran cold as his brother's hands wrapped around his throat, squeezing hard. "I wouldn't, Valor. I swear I wouldn't."

"Not gonna try to save me, little brother?" Valor bent over him, tightening his grip even more. He let out a thin laugh as Brave clawed at his hands. "Because that would be stupid."

"I know." Brave's eyes teared. Red spotted his vision. "Please stop—"

The band came in, shouting as they wrestled Valor off him. Skull helped Brave out of the motel room, cursing Valor under his breath.

His brother's cutting laughter followed him long after the door slammed between them.

"He thinks he's better than me. Thinks he's better than us all."

Pressing hard on his eye, Brave forced his mind back to the present. A present where he was so fucking lost. He'd *proven* he was better than Valor. Hell, not long after his brother attacked him, Brave stopped doing hard drugs. He'd practiced all the time, even though the rest of the band ditched him to party more often than not. Skull found him a vocal coach, stuck close when Valor was fucked up, and became his biggest supporter for years after.

Live On Satan's Time never got big, but they'd gained a decent following. Had a good run before Valor died.

And now Brave had Winter's Wrath fulfilling all his dreams. His hard work meant something. Fine, he and the guys weren't buddies, but they shared one goal. Were all willing to work hard to accomplish it.

Beyond that, nothing else mattered.

The door opened and Tate came into the rehearsal room, carrying a big white box. Not the one from the van. "Sorry it took so long. The van was gone, but I hunted down the owner of this place and he gave me this."

"That was cool of you, Tate. Thanks." Brave dropped the shirt. "I'm good, though."

Tate frowned at him as the cut proved him a liar and started bleeding again. Only a little, but enough to need patching up. "Sure you are. Shit, you probably need stitches. I ain't no doctor. Where's Malakai?"

"He's not a doctor either."

"No, but he's smarter than me. He could figure out how to fix you."

He could try. Brave shook his head. "I can do it myself if you don't want to."

"I *want* to, I'm just not good at anyth—"

"Stop talking shit about my favorite drummer." Brave's grinned as Tate ducked his head. Was hard not to love the kid. And, unlike the rest of the band, Tate didn't need more than a little encouragement now and then.

That I can do.

"Check if there's tape or something in there. Should work."

"Okay…" Tate opened the med kit on the floor, rifling through it until he found a small box of Second Skin. He held it up. "This good?"

"Perfect." Brave held still as Tate moved close, gently applying the clear bandage, legs framing one of Brave's, practically in his lap. His thigh brushing Brave's cock was a nice distraction from the throb of pain in his face.

That part of his body showing interest was bad news.

He tried to shift back.

"Hold still." Tate murmured, pressing against him a little more. "Just need to smooth it out a bit."

Shit. Brave wet his lips with his tongue, doing his best to ignore his swelling cock. It hadn't gotten any action in a while. And clearly hadn't forgotten how good Tate's tight, hot, willing body felt.

But Brave had fucked Tate when he'd been on a downward spiral. When he stopped giving a shit about everything and everyone. They hadn't even discussed that day since. Not alone anyway.

When he'd bared his damn soul to the band about Valor, about how messed up he was and what he was willing to do to fix shit, Tate had brought up them having sex once. Brave brushed the incident off as a one-time mistake.

Because using Tate had been a really bad idea. He'd wanted to hurt Jesse. Hurt Malakai. Not for any reason that made any damn sense, but what's done was done.

The way Tate moved his thigh against Brave's erection, he clearly didn't feel the same. The contact wasn't accidental. The kid wasn't good at being sneaky.

"I think you're done, Tate." Brave took a firm grip on Tate's arms when he wiggled even closer. "Stop."

"You sure?" Tate flashed him a wicked grin and glanced down at the outline of Brave's dick in his tight jeans. "No one's coming back up here."

"I'm sure." Brave pushed to his feet, setting Tate away from him. "Why you starting this shit again? You know it ain't happening."

Tate's grin faded. "Oh… I didn't know you didn't want me anymore."

Damn it, now I feel like an asshole. "Tate, you're fucking hot. Anyone would want you. And the right person will—"

"Shit, I'm not in love with you or anything." Tate raked his fingers through the long spill of golden-brown hair at the top of his head, letting it fall over the shaved part and forward to cover one eye. "I'm not looking for 'the right person'. Just figured we could have some fun."

"You can have *fun* with any groupie. Find a cute girl. Or guy." Why the hell were they even having this conversation? Tate knew how things were with the band. "I go near you and people get pissed."

"No one needs to know."

"The answer is no, kid. Sorry."

"S'all good." Tate shrugged and backed away from him. "But I saw how you looked at the new girl. You think the guys will be pissed if you mess with me? They'll go mental if you touch her."

"I wasn't planning to." And he really wasn't. He was no good for her. Or Tate.

Or *anyone*.

"Okay. Understood." Tate continued to the door. "But just so you know, the offer's on the table."

Long after the drummer was gone, Brave simply stood there, staring at the closed door. And picturing the one Tate had left wide open.

He should slam it shut. Forget about it.

The band was his priority. The one time he'd let his focus slip, he'd almost lost everything. He couldn't risk going there again.

But he couldn't deny Tate's offer was tempting.

"No one needs to know."

He'd been good for so long. Sure, he still fucked the odd groupie, but he was tired of the same old routine. Picking some random guy or girl for a quickie. Fuck, the last few times he didn't even get off. It was nothing but another performance. Another service to the fans.

For once he wanted pleasure that wasn't tied to who he had to be every minute of every day. He didn't know who he was beyond the band. He didn't have time to figure that out.

But some time with someone who didn't give a shit what his name was? Hell, even if they were using him, it would be a nice change.

Tate could give him that. No questions. No expectations.

For some fucked up reason, he remembered Malakai, leaning over him, whispering in his ear. That hard body that could hurt him bad. How fucked up was he that the idea turned him on?

If he was getting hard thinking about Malakai, one thing was very clear.

He needed to get laid. The way he used to.

No limits.

No holds barred.

And no fucking regrets.

Chapter Seven

This world was so messed up. One day, only a small portion spent with the band, and Shiori had to admit she was in way over her head. The information coming at her, from how to deal with the opening bands, to after parties and groupies and what was okay to do in the bus bathroom made her head hurt. The roadies were like family, but she shouldn't be alone with them. The guys in the band would respect her, but she had to watch what she said.

Shiori loved Danica. And Jesse was great. Being around Alder was still a little weird, but she liked him. He looked tired all the time, didn't talk much, but he was polite and treated both Jesse and Danica like they were his everything.

But after a couple hours with the three of them, she needed a break. She felt like a third—fourth?—wheel, and she couldn't add anything to Danica's sporadic rants about Sophie taking over her life, or how out of line Reese apparently was.

The band had decided to leave tomorrow, so Danica was staying at the hotel for another night. She'd convinced Alder and Jesse to join her. And, of course, Shiori should as well.

No 'of course' about it. Shiori cleared her throat.

"Please don't be mad, but I need to stay on the bus." Shiori looked down at her half-eaten plate of grilled chicken and vegetables. Danica had found them a quiet little restaurant in downtown Detroit. Had been really nice when Shiori asked what would be okay to eat.

Now that she was a contracted model, Shiori figured she should be more careful with her diet. She had no idea how she'd manage that on the road, but Danica promised to teach her.

Awesome. Danica would be with her for the beginning of the tour. Maybe longer.

But Shiori needed to figure out how to manage on her own. Just in case Danica *did* decide to take the opportunities Sophie had set up for her. She also sensed that the trio needed some time alone.

Danica frowned and set her fork on the plate she'd barely touched. "I'm not mad, but… Sweetie, today was rough. Why not give yourself more time?"

"If I stay tonight and it's horrible, I can still go back to the hotel. Or decide this lifestyle isn't for me and go home." Shiori took a deep breath. "Tomorrow we'll be on the road. I need to see if I can do this while I still have a way out."

"You'll always have a way out." Jesse cut a piece of steak, eyeing Alder and Danica's full plates and shaking his head. "But I get it. Time to take off the training wheels."

"Exactly." Damn, she was happy Jesse was here. He had a way of keeping things simple. And when he worded things just right, neither Danica or Alder tended to argue with him.

But this time, Alder decided to speak up. "You punched Brave. Are you sure you're ready to face him alone?"

Can't we forget I did that? Shiori had tried really hard to. No one had mentioned the altercation since, which gave her some hope. If she let herself think about it, she'd start packing her bags.

Fine, Brave had goaded her. Reese had pretty much demanded she hit him. In that moment she'd been so angry she'd reacted, not holding back. Something in her snapped and she'd checked out for a bit after. She remembered Danica leading her away. Remembered washing her hands in the bathroom. Seeing blood in the water. One of the rings Danica leant her had wicked little spikes on it. She'd hurt him.

Part of her wanted to apologize.

Another part wondered if he deserved it.

Which was cruel. Not like her at all.

She poked at her food with her fork, completely miserable. Given half the chance she would have faced him already. Forgetting what had happened would make her life easier. Facing him—and the rest of the band—with Danica backing her up even more so.

But she wouldn't gain their respect hiding behind Danica. She'd meant what she'd said to the other woman. Either she figured out if she could do this now or she might as well go home.

What else can I say to make them understand?

Jesse stood abruptly, grabbing his jacket from the back of his chair. "She won't be alone. I'll bring her back to the bus. Make sure she's okay and ask Malakai to keep an eye on her."

Alder's brow furrowed. "Malakai?"

Jesse inclined his head. "Yeah. Didn't you hear? She gave Tate candy when he was messed up. Malakai is her biggest fan."

He is? Shiori scrambled to pull on her own jacket, not sure what to make of how quickly Alder and Danica dropped the subject. Shortly after they were saying goodnight, grabbing a cab back to the hotel while she and Jesse took another to the bus.

Before Jesse could get out of the cab, Shiori put her hand on his arm. "I don't want you to come in."

"Why?" Jesse didn't seem upset. Or even overly concerned.

She took a deep breath. "I appreciate everything Danica's done. Everything she *will* do while we're on tour. But she can't fight all my battles for me. She can't force Reese, or the band, or the *fans* to like me. I have to do that on my own."

"And we've kinda taken over." Jesse sighed, gesturing for the cabbie to wait a minute. "I get what you're saying, but would it hurt to have Malakai nearby?"

"Is that going to be his new job?" Shiori shook her head, feeling more secure in her decision now that she had someone who got where she was coming from. "Danica wouldn't be working with the band anymore if they weren't safe to be around. Sophie wouldn't have signed me even on a trial basis. What do I need protection from? Someone being mean to me?"

Jesse's lips quirked at that. "Brave can be a bit of an asshole."

"I've dealt with assholes before."

"Yes, but you've never been stuck on a tour bus with a bunch of guys. You've never been dragged through a crowd by security because they've gone so wild you can't move." Jesse rubbed the back of his neck. "Shiori, I don't know you well enough to say how you'll adapt in the long run. But you can't do this alone."

He was right, and she didn't plan to. Except when it came to the band.

She pointed at the bus. "*This* I can."

He inclined his head and leaned back in his seat. "All right, slugger. You have Danica's number?" He smiled at her nod. "Don't be too proud to use it if you need to."

"I won't." She climbed out of the cab, giving a little wave as it drove off. Then she stared at the bus, parked in the middle of the empty lot behind the venue. All the other bands were already headed to Kansas City for the show in two days. The remaining scheduled date on the tour.

More dates were being added starting tomorrow, last minute and close together, which meant things would get crazy. If she made it through the night, this bus would be her home for the next two weeks. Possibly longer.

Excitement sizzled through her veins, warming her even though the temperature had dropped considerably. The idea of being out on the road, climbing up on stage surrounded by huge crowds, experiencing more than she'd ever dreamed possible...

She'd come for her sister and Hiro, but was it selfish to want a bit of this for herself? Her whole life she'd been trapped in a world where nothing really belonged to her. She'd given more than anyone should, paid a price to have some kind of security. To be loved.

Not the kind of love she needed, but the kind that kept her fed. Kept a roof over her head.

She didn't need that love anymore. What she needed was freedom.

Just a taste of it and she'd be ready to make whatever sacrifices she had to for Hiro's future.

Until then, she'd come this far.

No way was she turning back now.

Chapter Eight

The whiskey was tempting. Brave reclined on the leather sofa, watching Tate fill two tumblers while shimmying to some R&B he'd put on a few minutes ago. The drummer had ditched his shirt and was wearing faded jeans that rode low on his hips. Showing off his lean body. All those tight muscles and smooth skin.

Yeah, I need a fucking drink.

But Brave hadn't touched one yet. Sober him was conflicted enough. Drunk him made very bad choices.

And there was absolutely nothing to stop him from making them.

Hours earlier Connor had stopped by to say he and Malakai were heading to Kansas City with one of the other bands. Alder was with Danica, Jesse, and Shiori—probably all staying at the hotel.

Fate was either being kind or fucking laughing at him. He couldn't decide which.

Thankfully, Tate hadn't done anything besides put some music on and pour a couple drinks. Maybe he'd forgotten his offer.

Yeah, and maybe all my favorite characters will survive Game of Thrones.

A book. Yes. That was what he needed. Reading was the one thing he did that never got him in trouble.

He pushed up off the sofa and headed for his bunk.

"You crashing already?"

Brave reached into the space at the end of his bed to grab his new novel, shaking his head even though Tate couldn't see him. "No, just getting my book. Haven't gotten a chance to read much and I've been waiting for this one for a while."

Tate watched him return, sitting on the table and sipping his whiskey. "They made a TV show. Why bother reading the same shit?"

Normal conversation. This is good. Brave tapped Tate on the head with the thick paperback. "It's not the same. And you should try it sometime. Fucking ten times more intense."

Making a face, Tate shrugged. "Never got into reading. Malakai had me try the crime novels he likes, but they're boring."

"I didn't know Malakai liked to read."

"Told you he was smart." Tate looked down at his drink. "He could have done something awesome. Been a lawyer or a brain surgeon. But he got stuck taking care of his brother. Then me."

Brave sat on the edge of the sofa facing Tate and set the book down beside him. "Listen to me, kid. The man's fucking talented. He's one of the best bassists I've ever met. He dedicated himself to music. His choice. And a good one."

"Yeah… But he's had it rough."

"And still managed an amazing career." Brave put a hand on Tate's knee, giving it a little squeeze. "While watching out for your crazy ass. You know he likes taking care of you."

Tilting his head to one side, Tate met his eyes. "That's not why you hate him."

"I don't hate him."

"Are you afraid of him?"

Frowning, Brave shifted back, bracing his hands on his thighs. "No."

"Then why—?"

A soft knock sounded at the door of the bus. Motioning for Tate to stay put, Brave went to see who it was.

Barely visible through the window in the dim streetlights stretching across the lot stood Shiori. Wearing the same long thin jacket from rehearsal, hugging herself and bouncing a little like she was trying to keep warm. He quickly opened the door, stepping aside so she could pass.

Teeth chattering, she glanced over at him with a smile. "I was afraid you'd never hear me."

"How long were you out here?" He frowned as he took in the pallor of her lips and the sprinkling of snow in her sleek black hair. "No one came with you?"

"I told Jesse to drop me off."

"He *ditched* you in the fucking parking lot?"

"I *told* him to go." She rubbed her arms, her smile turning sheepish. "I was determined to spend the night on the bus, but not outside the bus. A few more minutes and I'd have called someone to bring me back to the hotel."

He shook his head, reaching to put his hand on the small of her back to lead her in. Recalling their earlier exchange, he hesitated. "Will you punch me if I touch you?"

Her lips slanted. "I don't know. Do I look 'desperate'?"

"You look cold." He slid his hand over her back to test her reaction. When she didn't pull away, he drew her a little closer. "And I'm sorry."

She opened her mouth, her eyes flashing in challenge. Then her expression softened and she laughed. "You said what you did so I'd hit you."

"Slap. Not punch." He grinned at the amusement in her eyes. He loved her spunk. Totally worth getting hit for a glimpse of it. "I deserved that, though. And I am duly warned not to fuck with you."

"Apology accepted then." She moved with him into the lounge and nodded to Tate. "You're looking much better."

"You showed up at the perfect time." Tate slipped off the sofa, going to the cupboard to pull out another glass. "It's a good thing you came. Have a drink with me? Brave was about to abandon me for his book."

When Tate poured Shiori her drink, she stood there for a long time staring at it. Brave was tempted to tell Tate to back off, but the kid was just being friendly. And considering the conversations she'd likely had with Danica, and Alder, and *then* Jesse, she didn't need someone else stepping in like she couldn't make her own decisions.

But keeping his mouth shut was hard when she took the drink and looked at him like she was sure she'd made a mistake. Her gray eyes, so full of innocence and uncertainty, made him want to take the glass away. Tell her coming here tonight had been enough. She didn't have to prove anything to anyone.

"I'm not sure I like whiskey, but I'll have a drink with you." She moved away from Brave and lowered to the sofa, rubbing her bare legs under her long jacket. Then she took a sip of whiskey. Her eyes widened. She moved fast to cover her mouth with her hand.

The glass slipped from her fingers, splashing Brave when he caught it midair.

Shiori looked mortified. "Shit! Oh, my God, I'm sorry!"

Tate fell over laughing as Brave dried his arm on his shirt.

He shot the drummer a cold look to shut him up, then turned to Shiori. "It's all right. Do you want to try it with some Coke?"

Tugging her bottom lip between her teeth, Shiori gazed up at him. "You're not going to tell me I shouldn't be drinking?"

"Do you want someone else telling you what to do?"

She shook her head. "No. That's the *last* thing I want."

"All right, then no worries." Brave retrieved a small bottle of coke from the fridge. Pulled out another glass to empty half the whiskey and fixed her a drink that wouldn't be too strong. "We'll all just hang out, have a drink, and relax."

"So you're joining us, Brave?" Tate took a swig of whiskey, his eyes full of mischief.

Time to set the kid straight. "I'll have a drink with you. *One*. And that's it."

Tate rolled his eyes. Glanced over at Shiori. "He used to be fun."

Shiori held her tongue between her teeth, looking amused. "What changed?"

"Band drama." Tate shrugged. Then shadows stole the playful light from his eyes. "And Alder... Alder almost died. Shit, I'm such an idiot. I'm fucking pushing you and you're trying to be a good brother."

"And doing a lousy job at it." Brave dropped down to the sofa beside Shiori. Fuck, him and Tate were all kinds of fun tonight, weren't they? He grabbed his whiskey and took a few long swallows.

He hadn't had a stiff drink in a while. The slow burn felt good going down.

Beside him, Shiori drew her knees up to her chest and sighed.

He shot her a sideways glance. "Not what you expected from a metal band?"

She shook her head. "It's not that. I just wish I knew a way to cheer you both up. Maybe if I'd left you alone..."

The way her voice trailed off got him curious. He relaxed back on the sofa, his lips quirking up at the edges. What did she think they all did on the bus? "We'd be having a wild party? Out vandalizing shit? What?"

Red spread over her cheeks. She looked at Tate, then back at him as though that was answer enough.

Which it was. And wasn't.

Unless he'd missed something.

And that would be very *very* bad.

Fooling around with Tate might not be completely off the menu, but would have to be totally on the down low. The band couldn't handle any more tension and both Alder and Malakai wouldn't care how willing the drummer was.

All they would see was Brave taking advantage of him. *Again.*

He was older. More experienced. Perfectly capable of finding someone else to play with.

The sexy mix of innocence and fire dressed like a Sailor Scout—he'd looked it up—sitting next to him would have been an easy target once, but one thing had been made very clear today.

She was off-limits. Just like Tate.

More than Tate, because while messing around with Tate would piss people off, doing *anything* with Shiori would jeopardize her career. She was on thin ice with Reese. Fresh to the lifestyle and new to the fans. He couldn't offer her anything worth risking all she was working for.

Tate cleared his throat. "I think what she's implying is me and you—"

"I got that." Brave chuckled and drank more whiskey. He couldn't finish it soon enough. "Not sure why?"

Emptying her own glass and holding it out to Tate for a refill, Shiori's lips parted. She pressed them shut and gave a little shrug.

Not so fast, sweetie.

He rested his elbow on his knee and his chin on his fist, brow raised. "Come on. There has to be a reason."

Thanking Tate when he returned with her whiskey and Coke, Shiori tipped it to her lips, likely for a little liquid courage. Then she met Brave's eyes. "I heard you talking to Alder."

"When?"

"That first night. Before Danica brought me to the hotel." She wrinkled her nose. "I didn't mean to eavesdrop, but Sophie and Reese were talking and I stepped away from them and saw you there."

He had a feeling he knew what she'd heard. He'd have to be more careful.

At least she hadn't told anyone.

He rubbed his jaw thoughtfully. "So it didn't bother you?"

Tate sat on the floor in front of them, looking totally confused. "Wait, what am I missing?"

"Alder was worried about you all being pissed at him. I told him letting you suck his dick might help."

"Me or all the guys?" Tate flashed a toothy grin. "Because I'm all for it either way."

Shiori's eyes widened. She clearly hadn't expected Brave to come clean about the conversation.

"Only yours. Then we discussed me doing it instead." Brave rolled his shoulders and sat up, polishing off the last of his whiskey. "I'm done, but I'd still like that answer."

Blinking fast, brow furrowed, Shiori stared at him. "What answer?"

"Did it bother you?"

He expected more blushing. Or one of her witty remarks.

Instead, she wrapped her hands around her glass, staring down at the liquid.

Maybe he'd gone too far. Fucking typical. Why hadn't he changed the subject? Ask her not to say anything and drop it. He couldn't see her repeating this to anyone. She might have spunk, but a lot of it was buried under shy.

"No, it didn't bother me." Shiori hiked her chin up. "Actually, I wouldn't mind seeing that."

And shy is down for the count.

Glass against his lips, Brave tried for another sip. Then remembered it was empty. "Yep, so I said I'm done."

"You did." She pressed her lips together, smothering a smile. "Good night, Brave."

He eyed the bottle of whiskey. Laughed as he gave in and took a refill.

Fuck it.

"I changed my mind." He licked a drop of whiskey off his bottom lip. "Things are just getting interesting."

One drink relaxed Shiori. Two made her daring. For the first time in days, she wasn't worried about anything.

Not that the worries had disappeared, but they'd faded to the background. Something that usually only happened when she hung out with Wendy, drinking cheap wine or some mix they'd come across on Pinterest and decided to try out.

Those nights they giggled, looked up dirty pictures, and Wendy told her, in detail, about the guys she'd been with.

Shiori didn't have anything to tell.

Her life had been split between school and taking care of Hiro. Elizabeth moving in gave her more free time, once Shiori had seen how good the woman was with Hiro, but she hadn't socialized in so long she wasn't sure where to start.

Wendy had dragged her to a couple of clubs, but Shiori always felt awkward. She hated the guys that came on to her. The crowded dance floor made her nervous. One roaming hand and she retreated to a booth where it was safe.

Another gulp of whiskey and Coke and the nagging worry of how she'd manage on a stage in front of hundreds, or even thousands of people…

All right, that gulp hadn't helped. Maybe the next one would.

"Slow down, little moon." Brave gently wrapped his hand around her wrist, easing her glass down. "The whiskey will catch up to you fast."

She cocked her head and nodded toward his glass. "But you're drinking it straight."

"Tons of experience."

"Experience I need?"

"Absolutely not. First tour some bands get shitfaced all the time. Or worse." Brave glanced over at Tate, who'd switched to beer and was shuffling through songs on his phone. Brave shook his head as yet another opening melody came out of the Bluetooth speaker before cutting off. "The lucky ones learn fast being constantly hungover on the road, or stoned at shows, can destroy your career."

"And the unlucky ones?" She really enjoyed talking to Brave. He was surprisingly patient and open. Didn't make her feel completely out of touch with his world.

Even though she was.

"Most don't last."

She inclined her head, understanding how that could apply to her. "So I shouldn't get too crazy."

"Oh, you definitely should. At least once." He gave her a slow smile. "Have fun. Go wild. Enjoy every fucking minute."

"But not so much that you regret it the next day. Or week." Tate sighed as if he'd heard all this before. Laying down on the floor, he placed his bottle by his hip and plunked an arm over his eyes. "You stay up for a lecture, Brave?"

"No. I'm waiting for you to suck my dick."

Shiori nearly spit out her drink at the look on Tate's face. Rolling over, he gaped at Brave. "You serious?"

"Nope."

"I hate you." Tate scowled and sat up. "If we've got to behave in front of her, why you keep bringing that up?"

"Who said you had to behave?" Shiori frowned at Tate over the rim of her glass when he glanced over. "Please don't. I didn't expect to be so comfortable here. But I am."

"You comfortable just talking, or...?" Tate folded his legs in front of him and set his empty bottle on the floor. "Let's play a game."

Brave huffed out a laugh. "Enough, Tate. We're not in high school."

"Who asked you?" Tate spun the bottle and grinned at Shiori. "It might sound lame, but it's fun. Not regular 'Spin the Bottle'. It's 'Truth, Dare, Bite or Kiss.'"

Her pulse quickened as she stared down at the bottle. Even *considering* saying yes was ridiculous. Brave was right. It was childish. Not something she'd ever had the chance to play, but she was too old for it now.

Then again, Tate was her age. He was part of this band and knew how to have fun.

She'd come here tonight to see if she could handle the band. Fit in with them.

Brave didn't want to do it.

He also didn't want to stay for a drink.

He had because of her, which her fuzzy mind couldn't quite figure out, but she liked it. What would he do if she said yes?

So far he'd been polite and sweet. Teased her a little, but like there was a line he wouldn't cross. A completely reasonable line she should respect. And did. Like the kiss on stage, he was acting in her best interest.

But he regretted the kiss. And what he'd said to her.

They had the chance at a fresh start.

What better than a bit of forbidden fun? She didn't expect it to go anywhere further. Whatever did or didn't happen tonight would end come morning. Reese had made it very clear what she wanted from Shiori.

Shiori wasn't Danica. Fans wouldn't like seeing her with one of their heroes.

The fans aren't here. Neither is Reese.

And this might be Shiori's last chance to completely let loose.

She slid off the sofa, across from Tate. "How do you play?"

Letting out a frustrated sound, Brave stood beside her. "I said no."

"Yes, you did." She tipped her head back and smirked at him. "And I already said good night once."

Rubbing a hand over his face, then muttering at the ceiling, Brave didn't move for a long time. Letting his hand fall to his side, he brought his glass to his lips, throat working as he gulped down the whiskey. He slammed the glass on the table so hard she thought it might break.

It didn't.

"What don't you two get? Shit happens and I'm the bad guy." Brave rubbed his fist against his lips, glaring at the bottle like it pissed him off. "This may be a game to you, but I'm already way past my third strike."

Hopping to his feet, Tate snatched up Brave's glass and filled it to the brim with whiskey. "Not with us."

The conflict in Brave's eyes reached past the sweet buzz in Shiori's head. She swallowed hard and reached up to take his hand. "There's no point to a game if it's not fun. For everyone. I get it. And I shouldn't want to do this. I thought I might leave after tonight. After talking to you, I don't want to. That's good enough."

Brave ran his thumb over her fingers, his expression softening in a way that made her wish they were the only two here. But that would be so much worse. Tate's playfulness kept things light. Brave's rejection would hurt if she'd been alone, wishing he would stay and forget all they shouldn't do for one night.

"You won't go?" Brave laced their fingers together. "Fuck, I actually did something right."

"More than you know." She bit her bottom lip as he settled down on the floor, one knee touching hers. "You're going to play, aren't you?"

He bowed his head. Shook it. Then chuckled. "Yeah, I guess I am."

Chapter Nine

The game was simple. Spin the bottle and the person it pointed to got to pick what they were willing to do. 'Truth, Dare, Bite, or Kiss'. If the bottle stopped between two of them, both took a turn. A shot for every 'pass'.

Brave eyed Tate, not sure how far the drummer was willing to go. Or, honestly, if there was anything he *wouldn't* do.

Shiori was a different story. Was she still trying to prove herself? Simply living for the moment? She'd only had two drinks, so she wasn't drunk, but definitely tipsy enough to go further than she normally would.

Which meant he got to play the game and be the ref. He was feeling the whiskey too, but still sober enough to throw down the red flag if needed.

There were limits none of them would cross tonight.

Including him.

Especially him.

He clenched his jaw as Tate sent the bottle spinning.

It stopped. Pointing at Shiori.

"Truth." She blushed and ducked her head. "Yes, I'm a total coward."

"It's the first spin." Tate shrugged, making Brave love him even more. "Since we were talking about blowjobs, what's the longest you've ever given one?"

Shiori fiddled with her short red skirt. "Ah…I haven't."

"Haven't given a long one?" Tate looked confused and Brave wanted to smack him until the drummer's eyes went wide. "Oh, you mean… *Never?*"

"Never." Shiori made a face. Then grinned. "Maybe you can teach me."

"Still learning myself, but I can try." Tate grinned back at her. "Your turn."

First few rounds were all truth and dare—the dare which had Tate wearing only boxers and Shiori sitting there in one of the band's T-shirts, soaking wet—but Brave had a hard time thinking beyond her first answer. He could tell she was innocent, but this was more. She had absolutely no experience.

And she was playing a fucked up game with two metalheads in a band.

And I'm fucking going to hell for letting her.

The bottle stopped, pointing at him after her next spin. He was tempted to go with truth again—she wasn't good at asking revealing questions—but he needed to up the ante.

This game was important to her. Whatever had held her back so long wasn't here now. But he was.

If they only had tonight, he'd make sure it was a night she remembered.

Setting his hands on the floor behind him, he leaned back. "Bite."

Without hesitating, she crawled over to him, bracing her hands by his hips as she rose up on her knees. He closed his eyes as her lips brushed his throat. Trembling, her breasts pressed against his arm, she inhaled softly. A warm caress on his skin, nothing but her breath, but enough to have his pulse pounding low. His jaw ticked as he forced himself to hold still.

This game was hard. With how many he played, this should be nothing, but his games only had one rule. Mutual satisfaction with zero expectations. He'd toyed with those he considered a challenge, but Jesse had been his last victim. After tossing the man's heart in the blender, he'd gotten a serious wake-up call.

No one was gonna tolerate his shit anymore. And he'd begun to hate the man he saw in the mirror. A man who carelessly destroyed others. Who would crush his own brother because lashing out was easier than facing the damage he'd done.

Putting himself in this situation had been stupid, but maybe he wanted to punish himself. He had no control over what happened tonight. He always took what he wanted. He wanted Shiori.

But he couldn't have her.

Which would be much easier to accept if he'd kept his distance. If he'd gone to bed with his damn book.

The graze of her teeth on his skin drew a rough sound from his chest. A little pressure and he ground his teeth together, fighting back a hot wave of lust. He wanted to lift her into his lap. Claim her lips and her body and get her out of his system. He never resisted temptation.

That had to be why he was painfully hard. Sure, he'd been on his best behavior lately, but that only meant he didn't fuck around in his own playground.

Shiori bit down, giving a nice edge of pain to the pleasure of her mouth on him.

He hissed through his teeth. Groaned as she flicked her tongue over the lightly throbbing spot on his neck.

"Stop." He gently nudged her away from him. "Careful, little moon."

She giggled, sitting back on her heels. "Sorry, I was enjoying myself."

"*Clearly.*"

"Why 'little moon'?" She settled back to her spot on the floor, her cheeks rosy red and her eyes shining. From the alcohol or the thrill of being a little naughty, he couldn't tell.

She didn't seem as affected by what had just happened as he was, though. Which was good. Safe.

He focused on her question. "Your eyes..." He shook his head and laughed, willing his blood to cool enough for his brain to function. "Just seemed fitting. I'll stop calling you that if it bugs you."

"It doesn't." She held his gaze for a long time, tugging her bottom lip between her teeth.

One taste. One more taste and he'd get the hell out of here. Take a long shower. Set temperate to artic.

"I think Brave's ready to call it quits." Tate smirked when Brave blinked at him. "Yeah, I'm still here."

"I know." Brave put his hand over the bottle. "And I'm not done yet."

He gave the bottle a hard spin, sitting back to observe both Shiori and Tate as they watched it go round and round. So far they'd had all the power. Kept the game light, completely stacked against him. Fine, he was sporting wood and could do fuck all about it, but he'd raised the stakes.

Either could back down. No harm, no foul.

He wouldn't.

They both swallowed hard when the bottle stopped. Shiori glanced over at Tate. Tate bit the tip of his tongue and shook his head.

Brave looked at the bottle.

Shit.

It had stopped between them.

I am so fucked.

If Shiori hadn't been so nervous, Brave's expression would be funny. He'd been both tender and distant, confusing the hell out of her after she bite his neck. For a moment she'd felt something between them. She thought he might kiss her. Try to seduce her.

He wouldn't have to try hard.

Letting herself even consider anything beyond this game was dangerous, but she couldn't help it. She let her gaze trail over his long, hard body, covered in black from his knee-high boots to the hair tightly bound at the nape of his neck. His face was pale, but his eyes were almost as dark as everything else about him.

There was challenge in his level gaze. He expected them to end the game before things went too far.

Tate wouldn't end it, but when she caught his gaze for some kind of direction, his eyes mirrored her uncertainty. They'd climbed into the lion's den. Both careless about the risk until the beast had them cornered.

Brave hadn't moved an inch. He'd trapped them without even trying.

She took a sip of her drink. Then another, meeting his eyes as she considered her options. No one would blame her for laughing and saying the game had been fun, but she was out. Nothing much had happened. She could face them tomorrow without a hint of shame.

But why be ashamed if she *didn't* retreat? Both men lived up the rock star image. The fans worshiped them, some up close and personal. Fine, she wasn't a member of the band, but she wasn't in her isolated bubble anymore. She'd escaped her cage, if only for a little while.

Tate had told her not to do anything she'd regret.

She'd regret not playing this game for all it was worth.

"Kiss." She settled back against the sofa, ready for whatever would come next. If Brave changed his mind and walked away she would deal. Her chest ached at the thought, but she didn't expect anything from him.

She knew better.

Innocent and stupid didn't go hand in hand. Whether this ended with a kiss or…or *more*, it would end. He wasn't a man looking for something long term.

And she wasn't a woman who could ask for it.

But tonight? Tonight she could have.

Brave's jaw ticked. He nodded once, then looked over at Tate. "And you?"

"Whatever you want, man." Tate rubbed his hands on his thighs. "Is this gonna be weird? I thought it would be fun. I'm not sure it—"

"Shut up, Tate. You're about to get exactly what you want from me." Brave pushed to his feet and moved to the sofa, settling down and patting the cushion beside him. "Come here, Shiori."

She slid onto the sofa, heat gathering within while goosebumps spread across her flesh.

He curved his hand around the side of her neck. Ran his thumb lightly over the tender skin of her throat. "We shouldn't do this."

No. He couldn't stop now. She'd accept any warning. Assure him she wasn't going to get her heart involved. It wasn't available. Not after what happened to Kyoko.

Love wouldn't have saved her sister's life, but her son would have his father.

The past was the past. She'd learned from it. What she needed from Brave wasn't sweet talk or promises. What they did tonight wouldn't change what she decided to share with him.

So far, he'd changed her opinion of him. In a good way.

He was a good man.

Cared about people more than he let off.

Not enough yet, but a good start.

As for tonight? She was done playing. "You owe me."

His brow lifted. Lips slanted, he shifted closer to her. "Do I?"

"Yes, you do. Our first kiss was 'too sweet'. Our second you were an asshole." She touched her bottom lip with her thumb. "I don't think I like it rough."

He made a gruff sound in his throat. Stroked along her pulse again. "I'm not gentle."

"But you were."

"My kiss was gentle. I was being careful. That's not me."

"I can go." Tate was sitting by their feet, looking uncomfortable. Like he knew he didn't belong.

Reaching out with his free hand, Brave latched on to the front of his shirt. "Tonight, Tate. You get what you want from me tonight. And never fucking mention it again."

Snagging his fingers in Brave's belt, Tate rose up on his knees, slamming his lips against the other man's as he tugged the belt open. Shiori watched them, forgetting how to breathe. Brave's strength as he tightened his grip on Tate's shirt. Tate's complete surrender to the moment.

Everything she wanted, so close.

As Tate undid Brave's jeans, drawing the zipper down, bowing his head, Shiori caught a brief glimpse of Brave's thick, hard dick before Tate's lips slid over him. Darker than his skin, with a smooth head that Tate focused on before taking him in deep.

"Now you've seen it." Brave's tone was soft, yet cold. Like he was keeping his distance. "He's good." Brave cupped his hand around the back of Tate's head, thrusting up into his mouth. "But this means nothing."

"Why?" She forgot the kiss she'd asked for, lowering her hand to Tate's shoulder, entranced with the way he moved. "You care about him."

"I do." Brave's relaxed his hold on Tate's head, letting the younger man glide over him freely. "But he's not mine."

"Do you want him to be?" She wondered what Tate thought about the conversation. He hadn't slowed down. Didn't seem to notice Brave's distraction.

Running his hand lightly over Tate's hair, Brave chuckled. "No. He needs someone stronger than I am. Someone that won't use him."

"You're using him?"

"I am. And he wants me to." Brave curved his fingers, putting a little pressure on her neck. Reminding her she was part of this. "Do you?"

113

"Want you to use me?" She snickered at his frown. He didn't get who she was. Not really. All he saw was the fragile girl with so much to lose. Not a woman who could play at his level. "You haven't been paying attention. All I want is a kiss. Are you offering more?"

"No." He brought his lips to hers, his tone low. "Not if 'more' means anything."

"It doesn't."

"Good." His eyes drifted shut as Tate moved over him faster. "I want you to feel what I do. Complete fucking freedom. It's good. So damn good."

"Show me." She was done being scared. That fear hadn't gotten her anywhere. But Brave's lips on hers sent her pulse racing, like she'd strapped into a car going so fast she couldn't see anything but a blur flashing by.

His kiss was deep, delving past the last of her restraints. His tongue touched hers and she moaned, splaying her hands over his chest as she rose up to take more.

She whispered against his lips. "Please... Show me."

Slipping away from Tate, Brave leaned her back on the sofa. He kissed down her body, lifting her damp shirt over her bare breasts. He curved a hand under one breast, lifting it to his mouth. His lips on her nipple shot a sizzling string of pleasure to her core. Her feet shifted restlessly on the floor as he shifted his attention to her other breast.

Fuck, she'd never known having a man's mouth on her breasts could feel so amazing. When he moved away from her, pulling her hips off the edge of the sofa, her breath caught.

He stopped suddenly, his grip tightening against her thigh. "Tate. Slow down."

"No." She smoothed her hand over his hair, pulling it loose. "You don't have a say. It's our turn."

With a gruff sound, he continued down her body. He tugged at her panties with one hand. The other rested on Tate's head. He had her bared to him in seconds, positioning one of her legs up over the arm of the sofa.

"You asked for a kiss." He breathed out a laugh, bringing his mouth to the base of her stomach, bracing his hand on the cushion by her hip. "You didn't say where."

"But you already gave me one." Not that she was complaining. She might be if she didn't want him exactly where he was. The brief urge to cover herself disappeared as he licked along the crease between her hip and her thigh. He sucked on the flesh right above her pussy, using his tongue and his teeth to make her squirm.

"I did." He ran his scruffy cheek along the inside of her thigh. "Do you want me to stop?"

"Brave." Her hips jerked as his tongue flicked over her clit. The tiny bundle of nerves sent off sparks of pure, desperate need. "Oh god…"

"I'll take that as a no." He traced his tongue between her folds, then back up over her clit as she writhed on the edge of the sofa, bitting into her cheek to keep from crying out. "So fucking sweet."

His mouth covered her, licking and sucking, drawing out the pleasure until it built up, coiling tight within. Bursting into a million flares, lighting her up inside and out, release tore a sharp cry from her lips.

He dipped his tongue into her, thrusting deep, drawing out the exquisite sensation until she lay beneath him, her heart pounding and her strength gone.

His grip abruptly tightened on her thigh. He cursed, pressing his forehead against her stomach and shuddering.

Rising up from his place on the floor, Tate leaned over her, kissing her as she gasped for air. His lips were slick and salty. He tasted like Brave and she wanted more.

With a low growl, Brave jerked Tate away from her. Made a frustrated sound when Tate whimpered and kissed him, both men above her, struggling for control.

Brave pulled away, chuckling as he ran his thumb over Tate's bottom lip. "You're not playing fair. What did you get out of this?"

"Everything." Tate nuzzled his head against the side of her neck. "Can we keep her?"

"Maybe." Brave slung an arm over Tate's shoulders, while idly brushing his fingers through her hair. "Still want to stay?"

Yes. But she shouldn't. Feeling good was shallow. Brave dividing his attention so quickly made it very clear that the game was over. And that's all this was. All it would ever be.

Exactly what she'd wanted.

But her body was not making this simple. How could she have his mouth on her and pretend nothing had changed?

You knew it wouldn't. Be like Tate. This was fun. It's over now.

"Mmm, definitely staying." She curled up on the sofa, moving just enough to cover herself with the shirt before closing her eyes. The shirt wasn't comfortable, but the damp material kept her from feeling exposed as the hum of pleasure drifted away.

"Good." Brave stroked her hair, which really wasn't fair. Tenderness from him was the last thing she needed.

And he didn't stop there.

"Tate, go get her one of my shirts." Brave leaned close, smiling when she peeked at him. "Come on, sweetie. Let's get you comfortable."

"I am comfortable." She sighed when he arched a brow at her. All right, sleeping in a wet shirt probably wasn't smart. And the leather of the sofa was sticking to her skin. "Ugh. Fine. But then you have to quit being so nice."

"Do I now." He helped her sit up, quickly changed her shirt, then lifted her into his arms. "I'll make you a deal. Tomorrow I'll be a jerk and make up for it."

Suddenly exhausted, she rested her head on his shoulder with a little nod. But when he carried her to the bunks, easing her onto one of the middle beds and tucking her in, she struggled to stay awake.

Tomorrow would be different. She could go back to focusing on her job. On her future and Hiro's. Keep her goal in mind and never stray from it again.

But tonight…

She didn't want tonight to end.

"What's wrong, Shiori?" Brave folded his arms on the edge of her bunk and rested his chin on them. "Talk to me."

"I think… I think I was wrong." She pressed her face into her pillow, frustrated. "I don't know how to feel about all this."

"Feel relaxed. Satisfied." Brave reached out to brush a strand of hair off her cheek. "Free."

"I'm not free."

"Maybe not." He rested his hand on her shoulder. "But you felt it tonight. And no one can take that away from you."

His words, the way he stroked her hair, speaking softly about the long ride to come, about the other bands, about random things she wouldn't remember, soothed her. She stopped thinking about what tomorrow would bring.

She was here. Now.

And that taste of freedom… Brave was right.

It was something she'd never forget.

Chapter Ten

Alder checked out the hotel room, happy that Danica had a couple nights here instead of cooped up on the bus. Nothing fancy, a junior suite with a lounge area, a small table, and two queen-size beds behind French doors, but on the rare occasions Danica, Jesse and him got a room, they had only a king-size with a chair in the corner.

The suite was for Shiori's comfort. Danica wanted to ease the girl into touring with the band.

He wasn't at all disappointed the new girl had decided to go all in tonight. Even though he'd brought up her confrontation with Brave, he respected her determination.

And he needed some time alone with his woman and his man.

Neither had gotten on his case too much about jumping the fan, but he sensed them holding back. Almost like...like they were hesitant to bring up anything that would piss him off.

Like everyone had been around Brave for years.

Which didn't sit well with him at all.

"Do you want something to drink? I can call for some tea." Danica moved to stand by the table, resting her hip against it as she watched him wander aimlessly around the room. "Or something stronger if you'd like?"

"Don't do that, Danica." He groaned when her brow rose slightly. She waited for him to clarify. "Don't be all careful talking to me. I won't break if you yell at me."

"I have no reason to yell at you." Danica frowned, folding her arms over her breasts. "I'm not happy that you jumped the barrier. I hate that you got in a fight. You scared me." She pressed her eyes shut. "But I'm not mad anymore."

"Anymore?" He moved closer to her, the distance between them like a chill settling deep in his core. When she sighed and wrapped her arms around his neck, the cold melted away. He buried his face in her hair. "So you were."

"Of course I was!" She playfully smacked him upside the head. "I'll never be okay with you getting hurt. But you made a choice and you'll face the consequences. I won't always be around to nag at you about acting like a twelve-year-old."

"Ouch. *Twelve?*" Alder made a face. She didn't have to nag at all when she said stuff like that. In a few words, she'd dismissed his behavior as reckless and childish. If he fucked up his career it was all on him. Fair enough. "Can I at least be legal?"

She rolled her eyes. "Sure. Legal and immature. Better?"

Not really. He hugged her tight, resting his head on her shoulder. "I'm sorry."

"I know." She leaned back, fingers laced behind his neck as he straightened. "We have more to discuss, but we'll wait for Jesse. How about that drink?"

"I'm good with water, but call for some tea. Jesse will probably have some with you."

"Herb tea then?" Danica's lips slanted. "He won't admit how much he enjoys a cup before bed, but whenever Brave or I make a pot, he has some. I'm not sure which is his favorite."

"Chamomile. He's getting over this fucked up idea that tea is for chicks." Alder held up his hands as her eyes narrowed. "I've never met his dad, but I've heard horror stories. The fucker would have put whiskey in Jesse's baby bottle if he could."

"I wish that surprised me."

"Yeah…well, he's been trying to get me to drink tea at night. Even messaged me some study about how it can help with insomnia." Alder snorted and shook his head. "Not convinced."

"Wait, he messaged you about it?" Brow furrowed, Danica leaned back a little more. "As opposed to just having a conversation?"

"He's getting better." Alder knew Jesse's issues with basic communication annoyed Danica, but that ran just as deep as the tea dilemma. Guys didn't discuss their feelings, or show emotions, or fuck other dudes.

Rejecting his father's narrow-minded views had taken Jesse years. He'd claimed his sexuality early on, but then hooked up with men who treated him like shit, almost like he was punishing himself.

Letting himself love Alder, and accepting the love Alder had for him for so long, was a huge step. Giving his heart to Danica as well was another. Jesse had come far in a short time, but sometimes his conditioning came back to haunt him.

Alder thought he had to be the mediator between Danica and Jesse at first. Make sure Jesse wasn't too gruff with her and she wasn't too impatient with him. They had a weird dynamic he still hadn't figured out, but even when they bickered, they had a strong connection. Respected one another enough to debate just about anything.

The way they made up when arguments got too heated was pretty fucking awesome.

No complaints here.

"I know he's getting better." Danica cupped his cheek. "Are you?"

"I'm fine." He had to be. He'd built up a wall within to block out all the shit he couldn't deal with. He slipped away from her as a dull roar sounded in his ears, his own pulse deafening him. One moment of weakness and the wall started crumbling. "I'm gonna call room service. Jesse shouldn't be long."

Danica's lips parted, but then she pressed them shut and inclined her head. She'd give him a brief respite, but she'd already mentioned having a discussion when Jesse got back.

One Alder wouldn't like, no doubt about that.

Their man returned just as room service was leaving. Jesse eyed the tray on the table, which had three mugs, everything they needed for tea, and a jug of ice water.

"Not sure we should go all wild tonight, we're heading out early." He walked over to the table, sliding his arm around Danica's waist and kissing her bare shoulder as she opened the envelopes of tea. "I delivered your girl, safe and sound."

"Did you talk to Malakai?" Danica paused with three sugar packages bunched in her fist. "Did she seem all right?"

"She's fine. But no, I didn't talk to him. She asked me not to."

"And you listened to her?"

"Yes. Because she's a grown woman and you've taught me well. 'Protective caveman bad.'" Jesse smirked as he traced his fingers along the waist of her tiny blue skirt. "Have I told you how hot you look today?"

Smacking his hand, Danica glared at him. "Don't try to distract me. Going from caveman to indifferent is not what I wanted."

Here we go again. Alder groaned and took over making the tea. If he waited for the two of them to finish arguing they'd all go thirsty.

"I wasn't indifferent."

"She's new to all this. She doesn't know what the guys are like."

"Neither did you."

"I'm older than she is."

"Not by much."

"Is Jesse allowed five sugars?" Alder bit back a smile as they both stared at him like he'd appeared out of nowhere. "I know this is foreplay for you two, but you both bitched about me not sleeping enough. I'm willing to try if you'll cut this shit short."

"Foreplay?" Danica's lips thinned as she pushed Jesse back and picked up the stainless-steel carafe to fill the mugs. "He can have all the sugar he wants."

"So you don't care?" Jesse shrugged and grabbed almost all the sugar packages from the dish.

"Are you serious right now?" Danica grabbed his wrist. Then she burst out laughing. "All right, this is getting ridiculous."

"Just a little." Alder mumbled.

Gaze softening, Danica slipped up against Jesse and whispered in his ear. "You *were* very distracting."

"Yeah?" Jesse gave her a hooded look. "I fucking miss being alone with you."

Alder shook his head.

Like he'd said. Foreplay.

"And Alder." Jesse latched onto the side of Alder's neck, pulling him close. "I miss this. No band drama. No watching for the press. Just the three of us."

Slipping her hand into the back pocket of Alder's jeans, Danica nodded, resting against Jesse's side. "I do too. But I told Alder we needed to talk when you got here."

Jesse's jaw hardened. He inclined his head. "You're right."

Why the fuck did I stop them from arguing?

"Not sure what needs to be discussed. I got in a fight with a fan. It's been dealt with. I won't do it again." Alder slipped away from them both. "Shiori is on the bus. She's a big girl and if she can handle Brave—which she clearly can—she's golden. Jesse is fine with three sugars in his coffee and tea. That it?"

"You aren't sleeping, Alder." Danica stayed where she was, resting her head on Jesse's muscular chest. But her expression changed. She looked sad. "You're...different. I don't know what happened, but I want to find out."

I'm fine. Just fucking fine. He took a deep breath, forcing himself not to say the words out loud. They were so automatic. What he'd been telling himself over and over.

But they weren't true.

They all knew he wasn't fine.

Convincing them otherwise was an escape. He wanted to shield them. Shield himself. Maybe if he managed to persuade them he'd start to believe it. Find a way to make it happen.

"No one will ever forget you."

The man closed in on Brave. Alder saw the knife. He lunged forward.

"I'm worn out. I know we weren't on tour, but all the interviews, practice, recording, did me in. Hell, the music video took *forever*." Alder's throat tightened. He kept his voice even, but with every blink, he was taken from the room. Back on that stage. He had to fight to stay in the present. "If this keeps up I'll get sleeping pills or something."

"You're having nightmares. Do you remember them?" Jesse raked his fingers through Alder's hair, holding him still. His touch centered Alder. The room came into focus. "Tell me what I can do."

Danica's firm grip on his hand anchored him even more. He was back with them. He needed to stay here.

But how could he tell them? He couldn't say it, but if a simple touch could chase away those nightmares, maybe all he needed was more. As their schedule got crazier, they lost their time alone. The stolen kisses and quickies weren't enough. The three of them hadn't been together, completely together, in months.

Tonight they could be. He could have them all to himself. He needed them.

"I need you." He brought his lips to Danica's, all the air leaving his lungs as she wrapped herself around him. Her lips, her tongue, her sweet, soft body invited him in, giving him somewhere to escape.

He tugged at the laces on her corset, lifting her onto the table as he lowered his mouth to her breasts. Both filled his hands and his blood pulsed fast and hard, driving down low as he flicked his tongue over a tight nipple.

"Alder." Danica tugged at his hair, gasping as her thighs tightened over his ribs. "Please talk to us."

"I need you. Please." He finished undoing the corset and let it fall on the table. "Please."

Danica stroked his hair, squirming as he sucked at one nipple, then the other. He could sense her uncertainty. Then the moment she relaxed and let go.

Jesse's lips brushed his throat. "Tell me what you need."

"You." Alder brought his hands to Danica's waist, holding on tight as Jesse's hands slipped down to unbutton his jeans. "I need you both."

Jesse hesitated. He was probably looking at Danica. Taking her lead.

"He's got a knife!"

Alder shoved Brave, turning to block the blade. A sharp pain and he was falling. The crazed eyes of the man above him never left. He went down with Alder. His fist pressed into Alder's chest. With the knife.

He couldn't fight the man. Couldn't move. A sharp, deep throbbing agony blinded him.

He heard voices all around.

Brave's was the only one he could make out.

"...leave him. It's me you want."

No!

The man wanted to kill Brave. Alder's eyes burned as he brought his trembling lips to Danica's stomach. He inhaled, losing himself to the scent of her. Spice carried on a cool breeze. And a fragrance unique to her. Addictive in every way. He could breathe her in forever and live on that alone.

Jesse's hand wrapped around his dick and he moaned, moving in his loose grip. The pleasure blurred the red haze in his mind.

"You want her, Alder?" Jesse tugged down Danica's panties. She helped. They both tempted him with that slick move. He pressed his firm length against Alder's ass. "You want me?"

"Yes!" Alder tried to open his eyes, but a few blinks and they teared. He couldn't let those tears fall. He lowered his head, pressing his eyes shut again. "No! I *need* you."

"After this, you tell us everything." Jesse fisted his hand in Alder's hair, tugging his head back as his teeth grazed Alder's throat. "One last escape and you tell us. You can't keep pushing us away."

"I won't." Alder brought his lips to Danica's as Jesse shoved his jeans down. In complete control, Jesse guided Alder's dick into Danica's slick pussy, driving him forward until he filled her. Alder lost himself to the enveloping pleasure.

Moving away for a moment, Jesse's shoulder brushed his thigh. He heard a soft rip. A zipper. A drizzle of lube and Jesse's fingers filled him, preparing him.

Only for a moment. Then a thick penetration. Jesse slammed in, driving him into Danica.

Heat and passion, the two people he loved surrounding him. He kissed Danica even as their bodies rocked together. Jesse knew what she could take. The rhythm that drove her wild. He drew it out, latching onto Alder's hips, forcing him to slide free of her. Then he fisted his hand around Alder's dick, slipping him back in.

Alder braced as he was filled and his dick sank deep into all that slick warmth. Danica held his face between her hands, biting his abused bottom lip hard, the sting stealing away the power of all the visions, all the pain. This pain was real. Was *now*.

And it was so fucking sweet.

Another thrust, Jesse into him, forcing him into Danica, and the world flashed white behind his closed lids. A sizzling current blasting out as he came, every nerve within lighting up until his whole body contracted, the power of pure ecstasy taking control.

Danica cried out, her pussy gripping him tight. Jesse slammed in one last time, his lips parted against Alder's shoulder as he shuddered.

"Tell them not to come any closer, I'll slit his fucking throat!"

Alder thought he'd gotten away, but he hadn't. His blood ran cold and his knees gave out. He latched onto the table, holding close to Danica. He wouldn't ruin this for her. For Jesse.

They were finally together.

"Don't let him die."

He heard his brother's voice, a desperate whisper. Almost dropped to his knees, but someone held him up. Lifted him, bringing him away from the stage slick with his blood.

Soft hands pulled his shirt away. He was naked, but not cold. A warm body pressed against him. Soft material covered him. A muscular chest pressed against his other side.

For months, everything after the knife flashed before his eyes was a blank. Almost like his mind filtered out the memory to protect him.

Once a week he'd get a little glimpse. Then more and more until every terrifying moment played on repeat in the silence. Darkness brought the blade into focus, making him blind to everything else. He couldn't even will his way back to the present. The pain paralyzed him.

The pain wasn't real. The scars were still faded. But when the terror swallowed him, the stabbing pain sliced deep. He felt the knife. Sliding into him slower than it really had. And blood flowed all around, deep enough to drown in.

Danica and Jesse thought he had nightmares. They were worried about his lack of sleep, but didn't pressure him because he snapped every time they showed concern. He'd drawn away from them, a little more every day, because he couldn't share this. He wouldn't let his horror infect them too.

But not telling them made the situation worse. Without knowing, all they could do was guess.

He swallowed hard, pushing up to sit against the headboard. Their eyes followed him. Jesse took his hand, lacing their fingers together. Danica wrapped her arms around his sheet covered thigh.

Both waiting. Both needing the truth.

So he told them.

"I remember. The night I was stabbed. I remember it all."

Chapter Eleven

Malakai surveyed the unruly crowd clogging up the snow slicked Walmart parking lot. The mild weather had the members of all five bands outside, enjoying the fresh air. Some had lawn chairs out and were hanging in groups, drinking.

The rest found ways to entertain themselves.

Roadies, security, and a few people with press passes gathered as random fights broke out between band members. Mostly harmless scuffling, but a few got pretty rough. And the attention of the crowd spurred them on.

On arrival last night everyone either crashed or disappeared to do their own thing. Apparently, this afternoon was dedicated to relieving tension that had built up during the long drive.

Not a huge deal in itself. Malakai had seen all kinds of drama during his years in the metal scene. Everything from who was fucking who to drug deals gone bad. Conflicts happened. He'd thrown a few punches when he'd been a dumb newb, but avoided getting into fights because shit went bad when he got violent. Besides, a guitarist didn't need to be fucking up his hands. Only an idiot would put their career on the line in a juvenile, masculine display like this.

He groaned as Connor stepped into the open space at the center of the crowd.

And we've found our next idiot.

Connor held up his favorite guitar, grinning as the crowd quieted down. He winked at a big breasted groupie who'd been hanging onto the lead singer of Gear-Core. Dude had a weird, made-up name he claimed was German.

Malakai was pretty sure his real name was Earl.

For the past hour, Earl had been placing bets. Anyone who beat him got the girl. Buy in was five-hundred dollars.

Connor's guitar was worth a hell of a lot more than that.

What the hell is he doing?

"This sweet thing asked if I'd fight for her." Connor jerked his chin toward Earl. "I don't have the money, but I've got this. What do you say?"

"Mk11 Warlock? You're putting up a 2k guitar for some pussy?" Earl looked stunned. "Are you fucking high?"

"Naw. It's called confidence, man." Connor stroked the mahogany body of the guitar, a crooked smile on his lips. "We got a deal?"

"Damn right we do."

Malakai shook his head as Connor handed his guitar to one of Gear-Core's roadies. He had a feeling this wasn't about getting laid. Connor was bored.

Judging him was easy, but Malakai recalled when he himself would take any challenge for the rush of adrenaline. He'd fought for as long as he could remember. Trained hard to hone skills he'd needed as a child and kept developing long after because he craved the control it gave him over his body. Over his life.

Discipline took longer to learn, but he'd finally reached a point where the rage that once overwhelmed him lay dormant for the most part. He ignored insults and posturing. He had nothing to prove.

To Connor's credit, the fight didn't last long. Earl matched him in size, but Connor ducked his wild swings, taking him down like a wrestler in slick move that had the man pinned beneath him, arm twisted at an awkward angle. Crying out, Earl tapped the pavement frantically. He refused Connor's offer of a hand up.

Shrugging, Connor strode up to the girl, claiming her lips in a deep kiss that had the crowd laughing and cheering.

Earl lunged forward, shoving the girl aside. He cracked Connor in the jaw before the guitarist could react.

For fuck's sake. Malakai moved closer to Connor, sure the man could handle himself, but not liking how the rest of Gear-Core circled him. They were some of the few bulked up meatheads in the industry, exercising obsessively and popping steroids which made them look more like body builders than musicians. When they went at Connor all at once, Malakai moved fast, cutting one off mid-punch.

Whipping the man around to face him, Malakai delivered a swift uppercut that sent him flying. One man down.

Four to go.

Two big ones restrained Connor. Another laid into him. And the crowd cheered them on.

Fucking savages. Red flashed across Malakai's vision as he lunged forward and elbowed one guy in the throat, stunning him long enough to tear another off Connor. The crunch of bone under his fist as he cracked the second man in the jaw gave him shallow satisfaction. He checked to make sure Connor was still in one piece. The man was family. Fucked up family that drove him crazy, but still his to protect.

And the dummy needed protection. He managed to get a few punches in, but he was shit at blocking them. A punch to the gut leveled him. Connor recovered quickly, but his opponent had grabbed a fucking pipe.

He swung it at Connor's head. Malakai threw himself forward, tackling the man. They grappled over the pipe. A familiar face cut through the blinding red haze holding Malakai, shouting words he couldn't hear beyond his deafening pulse. Someone trying to break up the fight. The man under Malakai twisted free. Punched up, missing Malakai.

And connecting with whoever was behind him.

"Son of a bitch!" Tate's voice. Malakai blinked as he spotted the drummer on the ground. One hand over his eye.

Growling, Malakai wrenched the pipe free.

Tate shouldn't be here.

Didn't matter. No one got to hurt him.

Not if they wanted to live.

Frantic voices came at him. Meaningless. He lifted the pipe. Hands closed on his arms. He wasn't sure how many were coming at him, but he had to defend himself. And Connor. And Tate. Fuck, there were so many people he couldn't even see the kid anymore.

He snarled, swinging back blindly with the length of metal. He struck someone and they let him go.

More hands, dragging him back. He struggled to get loose. His back slammed into a bus tire and a hand framed his jaw.

Jesse snarled in his face. "Snap out of it or I'm gonna knock you the fuck out, Malakai."

"Where's Tate?" Malakai tried to shove Jesse, but the man had his full weight on him. He was a big man. Strong and skilled. He hadn't survived prison by being a pushover.

"Danica got him out of here. They're with Tank and Skull. The other guys are taking care of Connor." Jesse's tone took on a hard edge. "You just fucking busted Brave's face open. I'm tempted to cut you out of the band. This shit *can't* happen."

Brave? Malakai took a deep breath, slumping against the tire. "Please tell me he didn't get hit with the fucking pipe?"

"I didn't see what the fuck you hit him with."

Malakai's heart stuttered. How could he have let himself lose control like this? "Is he all right?"

"He better be." Jesse pushed Malakai's shoulder into the tire and straightened. "I thought I could count on you. Thanks for proving me wrong."

What have I done? Malakai's stomach twisted as he looked down at his arm, at the streaks of blood on his skin.

Some of that blood was Brave's.

Jesse moved suddenly, cutting Alder off as he lunged at Malakai. "Alder, don't!"

"What the fuck were you thinking?" Alder slammed into Jesse, who barred an arm across his chest, holding him back. "He was trying to help!"

Skull grabbed Alder, restraining him and patting his shoulder at the same time. "It's over, boy. Come on, let's not leave the girls to deal with the blood."

The old man got through to Alder with a few simple words. And left Malakai to Jesse.

Who spared him one last disgusted look before walking away.

Still sitting on the ground, Malakai covered his face in his hands and groaned. He could still remember the last time he'd slipped over the edge. Back when he and Brave had been friends, they caught a few guys slipping something into a girl's drink. Called the guys out. Beat the shit out of them in the alley. Should have been enough, but one got back up. Attacked Brave from behind.

Malakai almost killed the man. Might have if Brave hadn't stopped him.

They might not be close anymore, but Brave knew him. Knew when he'd surrendered to the darkness. When he'd gone so far he couldn't pull back.

Which was why he didn't fight anymore. It was too easy to end up there.

How the fuck had he let this happen?

Connor was outnumbered.

The band was here. A few seconds and they would have stepped in.

I didn't know.

He'd lost it. And he shouldn't have.

And that's all that matters.

Someone moved close to him, carefully, shading him from the light glaring off the scattered patches of snow. He glanced up, then groaned. "Sweetie, you shouldn't be here."

"Probably not." Shiori knelt by his side. She took one of his hands in hers and pressed the bottom of her shirt against busted knuckles he hadn't noticed. "But you stuck up for me when you had no idea who I was. If nothing else, I owe you."

"I'm fucked up, slugger. I'm not good to be around."

"Tell me what happened." She dabbed at his knuckles with her shirt, not lifting her head. "I don't see you just grabbing a guy to beat on."

"I hit Brave with a fucking pipe."

"On purpose?" She met his eyes this time, inhaling slowly when he shook his head. "I didn't think so. What happened?"

For some reason, he couldn't put her off any longer. He told her, not sure the bare facts justified anything he'd done, but at least she was listening. He doubted anyone else would.

Fuck, for all he knew this might be the end for him. The band wasn't in a place where they could ignore his issues. Issues he'd tried to overcome.

And clearly failed.

"Let me get this straight. Connor was outnumbered. You stuck up for him." Her tiny nose wrinkled. "How is any of this your fault?"

"I don't...stop." He wasn't sure how to explain how the violent rage took over. How badly he could hurt people. "When Connor was surrounded, I just had his back. But then Tate went down. There were too many people. I snapped."

"You protected a friend. You were scared." She compressed his bloody knuckles with her shirt, her tone firm. "I might not be as strong as you, but I don't think I'd hold back if someone I loved was in danger."

Why was she trying to make this okay? It wasn't. He'd gone too far.

But she was sweet and innocent and saw something in him that wasn't there.

He let out a cold laugh. "I don't love Connor. Actually, I'm tempted to hit him too."

"If you want to go after him, I won't stop you."

"Being ganged up on was enough."

"You say that like it absolves him of any blame." She continued tending to the cuts on his knuckles. "It doesn't. He started the fight. You ended it. And you're both still breathing. I'd call that a win."

"Not for me. I don't do well with violence, Shiori. The man I become isn't who I want to be. I'm good at fighting. Too good to let myself lose control like that." He needed her to understand. He'd broken his own vows. "If the band is done with me, I've given them plenty of reasons."

"Not today you haven't." She increased the pressure on his hand, glaring at him like he was being stubborn and she was tired of it. "Stand up for yourself like you stood up for him. The band is stressed. They're always stressed and today it's your fault. Only, it isn't. And they have to know."

Almost made sense, from an outsider's perspective, but she didn't know the band. They wouldn't be so understanding.

Having someone in his corner was nice, though.

"Thanks, slugger." He eased his hand free and rose to his feet, looking around to see most of the crowd had cleared. "We should head to the bus."

She frowned at him. "Already? Shouldn't we give them some time to cool down?"

He shook his head. "Won't happen. And we have to hash this shit out before we hit the stage."

She stopped mid-step, bringing a hand to her throat. "I have to—"

"What's wrong?"

"I have to go on stage." She rubbed her arms. "Damn, I just… This is real now. With everything going on I hadn't really thought about actually being up there. I'm a little terrified."

Looping his arm around her shoulders, he pulled her to his side. She was too fucking precious. Her first performance and rather than getting ready, she was here, comforting him.

He enjoyed having her near. Fitting perfectly against him, relaxing as though his touch steadied her. As they walked her shivering eased off and her rapid little breaths slowed.

He watched her from the corner of his eye, smiling as the fear faded and determination took its place. He could tell her she'd be fine, but he'd known she'd figure that out herself.

All she'd really needed was to say she was scared out loud to someone who wouldn't judge her. Not that the band would. Or Danica.

But Danica represented all Shiori wanted to accomplish. Going to the other woman would be hard.

He had absolutely no problem being her shoulder to lean on.

Slanted smile on his lips, he squeezed her arm lightly. "How was the drive?"

Glancing up at him, she gave him a curious look. "You're not going to give me any advice? Tell me I can do this?"

"You know you can." He grinned at her. "And I'm a shitty dancer, so I've got no advice to offer."

Laughing, she spun away from him, walking backward. "You forget I've seen you on stage. You've got moves."

"Grinding against my guitar isn't 'moves'."

"No, but it's hot."

Hell, she needs to not say shit like that. The teasing glimmer in her eyes, the way her glossy pink lips slanted, tested the seal on the 'out-of-bounds' box he'd put her in from day one. She was simply being playful, but he liked it. He liked how easy she was to talk to. How, despite her innocence, she displayed a kind of fearlessness he admired.

Yes, she was afraid. But he didn't doubt for a second she'd succeed. Her kind of fearlessness wasn't reckless. It came from a core of strength. From an awareness of her own weaknesses. From seeing all possible scenarios, but not letting the worst of them hold her back.

He'd gotten his first glimpse when she'd been criticized by Reese after kissing Brave. That couldn't have been easy. Sure, he and Brave had helped her. Mostly Brave.

Still, she could have walked away then.

But she hadn't.

"Sorry, I didn't mean to make you uncomfortable." She patted his arm as they reached the bus. "You ready?"

Ready? He looked at the bus and groaned. Shit, how could he have forgotten, even for a moment? He'd fucked up. He was here to convince the band not to cut him loose. He didn't have the first clue what to say to them.

The sweet little thing by his side was very distracting.

And not for you. Don't forget that.

He wouldn't. He'd fucked things up enough for himself. No way would he drag her down with him.

The door opened. Malakai expected Jesse, but it was Brave who stepped out, a towel pressed to his cheek.

"Wanna give us a minute, little moon?" Brave smiled at Shiori, something in his eyes Malakai didn't like. A mix of tenderness and lust.

One she returned before brushing past him and hurrying up the steps onto the bus.

Maybe the son-of-a-bitch—and Malakai meant that literally—deserved that punch after all. He gnashed his teeth as Brave shut the door and faced him.

"What did you do, Brave?" Malakai clenched his fists at his sides. His mind was clear enough to keep him from lashing out, but just barely. "What the fuck did you do?"

Brave arched a brow. "Not the apology I expected."

"You knew better than to fucking grab me." Malakai growled, cutting across the distance between them. "The band wants to get rid of me for this shit? Maybe I deserve it. But *she* deserves better than whatever game you're playing."

"I'm not playing any fucking games. Cool it." Brave moved away from the bus. "This isn't about her."

"It is now." Malakai pressed his eyes shut. "Did you listen to a word Reese said? To a word *I* said after?"

"Yes, I fucking listened." Brave sucked in a rough breath. "I got it."

"That's not what it looked like. One wrong move and she's gone. Don't do that to her."

"What makes you think I would?"

"Jesse."

Brave sucked his teeth. "That was a long time ago."

"A long time…" Malakai let out a cold laugh, not sure why he bothered. "You're too fucking much. You played head games with the man your brother was—and *is*—in love with. You give yourself a free pass for that already?"

Nodding slowly, Brave smirked at him. "I'm too much? I'm standing here, bleeding because you flipped out and you're throwing old shit in my face. But hey, so long as you get to judge me, it's all good, right?"

"I'm laying out the facts. And asking you to leave her the fuck alone."

"Done." Brave gave an offhand shrug. "You finished? They're waiting for us. And for some stupid reason, I'm still gonna tell them not to toss you to the curb. Because that's the kind of asshole I am."

"Don't do me any favors." Malakai knew he was risking his career, but he couldn't handle owing Brave. The man would never let him live it down. And he'd use it every chance he got.

Maybe even for a clear path to Shiori.

Strong as she was, she stood no chance against Brave if he wanted her as his new toy.

Grabbing the front of Malakai's shirt, Brave jerked him close. "You sure? Be hard to watch out for her if you're gone."

And just like that, Malakai was trapped. He, who'd managed to steer clear of Brave's twisted games for so long. Brave was right. If they went in there snarling at one another the band's decision would be easy. Replacing Malakai wouldn't be all that difficult. He'd become a liability.

Without Brave's support, he might as well pack his bags.

"What do you want from me?" Malakai pried Brave's hand from his shirt. "A fucking apology?"

"No. I'm not stupid, man. I know how much you hate me." Brave glared at him. "I want you to go in there and make it fucking clear how much we need you. Because, like it or not, I know we do."

The last statement hit Malakai like a two-by-four to the head. Hating Brave had become second nature. The man gave him plenty of reasons. But he'd also just reminded Malakai all that mattered was the band.

A band Malakai had helped form.

One he'd fight for until his last breath.

Like Shiori, he didn't need to be told what he already knew. He had to fight. He belonged here. This band was his life and he wasn't ready to surrender the role he'd earned.

Brave being the one to make him see that chaffed, but he'd get over it.

He scowled at the other man almost out of habit. "You're right. I do hate you."

Rather than laughing, Brave inclined his head, his eyes tired. He dropped the hand holding the towel to his side, revealing the torn flesh along his cheekbone, cut open by the pipe Malakai had hit him with. Angry red and still seeping blood.

"I know."

Chapter Twelve

Being hated used to be fun. Hate was such a clean emotion. Direct.

And if Brave earned that hatred by doing whatever the fuck he wanted, all the better.

Then he'd gone and tried to change. And for what? All his efforts seemed pointless. His reward was guilt and second-guessing every decision he made.

No one cared. No brownie points for him.

Malakai, more than anyone, didn't trust the new him was real. And maybe he was right. Maybe it wasn't. Maybe Brave was just a horrible person. Selfish and cruel. On the same damn road Valor had been on, without drugs to make it nice and smooth.

Why should he care what Malakai thought? So what if the man was right?

Only…for months Brave had been trying to prove him wrong. And then Shiori came, fresh and new and seeing something in him that wasn't all bad.

He wanted to be the man she saw. It reflected the one he thought he could be. Made him believe he was on the right track.

Getting rid of Malakai would secure the illusion. He wouldn't have a constant reminder of all his fuck ups. Malakai had given him the perfect opportunity. Earlier, while he was still outside, the band discussed the risk he posed with his violent tendencies. Tendencies he'd tried to abandon, but one slip and all his past sins were in the spotlight.

Connor stuck up for him, but he didn't make a good argument. For either of them. He'd started the whole fight for a girl he wasn't that into. Oh, and he needed to find the guitar he'd wagered. Seriously, why was everyone so pissed?

Thankfully, he shut his mouth at a hard look from Jesse. Connor's admissions put his own standing with the band in jeopardy. As the tour manager, Jesse would report back to Reese and he didn't have anything good to tell her. Somehow, Jesse needed to prove he had control of the situation.

What better way than to eliminate the root of the problem?

On the surface, Malakai was an easy target.

But Brave needed him. He hadn't been talking shit when he'd said so. Not in so many words, he'd said the *band* needed him, but that was true too.

For Brave, it was more. Malakai was honest with him. In his anger, in the way he questioned Brave's every move. If Brave wanted to be a better man, no one else seeing he'd made progress would matter as much as Malakai.

Do you want to though? Seems like a waste of time.

He looked around the bus, catching Shiori's eye as she sat with Danica, speaking low about the routine they'd do for *S.L.U.T.* She flashed him a smile, still nodding at whatever Danica was saying. So far she'd been pretty good at pretending nothing had happened between them.

On the long drive to Kansas City, they hadn't spent a moment alone together. Danica had all kinds of guilt about letting Shiori spend the night on the bus without her. She gave them all shit when she saw Shiori wearing one of Brave's shirts. Shiori had left her suitcase at the hotel, which hadn't been a big deal until Danica pointed out if a single person caught her outside in anything of Brave's there would be talk.

Talk Shiori's career couldn't survive. Not yet. She needed to establish herself before rumors spread.

Fit with his decision to leave their night as nothing but an awesome experience for them all. Shiori followed Tate's example on how to behave and Tate seemed completely unaffected. Unlike the first time Brave had fucked around with him, when he'd seemed uncertain how to act. He'd adjusted to the idea of being used.

Which was fucked up.

Brave had never wanted to use the drummer again, but that night…hell, he wasn't sure why he'd given in to temptation.

But he had. And both Tate and Shiori were okay.

No harm done.

Until Malakai caught him looking at Shiori.

He couldn't even guess what the man had seen.

Except how much Brave wanted her.

And that he didn't like Malakai being the one she'd gone to.

Five people hovering over him and he'd been way too aware of Shiori's absence. When Alder joined them, paling at the wreck of his face, Shiori slipped away.

And clearly went to check on Malakai.

Because that's who she was. Malakai was alone. He needed her. Brave hadn't. Not then.

The band giving Malakai the cold shoulder pissed him off, but he wouldn't examine that feeling too closely. The man wouldn't appreciate his pity. Or his help.

Or pretty much anything coming from him.

Not that he had a choice.

"Thank you for joining us, Malakai." Jesse stood in the middle of the lounge, watching Malakai as he made his way up the steps. "Please have a seat."

Glancing around the room, Malakai's jaw ticked as he took a seat on the sofa next to Brave.

"As you all know, the band has dealt with…issues in the past." Jesse stared over their heads, rubbing his jaw. "We managed to overcome them, but things have changed. We have a label backing us. Sponsors. Which is awesome, but the privileges they provide come with responsibilities we can't take lightly."

On the other sofa, Danica and Alder sat close, Danica holding Alder's hand as he shot Malakai a cold look.

Sitting on Danica's other side, Shiori frowned. A few times it looked like she would speak, but then she sat back, hugging herself.

She didn't feel it was her place.

Brave knew it was his, but not yet. He'd let Jesse finish.

"I didn't approve Malakai and Connor coming here with another band. Still, that's on me. Excuses don't get you far in this business." Jesse folded his arms over his broad chest. "First of all, let's make it clear this won't happen again. Your actions reflect on the label. I can't tell you you're being stupid if you're off with a band still new enough to pull shit like this. And four of the five bands we're touring with fit that description."

Nods all around. The band would travel together. Not an unreasonable request.

"Now as for what went down today. Fights will happen. I get that." Jesse turned his attention to Malakai. "The man you attacked is in the hospital now. The band is tweeting about how you broke his jaw and knocked him out. Our fans and theirs are having fights on twitter about who's to blame."

"Malakai didn't fucking attack Bernie." Connor stood, jutting his bruised chin at Malakai. He held his side as he spoke through swollen lips. "I won that sweet piece of ass. She wanted me. The fuckers weren't happy that I beat their lead singer. They ganged up on me and Malakai had my back. What's your fucking problem? Any one of you would have done the same."

Connor wasn't the best defense for Malakai, but he'd made some good points. Brave watched Jesse as the man ran a hand through his wavy blond hair and sighed.

"There are a few dozen different clips of what went down. And you're right, I *would* have stepped in." Jesse rolled his shoulders. "But there are also videos of Malakai hitting Brave with a goddamn pipe."

My turn. Brave tipped his head back, meeting Jesse's eyes. "A few minutes on twitter and I can put a spin on that."

"Really? Better than the one trending now?" Jesse frowned at him. "I think it's #BravevsMalakai. Not all that original, but it's gaining steam. Fans think he wanted to take you out and this was the perfect opportunity. And I don't blame them."

"He didn't see me. Not even sure he looked." Simple truth. Brave knew Malakai had been in his violent haze. And he hadn't considered that before grabbing the man. *My bad.* "We stand united as a band and all the rumors won't matter. But if Malakai leaves we're adding fuel to the fire. It will confirm the band is broken."

"You're not broken." Shiori drew her knees to her chest, hugging them when all eyes turned her way. "Sorry, I know my opinion doesn't matter, but as a fan, all I see is what you show on stage. You're intense. There's so much going on under the surface. Anger and passion. It comes through in the music. Please don't lose that."

Her defense wasn't only for Malakai. It was for the band.

One they all needed to hear.

Brave was tempted to smile at her, but he couldn't chance everyone catching whatever Malakai had. Instead, he focused on their judge, jury, and executioner.

Jesse's brow furrowed. He looked at Alder, who'd dropped his gaze to Danica's hand in his. When Alder met his boyfriend's eyes some silent communication passed between them.

Tate cleared his throat, breaking the silence. "Malakai hasn't said anything yet. Neither have I, but mostly because I get why everyone's freaking out. Getting the label was awesome. We shouldn't fuck that up. But can we stop threatening to cut people? Wasn't cool when Brave went through his whole—you can be replaced—saga. We all belong here. This is us." Tate motioned to every member of the band.

Grinned as he included Danica, Jesse, and Shiori. "One for all and all for one, okay?"

"I second that." Brave wondered why Tate hadn't defended his self-appointed big brother before, but this made up for his earlier quiet. "The label knows it didn't sign choirboys. They probably won't say shit."

"I hope you're right." Jesse shoved his hands in the pockets of his worn blue jeans. "Connor, we know where you stand. Which means the majority is for Malakai staying."

"No. You get a vote. So does Danica." Alder didn't lift his head. His tone was rough, like anger had a stranglehold on him. "It's great that everyone's all good with what happened. Connor's busted up. And Malakai...*fuck*, he broke a man's jaw. He tore Brave's face open. He could kill someone, losing control like he does. Sticking together won't matter if one of us ends up dead."

"So you want him gone?" Danica reached out, cupping Alder's cheek. "I know you're upset, but he's your friend. You know he was only trying to help. It went too far."

"Yeah. I know." Alder lifted his head, his hard gaze fixed on Malakai. "And he can stay. But none of us gets to take our place here for granted. This is too important, we've all worked too fucking hard. Tate doesn't do drugs. Brave's cut back on drinking and being a dick."

Brave frowned. Sure, Alder had a point, but...all right, maybe he deserved to be called a dick. And worse.

"We've all made sacrifices. Made improvement. The urge to beat a man to death?" Alder let out a cold laugh. "Definitely needs to go."

And there it was. The root of Alder's problem with Malakai. A man had almost killed Alder. His target had been Brave. The man showed no mercy. Their lives had been expendable to him.

Alder couldn't separate Malakai's actions his attacker's. All he saw was the violence.

Connor slammed his fist into the dinette table. "Malakai wasn't—"

"Alder's right." Malakai spoke up for the first time, regret tightening his voice. He glanced down at his busted knuckles. "I stopped fighting because my lack of control scares me. I won't apologize for defending Connor. But I'll accept the consequences for my actions."

"How about therapy?" Tate ducked his head when everyone turned to stare at him. Then he shrugged. "I don't know. You were all on my case about getting therapy when I was high all the time."

Brave chuckled, recalling those unpleasant conversations. "You never went."

"I also don't do drugs anymore."

I guess we're not classifying weed as a drug? Not that Tate had even smoked a joint in a long time. The last was actually Brave's fault.

Best not bring that up.

"It's not a horrible idea." Jesse regarded Malakai thoughtfully. "Be hard on the road, but if you're willing, we actually have someone with us who's qualified."

Malakai arched a brow. "We do?"

"Yes. Ballz." Jesse chuckled when Malakai's eyes went wide. "He was a Mental Health Specialist. In the army. One of the reasons he's such a stickler for the rules. He's a good guy. Easy to talk to."

"He lets people call him 'Ballz', I figure he's pretty chill." Malakai rubbed the back of his neck and sighed. "Yeah. Okay, if he's up for it I'll talk to him."

While the two men discussed fitting therapy into the band's insane schedule, Brave watched Alder, who'd eased back against the sofa, one arm rested over Danica's shoulders. He seemed more relaxed. And very interested in this new information about Skull's brother, Ballz.

Considering Alder's sleeplessness, and how on edge he was all the time, he should probably see a therapist himself.

Probably should have after the attack, but no one had even considered it.

Not even Jesse, clearly, since he knew they had a shrink working security detail.

Or you, his shitty ass brother.

That would change now, but he wouldn't broach the subject in front of everyone. Malakai being pressured into therapy fucking sucked, never mind Alder. Suggesting a survivor of that kind of violence needed to rehash shit to fully heal? If he were Alder, he'd want to erase the little he remembered from his mind and simply enjoy living.

Brave would never let himself forget. Any more than he'd forget Valor's death. Those memories had changed him. Not all for the good, but he was stronger. Maybe even a little smarter.

"All right, so that's settled." Jesse smiled, though it didn't quite reach his eye. He looked worn out. "I'm going to check in with the sound crew. You guys—and girls—" He inclined his head to Danica and Shiori. "—should start getting ready. Be at the venue for sound check at 4:30."

With that Jesse took off, leaving them to follow their typical routine. Tate claimed the shower first, disappearing into the closet sized bathroom before anyone could protest. Connor mumbled something about going to the van to do work with his weights. Alder and Danica headed to the back lounge. Brave didn't want to know what they were doing.

If she could get his brother in a better mood, it was all good.

Alone with Shiori and Malakai, Brave did the one thing he hoped would settle some nerves.

He poured them all a drink, fixing Shiori's exactly like he had the other night.

"Should you be drinking after taking meds?" Malakai set his glass on the window ledge and frowned up at Brave.

Shiori let out a soft laugh. "He didn't take anything."

"I took a couple shots while Danica glued my face together." Brave's chuckle died in his throat at Malakai's wince.

He'd been trying to keep things light, but as much as the man hated him, he didn't like seeing him hurt. He cleared his throat, opening the freezer to fetch the man an icepack for his knuckles. Thankfully, they didn't look swollen. "Seriously, Grimm, I'm good."

Malakai's brow rose as he placed the pack over his right hand. "'Grimm'?"

Grimm? Brave wasn't even sure where that had come from. He shrugged. "Sorry, just slipped out."

"Because I remind you of guys who wrote twisted fairytales?"

"Naw. More the German meaning. I read somewhere it's 'fury'." Not exactly flattering. "Also, you can be pretty grim."

"I like it." Shiori sat forward, hands clasped between her knees. "Besides, the Grimm brothers changed their work to kid appropriate later on. It's all how you look at it. Grim determination isn't a bad thing."

Gaze softening, Malakai smiled up at her. "You have the determination part down pat. Thank you, by the way. What you said helped."

"I speak only truth." She smiled back at Malakai, then took a sip of her drink. Her phone buzzed in the pocket of the long jacket she'd draped over the arm of the sofa. She took it out, her smile fading as she stared at the screen, the phone slipping in her gasp. "Oh fuck."

Leaning across the narrow space between the sofa and the loveseat, Malakai eased the phone from her hand. Not something Brave would have thought to do. Shiori had punched him once for crossing the line.

The bassist seemed to have a whole different set of rules, because she didn't let out a whisper of protest.

Definitely some interesting dynamics between the two of them.

Brave wasn't sure he liked it.

Malakai handed her phone over, his expression hard with accusation. "Nice job, asshole."

What the fuck did I do now?

The message was from Sophie. A picture followed by 'Fix this'.

At first, he couldn't quite make out the picture. Parts were blurred. He enlarged it and groaned. Shiori's face was clear enough. The photo must have been taken when she was changing into his shirt during the game. Neither he or Tate had looked—things hadn't progressed that far then—but in the corner of the picture he was visible. So was Tate. The photographer must have been in a fucking tree.

The caption beneath the photo made it even worse.

"Who's the new S.L.U.T?"

"You're not dancing to that song." Brave handed her phone back to her and stood. He clenched his fists, resisting the urge to punch something. Or confront the fucker who'd put Shiori's career at risk. "You know the routines for the others. Do *Center Mass*. Go with a military look."

"And a hat and shades?" Malakai let out an irritated sound. "This looks like it was posted on twitter. It might not have gone viral because no one knows her yet, but the second word gets out..."

"I *know*." Social media was a fucking beast. Useful when they needed it, but toxic when they wanted privacy and personal shit leaked. He paced along the front of the bus, raking his fingers through his hair. "The fight might—"

"Distract them? Not likely. The attention it got already will be the end of it. Unless we play out the animosity. The band will love that." Malakai's tone was dry.

He also wasn't being very helpful.

"Scratch that. On stage, you're my best friend. Maybe more..." Brave's lips slanted. "Actually, that's not—"

"Happening. Go fuck yourself, Brave."

"You got a better idea?"

Malakai scowled and shook his head.

Smoothing his hand through his hair again, Brave sighed. "I might have something else." He went to the bathroom door and slammed his fist on the thin metal. "Time's up, drummer boy!"

The door swung open. Tate stepped out, butt naked, rubbing his hair with a towel. "All yours."

"Not now." Brave nudged him out of the way and slipped into the foggy bathroom. He wiped a hand over the mirror, meeting his own eyes in the reflection before the white sheen of condensation built up again.

He'd wanted to change. Then he hadn't. Then he'd balanced on the ledge between the two. A real change would mean more than a lot of talk and ditching a couple vices.

People would have to see the change to believe it.

And they were about to.

Chapter Thirteen

'Fix this.'

Two words that could mean only one thing.

Shiori had been stunned when she'd seen the picture. So stunned she hadn't said a word while Brave and Malakai discussed a diversion. All she could think was Sophie must be so disappointed.

Except...she'd only said those two words. Like she trusted Shiori *could* fix it.

But how?

Time to call in the expert. She texted Danica, figuring it would be less disruptive than knocking on the door where the woman had disappeared with her boyfriend.

Shiori: Not an emergency. Exactly. I need your advice.

Danica immediately came out, adjusting her pale blue, V-neck sweater. She glanced at Malakai, who'd moved to sit beside Shiori, then nodded toward the door.

"Let's head to the venue. I'll introduce you to our crew." Danica snatched both their jackets from the kitchenette bench, throwing them over one arm. She hooked her other arm to Shiori's as she started for the door. "See you on stage, love!"

Before Alder could answer, they were outside.

Pausing to pull on her jacket while Shiori slipped on her own, Danica met her eyes. "What happened?"

The explanation was embarrassing, but Shiori couldn't expect Danica's help if she didn't know the facts. Of course, she glossed over a few things. Like how the game had ended.

The other woman still looked pissed. "I *knew* Brave would pull something like this. Damn it." Angry red blotched her cheeks. "And all Sophie said was 'fix this'?"

"That's it." Shiori shoved her hands in her pockets and frowned down at the icy pavement. "But this isn't on Brave. He didn't want to play the stupid game. Tate and I pushed him into it."

"I doubt that."

Clenching her teeth, Shiori lifted her head. "You've done things on the road, with the guys. Did they force you?"

"Of course not." Danica shook her head and sighed. "I get it. You were having some fun. Please tell me that was the end of it? Right now this is a bump in the road. Between Brave and Tate, this could easily become a crater-sized pothole."

"It's the end." She did her best not to sound disappointed. Exploring more with Brave...hell, she wouldn't lie. It was tempting.

His fault, with the tucking her in and giving her those sweet smiles. Having him near made her whole body hum like a tuning fork, letting off the perfect pitch. As if preparing for a beautiful song missing only the lyrics.

A wonderful feeling, but one she couldn't indulge in. She'd strayed from her path, then found it again. And she didn't need any more bumps setting her off course.

Craters were out of the question.

"Good." Danica stopped by the roadies' van, putting her hands on Shiori's arms and turning her, giving her an affectionate little squeeze. "This isn't the end of the world. If anyone asks—and they won't ask you alone, I'm not leaving your side—say you've known the guys awhile and you're comfortable changing in front of them. I'll say I do it too. We'll make it such a nonissue; people will get bored."

"Bored works for me." Shiori squared her shoulders. "Anything that keeps Sophie from ripping up my contract."

Snickering, Danica moved to her side, slipping an arm around her waist. "She won't. She's dealt with drama so bad she had to catch the first flight to do damage control. She sent you a text."

This is low on her scale of disasters. That's good.

"Okay." Shiori took a deep breath. "I can do this."

"Yes, you can."

"Brave suggested I dance during *Center Mass* instead of *S.L.U.T.*"

"That is a *very* good idea." Danica laughed, lightening the mood. "And you'll look hot in uniform. I've got the perfect outfit for you."

Skull drove them to the venue, leaving the roadies and security to babysit the boys. They parked in an underground parking lot a block away and quickly walked over, heads down, hoping no one would recognize Danica and stop them.

Luck wasn't on their side.

"Danica! OMG, it's really you!" A girl ran up to Danica, bursting into tears as she reached for her. Danica caught the girl by the shoulders and smiled at her, which made the girl cry harder. "I was here last time Winter's Wrath was in town. And I loved your music video. I follow you on twitter. You wished me Happy Birthday!"

"Don't cry, sweetie." Danica wiped away the girl's tears. "What's your name?"

"Monica." The girl hiccupped. Her freckled face went red. "I'm sorry. You have no idea how much I love you. I already loved the band, but you...you joining them made me less of a freak. All the girls at school use your perfume. And your makeup. They'll die when they find out I met you!"

The girl was adorable. Maybe fifteen, with curly hair dyed an inky shade, black lipstick and eyeliner, and a snug Winter's Wrath hoodie covering her curvy body. She reminded Shiori of

Wendy, who got just as excited about meeting her idols. And wouldn't hesitate to run up to one either.

"They'll need evidence." Danica grinned at Monica. "How about a selfie? Post it on Twitter or Instagram and I'll share it."

"Can I do both?"

"Absolutely!" Danica took the girl's phone and handed it to Shiori. "Could you take a couple pictures?"

"Sure!" Shiori backed up until she had both women in view, snapping one photo of Monica gazing adoringly up at Danica. Another of Danica hugging her tight. A few more so the girl could pick her favorite.

Skull came up behind her. "How about one with Winter's Wrath's new dancer? You'll be the first to have a photo with her."

Monica let out a squeal. "Really? This is so awesome! You're gorgeous! And I'm so jelly!"

Before Shiori could say a word she was placed on Monica's other side. She tried to remember all Sophie's tips on how to stand. How to smile. Which side to angle her head.

Mostly she just lost herself to the excitement. Monica wasn't the only one completely blown away by the experience. Someone had taken a photo with her. Someone who wasn't friends or family.

This was different than the photos she'd taken for her portfolio. Sure, Monica was Danica's fan, but she could have easily brushed Shiori off like she was irrelevant.

She hadn't.

Which meant more than Shiori could say.

Still, she had to try.

Before Skull could lead them away, she hugged Monica. "Thank you. This is new to me, my first live performance with the band. You made being here even more special. And you can tell all the other girls I said so."

Eyes tearing, Monica shook her head. "No. Screw them. They can see you up on that stage and wonder what you're like. Wish they were you." She blinked and tears spilled down her cheeks. "I love how real you are. How real you both are. I'm not sharing that with anyone."

Monica rushed off to get back in the line which reached around the block. There was some excitement from the crowd, but metal barriers prevented anyone else from rushing them.

Anyone except the press.

On the other side of the venue entrance stood a small crowd of people with microphones and cameras. As Shiori and Danica approached, questions were shouted at them.

"There are rumors of a replacement. Is it true you're taking a break because you're pregnant?"

"Is there any truth to a lawsuit over a sex tape?"

"Has Alder asked you to marry him?"

"Are you the replacement? Have you seen this picture?"

The last stopped Shiori in her tracks. She moved closer to the reporters and glanced at the tablet the woman held out.

"Yes." She wasn't good at lying. And with Danica's cover story, she didn't have to be. "It's kinda creepy that someone was spying on us. I wasn't expecting that."

"So you admit you stripped in front of the band?" The woman held her mic closer to Shiori. "Are you already intimate with them?"

"Intimate?" Shiori cocked her head. "I'm not sure what you mean. We've been friends for a while. I've been getting changed in front of them forever."

Danica slipped to her side, snickering. "Oh my, is that a crime now? I guess we're both guilty."

Shiori's lips slanted. "So bad. On a bus all the time with the guys, we should totally hide our evil lady bits."

Busting out laughing, Danica hugged her. "You're adorable. 'Lady bits'?"

"*Evil* lady bits."

"True dat!" Danica glanced over at the reporters. "Oh, and I'm not pregnant. I just like tacos. And you can quote me."

With that the left the reporters behind.

Situation totally 'fixed'.

Malakai did his best not to move while Tate helped him with the mess he'd made of his black eyeliner, but he couldn't stop looking down the hall toward the bathroom.

Brave still hadn't come out.

Not since Jesse had returned to drive them to the venue, parking the bus in their reserved spot right across the street. Not even when Jesse had pounded on the door—twice—yelling for him to hurry the fuck up.

The rest of the band was ready. The sound crew was waiting for them, along with the VIPs who'd been led in about ten minutes ago.

"If I punch you, your eyes will be plenty dark." Tate dug his fingers into Malakai's jaw, forcing him to look forward. "Fuck, it's a good thing Alder lets Danica's makeup people prep him. Maybe they should deal with you too."

"Fuck no." Malakai shuddered. Alder did magazine ads and commercials. He used some powder to make his skin look perfect. And wore fucking lips gloss.

Lip gloss!

Letting Tate manhandle him, coming close to stabbing him in the eye with the liner pencil thing, was worth it if he could avoid that kind of primping. Just watching Tate use three different colors to hide the bruise around his own eye freaked him out.

To him makeup was torture. Done right it was like magic, but some of the shit people used looked like medieval devices. Like the contraption he'd seen Danica use on her eyelashes. He could total picture it being used to remove an eyeball.

One wrong move and a simple pencil could blind him. So he tried to stay *very* still. But no fucking way would he do all the powder and brushes and other shit. And lip gloss felt weird when he kissed a chick wearing too much. Slick, like motor oil smeared all over his mouth.

Every time Tate did his eyeliner, he tried to convince Malakai to use at least some 'balm'.

Not happening.

Why is Brave taking so long?

"Last warning. You love this bus, Brave." Jesse slammed his fist into the door. "Come out or I'm tearing this damn thing off the hinges!"

The lock on the door clicked. Brave stepped out, scowling at Jesse. "I'm done. Happy?"

Oh fuck.

Tate dropped the pencil.

Jesse backed into the wall.

Malakai slammed his fist on the sofa. "Are you mental? The fans are going to lose their minds!"

Moving into the narrow space of the lounge area, Brave glared at him. "That's the fucking point."

Latching his fingers behind his head, Malakai stared at the hack job Brave had made of his hair. Waist length strands chopped to just above his collar. And when he brushes his fingers through the chopped up bits he'd left, Malakai caught a glimpse of the closely—way too fucking closely—shaved part at his nape.

"You can't go on stage like that." Jesse pulled out his phone. "Hey, babe. We have an emergency."

Yelling came across the line.

"No. No one's hurt. I—"

Alder came out, spared Brave a brief glance, and snatched the phone from Jesse. "Hey, beautiful. Yes, Jesse is an idiot. I know." He punched Jesse in the arm. "Done. Now, seriously, Brave cut his hair." A high pitched shout had Alder holding the phone away from his ear. "I'll put him in a hoodie and send him over. I love you."

Stashing the phone, Alder looked at Brave. Then brought a hand to his face and rubbed his eyes. "I don't even want to know. Cover that shit up and let's get inside. Hopefully, Danica's people can fix it."

Hanging his head—the shorn hair falling forward and revealing where he'd cut himself with the razor—Brave turned to the bunk area, out of sight.

Stomach twisting with sympathy, Malakai lunged to his feet and followed. He moved behind Brave, gently brushing his fingers over the patchy, shaved hair at the base of Brave's scalp.

"I would have helped if you'd asked." Malakai pressed his teeth hard into his bottom lip as he took in the raw spots. That had to fucking hurt. And Brave already had a cut over his eye from Shiori and a gash on his face from Malakai.

Starting a damn painful collection.

Brave shrugged. "You know I don't ask for help."

"But…" Malakai pressed his lips shut. He'd never made Brave comfortable coming to him about anything. Never had a reason.

He wished he had.

He cleared his throat. "If it's any consolation, this should work. No matter how Danica's people manage to repair the damage, you're the face of the band and a drastic change to your appearance is a story. People will be talking about this for weeks."

Brave pulled on a hoodie, drawing the hood completely over his head to hide his hair. His dark eyes met Malakai's. "What if drastic isn't enough?"

"You have another plan."

"Yeah. It was stupid."

"It wasn't." Malakai slid his hand into the hood, curved his fingers around the side of Brave's neck. "One performance. I've done them with your brother. Not so much with you, but it doesn't have to be different."

"Stop." Brave reached up and grabbed his wrist. He glared at Malakai. "Don't feel sorry for me. I did this for her. She's worth it."

The way the man bit out the words... Malakai didn't believe Brave was using Shiori anymore. Maybe he'd finally woken the fuck up and seen what Malakai already knew.

Their lovers were faceless. Sex a shallow act in the closest dark space, with few words exchanged. Rarely any names.

Relationships involved two people with something to offer. And what did Malakai have? All his damage? His rage? There was nothing soft about him. And love was soft.

Shiori deserved love. A love neither he or Brave could give her.

Thankfully, she was strong enough to keep going on her own. Their support might be a bonus, but she didn't need them.

With or without them, she'd do just fine.

He wasn't sure what had happened that night between her, Brave, and Tate. Tate hadn't changed. Wasn't any closer to Brave than he'd been before. A fucking relief, because Malakai knew when Tate finally chose someone, nothing would hold him back. He was curious. Passionate. A little wild and young still, but that would pass.

When he fell in love, it would consume him. He got addicted to things. To ideas.

He hadn't reached that point with Brave.

Malakai realized he still hadn't answered Brave. "She is worth it."

"And what about us?" Brave smirked when Malakai frowned at him. "To save her, will you play my game? Can you handle it?"

"Can you?" Malakai still had his hand on Brave's neck. He tightened his grip, pulling Brave close. "You're not the man you were. This isn't your game. Not really." He leaned in, brushing his lips over the wound he'd caused. "Still want to play?"

"Bring it." Brave let out a low growl, pressing against him. "I always want to play."

"But this isn't about you." Malakai ran his fingers over the raw flesh of Brave's scalp. "And I'm doing this because I think you get that."

Resting his head on Malakai's shoulder as though it had all become too much, Brave laughed.

"I really do."

Sound check went fast. VIPs weren't happy, but they were promised time after the show to hang out. Made things better.

Next came an interview with a blogger who roasted bands—AKA ridiculed them for laughs—on his YouTube channel, pulling in more money from his huge following than most musicians he interviewed made in a year.

Malakai had never watched him, but Jesse warned them he wouldn't be nice. His thing was awkward questions, sarcasm, and randomly jumping up to shout insults.

Bigger bands begged for spots on his show. Fans loved him.

That he'd asked to be here tonight was cool.

But after five minutes Malakai hated the fucker.

"Legit question from twitter." The man, 'Trebble Joe', jumped up on his seat. "Danica Tallien is fucking two men. She's teased about it. Hands up if you're one of them."

Tate raised his hand.

Trebble Joe gaped at him. "You're doing that hot piece of ass?"

Alder growled. Brave held him down.

"No. I *wish*." Tate blinked at the camera. "I have a question."

"Go for it." Trebble Joe winked at the camera. "We're listening."

"What are you on? Is it legal? Can I have some?" Tate blew Trebble Joe a kiss. "That's all."

Thrown off, the blogger stared at Tate. Then rubbed his crotch. "I'm on tons of dick. Whose are you on?"

"Anyone who asks. But I like flowers first." Tate rubbed his lips. "And candy. And cookies. I'll suck your dick for cookies."

This interview wasn't going at all like the blogger had planned. He plopped on the sofa next to Tate and pouted. "I don't have any. But can you tell me something?"

"Sure!" Tate made a happy sound as Skull walked over and handed him a box of cookies. "Our man, Skull! He's the best!"

"You have a new girl." Trebble Joe leaned close to Tate. "And you saw her naked. Is she easy?"

Now he dies. Malakai moved to stand. Releasing Alder, Brave reached over to grab his arm.

Leaned close to whisper in his ear. "Give this asshole *nothing.*"

Tate blinked. "New girl? Naked? And I missed that? What's her name?"

Trebble Joe was visibly annoyed. He had no good material to show his fans. He tried again. "You saying you didn't see her naked?"

"*Who?* Am I supposed to remember?" Tate laid on the sofa, resting his head on Alder's lap. "I'm confused. And bored."

Alder patted his head. "Not sure who he's talking about either."

"The new girl!" Trebble Joe made a cutting motion with his hand when they all gave him blank looks. "Come on. You know who I mean."

"Time's up!" Jesse sounded way too pleased about ending the interview. "Thanks for coming. You're welcome to watch the other bands side stage, but I'm afraid my guys need to get ready to open their act."

"They gave me fucking nothing!" Trebble Joe ranted as Jesse led him away. "Give me something I can use!"

"You're interviewing the tour manager. That's pathetic. Get a grip, man." Jesse led the man backstage. "And you didn't even ask Brave about his hair. You're a horrible reporter. Sad."

"Did you just quote Trump?"

"No comment."

Once the YouTuber was out of hearing, Tate rolled onto the floor, clutching his stomach and laughing. "Did you see him? He's so pissed! He brought up Trump!"

"Not going there." Alder rubbed his hands on his thighs. "Look, I've had some time to think. And this crazy little drummer boy was right. Which is kinda scary." Alder grinned at Tate's huff. "We're in this together. The band doesn't get split apart. I'm sorry I went off like I did."

"It's all good." Malakai bowed his head as Alder pulled him in for a hug. "Think we should get Brave back to the hairdresser before she murders us all?"

"Hells yes!" Alder reached out, tipping the hood Brave had worn during the interview back. "I'm sorry. I love you, but… *Damn.*"

"I should have just shaved my head." Brave started walking fast toward the greenroom.

Alder hurried to catch up with him. "I'm glad you didn't. With the way you butchered your scalp you'd have ended up with brain damage."

"Fuck you."

"You mad I'm the pretty one now?"

Brave stopped short. Eyed his brother. "You're doing perfume ads. We all know how pretty you are. Go put on some blush and fuck off before I ruin your 'Bucky with the good hair' do with my fist."

"As opposed to Bucky fought a weed wacker look?" Alder held his hands up when Brave lunged at him and Connor held him back. "My bad. You were going for Brittney-Spears-changes-her-mind-mid-shave."

Tate slipped up to Malakai's side. Spoke softly from the side of his mouth. "Are they fighting?"

Was hard to tell. Brave wasn't struggling too hard to get loose. For the first time in weeks, Alder was smiling. Laughing. Sure, at Brave's expense, but he'd never done that before.

The two didn't joke around. Or give one another a hard time.

Malakai grinned and ruffled Tate's hair.

"They're acting like brothers."

Chapter Fourteen

Brave didn't know how Alder put up with all the primping. A little black around the eyes, sure. But apparently, the gash on his cheek looked better with some concealer to hide the bruised flesh around it. And the cut above his eye too. And since his hairline was all fucked up, they'd just cover it, and his entire neck, with black body paint.

If they make me look glam metal I'm not setting foot on that fucking stage.

The jacket they'd found to pull his 'new look' together was all right. Leather styled like armor at the shoulders, with straps across the chest. A pain in the ass to put on, but he liked the feel of it. He had his usual black jeans and knee length boots—these had thick straps along his calves that match the jacket.

Fine, he wasn't all fashionable, but he loved his boots. He brought about ten on tour and had a few dozen more at home. Danica teased him once that he was more obsessed with footwear than any model she knew.

She may be right.

About twenty minutes later the hairstylist, Kali, who'd resumed grumbling about his hair the second he returned to her *tender* care, patted his shoulder with a weary sigh.

"Well, you don't look like a toddler came at your head with a pair of scissors anymore." She turned his chair so he could look in the mirror. "What do you think?"

Checking out his hair he nodded and stood, giving her a quick hug before she yanked open the black barber cape she'd covered him with. "Looks great. Going for a Brandon Lee in The Crow style?"

"Actually, I was thinking River Phoenix from The Thing Called Love. Only edgier." Kali fussed with his hair. "I haven't seen The Crow."

"I'm gonna pretend I didn't hear that." He laughed as she shoved him toward the door. "Thanks, babe."

Letting out a little huff, she followed him. "Would you call Reese 'babe'?"

"Nope." He winked at her. "She ain't as sweet as you."

Kali snickered and shut the door behind him.

Humming under his breath, Brave made his way to the greenroom. He had some time to chill before they hit the stage and with his improved look, maybe the rest of the band would stop worrying about fan reactions. Sure, they'd talk. That was the point.

But no one would worry he'd gone off the deep end.

Tate spotted him first. He hopped to his feet, stepping up to Brave to stroke his freshly shaved jaw. "Ooo, soft. You're so purdy."

"Thanks." Brave brushed Tate's hand away. Went to the bar in the corner to grab a beer, surveying the room as he twisted off the cap. "Where are the girls?"

"Danica's stylist is still working on Shiori. Sophie's rejected every outfit they've tried so far." Alder sipped his own beer, eyeing Brave thoughtfully. The edge of his lips quirked. "Your new image Joker from The Dark Knight?"

Brave gave his darling brother a one finger salute.

Malakai chuckled. "You need your eyes checked, man. He could totally pass for Eric Draven."

"Who?" Tate grabbed a cookie from the tray on the table and stuffed it in his mouth.

"The Crow." Malakai frowned at Tate's confused look. "*Really*?"

Holding his beer to his lips, Brave stared at Malakai. He wasn't sure what shocked him more. That Malakai remembered the main character from the movie, or... *Did he just compliment me?*

No way. He was pointing out the obvious.

Snapping his fingers, Malakai arched a brow as Brave blinked at him. "Wake up, Draven. You look good. Now can you pass me a beer?"

"Uh, yeah." Brave took out another beer, handing it over, wondering if he should finish his own. He must be hearing things. "You calling me Draven now?"

"Sure." Malakai smirked at him, taking a long swig, then licking his bottom lip. "You still calling me Grimm?"

Not sure if I should. He shrugged, swallowing hard as he watched Malakai trace his thumb over the lip he'd just licked. What the hell was up with the guy?

If Brave didn't know better, he'd think Malakai was flirting. Which shouldn't faze him. Fuck, Tate did more than flirt. Even Connor had his suggestive moments. He'd fooled around with them both out of boredom.

But Malakai was different. He didn't play games.

He didn't have to.

Guys and girls threw themselves at him. He found the closest, semi-private area and did his thing. The few times the band had partied hard and gotten naked with groupies in a shared hotel room, Brave noticed how detached Malakai was with his lovers. They enjoyed every fucking minute—if the moans were anything to go by—but Malakai's eyes, his tone, were always cold.

His eyes weren't cold now.

And was it getting fucking hot in here? Brave brought his hand, cool and moist from the beer bottle, up to rub the back of his neck.

Alder snorted. "Well, that didn't last long."

Huh?

Malakai stood, grabbing a handful of napkins off the table, a knowing smile on his lips. "You made a mess."

Keep looking at me like that and I'm going to.

"Your hand." Malakai grabbed his wrist and Brave's stomach flipped. Lowering his voice, Malakai pressed the napkins into his palm. "Pull yourself together."

Glancing down, Brave's face heated even more. He'd forgotten about the paint on his neck. His entire hand was covered in black. He scowled and tried to rub it off. His hair stuck to the sweat slicking his face.

He brushed it back.

His stupid brother practically fell over laughing. Tate choked on his cookie. Connor slapped Tate's back, snickering.

Rather than join in, Malakai sighed and picked up a fresh napkin. "You're making it worse. Hold still."

"I can fucking do it." Brave stepped back.

Latching onto one of the straps on his jacket, Malakai jerked him forward.

The laughing from the guys stopped short.

"How about you let me show the guys we can get along." Malakai's lips thinned as he studied Brave's face. His gaze settled on the patched-up skin on his cheek. "Please."

The 'please' did Brave in. He held still as Malakai carefully wiped his cheek, trying to ignore the painful swell of his dick in his tight jeans, hoping the man didn't notice.

"Shit, this stuff doesn't come off easy." Malakai paused, glancing over his shoulder at Tate. "Pass me the vodka."

"Vodka?" Brave's brow furrowed, wishing Malakai would fucking finish and back off. "I don't mix, dude."

"Mix? You haven't even started your beer." Letting out a soft laugh, Malakai poured a bit of vodka on the napkin. "Remember when we had all that paint on us for the video? You all used some kind of oil to take it off, but I got an allergic reaction. So I used alcohol."

"Smart." Brave relaxed as Malakai fixed his face. He'd always admired how sharp the other man was—resourceful and all that, which came in handy when they'd been managing the band on their own.

And in situations like this.

The door opened and Jesse stepped into the room. "On in five." He blinked at Brave and Malakai. Looked over at Alder. "Should I be worried?"

"I'm not sure."

Alder speaking up made Brave realize all the guys had gotten real quiet.

He caught them staring from the corner of his eye and sighed. "Nothing to see here."

Jesse gave him a level look, then inclined his head. "He's right. Come on, we've got a sold-out show. Over a thousand people." He held up a hand when Brave's eyes narrowed. "Our Security detail is ready and the venue has its own guys. I spent an hour talking with the owner and assured him you'll all stay on stage. This place has a good reputation, and after the last show, he needed some guarantees that we wouldn't fuck that up. So don't, okay?"

"We'll be good," Tate said, sweetly, chomping down another cookie with a smirk.

Which clearly didn't reassure Jesse at all.

Dabbing at one last spot on Brave's cheek, Malakai turned to face their tour manager. "No fighting and no telling fans to fuck shit up. We got it."

"Good." Jesse hesitated, eyes on Brave. "They did a good job."

"Thanks."

Lips parted, Jesse gave him and Malakai another once over, then backed out of the room, letting the door shut behind him.

A few minutes later, the band headed to the stage. Everyone was in a good mood. Except for Alder, who kept shooting Brave dirty looks. If he was pissed about Jesse giving Brave a second glance, he could work that out with his man.

Brave didn't have time to worry about his brother's jealousy. As soon as Tate ran out to take his place behind the drums, the crowd went wild.

Connor and Malakai followed, the three of them starting up the opening of *Fallen Star*. Alder walked on stage, picked up his guitar, and flashed a broad smile as he cut in with the familiar chords.

Brave sauntered up to the mic and thrusting devil horns high. He grabbed the mic, growling as screams rose all around him. As he sang the world narrowed to the lyrics, to the rhythm, to the beat pulsing through him. What he looked like didn't matter. All the shit the band had to deal with was nothing but a scribble on the side of a page filled with words bleeding out from his very soul.

This was one of the first songs he'd written after LOST disbanded. Months after Valor died, when he still thought his future was fucked.

He lived for the music. Lots of bands talked shit, like they felt the same, then sold out, producing songs that appealed to the masses. Softer, with repetitive beats. Catchy stanzas with zero substance. The words were easy to remember, kinda like pop music.

Some even got turned into pop music, earning the bands royalties. Money and fame, the grand prize, right?

Fuck that.

Winter's Wrath was hardcore, intense, and that wasn't going to change. He'd heard a few covers of their songs done soft, but the best of those amateur musicians somehow managed to express the depth of the lyrics. Bring out the undertone of anger, or sadness, or defiance. He'd messaged a few to tell him how much he enjoyed their work.

Their replies were awesome. Every single one was excited to hear from him and asked if he'd mind them selling their covers. Without hesitation, he gave them the green light.

Imitation is the best form of flattery and all that.

But the real fans weren't satisfied with imitation. They wanted Winter's Wrath. They sang along, screamed his name, and reacted to every word with the emotion he'd hoped to inspire.

"When the blazing sun is gone,
So very long before the dawn
Your tiny light comes from on high,
We whisper wishes as you die."

The final notes trailed off and he let the fans repeat the chorus one last time. Stepping forward, he looked them over.

"How the fuck we doing tonight, Kansas City!"

Wild cheers flowed around him. This wasn't the biggest city they played in, but after a long span between events here, many had come from far and wide to see Winter's Wrath. Exciting and humbling.

But they didn't want his thanks. They wanted all the attitude he brought to every performance.

And he had no problem giving it to them.

"Not much to do around here, but you all ain't boring. You make your own fun, don't you?" He let out a low laugh into the mic. "I see some hot ladies in the front row, but they're being real quiet. Are the ladies here wild or what?"

On cue half, the women in the front row lifted their shirts, some flashing black bras, others bare breasts. And the roaring response was deafening. This wasn't a shy group. Everyone appreciated the display.

"Beautiful." Brave drew out a growly sound of approval. A soft sigh escaped a few red lips. "Now for the most important question…" He paused and the whole crowd leaned forward as one. "Where are my S.L.U.T.S?"

Devil horns up, every member of the crowd began chanting.

"Slut, slut, slut!"

This song was one of his favorites. He actually got the idea when a groupie named Olivia, who'd hung around with the band for a few stops on their first tour was jeered at by some girls standing in line. They called her all kinds of names.

She held her tears back until they got inside.

He hugged her and whispered in her ear. "They say that word like it's an insult, but you know what?"

Her tear reddened eyes met his. "What?"

"Slut stands for something. It's more than sex—though the sex is awesome." He winked at her and she blushed. "We don't let many people hang out with us. We trust you." He stopped walking. "Fuck, I need to write this down. Give me your hand."

Without pause, she held out her hand. He grabbed a pen from the pocket of his jacket and wrote the words. Sex. Love. Understanding. Trust.

Then he leaned in to kiss her forehead. "That's what it means, from now on. And don't you ever forget it."

Olivia had fallen in love with the drummer of another band not long after and had a couple kids with him, but she still kept in touch. And she'd never exposed anything she'd done with Winter's Wrath to the press, even when they'd offered her some good money.

Their trust in her hadn't been misplaced. And he remembered her, and others like her, every time he sang this song. Groupies were a special breed. Not opportunist like many believed. They loved the music, the lifestyle. The good ones had fed his muse over the years. When the guys were tired of him struggling with lyrics, the groupies were always ready to listen. Looking up at him with big eyes as though witnessing magic in the making.

They made him believe in the magic. That what he created with the band would last. The music was immortal.

As always, Danica came out during the chorus, wearing an outfit that had critics calling her a traitor to her gender. Women who dressed in shorts skirts and shirts that barely covered their breasts were shameless. Objectifying themselves.

Whenever she stepped on stage, Danica proved a woman could be powerful, no matter what she wore. She was sexy, had a presence none could ignore. And she gave all the haters a great big 'Fuck you' with a simple smile. She knew they were watching. And couldn't stop her.

Brave didn't watch Danica on stage anymore. Not like he used to. He was aware of her, shared the energy she pulled from the crowd, but his body didn't react like she was temptation on heels.

Which was odd.

Sure, her being with his brother *should* have set those limits a long time ago, but he'd always indulged himself. Always took what he wanted without a thought to the consequences. Showing the woman the respect she'd earned meant facing what a total asshole he was.

Had been.

Still am.

He wasn't ready to let himself off the hook. He still pulled some dick moves. But being able to see Danica strut around the stage and feel only admiration was cool. She was family. Would be his sister one day.

And she'd chosen a good man. Alder might be a little messed up, but he'd work things out. He had two people who loved him. Two Brave would have tried to steal away once just to see if he could.

His messed up way of showing he cared. If he could take them, they were no good for his brother. That Alder would have hated him had been icing on the cake.

Loving someone because they were blood was stupid. Brave had learned as much from Valor. A lesson he'd tried to teach Alder, without causing too much damage.

If Alder didn't love Brave, Brave couldn't hurt him.

But the stubborn fucker loved him anyway. More than Brave deserved.

Thank fucking god, because without Alder the band would have been torn apart when Brave tried to self-destruct.

Instead, they were here. A thousand eyes on them, unaware of how close Winter's Wrath had come to being nothing but a memory. Just like LOST.

A steady hand settled on his shoulder and his voice became husky. He hadn't seen Malakai move, but he sensed him there, at his back. There was a pause in the lyrics for Alder's provocative solo. Danica had the crowd in the palm of her hand. His brother kept them moving with the sensual draw of the melody, notes mimicking a pulse picking up as lust took over.

Just like Brave's was. He sucked in a breath as Malakai's hand slick down his chest. An excited murmur flowed in an undercurrent from the crowd, but he hardly noticed them as Malakai latched onto the front of Brave's jacket and twisted him around to face him.

This was an act. A diversion.

He had to remember that.

Guitar slung behind him, Malakai flashed an evil smile, tugging Brave's jacket straps while grinding against his thigh. He brought his lips close to Brave's ear, careful to keep clear of the mic.

"You look fucking terrified, Draven." Malakai lightly bit his earlobe, letting out a rough laugh. "Relax."

Relax? Is he fucking serious?

Malakai was *always* serious. And he was right. Brave had to be the slick player the fans knew or this little performance wouldn't work. Which he could have done with almost anyone but Malakai. Malakai had been a friend when he'd been too fucked up to be one back. An enemy when Brave needed someone to challenge his every move.

And now he was... *Fuck*, when had the man learned to move like that? Brave stared into Malakai's eyes, which always seemed to lack any color at all but black and white. But this close he could see a hint of blue, like the ocean at night when the water was almost completely still, but the slightest breeze revealed more. A quick glance and there was only darkness, but the faintest light bared the deep, rich shade.

Ever since he'd know Malakai, he'd been aware of only two sides to him. The calm and the rage. He'd learned to deal with each extreme, but what he saw now was something in between.

Something he hadn't built up a defense for. Malakai completely in control was cold and level. His anger like being shoved into an artic pool, so icy it burned to the touch.

Right now he was a bonfire in the middle of a frozen tundra, drawing Brave close to the edge, but warning him not to get too close. Those flames were dangerous. Unpredictable.

Brave could become hypnotized, simply watching them, but he'd forgotten his place, his purpose, long enough. He wouldn't be seeing this side of Malakai at all if Shiori didn't need them to shift focus away from her. They had to give the vultures something else to circle.

He curved his hand around the back of Malakai's neck, bringing their lips so close he could taste the other man's breath on his lips. A hint of the beer he'd drank while teasing Brave. The mint underneath.

The song was almost over. Time to end this.

Flicking his tongue over Malakai's bottom lip, Brave eased back enough to turn to the mic and whispered. "*Slut.*"

Unlike most of their shows, the crowd didn't immediately cheer. Uncertainty rolled around them in the silence. Then it got loud.

Really *fucking* loud. Cat calls, some grumbling, but mostly the fans sharing a moment of intimacy they didn't know how to absorb.

He couldn't blame them. He wasn't sure how to take it in himself. The second he released Malakai, the man returned to his place on stage, starting the next song with Alder, Connor, and Tate like nothing had happened.

Because nothing *had* happened. They'd done what they'd planned. Given the media something to talk about. An interesting story. A short clip of them touching, and dancing, and speaking softly. Tons to speculate about.

Not reality. Sure, it felt real to Brave, but he refused to let the moment sink in. Even though he wasn't close to Malakai anymore, he understood how his mind worked. Shiori needed saving. He'd saved her, no matter the cost.

Even if it meant feigning interest in a man he hated.

The next song was *Center Mass*. Which had a political slant, but was mostly a pragmatic look at the military, at police. At how, when threatened, their goal was to take down the enemy.

Both Danica and Shiori came out, thrusting their fists in the air. Danica had quickly changed into a tiny camo shirt and skirt, which was skin tight and provocative, but he couldn't tear his eyes away from Shiori.

Her legs looked like they went on forever with the skirt of her dress hitting mid-thigh. There was a strength to her every move. She looked like she was wearing the uniform from Top Gun, only sexier. A one-piece dress with a zipper down the front, parted slightly between her pert breasts, with no bra in sight.

Holy fuck, she was hot. He forgot to breathe and had to fight not to suck in air until the next break. Her black hair was sleeked back, bound in a neat little bun, and the length of her bare neck made his mouth water. Which was weird, because necks weren't usually his thing. He loved tits and ass. Hers were nice and round and he struggled not to stare, but he wanted to taste that smooth flesh. Graze his teeth along her throat and watch her shudder beneath him like she had when they'd played that stupid game.

A game he'd laughed at, but wasn't so funny anymore. He'd gotten to savor her, to hold her close. Gotten that one night he'd promised would be enough.

He'd lied.

As the chorus began Shiori tipped her head back, pulling her hair free of the bun in a smooth motion. She whipped her hair forward, dropping to her knees and dipping back. Running one hand down the center of her chest she toyed with the zipper.

It didn't move.

Brave let out a soft groan, which the rapid military beat Tate pounded out covered, but the sound in his own earpiece warned him he was too distracted from the song. If he fucked up now no one would care about Shiori's performance. They'd be focused on him.

This was her moment to shine. To prove she belong up here, with the band. She reflected everything Danica had been showing for so long.

The very image behind every word he'd written. Every one he sang.

He wanted her closer. Repeating his own lyrics in his face. Giving them substance. But this wasn't about him. As she leaped to her feet, clutching her chest as the drums mimicked gunshots, he could tell she was exactly where she belonged. Echoing the emotions of the fans. Making them feel like they were part of the music, like her dance mirrored all they wanted to say, without words.

She'd been told to earn her place, to make her presence known without him, or Danica, or anyone else holding her hand. Sure, she'd gotten some tips. She knew they had her back—or at least he hoped she did.

Her job was to entertain the crowd.

They were entertained.

A huge fucking win. One she'd accomplished on her own.

He'd lusted after a lot of women. And men. Even cared a little about some of them. Not enough to consider keeping them around, but he didn't see them to the door before the sheets were cool. He liked them.

But he'd never respected them. And it hadn't mattered, because the feeling was mutual.

Shiori was different, in so many ways. He spent more time thinking about her than he'd ever thought about anything or anyone. The only thing on his mind more than her was making music.

Not anymore. You've got writer's block, dumbass.

True.

Still, he didn't know what to do with how important she'd become. With how often he looked for her. How often she slipped into his thoughts. If he was just fucking horny he'd find a way to scratch the itch, but it wasn't that simple.

He cared about her. Respected her. Wanted to cheer her on from the sidelines.

Tonight, he was damn proud of her.

And nothing mattered more at that moment than letting her know.

Chapter Fifteen

I did it!

Shiori tried to contain her excitement as she stripped off her borrowed dress, carefully hanging it in the trunk closet with all Danica's costumes. Standing there in her bra and panties, she caught Danica grinning at her from the vanity where she was removing her dramatic eye makeup.

Screw it! Shiori squealed and did a little dance.

Danica laughed, tossing the makeup remover cloth aside as she rose, some black smeared around her eyes. But she was still so beautiful and her smile made Shiori feel all warm inside. Accepted.

"You were *amazing* out there!" The silk of Danica's black robe was cool against Shiori's bare skin as they hugged. "I was worried *Center Mass* might not give you enough to work with, but you owned it. I couldn't even keep up!"

Biting her bottom lip, Shiori drew back to meet Danica's eyes. "I didn't mean to upstage you."

"Take that back. If you performed that well without trying, I need to up my game." Danica winked at her, then returned to the vanity to finish cleaning her face. "Every city we visit needs the best we have to offer. The band works hard to make sure they give their all, no matter how often they've sung the same songs. We have to do the same. Make sure all those people know they're important to us. Our fans are everything."

"I know, but I'm not trying to replace you."

"Yes, you *are*." Danica shook her head. "I was pissed that Sophie forced my hand, but I signed those contracts. Because my career hasn't plateaued, even though I almost let it." She let out a heavy sigh. "I wanted to feel like I was essential to the band. Being with them means I don't have to leave Alder or Jesse. But…I began touring with them because I wanted a fresh platform. An image that wouldn't be overlooked. I want my accomplishments to mean something, to show others they can do anything if they keep aiming higher."

"You've done that." Shiori approached Danica, not self-conscious standing around half naked while the other woman emotionally bared so much more. She put her hand on Danica's shoulder. "You did that for me."

Danica's eyes teared. She blinked fast, putting her hand over Shiori's. "Thank you. But I don't think you needed much of a push to reach for your goals. You're fierce. Sweet, but unstoppable."

"I try." Shiori ducked her head and shrugged. "I was terrified to get up there. I thought I'd trip over my own feet and make a fool of myself. What you're doing is scarier. Your stage is the whole world."

Lifting her chin, Danica nodded. "It is."

"And Jesse and Alder will be fine. They're tough." Shiori smirked and wrapped her arms around Danica's shoulders. "I'll let you know if they cry themselves to sleep every night."

Snorting in a very un-model-like fashion, Danica swiped one last time under her eyes, giving Shiori's arms a squeeze before she stood. "If you can, record it. I'd like to see that."

"No, you wouldn't. You want to know they'll be okay."

"I really do."

"They will be. They have a badass metal band to lean on. And you can call every night." Shiori pulled her phone from her purse on the back of the vanity chair and checked the time. She usually called Hiro in the afternoon, but today had been crazy.

It was almost ten. He'd be sleeping now.

Her throat tightened.

"Shiori?" Danica rubbed her arms, bending down a little to catch her eyes. "What's wrong?"

Shiori sighed and put her phone back in her purse. "I didn't call my nephew today. He's only five and I've helped raise him. He was excited about me traveling with the band, but he always tells me about his day. When the fight and everything went down with Malakai...well, that's when I normally call."

"Is he with someone you trust? Someone who will keep him distracted?"

"Yes. My stepfather's girlfriend. He loves her." She smiled as she remembered who else would be with him. "My best friend, Wendy, was taking him out to a movie today."

"Do you think she'll still be up?" Danica patted her cheek when she nodded. "Then call her. She'll tell you how much fun he had and you'll feel better."

Shiori wasn't sure why it took a suggestion from Danica, but she grabbed her phone and quickly called Wendy. They didn't talk every day because Wendy worked full time and took art courses at night, but she should have considered giving her a shout after Wendy's text yesterday about taking him out.

The band's schedule was hard to work around. She didn't want to give them a bad impression by being on the phone while she was supposed to be learning their routines. But she'd find a way to keep in touch with the people she loved.

Wendy answered on the second ring. "Girl, I have been dying to hear from you! Are you alone? Do you have time to talk? Tell me *everything!*"

Snickering, Shiori thanked Danica softly when the other woman handed over her clothes, then took a deep breath. "I miss you! I'm with Danica."

"Oh wow!" Wendy paused. "Please tell me she's not a total bitch."

"She's awesome." Shiori giggled when Danica arched a brow at her. Wendy was loud, Danica had probably heard her.

"I've got to get ready for the afterparty, but I wanted to see how you're doing."

"You know I'm fine. And to get to the *real* reason for your call, Hiro is right here, fast asleep." Wendy lowered her voice as though she'd suddenly realized that the little boy was sleeping. "I think your stepmother needed a break. She was all excited when I suggested him staying with me tonight. He loved the movie. And he's so good! I thought he'd talk through the whole thing, but he just sat there, eating way too much popcorn and candy, sniffling every time the dog died."

"He's too little for that movie!" Shiori couldn't remember what the movie was called, but she had an idea what it was about. "Wendy, why didn't you take him to see a cartoon?"

"Oh stop. He loved it." Wendy snickered. "There were a lot of kids his age there. They were annoying as fuck."

"Nice."

"Hey, I suffered through it for our little guy," Wendy said, fondly. "Seriously, he's doing good. We watched a couple Winter's Wrath videos and he pointed at Danica, telling me 'That's what auntie's doing'. He's happy for you. I think you're his new hero. He said you're cooler than Spiderman."

"*Spiderman?* Wow, that's quite the compliment." Shiori smiled, wishing she was home so she could give her little man a hug. "So he's eating well? Sleeping enough?"

"Yes and yes. Elizabeth went on and on about everything she was doing to keep life 'normal' for him. She lectured me about keeping him warm. She's a pain in the ass, but she really cares about him."

"I know. I wouldn't have left if she didn't."

"Good. Then don't worry." Wendy let out a tired sigh. "Babe, I love you, but the kid wore me out. I'll call you tomorrow and you can talk to him. But try not to worry. Live up the dream. For both of us."

"I will." Shiori swallowed hard. "I love you. And give him a kiss for me."

"Love you too. Will do. G'night."

Ending the call, Shiori tried to blink back her tears, but she couldn't stop them. She was relieved, and homesick, and so grateful to Wendy for making her truly believe Hiro was in good hands. She didn't doubt it, but she couldn't help worry a little. She quickly pulled on her jeans.

What if Elizabeth got fed up, now that she'd be alone with him for days? What if he acted out because Shiori wasn't around and the teachers showed concern? Anything could go wrong and he could be taken away. Only her stepfather could fight to keep him, and she didn't need to owe him anything on Hiro's behalf. Or for Hiro to feel dependent on him.

So far Hiro only saw her stepfather as a man who ignored him. Hiro didn't like him. The little boy stuck close to Shiori when he was home, which thankfully, wasn't often anymore. Her stepfather had no interest in being around the boy.

The day that changed, Shiori would have to fight harder to get Hiro out of there. She'd drop whatever she was doing and they'd disappear. Somehow.

It hadn't come to that yet. Maybe it wouldn't have to.

After only a few days around the Trousseau brothers, she felt safe to say they could be trusted with the truth. But she'd have to be careful with her timing. The last thing she needed was for either of them to overreact.

Strangely enough, even though Brave had the worst reputation, he seemed the most levelheaded of the two. Talking to him was easy.

If only she could be near him without her stupid heart racing and her skin growing hot enough to let off steam. She tried to play it cool, but the second his dark golden eyes settled on hers, stupid little butterflies in her belly brought on the urge to touch him. Their one night together played on repeat every time she blinked.

If only she could talk to Malakai first. She couldn't explain why she was so comfortable with him. She could lean against him, feeling safe and warm. He didn't look at her with heat in his eyes. Didn't tempt her.

Let's hope he never tries.

She shook her head, tossing aside all the pointless 'if onlys'. She knew what she had to do.

"You ready?" Danica asked once they were both dressed, wearing *much* less makeup than before. Danica had put on a pair of fitted black jeans and a white tank, both looking like she'd taken a razor to the material. With big hoop earrings, her hair up in a ponytail, and gloss on her lips, Danica looked ready to pose for an edgy photoshoot.

Shiori wasn't sure her own outfit worked. Shiny black leggings and a translucent white shirt that fell off one shoulder. Her hair flowing free and dangling angel wing earrings. What she'd normally wear to a party, but this was her first appearance out with the band somewhere people could get close and take a good look at her.

Spinning around, arms out, she laughed. "I don't know. Am I?"

Chuckling, Danica stopped her spinning at patted her cheek. "Yes. You might feel overdressed when you see some of the groupies, but don't forget. You're not one of them."

The statement was hard to take in, but Danica had a point. They weren't better than the fans, but the fans were there to have fun. Nothing else. The band got to let loose a bit, but their every move was being watched. Danica and Shiori's even more so.

With that in mind, Shiori felt much better about her outfit choice. She might not look like a runway model, but that was okay. She wasn't one. Not yet.

Skull and another roadie drove them to the club to join the band who'd left right after the concert. She tried to play off their entrance into the Aura Nightclub like she'd been to after-parties thousand times, but she'd never been anywhere like this.

The place didn't look big from the street, but inside seemed *huge*. There were booths on either side of the area near the first bar, chandeliers overhead, and a flashy mix of neon lights and elegant fixtures. Gauzy curtains decorated the walls, along with small square mirrors framed in dark wood.

Music blasted from the back where most of the patrons danced between trips to the bar. Skull cleared the way for Danica and Shiori, leading them to a private room. Which she'd expected to be small. A bit quieter.

There were at least a hundred people in this room. Another bar, a modest-sized dance floor, and a pole on a round mini-stage.

Two shirtless girls were dancing on the stage—maybe they were strippers hired by the bands? If not, they were wasting their talents. Shiori could dance, but no way could she hang off a pole by her thighs.

Not that I've ever tried.

Snickering, Danica grabbed her wrist and tugged her to one of the tables in the far corner of the room where most of the band—Connor was off somewhere, as usual—was sitting.

As soon as they spotted her, the guys stood, holding up their beers.

Brave flashed her a wicked smile that imminently sent her temperature spiking to supernova levels. "Let me propose a toast. To Shiori, who made all the guys *and* girls in the crowd cream their pants."

"Not just in the crowd!" Tate laughed when Malakai punched him in the arm. "What? It's true!"

"Charming, boys." Danica shook her head. She pulled two beers from the bucket of ice in the middle of the table. After passing one to Shiori, she uncapped her own and raised it. "To Shiori, who's tough enough to deal with fans, agents, media, and all you crazy fuckers."

"Hear, hear!" Alder called out.

Cheers all around. Jesse slipped from his seat beside Alder, pulling Danica into his arms and kissing her before helping her into his vacated spot. Malakai stood and wrapped his arm around Shiori's waist.

He leaned close, speaking loud enough to be heard over the music, but soft enough that the words were for her alone. "You were amazing tonight."

"Thank you. Is it cocky to say I think so too?"

His eyes warmed, lightened under the neon glow around them, revealing the deep ocean blue that often passed as black. His smile softened the hard angles of his face.

"Not at all." He pressed his lips to her hair. "I'm proud of you. You should be too."

She bit her bottom lip, not sure what to say. His approval meant a lot to her. More than it should. He'd become her anchor in the band. A steady, secure presence.

Of course, everyone talked about how protective he was. He'd added her to his list of people to watch over. Which was nice. She appreciated it.

But she couldn't lean on him too much.

A little longer won't hurt.

"Malakai." Brave's tone carried an edge of warning. But his stiff smile didn't seem like he was angry with the other man. "Careful while there's so many people around."

Inhaling roughly, Malakai drew away from her and nodded. "Right."

The understanding between them went over her head for a few seconds, but then she recalled why they'd put on the hot act on stage. She already had one photo floating around somewhere, labeling her as the band's new 'slut'. Being too affectionate in public could lend credit to the claim of whoever had taken the picture.

Her skin cooled as she stood there, alone, not sure what to do with herself. She didn't want to be here anymore. Putting on a show onstage was one thing, but all the time? Second-guessing her every move?

"It'll be okay, slugger." Malakai gave her a brief smile before heading off to watch the strippers.

Patting the empty seat beside him, Brave caught her eye. "Come. Have a couple drinks, then we can take off."

Yes, please. She sat, careful not to get too close to him, and tried to open her beer. The cap scraped at her palm. Brave reached out, like he'd help, but she shook her head.

Gritting her teeth, she twisted harder. She didn't even want the stupid drink anymore. Damn it, she didn't even *like* beer.

"Can I get that for you?" A handsome waiter, with big blue eyes and neatly trimmed blond hair, approached, flashing straight white teeth and a little dimple.

No one could make a big deal out of her getting help from a waiter, could they? She sighed and handed him the bottle. "Thank you."

Grinning at her, the waiter twisted the cap. It didn't come off. He pulled a bottle opener from his pocket. "It's on good!" With a pop, the cap came off. "There we go. Would you like a glass?"

"No, thank you." No one else was using one—not even Danica, who was now sitting in Alder's lap.

Shiori wasn't jealous of her freedom.

Not. At. All.

"If you don't mind me saying, you don't look like the girls who usually hang out with bands like these. Let me guess..." The waiter tapped his chin with a finger as he studied her. "You're writing a book about metal bands?"

"Is this how authors dress?" She looked down at her clothes, wondering again if she'd messed up. Her image was all wrong.

"Some of them. They do prefer pajama pants, though." He leaned his hip against the table. "My mother's an author. When she's on a deadline pjs are her uniform."

"That's so cool. What does she write?"

"Horror novels. She's actually really good. I love her work." His voice softened and he smiled as though talking about his mother made him happy. He covered her hand with his. "If you give me your number I can send you a copy."

"Sure! That would be—"

"No." Brave moved close to her, glaring up at the waiter. "We need more beer. Wanna do your job?"

Lips parted, the waiter glanced over at the ice bucket, which still had a few bottles in it. Rather than object, he nodded curtly and grabbed the bucket. He brought it over to the bar.

Stunned at Brave's rudeness, Shiori turned sideways, eyes narrowed as he slouched back into his spot. "What the hell was that?"

"*That* was an asshole trying to take advantage of you." Brave's posture didn't change, but his jaw hardened as he stared back at her. "Do you give your number to every guy who asks for it?"

"Of course not! But this isn't about him! He was just being nice and you were...*rude.*" Not good enough. She bit back the urge to scream at him. His behavior was *completely* out of line. "I can't stand people who are assholes to servers. It's disgusting."

Brave shot up, bracing his hand against the table as he leaned over her. "I am *very* polite to servers. But fuck with what's mine and yes, I'm more than an asshole. I'm fucking dangerous, sweetheart."

Her jaw nearly hit the floor. Then she considered punching him again. The first time clearly hadn't been enough.

She'd read him all wrong. He wasn't the man she'd thought he was. Even though they couldn't be too close in public, even though they'd agreed their brief intimacy was a one-time thing, he thought he had some claim on her?

Hell no.

"I'm going back to the bus. This was fun." She shook her head when Danica pushed away from Alder, looking concerned—probably only now hearing the exchange over the music. She didn't need backup. And she refused to spoil Danica's fun because Brave was a jerk. "Enjoy your night."

She spun around, searching the crowd for Skull. Maybe he was outside? She couldn't go outside by herself. She wasn't stupid, no matter what Brave thought.

"Shiori?" Ballz approached her, a sharp glare scaring off the guy dancing close who'd reached out as though to draw her in to dance. Putting a hand on her back, he led her to a clear spot at the edge of the private room. "Is everything all right?"

"Yes, it's fine. I just..." She swallowed hard, her eyes burning, lashes wet. She would not cry. "I want to go back to the bus."

"Sure thing, hon." He grabbed his phone from his pocket. Held it to his ear, speaking loud. "Skull, you wanna come watch the guys? No, everything's fine. I'm driving Shiori back over... Yep, Tank's got them covered." A pause. "Okay."

"Shiori." Brave reached her side, frowning when Ballz moved between them. "What the fuck?"

"Do you want to talk to him, Shiori?" Ballz ignored Brave's curse, focusing on her. "Security hangs back while you're all having fun, but we pay attention. Tank texted me that there was some...'tension', between you. Our instructions when it comes to you and Danica is that you never feel pressured by any member of the band."

Wow... Shiori took a deep breath, absorbing this bit of information. Reese or Jesse must have put those instructions in place. Did they really think the guys were a threat?

Brave looked stunned. "I wasn't pressuring her to do anything."

"Good. Then you won't object to her leaving." Ballz folded his arms over his chest. "Shiori, this is your decision. Do you want to talk to him?"

Not right now she didn't. She was humiliated. Frustrated. Confused. She wasn't afraid of Brave. Hell, she almost wished he'd been acting jealous, rather than treating her like a possession. She couldn't think of anything he could possibly say to make this better.

"No." She turned her back on Brave. "I just want to get out of here."

Inclining his head, Ballz began to walk with her.

"Shiori, can I ask you one thing before you storm out?" Brave's shout was loud enough to have several people around glancing over curiously.

Fisting her hands by her side, she looked at him over her shoulder. "What?"

"I was trying to protect you." He approached slowly as he spoke, as though worried she'd run off. "Is that so horrible?"

"Protecting me? No. What's horrible is what you said."

His brow furrowed. "Why?"

Chin jutted up, she let out a little laugh. And she was the clueless one?

"I'm. Not. Yours."

Chapter Fifteen

"I'm. Not. Yours."

Brave watched Shiori walk away, knowing better than to push this any further with Ballz guarding her. His stomach twisted when he considered why those security measures had been put in place. They 'weren't to pressure' the girls? As if any member of the band would even consider...

Was this because of when he'd kissed Danica, way back when *she'd* joined the band? Fine, that was a dick move. He was ashamed of his behavior. He wouldn't have kissed Shiori like that if her career wasn't riding on him doing so.

But he'd never force her to do anything.

Except talk to me. He groaned, raking his fingers through his hair as he returned to the table. Right now, even pressing for a conversation would make him the bad guy. And he still wasn't sure what he'd done wrong.

Everyone stared at him as he sat.

Tate shook his head, handing over a fresh beer. "Relax. Chicks are weird. That waiter was totally playing her."

"You heard?" Brave took a swig of his beer as Tate nodded. "So I was right to step in?"

"Well yeah. I mean, what if he started sending her dick pics?" Tate cocked his head, a crooked, drunken smile on his lips. "Do you think she'd share them with me?"

All right, you're pretty desperate if you're looking for advice from Tate. Brave turned to his brother. "Did I fuck up?"

Alder arched a brow. "I didn't hear a fucking thing any of you said. Didn't know there was a problem until she got up. Care to fill in the blanks?"

By his side, Danica was shooting daggers at Brave. Stuck between Jesse and Alder, she looked reading to shove Jesse out of her way so she could tear Brave's throat out. "Quickly, Brave. I need to know how much pain you deserve."

"Down, girl." Jesse hugged her, confusion filling his eyes as Alder groaned and slapped a hand over his face. "What? *Hey!*"

Jesse shot up from his seat, his lap soaked with the beer Danica had poured on him.

"Maybe you should go work for a bit." Danica bit out. "I would be with Shiori if she hadn't made it clear she wants to be alone." She turned her glare back on Brave. "I need to know why. *Now.*"

While Jesse made himself scarce, Brave went over the exchange with the waiter. When he finished, Danica shook her head.

"There's more."

"Not really." He dropped his gaze to his bottle, pretty sure he had an idea of how he'd fucked up. "I basically told her no one messes with what's mine."

Alder brought both hands to his face, making a pain filled sound as he rubbed it. "Jesus Christ."

"Yours? *Yours?*" Danica strode around the table, murder in her eyes. "You stupid, selfish son-of-a-bitch." She looked over at his brother. "I'm sorry, Alder."

Alder made a dismissive motion with his hand.

Danica slapped her hands on the table in front of Brave. "You are fucking with her career. Yours is solid. You can say and do whatever you want. With one picture it's been made very clear she can't." Her tone sharpened. "So far *nothing* has happened that can't be undone. She gets what you two did together was part of a game. She can leave it at that."

"What if I can't?" A heavy weight settled on his chest, one that had been growing heavier ever since that waiter had started flirting with Shiori. One that had almost crushed him with her last three words. He didn't want things between them to be limited to the game they'd played.

He'd tried to deny it, but the idea of her with someone else trashed all his good intentions. Trashed the good vibes between them too, apparently. They were getting closer, naturally. Without sex, without anything but a connection he'd never felt with anyone before, pulling him in a little more every day.

Everyone was staring at him again, only this time like he'd lost his fucking mind.

The eyes that Alder loved so much he'd written a song about them, a unique shade of green that shone like the Northern lights, held his for what seemed like forever. Then all the anger seemed to leave Danica. She crouched beside him and took his hand.

"You can't mean it. Brave..." Danica sighed. "If you care about her, you will keep things professional. She's too new to this lifestyle to take the extra scrutiny a relationship with you would bring. I know it's not fair. I got to be with Alder. But I was established."

"She will be too." Brave truly believed that. No one could watch Shiori on stage and not know she was meant for great things. "You can see it."

"I can." Danica gave him a sad smile. "And if she's what's making you stupid, this will be even harder. But if there's anything worth having you'll wait. Let her shine on her own. Once everyone sees what we do, go for it. If you can do that I'll be cheering you on from the sidelines."

Fuck, why did his brother have to get with such a smart chick? None of the guys would have said shit.

All right, Malakai *had*, but thankfully, he wasn't here.

Without Danica's warning, Brave might have tried to earn Shiori's forgiveness. Figured out how to be the kind of man she needed. Found out what was so great about being with someone who did more than make his dick hard.

Someone who drew out his protective instincts—he'd have to work on those, apparently, caveman wasn't sexy—and made him think and feel. Someone he wanted to hold. Wanted to make smile and laugh.

He could have done all that.

And it would have ruined her.

Even if he learned how to be the man she deserved, being with him would affect her career. Which wasn't fair.

To *her*.

"So what do I do? Make sure she stays pissed at me? That she hates me?" The pressure on his chest was going to do serious damage. The idea of Shiori hating him made it hard to breathe.

What the fuck is wrong with me?

"No. Either way, you need to apologize." Danica patted his hand and straightened. "She's tough. If she needs to talk, Ballz is there, and we'll be heading back soon. Give her space tonight. Tomorrow, take her aside. Be a friend. Then *keep* being a friend."

"Got it." He could do that. Maybe. "But I'm a shitty friend."

"Hear, hear!" Tate raised his beer, breaking the tension with a laugh. "Sorry, I'm not as think as you drunk I am. This is sad. I like Shiori. I like you. You're cute together."

"Not helpful, Tate." Alder reached over and snatched Tate's beer. "You've had enough."

"Probably." Tate scooted over, laying on the bench and resting his head on Alder's lap. He was doing that a lot lately. "Wake me up when it's time to go."

Ignoring them, Danica rose and gave Brave a hug. Which he needed more than he cared to admit.

"We good?" She smoothed his hair back, looking concerned. "I'm sorry I freaked."

Brave let out a dry laugh. "You had every reason to. I'm happy you didn't hit me. Had my fill of that lately."

Brushing her fingers under the gash on his cheek, she nodded. "Yes, you have."

The silence around the table made him uncomfortable. He grabbed his beer and pulled Danica over to sit beside him, smirking when Alder sat up and scowled at him.

"So, bro. When you gonna marry this chick and make her my sister?" Brave snorted as Alder blinked at him. "What? You're not letting Jesse do it, are you?"

"No, but…" Alder cleared his throat. "Actually, I planned on asking her grandfather first." He turned to Danica. "I'm not sure of your traditions, but—"

"He'll love that." Danica's face lit up. She hopped out of the booth and skidded over to Alder, wrapping her arms around his neck. "I didn't know you'd even considered—"

"We haven't had time to—"

"Does Jesse know?"

"Not yet."

Their conversation continued, ending only when they started making out. Brave finished his beer while watching the dancers, not really seeing them. Exhaustion seeped into his bones and the heaviness still hadn't left. Instead, his chest felt like it was adapting to that pressure. Like he'd have to go on with his heart beating dully in the tight confines.

Since his brother was occupied, and Tate was sleeping, he didn't see the point in sticking around. Spotting Skull, he went over to see if he could get a ride.

The older man shook his head. "Tank just prevented Connor from getting in a fight in the alley. That boy is out of control."

"Need me to talk to him?"

"Naw. I'll deal with him." Skull eyed him skeptically. "You're not going back to the bus, are you?"

Did everyone know he'd fucked up?

Probably.

"I won't say a word to her. I just don't want to be here." Brave shoved his hands in his pockets. "How about I take a walk?"

Skull shook his head. "Not alone."

"I'll go with him." A heavy hand settled on his shoulder. Malakai. With the hood to his leather jacket up, giving him a smile he couldn't read. "We have a lot to discuss."

"Fair enough." Skull took off like everything was settled.

He clearly wasn't *that* worried about Brave's safety.

Heads down, they made their way through the crowd, careful to avoid the many fans wearing band T-shirts. That they made it outside without being jumped was nothing short of a miracle. Typically, the bands either stuck around until the end or had security clearing the path.

His new hairdo might have helped a little. People knew him by his hair and his face. Sometimes his boots.

Regardless, he knew his fans well enough to keep going once they hit the sidewalk. Without the crowd, it would be easier for someone to spot him.

They both slowed as they reached the end of the third block from the club.

Malakai remained silent.

Brave glanced over at him. "You got something to say to me?"

Nodding, Malakai shoved his hood back and stopped at the edge of an alley between two brick buildings. He folded his arms over his chest, his lips pulled into a thin line. "Shiori left because of you."

Not a question, but Brave answered anyway. "Yes."

"We've had this conversation."

"Have we?" Brave shook his head. "Because I recall you telling me to stay away from her. Not to use her. And I fucking did that." His pulse quickened as he met Malakai's hard, black ones. The color he'd noticed before seemed to have disappeared. "I *did* that, and I'll continue to do that. I don't need to be told again how I feel doesn't matter. I fucking get it."

"How you feel?" Malakai let out a bitter laugh. "Do you? Honestly, sometimes I wonder."

Grabbing the front of Malakai's jacket, Brave shoved him back into the brick wall. He couldn't fucking do this shit. Not now. Not with Malakai.

"Yes, I feel. I feel like I'm so fucking toxic I'll never have anything good. And I don't deserve to." He shoved against Malakai's shoulders, anger and loss twisting inside him so tight he couldn't breathe. "I've lost friends. Family. And just when I start to get some of that back…"

Malakai lowered his arms to his sides, watching him. "What?"

"I don't know. I fuck up again. Or life happens." He raked his fingers through his hair and paced away from the other man. "I think I'm going fucking insane. I hardly know her, but…there's something there."

"I know."

Brave stopped pacing. Lifted his head. "Say again?"

"There *is* something. Between you." Malakai leaned against the wall and sighed. "I really wish there wasn't. And I don't think it will be long before she's right where you are unless you close off everything you're feeling. You let her go, which is the most unselfish thing I've ever seen you do. The schedule might be tight, but you've found ways around that before. It would have been easy to try getting her out of your system with one last seduction."

"I can still do that." A lie. One that might save his sanity.

"But you won't."

"No. I won't." He really hated this whole being good thing. So far, it fucking sucked. "Few months ago I would have given you a different answer."

Malakai chuckled. "You wouldn't have given me an answer at all. We weren't on speaking terms."

"Dude, we talked." Sure, there had been tension between them. That animosity they'd held on to forever, but at least they'd been civil. Or at least civil*ish*. "I ask if you want coffee. You say yes. Good times."

"Yeah, was fucking awesome." Malakai rolled his eyes. "I'm glad we still have that."

For some strange reason, Brave got the impression Malakai hadn't come with him only to talk about Shiori. There some regret in his tone. He was acting all relaxed, but beneath the cool front was... Hell, he wasn't sure.

A few months ago he wouldn't have cared about that either. He'd been closed down for so long, conversations like this hadn't happened with *anyone*. The closest he'd come was harping on his brother about his health and safety, which got him nowhere. Aside from that, he did his job. Tried to write music. Found the well of ideas empty.

The life he'd lived before might have given him a few defiant, cocky, seductive songs, but he wasn't that man anymore. He had to find himself again to hear the music. When he was passionate, about pretty much anything, the lyrics came effortlessly.

Shiori had awakened some of that passion, but he had to shut it down.

Only one other had reached that side of him. The raw emotions he couldn't control. That he didn't expect.

Which had gotten the label of hatred for a very long time.

What the hell is it now?

He shook his head. This was Malakai. Best friend to worst enemy back to sorta friend. A little confusing, but Brave wasn't used to having friends. He wasn't an easy guy to like.

And claiming Malakai even 'liked' him was a bit of a stretch. Tolerated was an improvement.

A soft chuckle came from Malakai, drawing his attention to the other man's slanted smile. Malakai jutted his chin at Brave. "What's on your mind, Draven? Why so serious?"

"Keep it up and I'm going to start thinking you're a closet comicbook geek, Grimm." Brave inhaled slowly, surprised to find that pressure on his chest had eased slightly. Being near Malakai had a strange effect on him. Steadying at times. Then like he could tilt Brave's whole world off its axis.

"I am, but don't tell anyone." Malakai lifted a hand and rubbed his jaw. "Look, what happened on stage—"

"Was nothing. I get it." Brave's tone was sharper than he'd intended, but he didn't need Malakai pointing out the facts. Brave had figured them out himself seconds after his mind and body got all wrapped up in how good Malakai's touch felt. "Fucking believable though. You should consider acting if you ever get sick of playing guitar."

Malakai huffed out a laugh. "You thought I was acting?"

The pipe Malakai had nailed him with earlier had less impact than his question. What the hell was the man saying?

Staring off into the distance, Malakai continued. "You make a good enemy. Hating you? Fuck, that made sense. Whenever that hatred began to fade, you'd be thoughtless, or cruel, or selfish. Everything between us was black and white."

"What changed?"

"You did. I didn't notice for the longest time. I had such a clear picture of who you were in my head." Malakai's lips curved slightly. "The man I saw wasn't *you*. Not really. He was a man surrounded by walls built out of fear."

"I'm not fucking afraid." Rage bared its venomous teeth, the poison an antidote to the uncertainty within. Brave wasn't weak, wasn't the man Malakai was painting him out to be.

The type of man Malakai could accept, could care about. If Brave was damaged, he needed to be fixed. One of Grimm's favorite hobbies.

"You're fucking terrified." Malakai shrugged. "But whatever. Keep playing tough. You won't hear a damn thing I'm saying to you."

Sucking his teeth, Brave glared at the other man. "I hear what you're saying."

"Really? So you still think there's nothing?" Malakai hooked his thumbs to his belt loops, calm and irritating as fuck. "On stage, that wasn't an act."

"What does that even mean?"

"What do you *want* it to mean?"

Screw anyone who thought chicks were complicated. This man was like a jigsaw puzzle of code written in hieroglyphics. And he wouldn't give Brave a clue how to figure him out.

"Don't play games with me, Malakai." This little chat wasn't getting them anywhere. Brave was fucking done. If Malakai wanted to challenge him, Brave would accept. On his own terms. With one last warning. "You'll lose."

Malakai nodded slowly. "Maybe I would. Maybe I *will*."

Enough. Brave let the barrier between them fall, surrendering to his baser instincts. Instincts chained by all the promises he'd made. His vows to be a better man.

Being bad could be fucking fun.

He cut across the short distance between them, curving his hand around the side of Malakai's neck. He brought their lips close enough to touch and met the other man's dark eyes.

A low growl escaped Malakai as he latched onto Brave's shoulder, pulling hard and slanting his lips over Brave's in a violent, bruising kiss. A kiss that fit all the hatred simmering between them for years. His painful grip enhanced the blazing heat of his mouth, boiling over as his tongue touched Brave's.

Groaning, Brave pressed against him, trying to regain control as he fucked Malakai's mouth with his own tongue. The taste of him was addictive, like darkness and passion had a flavor, rich and heady, with a bite of cold. Instead of melting the ice between them, passion sank the sharp edge deep, piercing through the last layer of resistance.

The straps of his jacket loosened and he tipped his head back as Malakai brought his lips to his throat. Fingers roughened from playing guitar for years brushed the bared skin of his chest and goosebumps rose all over. Needing more,

Brave yanked open the rest of the straps. Grunted as Malakai turned them so Brave's back was against the wall.

Suddenly, Malakai drew away. He smirked, holding a hand up before Brave could protest. "Not here."

Grabbing Brave's hand, Malakai led him deep into the alley, which was dark and quiet in the dead of night. They stopped under black metal emergency stairs, well out of sight. Brave's back hit the wall and Malakai claimed his mouth, tearing open the buttons of the black shirt he'd worn under his jacket. Always so contained, the man's kiss was like they'd both strapped into a racecar, Malakai behind the wheel, going 0-60 in 2.4.

While Brave had been expecting Driving Miss Daisy.

Why? He wasn't sure. With others, Malakai treated sex like a basic necessity. The hint of emotion made Brave wonder if he'd be cautious, but he already had Brave's belt undone. His teeth grazed over a tight nipple as he gripped Brave's swollen dick and questioning motives required actual brain function. Which was gone.

"Fuck, Malakai." His whole body jerked as Malakai spit in his palm, using it to stroke his dick in his slick grip. His balls tightened and he inhaled as he fought the rising pressure. "Don't stop."

"I didn't plan to." Malakai continued lazily stroking Brave's dick as he braced his forearm on the wall by his head. "I want to fuck you so hard you'll keep your stupid mouth shut for a little while. But this will do for now."

"You're doing this to shut me up?" Brave ground his teeth as Malakai's grip tightened, moving over him faster. "God damn it, I—"

"Can't scare me with sex. This?" Malakai flicked his tongue over Brave's bottom lip. "This is fucking nothing. You're a good looking man. I'd have fucked you already if I didn't hate you." He kissed Brave again, slowly this time, drawing it out as he ran his hand up over the head of Brave's cock. The pleasure, mixed with all the promise behind that kiss, brought the sensation to a level not limited to touch.

Pulse pounding, Brave panted against Malakai's lips, eyes pressed shut as a violent shudder passed over him.

"Do you feel me, Brave?" Malakai brought his lips to Brave's throat, his voice soft. "I told you what happened on stage wasn't an act. I felt you. More than hate or lust. Maybe a combination. And something else."

"What else?" Brave hoped Malakai had a name for 'it', because he didn't. Not yet. "What are we fucking doing, Grimm?"

With a deep laugh, Malakai kissed him again. "Some crazy shit. You having fun yet?"

"Oh yeah." He grinned, feeling lightheaded. The pressure had built up to the point the throbbing of his dick matched the flashes of red behind his closed lids. "I'm gonna come."

"No. You're not." Malakai released him, firmly holding his shoulders when he swayed. "Easy there."

As the cold wrapped around him, Brave's lips parted. The painful throb in his dick hadn't subsided without stimulation. If anything, it got worse. The mutual desire had been an illusion. Abrupt rejection hurt like hell.

What the fuck is this? Revenge?

He'd thought Malakai was telling him they had…fuck, *a connection*. Potential for more. Was he messing with him? He glared at the other man.

"Don't look at me like that. Patience is a virtue." Malakai stepped back, crossing his arms over his chest. "I won't fuck you in an alley. Maybe behind the bus. We'll see."

We'll see? Brave snarled through his teeth, shoving his dick—a little too hard, which pissed him off more—back in his jeans and quickly straightened his jacket. "You must be on some good drugs if you think I'll let you touch me again."

"We came out for a conversation. We had one. Cut the drama." Amusement lightened Malakai's tone. "Is this a good time to tell you I love you?"

"I fucking *hate* you." Brave slammed his hand into the center of Malakai's chest. "You think you can do shit like that to me? Don't you know—"

Spitting out a laugh, Malakai caught the punch he threw mid-swing. "Know who you are? What you can do to me? 'You're hot all scary. Tell me what you're gonna do. I'm already hard.'"

His own words being thrown back at him twisted the knife of rejection even deeper. He should have been ready for this. Malakai had his own set of rules. Brave had broken them, and the man made him pay.

"You made your point." Brave turned away from Malakai, his already battered heart feeling like it had been dragged down a road covered in glass. "Everyone should be heading back. If not, I'm taking a cab."

He made it to the end of the alley before Malakai's soft words followed him, tearing apart his assumptions. Leaving him even more lost.

"I do love you, Brave." Malakai was close. Almost close enough to reach back and touch. But he didn't. "But I don't trust you."

"Good. You shouldn't."

"Just so we're clear." Malakai moved slowly past him, not looking back. "I haven't given up on you. You're always talking about games. Let me know when you hit reset on this one."

Chapter Seventeen

That hadn't gone as planned. Malakai stared out the window as Skull drove him, Brave, and Tate back to the bus. Tate had woken long enough to be guided to the van, then passed back out. Skull was humming along to some depressing old country music.

And Brave? Brave was sitting in the seat behind him. Likely contemplating his very painful death.

The idea had been to get Brave alone. Lay his feelings out like the cards of a gambler chasing the river. After calling all in. With his heart.

Instead of waiting for Brave to raise the bet, call, or fold, Malakai had set the table on fire and suggested Russian roulette. Pulled the trigger and called neither of them dying a win.

In other words, a clusterfuck.

Still a few bullets left. Wanna try again?

He wondered if Brave would be less pissed if he knew he wasn't the only one sporting the blue balls of agony. Probably not. Thing was, the man deserved at least half the blame.

Why did he have to bring up his damn game?

Malakai *knew* this shit was real. He saw it in Brave's eyes. Felt it in his kiss. Their hatred had been overpowered by the bond they'd ignored since the band's inception. If they'd stayed friends, they'd have more now. But they hadn't. They'd smothered their feelings, trying to kill them.

Instead, those feelings had broken free, ready to do some damage.

As soon as they pulled up beside the bus, Brave got out. Malakai expected him to head inside and be a dick to everyone before crashing for the night. Instead, he went to the other side of the van, opening the door and speaking softly to Tate.

Frowning, Malakai got out, blinking as he watched Brave pick Tate up like the kid weighed nothing. He carried Tate to the bus, struggling to open the door while not jostling the drummer too much.

Skull ran over and opened the door for him.

Once they were all out of sight, Malakai started for the bus. Then groaned and headed around it, sitting on the bumper with his hands in his pockets. He stared into the dark woods, thick enough to block the light from the highway beyond. The stillness centered him. Made sorting through his muddled thoughts simpler.

He'd asked Brave to reset, but that wasn't what he wanted. He needed them to keep moving forward, instead of slipping back to status quo every time things got scary.

He'd accused Brave of being afraid. And he was.

But he wasn't the only one.

Footsteps came toward him and he lifted his head, hoping to see Brave, but not expecting to.

Brave gave him a tight smile and came over to sit on the bumper beside him. He settled there, looking more relaxed in a white band hoodie and a pair of black jogging pants. Rubbing his thighs, he let out a heavy sigh. "I'm sorry."

Malakai knew he was hearing things. "*You're* sorry?"

"Yeah… I was being an asshole. *Again*." Brave brought a hand up to massage the back of his neck, which still had black smeared on it. "Honestly, this whole behaving myself thing is driving me fucking crazy. I wanted to stop. Seemed safest with you."

Shit. I'm *the fucking asshole*. Malakai groaned and tugged Brave's hand away from his neck. He curved his hand over the same spot Brave had been rubbing, digging his fingers into the tense muscles.

With a pleasure filled moan, Brave leaned forward and continued talking. "I fully expect to die alone. Like Valor."

Going still, Malakai stared at him. "That's not happening. I ain't going anywhere."

"You say that, but I know you, Malakai. You've been looking out for Tate for years. Made him family. Alder too. And Connor…" Brave shook his head and laughed. "We've got a nice little collection of damaged fuckers who need you. Need someone willing to stand up for them when no one else will. Shiori…" His throat worked as he swallowed hard. "She'd be better off with someone like you. You'd be cool waiting as long as it took."

And he had to bring her up. Malakai massaged Brave's neck, snorting under his breath. "I probably would. But I'm stuck in the friend zone."

The muscles under his hand tightened. Brave gave him a hard look. "You want more?"

"Doesn't matter what I want. Neither of us can give her what she needs, so it's a nonissue. Don't make it one." Malakai slid his hand under Brave's hoodie to work on the corded muscles of his traps. "This is about me and you. Where do you stand?"

"I want you." Brave took a deep breath. "But, yeah. There's more. It would be cool…" He gestured from himself, to Malakai, then back. "This."

Cool. What was Malakai supposed to do with 'cool'? "So…friends?"

"I don't fuck my friends."

Malakai arched a brow.

"All right, sometimes I do." Brave tipped his head back. "What do you want me to say? You wanna go on a fucking date? I ain't getting you flowers."

"Just for that, I'm getting you two dozen, you ornery bastard." Malakai chuckled as Brave's cheek went red. "If it helps, I don't 'date'."

"Neither do I." Brave frowned. "We didn't go through all this stress to be friends-with-benefits, did we?"

The question eased some of the worry twisting Malakai's guts. It didn't sound like an arrangement Brave wanted. But they were both too old to start calling each other 'boyfriend'. And partners sounded like a business thing.

"From what I overheard, you're fond of 'mine'." Malakai grinned as Brave reddened even more. "I'm good calling you mine."

"I'm good with that too." Brave went still, then made a face. "Makes for a weird introduction, though. 'This guy is mine.'"

"Gets straight to the point."

Brave inclined his head. "True. But Alder calls Jesse his boyfriend."

"Alder's a kid."

"He's two years younger than you." Brave smirked, eyes drifting shut as Malakai dug his fingers deeper into the muscle of his shoulder. "And Jesse is older than I am."

Strangely enough, Brave pushing for some kind of definition to their relationship made him happy. Happy enough to go with whatever worked.

He shifted his hand to Brave's other shoulder. "So you want to make this all official?"

"Will that help with earning your trust?" Brave reached up and wrapped his hand around Malakai's wrist. "Fucking hit me when you said that. Next time, use your fists."

Eyeing the fresh wound on Brave's cheek, Malakai shook his head. "No can do. But you're getting there, Draven. I'm starting to trust you. Coming out here to talk? Made a *huge* difference."

Brave nodded, releasing Malakai's wrist. "I can't promise I won't fuck up again."

"I can handle you." Malakai listened, taking in the quiet of the night. And considering how he could make up for what happened earlier. He brought his hand back to Brave's neck, this time slipping his fingers up into his hair. "Everyone gone to bed?"

"Pretty much. Alder, Jesse, and Danica are in the back lounge. I should have gotten a bed put in back there. It's not fair they have to sleep apart." Brave's jaw hardened. "She's leaving and it's going to wreck my brother."

No matter what Brave thought of himself, he'd become a good man. Malakai gave the man's hair a little tug. "He'll have Jesse. And you."

Releasing a rough sound of need, Brave yanked Malakai off the bumper while slamming their lips together. Malakai brought his free hand up to tangle both in Brave's hair. He set his legs on either side of Brave's thigh, hissing as his erection pressed into the hard muscle.

Brave hooked his fingers to the bottom of Malakai's black hoodie, lifting it with the T-shirt underneath, breaking their kiss just long enough to pull both off. He tossed them aside and ran his hands down Malakai's chest with a low hum of appreciation.

"I used to hate when you took your shirt off. Fuck, man, these muscles." Brave curved his hands around Malakai's waist, brushing his thumbs over his abs. "I've never seen you work out."

"Connor has a travel punching bag. Solid frame. I use it every morning before you're even out of bed." Malakai closed his eyes as Brave lowered his lips to his chest. "I should have ditched my shirt more often. We would have gotten along better."

Chuckling, Brave licked up to his nipple, already hard with arousal. "Coming from the guy who wanted more than sex."

"*More* than. I still want it." Malakai tipped his head back as Brave tugged the nipple between his teeth, sending a shock of pleasure shooting down to his balls. "If you're gonna try edgeplay, warn me. What I did to you was cold."

"Don't know what edgeplay is." Brave shifted his attention to his other nipple. His hand moved down to rub Malakai through his jeans. "And it wasn't cold. Was hot."

"Mmm." Malakai tugged Brave's hair, bringing his head up so he could whisper in his ear. "You still want me to fuck you? Here's good."

Brave went still. "I don't bottom."

"You were with Jesse." Malakai shook his head. "*He* doesn't bottom. His first time was after some fucker slipped something in his drink."

Brave's lips parted. "Jesse was raped?"

"This is me trusting you. Don't fucking repeat that. I don't think he remembers telling me." Malakai's brow furrowed as Brave went white. "Jesus, Brave… What did you do to him?"

"Shit I can't make up for, but I'll try." Brave slammed his head back against the back of the bus. "Damn it, what's wrong with me? He was…he told me he didn't—"

"Hey." Malakai shoved his anger aside and braced his hands against Brave's shoulders. "He's good now. Your brother and Danica have him. And I've got you." Malakai inhaled roughly. "Why don't you? It's more than a preference."

Brave lowered his head, his shortened hair falling over his face. "Valor caught me once. With the drummer." He rubbed his hands on his thighs. "He let us finish, then made it clear what he thought of me being 'gay' *and* 'some guys bitch'."

"What do you mean, made it clear?" Brave never talked about Valor voluntarily. Any mention of his dead older brother got him lashing out. Kept him in a vicious mood for days.

"He beat the fuck out of me. While the band watched. Told us all if he ever walked in on 'that shit' again, he'd buy a gun and write our names on every bullet." Brave's shoulders lifted and he laughed. "Cole got there in time to…calm him down. Valor was high as a kite. Didn't remember fuck all the next day. Asked me if I got run over by a truck."

"He do that a lot?" Malakai knew Brave loathed his brother. Or he did *now*. But he'd thought the animosity came from Valor almost getting every member of LOST killed searching for him when he'd disappeared into the woods one night, strung out on LSD. Valor had been the only fatality, but not the only victim.

Brave had been young when he'd joined Valor's band. Vulnerable to a man who should have looked out for him. Sounded like Valor was his father's son. Only worse.

"When I was stupid enough to get in his face?" Brave shrugged. "He'd put me in my place." He brought his hand to his throat. "I learned to keep my mouth shut."

"There's more."

"There isn't. Brothers fight." Brave's tone turned cold. "Way to kill the mood."

Before Brave could rise, Malakai secured Brave's shoulders against the bus, all his weight on his hands. They would finish this conversation. "Don't fucking do that. I can't read your damn mind. I figured you were versatile because what I know about Jesse. If you're not, that's fine."

"Is it?" Brave bit out the words like a challenge. "You'd let me fuck you?"

Maybe Brave was right. He'd killed the mood.

His dick hadn't gotten the message, but he'd had his own bad experiences. Letting Brave fuck him while he was pissed off?

Fuck no.

"I've had two men fuck me. They were a lot like you." Malakai gritted his teeth. "So no."

"What do you mean, 'like me'?"

"Angry and lashing out. First guy when I was sixteen. He was twenty years older than me. Fucked me raw in a bathroom stall." Malakai's lips twisted as he remembered that painful experience. "I was lucky. Guy at my school came in right after he left. Told me I should get checked because the man fucked a lot of students."

"Students?"

"Yeah. He didn't rape me, so don't make it a thing. He was nice until that day. Sucked dick like I was paying him. I passed gym even though I skipped all his classes." His high school diploma had been worth not ratting the sick fuck out at the time. He'd learned later that the teacher messed with the younger students too. He ended up in prison when a thirteen-year-old went to the cops.

Brave took a deep breath. "Sixteen."

"Yeah. But the band has us do blood tests. You know I'm clean."

"This isn't about you being 'clean'. Even if you...if you got something from him I'd still love you." Brave wrapped his arms around Malakai, holding him close. "We've all got our damage."

"I don't." Malakai tried to pull away, but Brave tightened his grip. "Let go."

Hands falling to his sides, Brave leaned back, watching him as he straightened and paced away. Sure, he could see how some might see his teacher fucking him as a problem. And maybe it was. Since then, Malakai didn't get close to anyone. He wouldn't claim to be better than Brave in how he treated the people he fucked.

Making sure they knew they were being used didn't absolve the fact that he was using them. That he barely said a word to them before he sent them away. Sometimes with a roadie if they made things weird.

"You know, I'm practically a virgin." Brave rested his hand lightly on the bumper by his hips. "Never thought about that before."

Malakai choked out a laugh. "Dude, in no way, shape or form are you a virgin."

"Isn't there a seven-year rule?"

"Maybe? If you're becoming a nun?" Malakai was fucking tired. And for some reason, he couldn't stop laughing at Brave's claim. "What are you getting at?"

Brave looked him dead in the eye and the laughter died in his throat. "I want another first. And go ahead and laugh. It's lame. But...he's not here. He can't ruin this."

If Valor wasn't dead, Malakai would hunt him down. With all the damage Brave had done, it was easy to cast him as the villain. But Malakai saw the young man he'd been. His older brother holding his life, his future in his hands.

And he'd tried to crush it all.

Between Brave's parents, and Valor...no wonder he was so fucked up.

Brave was trying to change. To do better. He'd asked Malakai to be part of his new beginning. And unlike others in Brave's life he should've been able to count on, Malakai wouldn't disappoint him.

Eyeing the woods spread out behind the bus, and glancing at the dark parking lot, Malakai tried to think like the sleazy photographers who'd foam at the mouth for a chance to catch them in the act. But even with night vision cameras, the trees were too thick for a clear shot. No one could see them without being spotted themselves.

This was as much privacy as they were going to get for a while. He returned to Brave, latching onto his wrists, pinning them over his head against the bus with one hand. Framing Brave's jaw with the other, he kissed him, long and hard, delving deep into his mouth with his tongue, letting his body offer reassurance words couldn't.

Pressed against Brave, Malakai was so damn hot he could manage a snow storm butt naked. But when he lowered his hand, bringing it up under Brave's hoodie to touch his bare skin, his flesh was cool.

"You're fucking freezing." Malakai moved between Brave's thighs, speaking between hungry kisses. "We should go to a motel or something."

"We're leaving too early." Brave's hips moved restlessly, lifting to grind against Malakai. "I'm fine. You'll fucking kill me if you stop again."

"I won't." Malakai groaned as he reached between them to stroke Brave's dick through the smooth material of his jogging pants. "I'm trying to make this good for you, but fucking you behind the bus, in the cold, ain't the best idea."

Brave shuddered, thrusting up into Malakai's loose grip. "Sounds perfect to me. Do you have…" His steady motions faltered. "Damn, this is weird. Usually, I'm the one pulling out condoms and lube. I don't have my wallet."

"I've got mine." Malakai pulled it from the back pocket of his jeans, slapping it onto the bumper beside Brave when the other man brought his lips to his throat and sucked hard. "You're gonna have to stop that if you want me to find anything."

Huffing out a laugh against his neck, Brave flipped open Malakai's wallet, tugging the condom and pack of lube from the slot under his credit cards one-handed, without even looking. "Amateur."

"Fuck you."

"Yeah. Within the hour if you don't mind?"

Shaking his head, Malakai backed up, unzipping his jeans and pulling out his throbbing cock before grabbing the condom. He brought the wrapper to his mouth to tear it open with his teeth, pulse racing as he caught Brave licking his lips while looking down at Malakai's dick. The open package almost slipped from his fingers.

Brave gave him a crooked smile before pushing away from the bus and taking the condom from his hand. "Where's that detached attitude, Grimm? You're usually cool as fuck when you're seducing a man."

"Don't." Malakai's mouth went dry as Brave knelt in front of him. "We've brought up enough of the past."

"Yes, we have." Brave fisted his hand around the base of Malakai's shaft, brushing his lips softly over the tender head, drawing a curse from his lips. "I want to taste you before you fuck me. Do you mind?"

Hell no. Malakai sucked in air through his teeth as Brave traced his thumb along the underside of his glans. The man seemed to be memorizing every inch of him, testing his reactions with gentle torment.

With level breaths, Malakai retreated from the rush of arousal threatening to cut things short. He'd mentioned edging to Brave because he'd done it before. Because sex had bored him for the longest time. Being bisexual should have given him sufficient variety to hold his interest, but he never connected with anyone long enough to want to experiment.

Quickies limited what he could do, even with a partner willing to try anything. Threesomes and moresomes were fun for a while, but even that got monotonous until he taught himself to control his body. Fucking three people in a row, giving them multiple orgasms, still hard after the last man—or woman—standing was completely drained, then claiming his own release gave him a twisted sense of power.

Brave bringing him to the brink this fast proved something had been missing before.

Still, he was up to the challenge.

"You're nice and thick." Brave replaced his thumb with the tip of his tongue, gazing up at Malakai with an evil glint in his eyes. "Good length. Will feel amazing when your dick hits the back of my throat."

"Jesus." Malakai tried to ease past those soft, teasing lips, but Brave tightened his grip, holding him still.

"I have one request before I start."

Malakai nodded, positive Brave on his knees could replace torture as an interrogation tactic. He'd do or say anything Brave wanted to get him to continue.

Brave licked up his length, then flashed a wicked smile. "Don't. Move."

The command sent a resistant shudder through Malakai, but he inclined his head, gritting his teeth as Brave's slick lips slid over him. Brave's tongue slipped along his length, hot pressure stimulating every inch as it disappeared into his mouth.

Malakai's palms itched to cup the back of Brave's head, not forcing him to go faster, but to move with him. Let him know how goddamn good his mouth felt. An exchange he'd never needed before.

He left his hands where they were. He had a feeling the 'Don't. Move.' rule included his hands. If he ignored it, Brave might stop.

Under the same circumstances, Malakai would.

The grip on his cock eased. Brave's hands curved around his hips. And his lips slipped down his length. The sensation of Brave swallowing around him was erotic as hell. His pulse throbbed hard and low, and Brave kept up a rhythm to match, as though driven by the beat. Guiding it faster and faster as he circled his tongue all the way up, sucking at the tender ridge before starting all over again.

And that control Malakai took so much pride in? Yeah, about to die a shameful death. His balls tightened as the current of need sizzled through his veins, spreading to every part of his body. His toes curled in his boots. His fingers twitched and he fisted his hands to keep them where they belonged.

Fuck this. He growled and delved his fingers into Brave's hair, pulling him away from his dick, bending down to kiss him before laughing against his swollen lips. "You want me to come in your mouth or you want me to fuck you?"

"You mean I can't have both?" Brave smirked, rolling the condom over Malakai's length. He rose, returning Malakai's kiss with a hungry one of his own. "I've heard stories."

"Yeah?" Malakai sucked Brave's bottom lip, sliding his hands down Brave's back and under the waist of his jogging pants to grab his bare ass. "What stories?"

Brave's eyes drifted shut. He inhaled roughly as Malakai lowered his fingers, grazing between his ass cheeks. "That you last so long you can't be human."

"I never felt human...or even *real* with anyone else." Malakai rested his forehead against Brave's. "You remind me that I am."

Slanting his lips over Malakai's, Brave replied with raw emotion, digging his fingers into Malakai's shoulders, revealing so much Malakai knew he'd felt the same. They'd both let sex become a distant thing, with people who couldn't reach beyond what they showed the world. A passion that echoed what they shared on stage, but nothing more.

Malakai might regret letting Brave in so deep, but he didn't care. Bring on the damn pain and scars. He was finished with shallow shit. The worst that could happen would be them hating one another again.

Pulling away, Malakai turned Brave, taking his wrists to place his hands against the back of the bus. He pressed his chest against Brave's back as he licked and sucked along the curve of his neck, breathing in the intoxicating aroma of beer and a hint of citrus, mixed with the deep familiar scent of the man who'd never been too far. The lingering scent he'd come to crave.

When Brave moaned, Malakai nipped his earlobe, then whispered to him. "Real is so much better. No matter how good having a warm body under you feels, when you're holding back part of yourself, the part that can get hurt..." He hooked his thumbs to the waist of Brave's jogging pants, dragging them down slowly. "You become numb inside. The experience lacks something...something I didn't know I was missing."

"Do you feel that now?" Brave met his eyes over his shoulder, licking his bottom lip as Malakai retrieved the packet of lube from where he'd left it on the bumper. "With me?"

"With you? The man who wrecked my perfect record of being in control?" Malakai drizzled the lube on his palm, coating his dick, then adding more so his fingers were nice and slick. He kissed Brave as he brought them down, circling his hole with gradual pressure, groaning as Brave let him in. "I feel it. I feel *everything*."

Brave shifted slightly, bowing his head between his arms, his whole body trembling. "I'm almost there. Don't give me a chance to back off because I'm fucking terrified." He widened his stance, exposing himself even more. "Make me feel it too."

Brave didn't brace himself as Malakai's dick pressed against him. He relaxed, pushing back, focusing on the stretch, the burn, on every sensation as if he'd never been taken before. The man was fucking hung, and the slow penetration rode hard on the edge of pain. Malakai added the last of the lube, teasing the ring of muscle with shallow thrusts.

He'd joked about being a virgin, but not about this being a first. His heart never got wrapped up in what he did with his body. He left it riding the pine, with no promise to ever let that vulnerable side of him in on the game.

The games were over and his heart was first up to bat. Beating hard, consuming every fucking moment like neglect had left it starving.

He was terrified.

In over his head already.

And the rest of him didn't seem to know what to do.

Sure, his dick was hard and ready for anything, but his skin was oversensitive, every touch from Malakai a shock, like the man was made of electricity. His fingertips, his lips, his body sent a current riding along Brave's nerves.

His brain had short-circuited long ago.

The functioning side tried to take over, but he denied it. He'd asked Malakai to make him feel.

He was doing just that.

Rocking against him, sinking deeper, then easing back, Malakai whispered words he couldn't make out, but the gentle assurance translated in his tone. He'd mentioned fucking Brave again and again, but he wasn't. Instead, he used his body to bring them together on another level.

Almost like the dam of hate they'd built had been rigged with dynamite. One spark and the explosion broke a hole in the cement, crushing the barrier under the weight of the water, all obliterated in an instant.

What hurt the most was neither of them had lit the fuse.

Shiori had inadvertently struck the match. If they didn't both care about her so much the barrier would have been reinforced until nothing short of a nuclear blast could tear it down.

He hadn't liked the idea of Malakai sharing his feelings for her, but in some fucked up way, knowing the man was struggling with him helped.

"Stay with me, Brave." Malakai pulled out completely, wrapping one hand around Brave's throat. "Fuck, I don't think you even realize you're pulling away. Whatever's on your mind can wait." He put some pressure on Brave's throat as he penetrated him once again. "You're mine. All of you. And I will give you *exactly* what you asked for."

As if to emphasize his point, Malakai bit into the other side of Brave's neck, adding sharp pain to the onslaught of sensations. He filled him, restricted how much he could breathe, and marked him all at once.

Clenching around the fullness, Brave rasped in air, sweat beading at his temples as he shuddered, completely overwhelmed. He'd never given anyone this much control over him.

Wouldn't have trusted anyone enough to try.

Malakai gave him what he needed, taking all he offered, using the knowledge he'd gained over the years. He knew Brave's triggers. Knew how to avoid the bad ones and use the good to breach all those closed off parts of him.

When Malakai's pelvis settled against him, Brave bucked his hips restlessly, all his focus on that deep penetration. He bit out a word he hoped sounded like "*More.*"

The response told him Malakai had heard. Grinding in deeper, Malakai released his throat and wrapped a hand around

Brave's dick. He stroked him as he withdrew, then drove in hard. In and out, angling to hit a spot that sent flashes of white across Brave's vision as his muscles clenched with each thrust.

"Fuck, you feel good. You're not cold anymore." Malakai ran his lips along Brave's throat. "So fucking hot."

Bearing down, Brave gritted his teeth as Malakai shifted back. Calloused fingers dug into Brave's hips as Malakai withdrew until only the head of his dick remained inside. His pace changed, building up to a merciless rhythm marked by the slap of skin on skin. Slamming in, gliding out, over and over until all the pressure, all the stimulation, hit like a meteor on impact with the Earth.

Brave came hard, pleasure tearing through him, rocking his whole body with each aftershock. He brought his fist to his mouth to muffle a shout as Malakai drove into him one last time.

"I will hurt you if you fucking move." Brave rested his head on the bus, jerking as Malakai wrapped his arms around his waist, dick shifting just enough to send another tremor through him. "*Please.*" Maybe if he asked nicely? "Please stay still."

Sucking lightly at the side of his neck, Malakai chuckled. "I am trying very hard. With the way you're holding me, I'm not getting anywhere without serious damage."

Brave's lips curved. He twisted his head sideways, giving Malakai a lazy kiss as his body settled. Malakai ran a hand over his stomach, up to his chest, holding him like he wasn't in a rush.

This was probably the longest time Brave had spent with anyone besides Jesse after sex.

His smile faded and he drew away from Malakai, pulling his jogging pants up the second Malakai was free from his body. What they'd done had been fucking awesome, but did he really deserve to feel this good?

How many people had he hurt before he'd considered changing?

"Hey." Malakai brought a hand up to his shoulder and squeezed. "Talk to me."

"Not sure what to say. This was…" He leaned against the back of the bus, shaking his head. "Incredible. And I feel guilty."

He expected Malakai to give him all the reasons he shouldn't. The past was in the past. Do better now.

Instead, he tugged Brave around to face him. "So do I."

"That's helpful."

"It's not meant to be. We've both done shit we'll have to live with." Malakai sighed and rubbed the back of his neck. "Hopefully, the people we've hurt can forget about us. But remembering them is the price we pay. Most of the people I've been with knew the deal. Others…I could tell they thought they'd be 'the one'. What we shared would be special and I'd ask them to stick around. I knew, and I didn't care."

Brave nodded. He'd done the same. "How do we fix it?"

"We don't. We accept that we were assholes." Malakai smirked, reaching out to tuck a strand of hair behind Brave's ear. "I know who you were and who you are. And I love you anyway."

No matter how many times Malakai said those three words, Brave would never get tired of hearing them. They didn't erase the guilt, but he put it where it belonged, with all the other lessons he'd learned.

Catching Malakai's wrist, he held his hand against his cheek. "I love you, too."

For a few beats, neither of them spoke.

Then Malakai laughed. "Enough of all the emotional shit. I'm still not used to it. Ready to go in?"

"Yeah." Brave gave himself a little shake. As much as he enjoyed the closeness they'd found, they both needed to figure out how to manage their new intimacy.

Which meant more than talking and fucking and being all sappy. They'd have to deal with the band. With how to act in public.

This could get weird.

But he was ready to handle whatever challenges they'd face.

As they made their way to the door of the bus, he glanced over at Malakai, needing his take on things. "So how we doing this? Band meeting? Do our thing and explain if anyone asks? A statement to the—"

"Your bunk or mine?" Malakai held up a hand when Brave frowned at him. "Dealing with the fallout tomorrow. All I know, right now, is I want to wake up next to you."

"Fucking bunks are small."

"You telling me no, Draven?"

Brave grinned and shook his head. "Not sure I know how anymore."

"Good. Because I'm claiming this as another first. I've never slept—as in actually sleeping—with anyone before." Malakai's lips curved slightly. "I just hope you don't snore."

Chapter Eighteen

Last night's performance had been featured in a wicked review on the Rolling Stone website. An amazing accomplishment, Winter's Wrath never got a mention unless they had a new release coming out.

Reading the article for the third time, Shiori looked up from Danica's laptop, not sure why the other woman, sitting across the table from her with Jesse and Alder, was scowling into her coffee.

"I'm missing something." Shiori took a sip of her own coffee, now lukewarm and bitter enough to curl her tongue. "This is good publicity, isn't it?"

Jesse raked his fingers through his rumpled blond curls and shook his head. "I'm not sure. Reese called and she's cautiously optimistic. She's waiting to see how the public reacts."

"Because they're speculating about Brave and Malakai being gay?" Shiori rolled her eyes. "That's stupid. Every fan I know suspects you're all bisexual. No one cares."

"Because it's not PC to make it a big deal, but that doesn't mean it won't affect sales." Jesse rolled his shoulder, looking tired. "There's still an attitude in the metal scene that isn't inclusive. A little homoerotic flirting to tease the ladies is acceptable. What they did was clearly...*more*."

"That's not the point." Danica reached out, taking her laptop and snapping it shut. "Their little display is all anyone's talking about. You're not mentioned at all."

"So...Reese isn't impressed with my performance?" Shiori bit hard into her bottom lip when they all avoided meeting her eyes. "I was on for one song. I thought I had at least a week to prove myself?"

Danica reached out, covering Shiori's hands with hers. "You *do*. This isn't a reflection of your performance; you were amazing. Sophie's likely working on an angle to get you more exposure as we speak. I'm just...damn it, why did they have to steal the spotlight?"

Biting back a laugh, Shiori turned her hands to squeeze Danica's. "Because *they're* the band. Besides, I knew they'd planned to do something to take the focus off the pictures—"

"*We* had that covered!" Danica's eyes widened. "Oh, I almost forgot. Our little encounter with the press *was* mentioned. A short piece on a fashion blog, but you're in there!"

Danica pulled up the blog on her phone, then passed it to Shiori.

Just one of the guys and 'evil lady bits'

I have to say, the impromptu interview with the ladies of Winter's Wrath impressed me. When the press tried to shame their new dancer—who will presumably be taking over for Danica Tallien while she's strutting on the catwalk and shooting commercials for two new fashion lines and a coveted makeup ad—both women laughed off the assumption that they had to be sleeping with the boys to change clothes in front of them.

Honestly, it never occurred to me, but when you're stuck on a bus for days at a time, where do you find privacy? The idea that whipping off your shirt is no big deal is usually reserved for men, but the two models clearly feel comfortable around the band. Which was a refreshing statement.

I'm looking forward to hearing more about the new stage performer, Shiori Ayase, over the next few weeks. The girl has spunk!

"Oh wow…" Shiori's cheeks heated. Sure, she'd expected to eventually have her pictures out there if she succeeded as a model, but being mentioned on a big blog made the whole experience more real somehow.

Back in her regular life, when she was on social media, she hardly got likes on stuff she posted. Of course, she hadn't shared many pictures—Sophie wanted her to work on her selfie skills—but it never felt like anyone cared what she had to say. She'd get one like from Wendy and that was pretty much it.

"I'm sending this to you. You need to share it." Danica sounded excited for the first time that morning, as if it had just occurred to her the situation wasn't hopeless. "Reese should be letting us know the next stop on our tour later today. We'll brainstorm for different ways to elevate your platform."

"That works." Shiori snatched her phone out of her purse when it buzzed, immediately sharing the screenshot of the article with a quick *'OMG, how awesome is this?!'*

Within seconds, her notifications were going off as 'friends' from high school started liking and commenting. Shiori's lips parted.

Chuckling, Danica pointed at her phone. "You'll want to turn the notifications off or they'll drive you nuts. We'll take some pictures together today for you to put up and I'll share them. Sophie also wants you to check out the fan page she set up for you and engage with people there. Things are about to get crazy."

"How am I gonna keep up and learn all I have to on the road?" Shiori hadn't expected this lifestyle to be easy, but suddenly it seemed impossible to manage. "I'm practically social media illiterate. Wendy had to teach me how to stop posting every time I hit a new level on Candy Crush. And I think I lost some friends by accidentally asking them to join me in the game twenty times in one day."

Alder snorted. "I'd definitely unfriend you for that."

Danica smacked him lightly in the chest with that back of her hand. "*Not* helpful." She turned her focus to Shiori. "Things will move fast, but that's part of why you're here with me. I'll give you some tips. You *don't* have much time to negotiate social media, but a few minutes throughout the day will do wonders. As for your fan page and Instagram, Sophie has people on staff to keep those active. It sounds like a lot, but it's really not."

Inhaling slowly, Shiori nodded. Glancing at her phone, her eyes went wide. "I have fifty new friend requests."

"You trust Jesse to vet them?" Danica smiled at Shiori's nod. "Okay, give him your phone. We need to go shopping. Now that you've caught the attention of the fashion world, they'll notice if you're wearing my clothes."

"I have my own clothes." Sure, she'd packed quick, but she still had some nice outfits.

Lips parted, Danica went still. Then nodded. "I know you do, sweetie. I'm not criticizing your wardrobe. But… You do know Sophie set up a clothes budget for you? She does for all the new models. She did it for me and made suggestions—but we also have fashion experts to help us make good choices. If you'd rather shop with one of them—"

"No!" Ugh, this was not easy. Shiori knew what she liked wearing, but she was open to suggestions. And she'd take Danica's over anyone's. Only…being told what to wear would take some getting used to. "I'd love to go shopping with you. I'm used to being careful how I spend my money. Sophie did tell me I'd have a special account for expenses, but I haven't even set up the card. Things have just been going at light speed."

"They will, but you've got this." Danica slid between Alder and the table, grabbing Shiori's mug and moving to the sink to dump out the coffee and fix her a fresh cup. "You've already proven you can make smart choices. Stick to that and you're—"

"Good morning." Brave ambled out from the bunk area, sleepily rubbing one hand over his face. "We having a meeting?"

"Someone would have gotten you up." Alder frowned at his brother. "Where the hell did you go last night?"

"I was outside getting some fresh air." Brave rested his hip against the fridge as Danica held out a steaming mug of coffee. "Thank you, sis. Need this."

"You're welcome." Danica stopped by his side, holding Shiori's coffee cup and studying him with a shrewd look in her eyes. "Have you spoken to Malakai this morning?"

Brave frowned. He set his mug on the counter. "About what?"

"About you both being mentioned by Rolling Stone. Reese is considering how to best publicize your stunt on stage."

"Our 'stunt'?" Brave paled. "Is that what she's saying?"

"Yes. How else is she supposed to take it?"

"I…" Brave's brow furrowed. "I don't know. Where is Malakai? He wasn't there when I…I mean…I just got up."

"We know." Alder stood, eyeing his brother. "Are you all right?"

"Yeah. I just…*fuck*, I'm not awake enough for this." He rubbed his face again. Then his eyes met Shiori's. "Hey, little moon. Can we talk?"

She wasn't sure what to make of Brave's strange mood, but she was curious about what he had to say to her. Pre-coffee his guard was down. His words raw and honest.

If they were going to talk at all, it would be now. Before he had time to prepare. While he was still too sleepy to hold back.

"I'd like that." She was still wearing the Harley Quinn nightshirt and the big slipper boots she'd packed. It was pretty warm on the bus, but outside, not so much. And that was the only place they could be alone.

Last night she'd dropped her jacket on the sofa, but it had been moved. To where, she had no idea. Her suitcase was tucked at the far end of her bunk and even after days on the bus, she still hadn't really explored. Was there a closet somewhere?

"Here." Brave grabbed a big hoodie slung over the arm of the sofa and handed it to her. "It's not that cold."

The hoodie was his. She could tell the second she pulled it over her head. His scent had become so familiar a whiff threatened her careful detachment. She wanted to hold the sleeves to her face and breath in, but she was still mad at him.

And she had to figure out how to work with him being a complete jerk. So no sniffing or being happy that he'd brought up talking first. They would discuss how to be civil. Agree on a professional relationship. End things on a lighter note than they had last night.

Reasonable, but the idea of being so cut and dry made every step heavy as she followed him off the bus. She'd had a long time to think about his reaction to another guy hitting on her. She wasn't naïve. The waiter had opened up the conversation because she'd been an easy target. She got that. *Now.*

Giving him her number might not be a big deal, but seeing how quickly people reacted to her in public gave her pause. Brave had lived this life for a long time. Maybe he was being protective because he'd made the same mistakes.

That didn't excuse his rudeness, but she'd hear him out. He was the lead singer of a band she hoped to work with long term. Holding grudges wouldn't get her anywhere.

Outside was noisy. The other bands were packing up and saying goodbye to one another. Since Winter's Wrath had nothing scheduled yet, the more well-known bands had jumped on other tours. While the smaller ones were heading back home. Last minute schmoozing might lead to future opportunities.

Brave offered his hand, flashing her a hesitant smile. "The roadies usually go out for breakfast together. They probably took the bigger van. Not sure you've seen much of our original one? We won't be bothered here."

The roadies' smaller van, which was parked next to the small truck the band rented to carry merch and supplies, was cut off from the activity around them. Would give them privacy she wasn't sure she wanted

Privacy would give them a chance to work out their issues, but could she remain detached without anyone around to remind her how much damage he could do to her career?

Before last night, she'd wanted to talk to him. Maybe that time had come. No more secrets. How she felt about him didn't matter.

She took his hand and let him lead the way.

He turned on the van, letting it run as he stepped around the back and opened the doors. Inside was a setup that reminded her of every hippie movie she'd ever seen. Big, long fluffy cushions set up around the open space with beanbag chairs. Christmas lights strung along the walls of the van. He pressed a button and a neon sign lit up behind the driver's seat, reading 'Exit' with an arrow pointing to the side door.

Corny, but oddly charming. She let him help her up and settled on a black, Batman beanbag chair.

After pulling the back doors of the van shut, Brave plunked down on another beanbag chair bearing the Captain America shield.

Shirtless, wearing nothing but jogging pants and a pair of worn sneakers, Brave rubbed his scruffy jaw. "I was out of line last night."

"Okay." She frowned at him, not sure what she was supposed to say. Were they done already?

"Shiori…" Brave sighed, sitting forward, his long legs folded in front of him. "I need to be straight with you."

"Please do."

"Damn it, don't do that." Brave let out a frustrated sound. "I care about you. I'm trying to do what's best for you, but that means not admitting any of this. Not saying I wish things were different. I wish I'd met you and could ask you out and just get to know you. You ready to shut me down the second I say you're not like other girls I've been with?"

"Yes." Shiori held his steady gaze, digging her nails into her palms. "I have to tell you something, And after last night, I didn't want to."

"I'm sorry."

"Don't be. It doesn't change anything." She pressed her eyes shut. "Almost six years ago there was a girl who fell in love with a man like you. She was almost sixteen. Met him at a concert. She loved his music. She was looking for a way to escape the life she was trapped in."

Brave went still. Motioned for her to go on.

"The guy was into her, but she was young. Innocent. Not a groupie he could toy with. He asked her to join him on tour. Told her she was different. That he needed her close." Shiori's eyes teared. "She was so good. So sweet. She believed him when he told her she was special. He was gentle, but he wanted her. He ignored every other woman. Said he would be a better man for her. He seduced her one night, in the parking lot. And she remembered that night as a beautiful experience."

"I don't understand—"

Shiori held up a hand. "She was my sister. She called me while she was with the band. Told me she was in love."

"Your sister?" Brave's jaw hardened. "No. There's no fucking way. I've done some fucked up shit, but I've never been with a girl that young."

"Not that you'd have been able to tell. My sister hardly ever got carded. She could pass for older." She took a deep breath. "But it wasn't you. It was Valor."

"Damn it." Brave's lips drew in a thin line. "Please continue."

She gave him a stiff smile. "He sent my sister home when he was done with her. Months later, she was still waiting for him." Her voice broke. "The doctors told her carrying the baby to term would be dangerous. She didn't care. She hoped she'd make it, just like she hoped the man she loved would come back for her." Hot tears trailed down her cheeks. Brave reached out, but she shook her head and dried her face with her sleeves. "She made me promise one day I would tell you. Tell *him*. It was my choice to wait. To get to know you and Alder first."

"Valor has a son." Brave pressed his fist to his lips and sat back. He stared at the floor, his other hand clenched on his knee as though shock and anger had taken hold. His jaw ticked. "I don't understand. Even while Cole was with us, he would have looked into it. Would have made sure the kid had everything he needed. Why wait? Why tell us now?"

Hugging herself, she considered her answer carefully. "The opportunity came at the perfect time. My sister and I were isolated our whole lives. Our mother was estranged from her family when she died and our stepfather doesn't have any. I want better for Hiro."

"His name's 'Hiro'?" Brave looked up at her, a soft smile on his lips. "From Big Hero 6?"

"No, that wasn't out yet." Shiori let her arms slide down around her knees. "She named him after some painter she liked. I'll have to read up about him before Hiro gets old enough to ask."

"How old is he?"

"He'll be six in two months."

"Do you have a picture of him?" Brave laughed when she looked down at her borrowed hoodie. "Your phone's on the bus. Right." He took a deep breath. "Wow…I'm not sure what to say. Does he need anything? Anything at all and I'm on it. We should go back to Detroit and—"

"You can't cut the tour short, Brave." She leaned over and took his hand. "But I'll bring you to meet him soon. Alder too."

"Is he with someone who will treat him good? Your stepfather isn't an asshole, is he?"

Wasn't that the million-dollar question? She chewed at her bottom lip. "He's...he's not really interested in Hiro right now, but his girlfriend is amazing with him. And my best friend, Wendy, stops by as often as she can to check on him." A temporary fix. She hoped Brave and Alder might have a more permanent one. "What about your parents? They'll want to meet him, won't they? Being blood, they might be better for him to grow up with?"

Brave's expression darkened. "Oh, they'd definitely play the part. Hell, they manage to pretend they didn't give Alder up for dead after he was stabbed."

Ouch. Shiori withdrew her hand. "But, were they good parents? I'm sure they were scared for their son. They've already lost one."

"Yes. The only one they really cared about." Brave sighed, shifting forward to kneel in front of her. "I wish I could tell you Hiro will have the perfect, ready-made family. But I won't pretend my parents are good people. The photographer who shared that picture online? I'd suspect my mother if she wasn't covering political scandals in Washington. And my father disapproves of my 'lifestyle'. Take that in any way you choose, you'll be right."

"But as his grandparents, they could fight for him." Her throat locked as the hope she'd grasped for turned to dust. "They did a good job with you and Alder."

"I spent more time raising Alder than they did." Brave's lips twisted. "He turned out good because that's who he is, I don't get any credit. And they get even less." His brow furrowed. "But why would they need to fight for him? Isn't he safe where he is?"

Shiori nodded, certain she still had time to come up with another plan. This job would give her the money to get her own place. Her stepfather could hire a better lawyer if she brought him to court for custody, but maybe it wouldn't come to that.

"He's safe. And if Reese decides to keep me, or Sophie finds me other work, I'll have enough to support him." She ground her teeth. "If I can prove I'm a fit guardian."

"Hey." Brave brought his hand up to her cheek. "You really don't want your stepfather raising him, do you?"

"No." Shiori wasn't sure Brave would understand, but she had to tell him something. Enough of the truth to avoid too many questions. "I was a little older than Hiro when my mother died. It happened so suddenly—no one expects a woman in her late twenties to have a heart attack." She pressed her eyes shut to hold back more tears. "My stepfather didn't have a lot of money, but he kept a roof over our heads. Made sure we had food to eat. And reminded us every day how much of a burden we were. Kyoko got the worst of it. She tried so hard to take care of me and the house, but he'd cut her down with a few words and make her feel worthless."

"He sounds like a real piece of work." Brave smoothed his hand over her hair. "You're afraid he'll do the same to Hiro."

She nodded. "I never want Hiro to feel he owes that man anything. My stepfather has a job that takes him away for months, so that helps, but Hiro already knows to avoid him. He never asks for anything. If not for Elizabeth, he'd be miserable. She can't have kids, so she lavishes attention and affection on him."

"But she's just the girlfriend. If they break up…"

"Hiro only has me." Her lips thinned. "She's useful to my stepfather while he's away, though. Taking care of Hiro and the house. I don't think she realized she's being used. She doesn't like me, so it's not like I can warn her."

Brave sighed and pulled her into his arms. The strength of them around her eased the tightness in her chest and she didn't think twice before resting her head on his shoulder.

She couldn't lean on him too much, but right this minute she'd accept his comfort. Hugs were the best kind of medicine.

They didn't make problems go away, but the weight lightened a little all wrapped up in warmth. As if the hug transferred a little strength, recharging her enough to keep moving forward.

"I'm glad you told me about Hiro. And about *you*." Brave pulled her into his lap as he leaned against the beanbag. "You're not alone anymore. You decide how you want to take care of Hiro and I'll help however I can. I know Alder will too. Hiro will never feel unloved, or like he's indebted to anyone."

"That's all I want."

"But since your sister was so young when she had him, I'm guessing your stepfather has legal guardianship?"

"Yes." She lifted her head to look up at him. "I consulted with a lawyer when I turned eighteen and she told me I'd have to have a stable income, a place of my own, and prove I'd be better able to provide for my nephew. I started applying for jobs everywhere, but it was hard to find anything around the hours when I needed to be home with him. I was stuck."

Brave inclined his head. "I can't even imagine how hard that was. You should have been able to get out. Start your own life. But you chose to stay for him. He's lucky to have you."

"Not lucky." She frowned, rejecting the idea that any kid should feel grateful to have someone who loved and cared for them. The thought had her stomach twisting. "Every kid should have someone who puts them first."

"But not every kid does." Brave rubbed her arms, and kissed her hair. "Shiori, if you're worried about him I'll tell Reese not to add more dates. We can hold off on the European tour. I can get in touch with some lawyers and—"

"No." Shiori smiled to soften her words, sliding off his lap and turning to face him. "I'll accept your help if it comes to that, but it hasn't yet. I need to prove to myself I can do this. Part of me imagined your parents would be better for Hiro than me, but if they're not I'll do whatever it takes to give him what he needs."

"I respect that." Brave rested his hands on his thighs. "So...do you want to tell Alder, or should I?"

She laughed and shook her head. "You can tell him."

Brave grinned and reached for the door. He paused halfway. "You have enough on your plate, so I don't want to add to it. But I need you to know...I'm waiting for you. Waiting for when you have the life you're working so hard for." He squared his shoulders and glanced back at her. "I won't claim you. I won't get in your way. But when you want me to step up to your side, when it's our time." He held her gaze, his words a gentle promise. "I'll be there."

Her heart stuttered at the intensity in his eyes and it took all her strength not to tell him she wanted him there now. Had Valor said such sweet things to her sister? Kyoko had been so young, so desperate for love and support, he wouldn't have had to try very hard to win her over. Shiori wanted to believe she was less vulnerable, but she didn't trust how easy it would be to accept everything Brave offered.

But if he was still around when she reached her goal?

Well, if he was tempting today, he'd be irresistible by then. Or even tomorrow.

As he stepped onto the pavement, she slid over and grabbed his hand. "Brave..."

"Don't say anything. I've already proved I suck at keeping my distance." His lips quirked at the edges. "I'm trying to avoid doing anything else I need to apologize for."

"I just wanted to say thank you." She bit her bottom lip, stuffing her hands into the pocket of her borrowed hoodie. The material was heavy and warm and his scent surrounded her. She was tempted to keep it. She took a deep breath. "For understanding."

"No problem. Just don't friend zone me. That's Malakai's thing."

"Malakai?"

"Forget I said that." Brave shook his head and started for the bus. "Let's go tell my baby brother the good news."

Half running to keep up with his long strides, Shiori climbed onto the bus a step behind him, blushing as their entrance drew every eye in the room. Danica had her laptop out on the table in the kitchenette, and Jesse was beside her, with a brush in his hand, looking like he'd been brushing her hair while she worked.

Alder was sitting on the sofa, holding his guitar, the last chord he'd played still hanging in the air.

Connor and Tate were on the loveseat, playing a videogame. Their characters died as their attention shifted to her.

Malakai wasn't there. She wasn't sure where he'd gone, but she missed him. Brave's comment about him being in the 'friend zone' bothered her for some reason. Yes, he was her friend. But putting it like that sounded wrong. He'd become so important to her, so quickly, she couldn't put a label on how much he meant to her.

Don't make it complicated. Things are messed up enough already.

Stopping in the middle of the room, Brave flashed a broad smile and cleared his throat. "I'm not sure how to say this. I've got some awesome news." He paused, and spread his arms wide. "It's a boy!"

Alder almost dropped his guitar as he shot to his feet. He stared at Shiori. "There's no fucking way you'd know this soon. And…" He pulled off his guitar and handed it to Tate. "Damn it, Brave! What the fuck is wrong with you?"

Shiori groaned, slipping past the brothers to sit beside Danica. "I may have to kill him."

"I may help you." Danica's brow lifted. "What's going on?"

Before Shiori could answer, Brave pulled his brother into a headlock. "We're uncles. Valor actually left something good in this world. But thank you, now I know what you really think of me."

"What the hell are you talking about?" Alder wrestled free from Brave, turning to Shiori again. "You knew Valor?" He paled and shook his head. Glared at Brave. "Dude, this isn't funny. Even if he messed with her right before he died she would have been…what, thirteen? Fourteen?"

"I never met Valor." Shiori wanted to throw something at Brave. His happy 'announcement' had made everything awkward and confusing. "But my sister was fifteen when she did. I doubt he asked how old she was. The point is, you have a six-year-old nephew."

Alder sank onto the loveseat, almost sitting in Tate's lap. "Valor has a son?"

"Yes."

"Are you sure?"

Shiori's lips parted. "*What?*"

Tate groaned and smacked Alder upside the head.

Alder winced. "What the fuck?"

"You hit me when I say stupid shit." Tate scowled at him. "You totally deserved that."

"I really did." Alder rose, stepping up to Shiori and taking a knee, looking so torn she couldn't be too mad. "I'm sorry. This is just… Your sister deserved better. Valor should have left her alone."

"He should have, but they had a beautiful son and that's all that matters." She needed to focus on Hiro. Talking about her sister with Brave had already left her raw. "I had a lot of reasons to take this job. One of them was to meet you and Brave. All I know of your family is that your brother used and abandoned my sister. I wasn't sure you'd even care that you have a nephew, but it didn't take long to see otherwise."

"Did your sister ask you to…?" Alder exchanged a look with Brave and went still. He bowed his head. "She's gone."

"She died right after he was born." Saying that never got any easier, but Shiori quickly explained her plans to support Hiro herself. Not revealing all she had to Brave, but hopefully saying enough so the band would understand why she was here. She hadn't meant to keep secrets from them. She still intended to do the job she'd signed on for.

Danica hugged her from behind and rested her chin on Shiori's shoulder. "One way or another I was going to help you establish yourself, but it's even more important now. Reese is sending us to New York in three days. We're headlining for Horizon and they pull in a huge crowd. You're going to put on a performance no one will ever forget. Offers will come in like crazy."

"I hope so." She had to face that her plan had been naïve. Coming on tour with the band had seemed so perfect. Fine, she hadn't assumed anything, but she wouldn't lie to herself. There'd been this perfect scenario in her head where Brave and Alder would tell her how amazing their parents were. Real grownups who'd have all the answers. Who would take over and give Hiro safety and stability and everything she didn't have the slightest clue how to provide.

Instead, it had become very clear that while the men would do what they could, Hiro's future was on her shoulders. Family wasn't a puzzle piece that would suddenly fit into place.

She'd been scared. Overwhelmed. Alone.

That she wasn't anymore was something, but not everything. She still had a lot of work to do.

But the path was clearer. Probably the most important lesson she'd learned.

All her hard work would pay off. She'd needed a job and she had one. She'd needed support and she'd found it.

"Shiori, I'm sure Brave told you this, but please know you have me. You have the band." Alder took her hands in his, his tone solid and clear. "You've dealt with a lot on your own and I admire your strength. And you'll need that going forward. But my nephew will have what neither me or my brothers did. I get that you have a lot to prove. What happened between Valor and your sister…damn it, nothing I can say or do can make that right. But that little boy is loved. We've all got our issues, but he won't suffer for them. You're in charge here. You tell us what to do and we're on it."

She nodded and smiled, excited for Hiro to get to know these men. Even if she'd been wrong about them being able to swoop in and make everything right, she hadn't been wrong about how important they'd be in his life. He'd have good men to look up to. Love that wouldn't cost him a thing.

"I'm glad I could finally tell you." She sighed and turned next to Danica, setting her phone on the table. "I should get started on the social media thing. Or…" She unlocked her phone, glancing over at Brave and Alder. "Would you like to meet him? He loves video-calls. It's not the same as meeting him in person, but it's a start."

"We'd love to." Brave stepped up to her side, jostling a little with Alder when his younger brother squeezed in, both trying to fit into the small space between the table and the bench.

Snickering, she face-timed Wendy, who started saying hello, then froze, lips parted when she spotted the guys behind her. They must have waved or something, because Wendy squealed and the screen turned the color of her red sofa cushions.

"Wendy!" Shiori rolled her eyes as the screen changed to show a hand. "What are you doing?"

"Sitting here in my PJs with bedhead and no makeup!" Wendy let out a mortified groan. "Why didn't you warn me? I thought you loved me?"

"I do love you."

"You let the lead singer of Winter's Wrath see me like…like *this*. I'm revoking your best friend card."

"I'll bring you something cool when I come home." Speaking to Wendy's hand, while on speaker phone in front of the whole band was weird. Her cheeks heated as she sensed their eyes on her. They probably thought she and Wendy were nuts. "I'm going to New York in a few days. Tell me what you want and it's yours."

"Dude, she's a fan. How about I give her some drumsticks?" Tate popped up on the table in front of Shiori, tipping his head to look down at the phone. "I'm still in my PJs too if that helps. Very manly panda ones."

"Is that Tate Maddox?" Wendy peeked through her fingers. "Would it be weird to ask for the PJs?"

All the guys burst out laughing. Beside her, Danica's cheeks reddened as though experiencing vicarious humiliation.

"*Very!*" Shiori ducked her head when Brave squeezed her arm. His sympathy made the embarrassment even worse. "Is Hiro nearby? I wanted him to meet his uncles."

"You *told* them?" Wendy moved her hand, her green eyes wide. "That's awesome! One sec, I'll get him. He was playing with Raccoon before." The red material filled the screen again with a soft *Plunk,* as though Wendy had tossed the phone aside. "Hiro!"

Brave crouched down, frowning at the phone. "He's playing with a raccoon?"

"No, Raccoon is her kitten." The heat covering her cheeks spread over the rest of her as she met Brave's eyes. Having him this close wreaked havoc on her senses. How he'd thought she could *ever* stick him in the friend zone was beyond her.

Little footsteps and laughter sounded, bringing her attention back to the screen. Hiro's adorable little face appeared. "Auntie!"

"Hey, baby." God, she wished she could hold him. They'd never spent this much time apart. Keeping busy made the time pass faster, but the separation hit her hard the second she looked into his big, golden-brown eyes. "Remember how I told you I'd be dancing for Winter's Wrath?"

"Like the lady in the video?" Hiro's overgrown black hair fell over his forehead. "Did you get to dress all scary?"

"Not yet, but maybe soon."

"Cool!" Hiro bounced on the sofa, giggling when Wendy shouted for him to be careful. Then he peered at Shiori, looking past her and whispering. "Are those guys in the band?"

"Yes. And there's something else I need to tell you about them." Shiori cleared her throat. "This is Brave." She turned the phone slightly. Brave waved. "And Alder."

"Hey, buddy." Alder crouched down beside his brother.

"They're your uncles." Shiori caught Hiro's confusion right away and smiled at him. "You know how Mommy was my sister?"

Hiro nodded.

"Brave and Alder were your Daddy's brothers."

"Oh." Hiro's tiny nose wrinkled. He cocked his head, as though taking in the information. He was a smart kid, she had no doubt he'd catch on quick. Pushing his tongue into the space where he'd lost his tooth, he eyed the men. "Is my daddy there too?"

Oh no. Shiori schooled her features, hoping the men wouldn't react badly to the question. Hiro *knew* his father had died, but sometimes asked when he'd come back. He didn't seem to understand death was permanent.

"He's not here, sweetie." She inhaled slowly. "But just like Mommy, he's always watching over you."

"From heaven." Hiro sighed and plunked back on the sofa, holding the phone above him. "I want to go to the park, but Wendy says it's too cold. Will my uncles bring me to the park?"

"Do you want to ask them?"

"Yes!" Hiro brought the phone close to his face. "Jeffrey says his uncles bring him to baseball games and camping and fishing and all kinds of things. And they let him eat ice cream for breakfast."

Brave grinned as Shiori held the phone facing him. "We'll do tons of fun things, sport. Don't tell you auntie, but I'll get all kinds of ice cream for when you come visit."

Alder squished in, a huge smile on his lips. "Do you like cake? Cookies? I'll get all your favorites. And I love baseball."

"He really doesn't. You'll have to teach him." Brave slung an arm around Alder's neck. "But camping we can all do together. You can come hang out on the tour bus. Maybe Uncle Alder can teach you how to play guitar."

Sitting back, Shiori relaxed and watched the Trousseau brothers answer a million questions from their nephew with so much enthusiasm she couldn't wait until Hiro got to meet them in person. All three grumbled when Jesse gently reminded them that the band had to hit the road.

Wendy saved them from a long goodbye when she grabbed Hiro and flung him over her shoulder, stealing the phone away as he giggled. "We're about to make pancakes, so we've got to go. I'm taking Hiro home around six, but you can call a bit later if you want."

"I will. Thank you, Wendy." Shiori blew her best friend a kiss and ended the call. Blinking fast, she slid off the bench as Brave and Alder rose. Homesickness hit her like a battering ram straight to the chest. If Hiro hadn't looked so happy, she'd have a hard time not packing her bags and heading home.

Big arms surrounded her, pulling her against a solid chest. "He's doing good, little moon. Your friend, Wendy, is great with him."

"I think she's totally earned my PJs." Tate chimed in as he unbuttoned his pajama top. Dark blue, with panda heads all over it, which matched the pants. "They're super comfy."

"I second Wendy getting those fucking goofy PJs." Connor made a face. "I'm tired of seeing them."

"Which is why I have three sets!" Tate smirked as he folded the top. He hooked his thumbs to the bottoms.

"Tate!" Every single person in the room yelled at him at once.

He shot them an innocent smile. "What? I'm just getting Wendy's present ready for her."

Shaking her head, Shiori glanced up at Brave. His expression shifted, eyes troubled. He moved away from her, staring down at the blank screen of her phone as though still seeing Hiro there.

His throat worked as he swallowed. "He looks like Valor."

She grabbed her phone, holding it to her chest. Brave's feelings for his brother were pretty obvious. All the joy from him having spoken to his nephew faded as he lifted a hand to rub the back of his neck, frowning at the floor.

Alder stepped up to her side. "So what? He also looks like you and me. And our father."

"Yes, but..." Brave let his hand fall to his side. "He'll ask us about Valor. We can't tell him the man was an asshole. That he was a violent drug addict."

"No fucking kidding." Alder glared at him. "What are you getting at?"

Brave's lips thinned. "I'm going to have to think of something positive to tell our nephew. Shouldn't be hard for you, you thought Valor was a goddamn saint for most of your life." His jaw ticked. "I'll have to either make something up or..." He groaned. "I don't know, all right? I've got nothing."

Backing up, Brave held up a hand when she moved to follow, then spun around and quickly left the bus. Everyone went still. Silent. As if unsure how to react.

Nails gouging her palms, she started for the door. Danica caught her hand, slipping out of the booth quickly. "You can't go after him. The press is hanging around, doing last minute interviews and digging for dirt."

This was getting ridiculous. Shiori gently twisted free. "I won't give them any. I know what I stand to lose. But part of the reason I'm here is so Hiro has family. This is his family, which makes it mine too. I take care of my family and if the damn tabloids want to make something of that, then let them."

Without wasting another second, Shiori made her way off the bus. Her whole body shook as she searched the throng of musicians and roadies and press for Brave, not sure ignoring Dania's advice had been the best idea. Danica was only trying to help, and Shiori was grateful, but she drew the line at not even being able to talk to Brave in public.

If the media could make a story out of any interaction they'd find a way, no matter how careful she was. A career that couldn't survive manufactured drama wouldn't get her very far.

I have to stop being afraid of what people will think of me.

A camera flashed and she glanced over, giving the man with the camera a sweet smile. He grinned at her and took a few more pictures.

Time to show them what I'm made of.

Chapter Nineteen

Hands stuffed in his pockets, Malakai kept pace with Ballz as they made their way back to the parking lot where all the buses were parked. He'd gotten up before everyone, careful not to wake Brave, and decided to go for a walk. Fine, he didn't want to keep their relationship a secret, but there were better ways for the guys to find out than seeing him climbing out of Brave's bunk.

Ballz had spotted him and suggested grabbing breakfast. Malakai figured Jesse told him about the whole anger management thing, so he hadn't been thrilled to spend time with the man. Therapy over eggs and bacon would fucking suck.

Instead of the conversation being all deep and probing, it had been…normal. They talked about the same random shit they would any other day. No questions about his childhood. No 'so how does that make you feel?'

He slowed, glancing over at the other man, who couldn't be more than forty. Ballz still had military written all over him. Buzz cut, muscles, and his black shirt and jeans could pass any inspection. The roadie/bodyguard intimidated crazy fans with his cold stare, but with the band he was laidback.

Hadn't been hard to talk to until Malakai started worrying about being studied like a bug under a microscope.

"Did Jesse talk to you about me?" Might as well put it out there. They were running out of time.

Ballz's lips curved slightly. "I was wondering when you'd ask."

"*And?*"

"He did."

"But you haven't asked me anything." Malakai shoved his hands into the pocket of his thin leather jacket and scowled. "Shouldn't you be evaluating me? Digging into my past?"

"Do you want to talk about your past?" Ballz arched a brow when Malakai stared at him. "I've always found the most difficult people to work with are the ones who're forced to get help. If you don't think you need to work on your issues, nothing I say will make a difference."

Shoulders hunched, Malakai nodded. "That makes sense. But I know I'm fucked up."

"Because you like hitting people?"

"I don't fucking like it." Malakai ground his teeth. "I don't fight for the fun of it, I just won't put up with bullies thinking they're too big to be taken down."

"Proving they don't have that power feels good." Ballz held up his hands before Malakai could protest. "Not judging, I've been there. When you're finally in the position to stand up to the assholes that looked down on you? To show them you won't take their shit? It's amazing."

"It sounds like you're telling me I'm not doing anything wrong." Malakai cocked his head. "I go so crazy I could kill someone. That's a problem."

Ballz inclined his head. "I'm glad you agree. Now the question is, who are you fighting when you lose it? Not the person you've got down on the ground, who can't get back up. You mentioned bullies. I'm guessing you're not a fan."

Rolling his shoulder, Malakai tipped his head back. "Who is? We've all dealt with them at some point."

"To some extent, absolutely." Ballz steady gaze speared him, those deep azure eyes digging up shit Malakai hadn't thought of for years, without even trying. "But most of us either win a battle against them, or within ourselves. You lost. I'm not sure how badly, but you haven't forgotten. Every time you fight, you're pulled back to that moment."

He had lost. Not just a fight. The one he needed to win. If he'd been stronger he could have avoided so much pain.

A steady hand settled on his shoulder. Ballz gave him a level look. "It's up to you if you want to tell me what happened. You're not like the soldiers I worked with. I consider you a friend. I cared about every man and woman who came to me, but we never spent more than a few hours together. My job was to recommend the best therapy for them. Most I never saw again."

Obviously not the case here. Whatever Malakai told him, they'd be traveling together for weeks. Maybe months. Even with the band, Malakai always controlled how much they knew about him. He held back a lot because he liked how things were. He was tough, but looked out for Tate. And Alder when the kid needed him. He didn't put up with bullshit. He fucked who he wanted and no one cared because that was the lifestyle. He never mentioned family, but he wasn't the only one. Some topics were off limits for them all.

One night, when the band had been together for a few weeks and he and Brave were still friends, he'd mentioned his brother. He couldn't remember why he'd done it, but he was in a weird place. Tate was high on something and Malakai and Brave took turns watching over him after he passed out.

Malakai was fucking terrified Tate wouldn't wake up. He finished half a bottle of vodka just staring at the kid, making sure he was still breathing.

While he puked it all up, Brave rubbed his back and told him Tate would be fine. He'd been hungry, then sleepy. Probably just shared a joint with another band. If it helped Brave would ask around.

Rubbing his eyes with his thumb and forefinger, Malakai recalled what he'd said to Brave that night. And more. "I was really poor growing up. My father was an accountant, but he couldn't find work. He'd been fired from some company for doing shady shit, but I never knew the details. I didn't know him very well. My mother worked two jobs. At a call center during the day, and waiting tables at night. She was amazing. They both died in a car accident when I was ten. Me and my brother were sent to the same foster home. Not a bad place, but they had a lot of kids."

Here was the talking about his childhood. And Ballz hadn't even asked.

But he kept going, because the rest didn't make sense without it.

"School was always rough, but going to a new one in the middle of the year…it was bad. My brother, Eric, was picked on a lot. I tried to protect him, but I was scrawny and just got my ass handed to me." He let out a bitter laugh. "Eric stopped telling me when some asshole was fucking with him. But he'd made friends, so things seemed okay. Then he started selling drugs."

He pressed his eyes shut. He'd been so fucking mad at Eric. Seen him hanging with the same kids that used to bully him. When he told Eric to stay away from those fuckers, his brother laughed at him.

"He loved having money to burn. He partied all the time, getting drunk and high. I didn't know him anymore." Malakai felt like a hand had wrapped around his throat. Squeezing hard as he recalled saying those very words to Eric. "I'm not sure what happened, but one day he came to me, freaked out, saying he was done. He'd wanted the bullies to stop targeting him, so he'd found a way to be part of their pack. He knew if that changed he'd be right back where he started. I told him not to worry. I had his back."

After a long silence, Ballz inhaled roughly. "Neither of you had anyone else to go to."

"No. Our foster parents were taking care of little kids. They couldn't help us. We were afraid they'd ship us off if we brought any trouble into the house. We weren't wrong." He let out a rough laugh. "Eric cut ties with his 'friends' and they came after him. I was there, like I'd promised. I fought hard. I wasn't big, but I went fucking nuts. Hurt a few of them. But there were so many and they got to Eric. By the time the cops showed up... He didn't die right away. He was in a coma for months. I was shipped off to a group home. They let me visit him. They told me it wasn't my fault."

"You didn't believe them."

"How could I?" Malakai raked his fingers over his scalp, hating that he could see Eric lying there, so clearly, when he'd managed to keep that image out of his head for so long. "If I'd been stronger I could have stopped them. What the fuck did my promise mean if I was too weak to protect him?"

Folding his arms over his chest, Ballz stared at him. "What do you think it meant?"

Isn't that obvious? "Absolutely nothing."

"And as long as you believe that, you'll never forgive yourself for what happened to him." Ballz's tone hardened. "I like giving homework, so here's yours. I want you to remember when your brother trusted you enough to tell you what he was doing. When he turned to you because he knew you were strong. That you believed he could do better. Try to see the young man who earned that trust."

Malakai's brow furrowed. What kind of homework was that? "None of that saved him."

"And you losing control doesn't save him." Ballz shrugged. "You're not going to fix this overnight, Malakai. And this won't be easy. But if it helps, you're not as fucked up as you think you are."

"Yeah? Tell the guy whose jaw I broke." Malakai's stomach twisted. His own actions made him sick. He couldn't even remember which guy he'd put in the hospital. "Pretty sure he doesn't feel the same."

"Oh, you don't get a free pass on that. You lost it. You hurt someone. Let that sink in." Ballz's tone cut deep, as if he wanted Malakai to feel every word. "Every time you get in a fight—there's no guarantee it won't happen again. I'm not trying to turn you into a pacifist—you'll need to face the damage you've done. Whether or not you've got the high moral ground, you're hurting someone. And if you don't stop, you're no better than the people who killed your brother."

Fuck. Malakai blinked at Ballz. "You were paid to do this? No offense, but you really suck at it."

"Do I?" Ballz smirked. "I've counseled men who were ready to snap because they'd blown some other guy's brains out. And they could describe it in detail. Some of them needed to go back out in the field and one moment of doubt could cost them their lives." His shoulders lifted. "Whole different world. And I won't blame you if you'd rather talk to someone who'll prescribe hugs and tell you nice happy things. But in my professional opinion, you don't need shit sugarcoated."

Trying hard not to laugh—weird ass reaction—Malakai shot Ballz a slanted smile. "I prefer your approach. Even if it's tough love."

Ballz snorted. "You have no idea what 'tough love' is, music boy. Now hurry up and get your ass on the bus. Do your fucking homework. And we'll discuss this again in a couple days."

A sharp nod and Malakai quickened his pace. Then stopped. This had been good, right? He'd never told anyone the whole story about his brother, and facing the impact gave him a lot to think about.

But he wasn't 'fixed'. Anything could happen over the next few days. He glanced back at Ballz. "What if shit goes bad again? What if I—?"

"You'll either be with the band or one of us bodyguards. I'm not setting you up for failure, kid." Ballz smirked when Malakai frowned at the 'kid' label. "Play nice with the other boys and you won't get in trouble."

Malakai's lips thinned, but he nodded again. He shouldn't need the reassurance. Someone else watching him to make sure he didn't snap.

Better that than another chance he'd go too far.

The soft sound of running drew his attention and he turned as Shiori reached his side. Out of breath, with sweat beaded at her temples as if she'd taken a few sprints around the parking lot, wearing a hoodie too thick for the mild temperature.

Waving Ballz ahead, he drew her aside as buses began pulling out of the lot. "Hey, slugger. Getting some exercise in?"

"No, I'm looking for Brave. I got off the bus a few seconds after he did, but I still lost him." She scowled and looked around again. "Everyone's ready to go. Where the hell is he?"

"Depends *why* he took off." Malakai studied the parking lot, noting only a few of the newer bands remained. Brave didn't know them, so he wouldn't have stopped for a long goodbye.

Shiori tugged her bottom lip between her teeth. "I introduced him to his nephew. *Our* nephew. Valor and my sister's son."

"Oh..." Malakai tried to process the information, his mind tripping over all the missing details. "Did Valor... When he and your sister were together, was it consensual?"

"What?" Shiori blinked at him. Her lips parted. "Yes! Kyoko loved him. She was young, but... No, I guess there's no 'but'. What he did was *wrong*. I don't think he knew she was only fifteen."

"Still a 'but', sweetie." Malakai shook his head. One thing he and Brave had in common—most of the band did, as far as he knew—was sneakily finding out how old someone was before fucking them. Still heartless, but better than ending up with jailbait.

Excuses didn't matter when you messed with someone too young to *give* consent. And either way, he'd never been turned on by anyone who looked like a child. Shiori was the youngest woman he'd ever been drawn to, but she had a maturity to her. Her eyes told him she'd experienced life, despite the innocence that lingered because she hadn't lived *his* extravagant life.

Latching onto his hand, Shiori started toward the edge of the parking lot. "Doesn't matter. We have to find him."

"I need to know how upset he was." Malakai turned his hand in hers to pull her back to him. "Was he thoughtful? Angry? Being a total asshole?"

"He was…" Shiori's brow furrowed. She pressed her eyes shut. "Sad I think. He was happy to meet Hiro. To talk to him. But after we hung up he mentioned how much Hiro looks like Valor. And that he couldn't tell our nephew what a horrible person his father was."

Not good. If Brave had been pissed or lashing out, Malakai would check the closest bars. A few drinks, hitting on a waitress, and Brave would be his sweet old self again.

When reminders of Valor cut him deep, he needed to be alone. Or do some damage. With everyone else on the bus, the former was more likely.

Brave knew they were leaving soon. He wouldn't have gone far.

Malakai eyed the trees behind the bus. "Come with me."

The tightness of Shiori's fingers laced with his made his pulse erratic. He'd managed to keep their contact friendly. Quick hugs. A pat on the back. A brief press of his lips to her silky soft hair, which carried the fragrance of lilies floating on a vibrant stream.

She tested his control in ways no one else could. Brave came close, but Malakai had clearly failed at keeping his distance from the man.

With Shiori, failure wasn't an option. The tabloids would paint her as another groupie. She still hadn't had enough of a chance to prove herself. Hell, even walking with her, holding hands, could ruin her credibility as an independent, up-and-coming face in the fashion industry. Her connection to Danica was an asset.

Being too close to him wasn't.

"I'm sorry." He eased his hand from hers, clearing his throat as they reached the edge of the trees. "I should have warned you holding hands could—"

"I don't want to hear it." Shiori's jaw ticked. She shot him a narrow look. "This is about Brave, not my fragile career. Where do you think he went?"

He blinked at her, then inclined his head, looking over the tightly wound branches, like he had last night, only now the wall of trees was clear in the light. He walked along the edge of the parking lot and grinned as he found a path a few steps away from the back of the bus.

"This way." He started forward, glancing back once to make sure Shiori stuck close. She wouldn't get lost, it was a small expanse of woods between the parking lot and the highway, but even without snow, the frozen earth wasn't easy to walk on.

Shiori picked her way down the slight slope, widening her strides to cut ahead of him as she caught sight of Brave a few yards away, sitting on a boulder. Without a word, she wrapped her arms around Brave's neck.

Brave went still, looking up at Malakai uncertainly.

Malakai smirked. "Go ahead and tell her she can't hug you. I dare you."

"This isn't funny." Shiori eased back, cupping Brave's cheeks in her hands. "I don't know everything about Valor, but I can see talking about him isn't easy. And you don't have to. Hiro won't ask many questions."

"I know." Brave took her hands in his and lowered them, his lips curving to one side. "It just hit me how…unfair this will be for him. He deserves better."

"He *has* better."

"You're right." Brave inhaled roughly. "I needed a minute to get my head on straight. I didn't mean for you to worry."

"You don't get a say in that. I care about you." She leaned closer to Brave. "More than is smart."

Clearing his throat, Malakai stared off into the distance, a thin smile on his lips. No reason for him to be here anymore. "I'll head to the bus. Tell the band you won't be long."

A hand latched onto his wrist. Brave frowned at him. "You're not going anywhere. Not until you tell me why you slipped out of my bed this morning."

Shiori's eyes went wide.

Malakai groaned and tipped his head back, eyes shut.

And Brave let out a soft laugh. "No one is leaving. The three of us need to have a little chat."

Heat crept up the back of Shiori's neck as she tried to free her hand and Brave tugged her against his side. She shouldn't have come. Or, maybe she should have, but without revealing way too much.

She'd been hurting for Brave and needed him to know how she felt.

Even though it *wasn't* smart.

Even though nothing could come of it.

She had to tell him.

Apparently, he hadn't been lonely for long. His whole 'I'll wait for you' speech had been nice. Sweet and romantic enough to have her questioning if she really needed to stay away from him. No one had ever tempted her to veer off course like he did.

But he risked *nothing* with all his talk about wanting her. One way or another, he'd be fine.

With Malakai. Who he'd hated until recently. Who she was trying very hard to stay friends with while her emotions ran wild. She was allowed to have friends.

Only friends.

While they could have anything they wanted.

"You two should talk. After you let go of me, because I'm getting that urge to hit you again." She cut out each word like a knife carving ice. She needed to be cold. Detached. Her heart couldn't absorb any of this.

But she breathed a little easier when Brave released her.

He pushed off the rock, his soft words all that stopped her from leaving. "Little moon, I won't lie to you. I have no fucking clue what I'm doing."

"That's helpful." She folded her arms over her breasts, noting Malakai standing a few feet away, mirroring her posture. "If it's any consolation, you don't have to explain a thing to me. *We* can't happen."

Brave inclined his head. "Maybe not. But by that reasoning, neither can Malakai and I."

Malakai's eyes narrowed. "Is that so."

"I didn't like waking up to find you gone. And I do want to know why you disappeared." Brave rolled his shoulders. "But it's a good thing you did. Our performance on stage worked. The attention was off Shiori." He paused, his jaw hard. "All of it."

This she already knew, but clearly, Malakai didn't.

He glared at the ground, nodding slowly. "We stole the spotlight."

"Last night, yes." Brave's lips pulled into a thin smile. "And if we make a thing of our relationship, the media will be all over us. The fans will be watching us on stage. We'll be a huge story."

"And her joining the band will be nothing but a footnote." Malakai's tone turned bitter. "If that."

All right, this was ridiculous. She still felt like she'd been played, but the men didn't sound like they'd hooked up because they had the freedom to do whatever they wanted.

While she'd been setting up her limits, focusing on her goals, Malakai and Brave had grown closer. She'd been happy to see them getting along. Relieved as the tension between them faded away.

What if their feelings for one another had caught them off guard? Could she fault Brave for turning to a man he'd known for so long?

Being pissed was selfish. Expecting them to put their relationship on hold to further her career even more so.

I won't let that happen.

"The solution is very simple." She unfolded her arms and tucked her hands into the pocket of her borrowed hoodie. "I'll ask Sophie to find me another job."

"*No!*" Both Brave and Malakai shouted at the same time.

Her brow lifted. "Neither of you have a say."

Malakai stepped forward, his throat working as he swallowed. "You're right. But…" His lips curved slightly. "I'm usually the rational one—when I'm not throwing punches." He rolled his eyes as Brave touched the healing wound on his cheek with an exaggerated wince. "Any argument I have against you leaving will sound good. Might be convincing." Letting out a soft sigh, he took her hand. "And wouldn't be fair. You have to do what's best for you." He brushed his thumb lightly over her knuckles. "But I want you to stay."

Asking why would be opening a Pandora's box she wasn't prepared for. She should hug him and smile and go on with her day. Nothing had to change.

He and Brave were together.

She had plenty on her plate.

Complications were to be avoided at all costs.

The limits she'd set for herself, and had let others set on her, started feeling like a tight collar around her neck. Responsibility a leash constantly tugging her to heel.

Would a little taste of freedom be so bad?

Another one? She bit the tip of her tongue, thinking back on the night with Brave and Tate. She'd had her moment. Been wild and reckless and promised herself that would be enough.

But it hadn't been.

She didn't know what she wanted. From Brave *or* Malakai. Maybe all she needed was a chance to explore her feelings, even if she ended up right back where she'd started.

Focused on her goals. Building a solid career. Providing Hiro with a safe, happy life.

And maybe, just maybe, she could have both.

Both everything Hiro needed and some amazing experiences. Not both men. Of course not. A simple relationship was out of her reach right now, never mind...

Shaking her head, she shoved away all her jumbled thoughts and grinned at Malakai. "You're a great friend. I don't want to go either, but we have to—"

He put a finger over her lips, his eyes darkening. He didn't move closer. His finger left her lips, so he wasn't even touching her. But his gaze brushed her skin like a soft caress. Goosebumps rose along her flesh at his low laugh.

"We don't have to do anything." He shook his head and tucked a strand of hair behind her ear. "It's nice to know you consider me a 'great friend'."

Her mouth went dry as erratic butterflies danced around deep within. She'd been worried about Brave, but at least he played fair. She had no defense against Malakai. He wasn't playing at all.

"Good." She wet her bottom lip with her tongue. "That's good."

He gave her a slow smile. "I'll be only a friend until you ask for more. Deal?"

She nodded. Sounded like a *much* safer option. "Deal."

With that, he turned and started towards the bus, tossing back a casual, "Time to go."

Her body wouldn't move. Her brain had taken a hike. All the confusion was gone, leaving only deep desire burning low, like a kindling flame waiting to be stroked.

Brave eased close to her side, slipping one hand around her waist, his lips curving slightly as she glanced up at him.

"He's worse than any drug. I doubt anyone could resist him when he gives them a taste of that fucking high." He leaned close and kissed her cheek. "Good luck."

Chapter Twenty

Shiori's first time on the bus had felt like an adventure. Danica teased her about staring out the window like a kid, but she'd never been on a road trip, so she wanted to take in all the sights.

This trip, she'd started with the same excitement, but it didn't last. The drive was taking *forever*.

She checked her phone and slumped on the sofa, biting back the urge to demand how only three hours had passed. Asking 'Are we there yet?' was only funny the first time.

Tate had ruined the joke in the first twenty minutes. Jesse was a patient man, but after the fifth repeat, he'd threatened to pull over make Tate walk.

The drummer was now playing video games with Danica and Alder. They'd asked Shiori to join them, but the only game she'd ever played was *Disney Infinity* with Hiro. *Call of Duty* wasn't her thing. Besides, the trio had some fierce competition going on.

There had to be *something* for her to do. She wasn't a child. She could entertain herself.

Only, playing Candy Crush on her phone didn't cut it. And she'd been told to stop reading comments on the picture she'd shared of her and Danica. Within a few hours, social media had become a scary and overwhelming place. Wendy had even called on her lunch break, freaking out over some of the nasty things people were saying.

She hadn't been happy when Shiori begged her not to engage. In her words, as Shiori's best friend, it was her *job* to annihilate those assholes. But Danica had said to ignore them. After Shiori told Wendy to check Danica's page, her best friend let the subject drop. Danica had over a million followers. Some of her fans defended her and the conversations turned downright feral.

Dropping her useless phone on the sofa, Shiori stood and stretched, jumping when Alder shouted and punched his fist in the air. She snickered as both Danica and Tate playfully smacked him. At least they were having fun.

Ambling over to the kitchenette, she smiled at Connor, who was eating straight out of a big tub of double fudge ice cream that had his name written on the side in big letters. He winked at her and held out his spoon.

"Want some?" He shrugged when she shook her head. "Cool. Just don't worry about the labels. Jesse is all pissy about me eating 'Tate's' food. He figures we need shit separated, but Tate don't mind sharing, right, buddy?"

Not looking away from the TV, Tate shouted back. "Don't touch my cookies, Con!"

"I won't." Connor grinned at Shiori. "See?"

Shaking her head with a laugh, she clicked on the kettle, listening for any clue of what Brave and Malakai were doing in the back lounge. They'd disappeared in there hours ago and she hadn't wanted to disturb them. No one else seemed the least bit curious about their being alone and quiet for so long.

She pulled out a mug and rested her hip against the counter, careful to keep her tone light. "Do we need to worry about our lead singer?"

Connor's brow furrowed. "Because he's with Malakai? Naw, they ain't quiet when they fight. Quiet means they're working on music. It's hard to hear with the game blasting, but

Malakai's been strumming the same notes over and over for the past hour."

Holding still, she tried to block out the shouts, gunfire, and bombs behind her. Very faintly she made out the deep thrum of the guitar. She loved Winter's Wrath's music, but she'd never considered what went into making every song. From the lyrics to composing parts for every instrument—they were creating art, which must take hours. Maybe days.

She'd always assumed they created the music when they weren't on the road, which meant she'd only hear the finished product.

Glancing at the door that led to the bunks, she chewed her bottom lip uncertainly. "Do you think they'd mind if I watched them for a bit?"

"Not at all! Go on in, just don't talk to them if they're in the zone. Malakai and Alder get grumpy when they're yanked out, and Brave..." Connor ate another spoonful of ice cream, eyeing Alder thoughtfully. "Alder's not in there, so Brave's probably working on a darker piece. He hasn't been able to write shit in a long time. If he's onto something, you don't want to mess with that."

"Maybe going in at all would be a bad idea then." The music was more important than her curiosity. "Do you have a book or something I can read?"

"Unless you're into Penthouse letters, I got nothing for you." Connor's lips slanted. "But Brave has a dozen in his bunk and like five million on his reading thingy. You should ask him."

"I'm trying *not* to bother him."

"And I'm telling you, you won't be." He pointed firmly at the door. "Go."

Ugh, stubborn man. She shook her head and opened the door, closing it firmly behind her and padding softly down the walkway between the bunks. The noise from the TV was muffled in here, but she couldn't hear the guitar anymore. She approached the door, hearing Brave's voice beyond, tempered with frustration.

"I don't know what's wrong with me. The melody is on point, but…" He groaned. "It's missing something."

"More than the other instruments?" Malakai's tone was calm, as though he was trying hard to help, but didn't want to push. "You're stuck on these two songs. Maybe we should work on something else."

"There *is* nothing else."

A dull ache welled up in her chest at the defeat underlying Brave's words. This was more than frustration. Almost as though failing to finish the songs was tearing him apart.

But Malakai was with him. Malakai understood the process.

Nothing good will come from me going in there.

She turned to head back to the front lounge.

The door opened behind her. "I'll get you a drink. Maybe if you're more relaxed you'll—" Malakai smiled as she spun around to face him. "Hey, beautiful. You coming to keep us company?"

The way he said *"beautiful"* filled her with a warmth that radiated through her skin, like a sunrise within which couldn't be contained. His eyes took her in like he could see the glow.

Brave was right, the man was like a drug. An aphrodisiac she'd consumed in small doses at first because he'd diluted it so much. The only effect had been a nice little buzz.

Without warning, he'd upped the dosage. A taste wasn't enough.

And *"luck"* wouldn't save her.

Malakai arched a brow and moved closer. "Shiori, this is going to be a very long ride. I don't want you uncomfortable around me."

"I'm not."

"Really?" He reached up and brushed his fingers across her cheek. She shivered, biting her lip as sparks of desire danced along her nerves. He lifted her chin with two fingers, giving her a hooded look. "Ah, I see."

"See what?" She swallowed hard, pulse racing, palms going damp. Her body was not cooperating with her efforts to play it cool.

Little creases formed around Malakai's eyes as he smiled. "Are we still 'just friends', sweetheart?"

Just friends. Yes. That's safeish.

Sorta, in a not-the-least-bit kind of way.

But she managed to nod.

"Then no worries. Go sit with Brave. I'll bring you a drink as well."

A drink. Damn it, she'd forgotten her tea.

Hopefully, he'd bring her something stronger. Earl Grey wasn't gonna cut it.

Losing his touch almost tipped her off balance, but she managed to reach the room without making a fool of herself. Once inside, the bus decided to be helpful, jerking as the tires hit a rough patch of road.

She stumbled and Brave jumped up, latching onto her forearms to steady her.

"You all right?" Brave guided her to the sofa, his gold-brown eyes never leaving her face. "Are you overheated or did Malakai get to you?"

Folding her legs under her as she sat, she let out a breathless laugh. "You warned me he would."

"I did, didn't I?" Brave settled at her side and slipped one arm around her shoulders, tucking her close. "I should be jealous."

The fact that he wasn't seemed to confuse him. She rested her head on his shoulder, relieved that his touch wasn't driving her crazy. His presence still unsettled her, but the warmth that pooled in her core wasn't overwhelming. Almost as though her body had accepted he belonged here with her, while giving into her brain's firm *"This is all you can have."*

So long as Brave accepted that as well, she'd be fine.

A naïve, starry-eyed side of her wished he *wouldn't* accept, but she did her best to ignore that wistful little voice in her head.

Brave ran his hand lightly up and down her arm. "I'm glad you came back here. I'm trying to focus on the music. And our man is good at keeping me on track, but—"

She tipped her head up to frown at him. "'Our man'?"

"Mmhmm." Brave's lips curved slightly. "He's claimed us both. There's no point in fighting it."

"That's not how relationships work." She closed her eyes and sighed. "And I'm not in this equation. Neither of you can 'claim' me. But you *can* be together."

"Not without ruining your career."

"That's such bullshit." She scowled at his chuckle. "How is any of this funny?"

He kissed her temple and gave her a light squeeze. "It's not. You just don't swear often and it's cute."

Releasing a rough *Hmmph, she* drew away from him. The distance between them didn't feel right, but he wouldn't take her seriously without it. "Brave, I know what I need to do. I can't let myself fall for you. I can't let Malakai tempt me. And I *won't* let my ambitions ruin what's building between you."

Sliding a hand behind her neck, Brave leaned in, his steady gaze holding hers. "You can have everything, little moon. I won't pressure you, I promised I'd wait and I meant that."

"You didn't wait very long."

"You *are* jealous."

"No, I—" Ugh, this conversation was getting them nowhere. "I'm not like you. I won't have many opportunities. I *need* this one. And even *if* I believed I could be with you, in secret, without affecting my career, there's no way I could handle both you and Malakai."

He smiled as if she'd given him the answer he'd been hoping for. "I have no problem keeping this private."

"What exactly is 'this'? The three of us?" She shouldn't like the idea. It was completely insane. "Has anyone ever told you you're greedy?"

"Yes." He shrugged, as if the label didn't trouble him at all. "Would you rather I dump our man?"

"Stop calling him that!" All right, he had to not be touching her. His touch, along with this messed up fantasy he offered, was making it very hard to be rational.

But she didn't pull away.

Part of her wanted to be convinced.

"You didn't answer my question." Brave's tone deepened, taking on a rough edge, as though he didn't like what he was saying. "Do you want me to leave him?"

"No." She swallowed hard, torn between the longing to share what the men had and the knowledge that it was impossible. She glanced at the door, grateful Malakai hadn't heard their exchange. Brave even suggesting casting him aside made her heart hurt. "I can't believe you'd ask me that."

Brave stroked the side of her neck, wetting his bottom lip with his tongue in a subconscious way that brought all her attention to his mouth. "I knew you wouldn't say yes. You won't make me choose, any more than I'll make you."

"I don't have a choice at all." Which she hated a little more with every repeat. Being a model, she had to watch what she ate, but the odd treat wasn't forbidden. She had to dress a certain way in public, but she didn't have to burn all her leggings and comfy T-shirts.

What kind of life was she living if she denied herself any pleasure? Sure, she'd have to be careful, but how careful? So careful that she had to sit back and watch Brave and Malakai enjoy everything she wanted because she wasn't part of the band? Because she was a woman?

"Ease off, Brave." Malakai stepped into the room as Connor held the door for him. Setting the three glasses on a table at one end of the U-shaped sofa, Malakai eyed Shiori with concern. Then he frowned at Brave. "Don't make me tell you again."

Brave's eyes narrowed, but he slid away from Shiori. His lips parted. Then he shot Connor a pointed look.

Connor held his hands up. "I'm out."

He retreated, shutting the door behind him.

Malakai handed Shiori a glass of clear, bubbling liquid. He grinned when she glanced up at him. "It's white rum and diet sprite. One of Danica's new favorites. I thought you might enjoy it."

"Thank you." Shiori took a small sip, savoring the hint of spicy rum mixed with the subtly citrusy soda. "Mmm, Danica has good taste."

"That she does." Malakai picked up the other glasses, both filled with dark soda, likely whiskey and Coke. He held one out to Brave. "Stop glaring at me. I won't fight with you over this. You will give her space to decide what she wants from us."

How could he say '*us*' so casually? Her brow creased as she took another sip, trying to maintain her composure. "This has to be the weirdest conversation I've ever had."

"I'm not surprised." Malakai smiled at her over the rim of his glass. "If it helps, the conversation is over. For now." He sat on the sofa beside Shiori, reclining and resting his ankle on his knee. "Brave's finally made some progress. Ask nicely and maybe he'll sing for you."

She turned to Brave, Malakai's calm putting her at ease. No decisions had to be made right this instant. And Brave had to focus on the music.

Fluttering her eyelashes, she gave him her sweetest smile. "Please?"

Rubbing his jaw, Brave met her eyes with a wry grin. "Damn, karma works fast. All right, little moon. I'll give you an exclusive preview. Maybe you can help us figure out what's missing."

He rose from the sofa, took a swig of his drink, then cleared his throat. His whole bearing shifted, as if the music had taken hold, bringing him somewhere just out of reach. The same way he looked on stage, surrounded by thousands under blinding lights.

His voice held the same power as he sang.

Another hit could kill me,
Seeping in my veins,
Warping me into the unknown.
I still let you in.
Feel your fangs slip deep,
Give me some fucking more.
Delicious poison is all I'll ever need.

A heart that could die for you,
Grows lifeless and cold.
Another offering to make you mine,
Sweet venom in my blood,
Smiling as you rip me apart,
This is the death that they call love.

Her pulse slowed, following the hypnotic rhythm, as though she couldn't breathe unless he did. This song wasn't like any she'd ever heard from the band. There was a movie she'd seen once with music of the same haunting quality. A chill skittered down her spine. She shivered as goosebumps spread over her arms.

Brave's voice affected her in a way she couldn't understand. Whether deep and seductive, a luring whisper, or a gritty battle cry, he had a talent for trapping any who listened to him in the emotion he conveyed.

This song held a twisted undercurrent of lust. Irresistible. Alluring. The chill evaporated as heat pooled in her core and she clenched her thighs as he finished the final verse.

His wicked grin proved he knew exactly what he'd done to her. He took another sip of his drink and licked his lips. "Not bad?"

"I don't think your ego needs any more stroking." Her cheeks flamed at his sultry look. Why had she used the word 'stroke'? There was no way it could be innocent between them. She quickly changed the subject. "Different from your usual style, but I love it." She tugged at her bottom lip, searching for the name of the movie it reminded her of. "Did you ever see that Anne Rice movie? With the vampire who plays the violin?"

"Queen of the Damned?" Brave's brow furrowed at her nod. "I haven't seen that in a long time. It's not *too* much like that music, is it?"

"I know what she's talking about. Korn does some of the songs I think, but we've got a different sound." Malakai tilted his head to one side. "We might switch up fangs for syringe, though. The song has an interesting double meaning. Could be about addiction to love or drugs."

"Fangs are sexier." Brave sat sideways on the sofa, facing both her and Malakai. "The rest can be implied without spelling it out."

Malakai's lips thinned. "Or you'll have people thinking it's about a vampire."

Shiori bit back a smile as the two went back and forth, debating lyrics, whether Alder should sing the chorus, and lastly, whether they should do an acoustic version first. They weren't exactly arguing, but their passion was contagious. She wished she could add something useful to the discussion, but she was happy just being here to witness art in the making.

A much messier process than she'd ever imagined.

Finally, Brave turned to her. "What do you think?"

Her eyes widened. Of which topic? They'd been jumping from one to the other so fast she had whiplash. "Well…fangs *are* sexier than syringes. And there are always new vampire movies. Maybe they'll use you for the soundtrack."

"That would be fucking cool." Brave polished off his drink. "What do you say, Grimm? Shall we tempt producers with our sexy new song?"

Shaking his head, Malakai laughed. "No objections here. But unless you're doing it *acapella*, we need to get some notes down."

Brave gestured to Malakai's guitar, resting against the sofa. "You're up, stud. Show her what you've got."

Slinging his guitar strap over his shoulder, Malakai adjusted his guitar, strumming it once before glancing over at her. "This is the raw core of the melody, but it will give you a good idea of how it will sound with the pieces in place."

Knees drawn to her chest, she nodded. Her gaze followed his fingers moving over the strings as every note vibrated through her. Malakai's expression was intense, but he handled the guitar effortlessly, as though it was part of him.

Time breezed by as she listened to him, then both men together, go over the song again and again. The repetition never got boring. Every miniscule change, their explanations of how it made the song better, fascinated her.

But being with them did something to her she hadn't expected.

Sex and relationships weren't brought up again. They were all simply together, enjoying each other's company like this was where they belonged. All that had been so scary before seemed easy. They weren't being too reckless or too careful. This wasn't an insane world where she didn't fit in. She had her place.

What they all wanted was within her reach.

All she had to do was take it.

Chapter Twenty-One

Almost two full days on the bus and Malakai was torn between relief that they'd finally gotten to New York, and the strangest urge to tell Jesse to keep driving for another twenty hours. Or more.

He usually got so tired of being around the band after a long drive he'd ghost the second the bus parked. Spending all his time with Shiori and Brave had been different.

Testing his willpower, giving him blue balls, kinda of crazy-making, but so much more. He already missed claiming the back lounge for hours, watching Brave write lyrics while Shiori snuggled up next to him. Or cleaning his guitar while Shiori read one of the books Brave had gotten her into—they both enjoyed high fantasy, how about that?

Shiori's head on Brave's lap, Brave stroking her hair between turning the pages of his own book...

Watching them brought a sense of longing and tenderness and protectiveness Malakai had never felt all at once. More and more he craved what seemed so natural. The three of them fit perfectly.

Shiori had been right to point out that this wasn't how relationships usually worked, but they weren't in a usual situation. Besides, they didn't have to look far to see how three people could share a stronger love than most couples ever knew.

Alder, Danica, and Jesse faced challenges, but they'd found a balance. They weren't exactly hiding, and yet, they managed to keep their relationship from becoming a focus of the media.

Not that difficult, actually. Malakai knew famous singers whose fans thought they were single, even though the guy had two kids and a wife of ten years, or the chick was engaged to her manager. Sure, when shit hit the fan the tabloids dug up every bit of dirt they could find, but the spotlight didn't own their entire lives.

On the bus, exposure was limited. Shiori had relaxed, taking silly selfies with him and Brave—and the other members of the band—and opening up about her hopes and dreams. She'd started with a sort of hero-worship for Danica, wanting to follow in her footsteps, but recently started talking about her role in the band in a different way. She had ideas for music videos that were really cool, and showed them pictures on DeviantArt that would make for wicked album covers. She laughed every time she made a suggestion, like she had no faith in her abilities, but her confidence was growing.

The point was, she was invested in the band's success. She wanted to continue working with them, in any way she could be useful. Even if he wasn't falling for her, he'd have been excited to see what she had to offer.

Still sitting in the back lounge, Malakai sighed as he picked up his guitar and carefully laid it in the black velvet lined case. Accepting his feelings for her made the trip ending even harder. He hated uncertainty. Couldn't stand losing control over the next step he'd have to make.

But back in the real world, he couldn't keep Shiori close. Even Brave had realized no matter how sweet and seductive he was, she had to decide if being with them was worth the risk.

Because, like it or not, there was a risk. One they didn't have to face.

The door to the back lounge opened. Jesse slipped in, a knowing smile on his lips.

"Figured I'd find you in here." Jesse folded his arms over his chest and leaned against the door frame. "Everyone's heading to the hotel. We'll be here for a few days—we're doing three shows in the area—so rooms are covered. Reese haggled for a nicer hotel, but we only have four rooms."

Malakai frowned, doing the math. "You're obviously staying with Alder and Danica."

"Yes. And I stuck Tate with Connor. Which should be fun." Jesse's lips quirked. "I put you and Brave together. I figured you wouldn't mind."

"I don't." Malakai's frown deepened. "So Shiori's alone?"

"Officially, she's sharing with Danica, but it's in her contract that she never has to share a room at all. Reese was grumbling this morning about Sophie demanding a separate room for both Shiori and Danica, and how 'the woman' knows Danica doesn't need one." Jesse smirked. "The details are boring, but the suites Reese is putting us in? Fucking awesome. Two executive suites. You guys have junior ones, but they're still nice."

"Better than the bus." He didn't really mean that. Leaning against the side of Shiori's bunk, speaking softly to her as she fell asleep, was worth crawling into a rectangular box and sleeping on a thin mattress.

Fine, they'd be on the road again at the end of the week, but it was going to be a very long fucking week.

"Mmhmm." Jesse smirked, looking him over. "And I thought you'd be happy, having Brave to yourself."

Malakai chuckled darkly. "Sure. Keeping him trapped in our room will be the highlight of my life."

"True. And I don't envy you." Jesse shrugged and pushed away from the doorframe. "But you might not have to. Either way, time to pack your shit and get in the van."

Within ten minutes, Malakai was hauling his guitar and luggage off the bus and into the van. The roadies had already taken off, staying in a nearby motel. The band made sure they were comfortable, and got some time to wind down. Not all bands could afford to get their roadies rooms, but over the years Winter's Wrath had worked it into the budget.

Skull and Ballz would stay on the bus, but that was their choice. Ever since Brave had bought the new one, they spent all their free time doing maintenance. With Skull he kinda got it. The man made Malakai's protective urges seem negligent. He wanted the bus running perfectly. Needed to control who came close to the vehicle where the band spent most of their time.

Ballz was still an unknown. Shrink and bodyguard by day, mechanic when he could be doing other shit?

As if Malakai's thoughts had called him, Ballz approached before he could climb into the backseat of the van.

"How's that homework I gave you going?"

Malakai cringed. He wouldn't lie. He hadn't followed through enough to get passing grades. "My brother is dead. I'm having a hard time finding anything I did making a damn difference."

Inclining his head, Ballz smiled. "Good."

"Good?" Malakai blinked and shook his head. "How the fuck is that 'good'?"

"You haven't spent as much time going over what happened as I'd like, but your response tells me it's been on your mind. Even subconsciously is progress." Ballz's shoulders lifted dismissively. "Nothing I say will bring him back. But how you perceive your relationship, your guilt, might change."

The man was too smart for his own good. And for Malakai's peace of mind. He sighed and leaned against the van. "The guilt is what's fucking with me."

Ballz's lips quirked. "Like I said. Progress."

Those words stuck with Malakai long after he squeezed into the backseat beside Tate, trying to give the kid his full attention while the drummer bounced in place, shifting from topic to topic so fast Malakai couldn't keep up. Tate didn't do well on long road trips. He got twitchy and needed to be set loose ASAP. Which always freaked Malakai out.

Best case scenario, Tate would find a hot older woman to entertain. Sometimes he found a good one who rocked his world and didn't leave him feeling used. Not that Tate would ever admit he felt like a piece of meat. He just got moody and went on the prowl for the next hookup. Like each new one could erase the last.

In a way, Tate had stepped into the shoes of Malakai's brother, but watching over him was a form of torture. He couldn't stop Tate from getting hurt. He could only be there to put the pieces back together.

But there were pieces left to put together. And in the end, that was all Malakai could ask for.

The van pulled into the underground parking of the hotel and everyone got out. Except Brave and Alder. Brave latched onto Malakai's arm, going still when Alder sat there, watching them.

Brave cleared his throat. "I didn't hear everything you said to Ballz, but I caught a bit. About your brother."

Jaw clenched, Malakai looked down at Brave's hand. They were intimate enough the restraint shouldn't bother him, but with this subject on the table? He needed the option to leave.

Air came a little easier when Brave released him. Malakai folded his arms over his chest. "What of it?"

Brave sat back and sighed. "When shit got really bad, I brought up your brother. Said you could have mine. That was fucking low."

"I never told you my brother was dead."

"You didn't have to. I knew he'd been on drugs. That something bad happened. Knew enough to get why you're so protective of Tate." Brave lowered his gaze, pressing his eyes shut. "I'm sorry."

"Don't be." Malakai caught Alder's eye, returning his slight nod. There was a reason Alder had stuck around. He needed to hear this. "Just do better."

He climbed out of the van, grabbing his guitar and suitcase, trying to get out of there fast so the brothers could talk.

But he couldn't avoid hearing Alder's heavy sigh. Or the way his voice broke when he finally spoke up.

"Brave, I-I need to tell you something." Alder sounded on the edge of falling apart. Like he needed his brother, but wasn't sure he should. "Can we leave our stuff here and take a walk?"

The urge to stay sliced through Malakai with every step he took away from the van, but he forced himself to keep moving. Alder wasn't his brother, any more than Tate was. He couldn't fix the mistakes he'd made by hovering over the two youngest band members. Being protective was one thing, but he couldn't attack anyone who upset them. Who hurt them.

Especially not Brave.

The man was trying to be there for his brother. He wasn't perfect, but he had the chance to 'do better'. Which was the only advice Malakai could give him.

He wanted to keep Brave from fucking up. From damaging the bond he'd finally built with Alder. He wanted to show him how to earn his brother's trust. And keep it.

Because once he lost it, he might not get another chance.

Chapter Twenty-Two

New York had a pulse unlike anywhere Alder had ever been. Those who lived there carried the rapid beat, always having somewhere they needed to be right that second. One glance and the tourists stuck out, off from the allegretto pace, wide-eyed and out of rhythm. He'd heard it took years to come off as a 'real' New Yorker.

Alder loved the city, and he'd been here often enough to walk down a street without getting dirty looks for slowing people down, but he still didn't fit in.

Which was becoming the norm for him. Some days he didn't feel like he fit in his own skin. But being here gave him a good distraction from the quicksand of memories inside his skull.

Brave, being the new Brave, walked by his side silently. Once he would have filled the silence with cutting remarks if he'd agreed to come at all. When they'd started mending their relationship, he'd done a complete 180, always careful, always asking how Alder was. What could he do for him? Was there anything he needed—anything at all?

Neither the man Brave had been, nor the one he'd tried to become, were his brother. Alder hadn't known how to be around that man.

But this guy right here? This one he could live with. He joked around with Alder like he wasn't fucking fragile. The rare times things got serious, he really listened. He didn't show concern out of misplaced guilt. He actually cared.

Turning a corner off the main street with the thinning crowds, Alder slowed. He shoved his hands in the pockets of the thick, black wool jacket all the guys—except Brave—teased him about. Hell, he'd gotten it free after doing a Kenneth Cole ad. And it was fucking sharp.

He glanced over at Brave. "I don't look like a tool, do I?"

Stopping short, Brave stared at him. "Huh?"

"The jacket..." All right, starting with a safe subject seemed kinda lame now. He shook his head and kept walking. "Never mind."

"Alder." Brave caught up with him, putting a hand on his shoulder and maneuvering him off the sidewalk, in front of an apartment complex. His forehead creased as he studied Alder's face. "You don't look like a tool. Connor doesn't even own a jacket—the dumbass is gonna freeze in that rank hoodie he always wears. And Tate wears a bomber jacket that went out of style before he was born. Seriously, you're fine."

"Okay." Alder inhaled roughly. Dropped his gaze to Brave's crazy, knee length boots. They seemed to be made of more metal than leather. He pressed his eyes shut and forced himself to stop dodging the subject. "My jacket's not why I wanted to talk to you."

Brave's lips quirked. "I figured as much."

Alder swallowed hard. Damn it, why was this so difficult? Wasn't like Brave didn't know he was fucked up. Was Alder's damage that big of a deal?

Their resident head shrink, Ballz, seemed to think so. They'd had a few long discussions which resulted in a *'In my professional opinion, you need to see a psychiatrist.'*

Those words had freaked Alder out. Ballz explaining he'd made the same suggestion to soldiers he'd worked with didn't help. They were *soldiers*. Alder wouldn't even consider what he'd gone through being on the same level as men and woman who got shot at every day.

Ballz had three words for him.

"Focus on you."

Whatever that meant.

"You know, you're a lot like dad in some ways." Brave held up a hand when Alder frowned at him. "Not in being a judgmental bastard who doesn't know how to love. He wasn't always like that. He and Mom are toxic together. Because he's so cold, she threw herself into her work. Because she's calculating and obsessive, he became completely detached."

"Not hearing how I'm like him."

"You get lost in your own head. I remember when I was a kid—you were still in diapers—and Dad came home early from work. Grandpa had just passed away. He sat in the kitchen for hours, drinking coffee and staring at the wall. He didn't cry. His jaw just hardened whenever anyone came in the room." Brave's lips thinned. "Mom found out from his sister that night. And she started yelling at him. Telling him he was selfish for not telling her. He just sat there, nodding. Then he got up and walked out." He let out a bitter laugh. "I started crying. Valor told me to shut up because I was upsetting our mother. I loved Grandpa—he was the one who got me listening to old jazz music, used to sing with me and tell me I had some good chops."

"I wish I'd gotten a chance to know him." Alder rubbed his jaw, trying to remember either of their parents ever discussing their grandfather. "What happened when Dad came back?"

"He apologized to Mom. Didn't take a single day off work. We went to the funeral a week later and it was like he'd completely shut off his emotions. He checked to make sure *Mom* was okay. That all the arrangements ran smoothly." Brave rolled his shoulders and sighed. "You do that. You worry about everyone else. You'll focus on details, on distractions, and refuse to deal with your own feelings."

Alder nodded slowly, fidgeting with the buttons of his jacket. He lifted his head to meet Brave's eyes. "That night…what happened on stage. I remember."

Brow furrowed, Brave seemed to absorb his words. His lips parted and the color left his skin. "Jesus, Alder. When… How much…" He pressed his lips shut and put his hands on Alder's shoulders. "Tell me everything."

'Everything' was a lot. But Alder told him. More than he'd told Danica and Jesse—he hadn't wanted to hurt them with the painful shit. More than he'd told Ballz, because opening up to a shrink was nerve-racking.

Needing his big brother might be childish, but, as fucked up as their relationship had been for years, Alder never forgot who'd been there for him when he was little. Who'd taken care of his skinned knees and taught him how to throw a ball. Who'd explained what sex was and didn't bat an eye when Alder confessed he was bisexual. The one person who'd always been family.

Alder's eyes burned with unshed tears as he described the moment the knife had sliced into him. How hot his blood felt pooling around his body. Being scared for Brave while all his strength drained away.

Then darkness. Not a peaceful darkness, but one that trapped him. He couldn't move. Couldn't breathe. He knew he was dying.

At one point, he'd thought he was dead.

No bright light to walk toward.

Just nothing.

A cage of nothingness, where he could hear the people he loved speaking softly, but they were so far away. He was sure he'd slept, but when he was close to consciousness he imagined his body being placed in a coffin. Lying there, aware as he was lowered into the ground. Screaming without a sound as he was left in a grave, sensing his body rotting around him.

He shuddered as he tore himself away from the morbid images that were still so clear. "I don't sleep because the nightmares are so fucking bad. I'm being stabbed again. Being buried. Sometimes both if I can't wake up. The worst thing is I don't have to be asleep to see it. Without warning, I'll just…"

He ground his teeth. "When I'm distracted I'm usually fine. I've been trying to keep busy, but when people ask why I'm being weird it reminds me there's something wrong with me."

"Alder, there's nothing..." Brave shook his head and pulled Alder into a tight hug. "Fuck, I'm glad you told me."

"When I die, I want to be fucking cremated, okay?" Alder released a shaky laugh, certain he sounded crazy. "Let's not dig too deep into how that would feel if I'm not really dead."

Brave's grip tightened. "If that's what you need to hear..."

Alder rested his head on his brother's shoulder. "I don't know what I need to hear. I just needed to tell someone. And I feel like an asshole for laying all this on you. Danica and Jesse know most of it, but not...not everything."

"I'm always here if you need to talk." Brave rubbed his arms and shifted back a bit to meet his eyes. "What happened was bad. Really bad. I don't think you're an asshole. I think you're trying to figure out how to deal with this in a way that's best for everyone else."

"Maybe..." Getting everything out was a relief, but fucking exhausting. He rolled his eyes and shrugged. "This is gonna sound stupid, but I really want to change the subject."

"Doesn't sound stupid. You call all the shots, bro." Brave hooked an arm around his neck and gave him a loud kiss on the cheek. "Not sure if I'm supposed to ask, but have you talked to Ballz?"

"Yeah. He suggested some coping mechanisms. I'm doing yoga with Danica when we have a chance. And breathing stuff when I freak out." Alder left out the whole seeing a psychiatrist thing. They'd discuss that later. Right now, he was done. "I hear you're working on a new song?"

Brave frowned slightly, but he inclined his head. "Two. And they're awesome, but..."

"Still missing something?"

"Not sure what, though." Brave's arm slipped from Alder's shoulders as they turned back the way they'd came. They had to catch a cab to the hotel. Hopefully, someone had brought their stuff up to their room. He was fucking beat.

On the crowded street near Time Square, they worked their way through the press of bodies, eyes on the road. Alder spotted a cab and nudged Brave, but Brave held up a finger, cocking his head to one side as though listening to something.

His face lit up and he took off with a wave for Alder to follow.

Where the fuck is he going?

At the corner of the street, a tall black man in a hoodie was playing the violin, a blue ball cap on the ground by his feet for change. A small circle of people had formed around him, and children rushed forward, tossing dollar bills into the hat. The man flashed each one a smile without slowing the wicked pace of the bow slashing across the strings.

The song he played was *The Arena* by Lindsey Stirling. Alder had started listening to her stuff after Tate showed him the video, which was awesome. He now had all her albums. Not that he'd shared that bit of information with anyone.

Dubstep and metalcore didn't mix.

Stepping right through the crowd, Brave pulled out his wallet. He flashed a hundred-dollar bill.

The violinist eyed him, then shook his head as he finished mid-note. "Dude, I'm not taking your money."

Brave frowned at the bill in his hand. "Why the hell not?"

"You're Brave Trousseau."

More people gathered, some recognizing Brave and letting out little screams. Alder pulled his hood up, hoping they'd miss him. He didn't mind the attention on stage, but it always weirded him out in the street.

"I am." Brave held out his hand. "And you are?"

"Dariel Boyd." The man straightened, holding his violin loosely at his side. "I do a cover of your song, Subsist. Be cool if I could play it for you."

"Be even cooler if I could sing along." Brave shot the man a sly smile when his eyes went wide. "Then I've got an offer you can't refuse."

Dariel smirked, turning the mic toward Brave. "Music first. Talk after."

Folding his arms over his chest, Alder leaned against the closest wall, not sure what should worry him more. His brother quoting the *Godfather* to a random street performer.

Or what Reese's reaction would be to whatever this 'offer' was.

All the chaos in Brave's mind settled the second he heard the violin. A huge claw still dug into his chest as he tried to absorb everything Alder had told him, but Alder wanted a distraction. He'd asked about the new songs.

Brave couldn't fix what had happened to his brother. He couldn't take away the scars, or the nightmares. He couldn't erase the memories he'd hoped Alder would never have to deal with.

But he could give him the music.

This wasn't the first time Brave had considered adding a violin to the band, but he'd never gone further than watching a few popular YouTube videos to see if anyone clicked. When none did, he moved on with his life.

The way Dariel played grabbed Brave by the throat and made it hard to breathe. He only got this excited when a song came together he knew would be a hit. The more he heard, the more he felt like he'd found that missing piece.

Fucking crazy to get this worked up about a guy he'd just met. Especially since he wasn't thinking with his dick.

Stupid thing had to be broken though, because Dariel was fucking hot. But Brave didn't waste any time wondering why his body didn't react to the other man. Fans would. They would lose their minds the second he made his debut.

Yes, he was already thinking that far ahead. Dariel obviously liked Winter's Wrath. He knew their music. He played their songs like he belonged on that goddamn stage.

People all around had their phones out, recording him and Dariel as they worked their fucking magic. By the end of the day, Winter's Wrath's fan page would be filled with questions about 'the new guy'. Probably asking when they'd see him again.

And Brave hated disappointing his fans.

He set that aside as one of the points he'd bring up to Reese if she—for some crazy reason—didn't understand his vision.

When the song ended, people started shouting requests. He smiled as he leaned close to the mic, using his sly, sultry tone to get their attention. "I hope you've all got tickets to our show tomorrow night!"

Everyone cheered as if they did, but he counted only about a dozen people who were definitely hardcore fans. The rest were caught up in the excitement. Which made them *potential* fans.

"Now if you don't mind, I need to steal this man for a sec." Brave turned off the mic and grinned at Dariel. "You're fucking incredible."

"Thank you." Dariel snatched up his bill stuffed ball cap and emptied the money into the violin case laying open on his amp. "Look, you stopping to sing with me was…*amazing*. But I don't know what you could offer that I'd—"

"I want you to join the band." Brave held up his hand when Dariel looked ready to interrupt. "Hear me out. I've been looking for a way to add another layer to our sound. You're it. We're working on a new album and the violin would give the music the depth it's been missing."

Dariel nodded slowly. "I can see that. But I'm gonna have to pass."

This couldn't be happening. Brave pressed his eyes shut, rubbing his temples as he tried to make sense of what Dariel had just said.

Stepping up to Brave's side, Alder placed a hand on his shoulder as he addressed the violinist. "Hi, Dariel. I'm Alder. The sane Trousseau brother. And I understand this all sounds nuts."

"Just a little." Dariel placed his violin on top of the money in the case. "If you're holding auditions, I'm so there. But like this?" He motioned around him, at the thinning crowd, then to himself. "To be blunt, I'm working my ass off for a real chance to get noticed. I have a good following on YouTube. I've had offers. I took a look at the contracts and said no because they wanted me to change too much."

"We're not asking you to change." Brave looked over at Alder, who was shaking his head as though to tell Brave he needed to back off.

Dariel wasn't saying 'No' to Alder, so maybe he should let them talk. So long as his brother figured out how to close the deal.

"I appreciate that." Daniel's lips spread into a warm smile that would drive Winter's Wrath fans out of their minds. Then he sighed. "And I'm tempted, but your manager won't go for it. I'm not getting my hopes up for nothing."

Alder approached Dariel slowly, his tone low. "I get it. Two metal heads coming at you like this doesn't seem legit. And we do have to work things out with our manager. But she trusts Brave's instincts. Consider this another offer. I'll leave you my number. We're here for a few days. If you want to come meet the rest of the band and take a look at the contract, give me a call."

Brave was damn proud of his brother—he was handling this like a pro. He coughed to cover a laugh when Alder stuffed his hands in his pockets, coming up empty. No matter how often Jesse got on his case about carrying a pen and a sharpie for signatures, he always forgot.

Shooting Brave an amused grin, Dariel pulled his phone out of the pocket of his hoodie. "Just give me the number, man. I got a sharpie if any of your fans, still hanging around, want you to sign something."

Thanking him, Alder recited his number, his expression curious. "I don't get many requests to sign stuff unless we're at an event. Do you?"

"Sometimes, if people follow my channel." Dariel leaned close to Alder, his lips curving at the edges. "Usually some hot twink wanting some action though."

Alder's cheeks reddened as he nodded. "Yeah, I can see that."

"Damn, you're perfect." Brave watched Dariel beckon the fans over, moving to his side as they surrounded Alder. "You know how to work a crowd and you have no shame."

"I'm a pansexual guy that got kicked out of the army a year before DADT was repealed. I give zero fucks about what people think of me." Dariel's expression hardened. "That gonna be an issue?"

"Absolutely not." Brave knew Reese liked keeping their sexuality low-key, but when his relationship with Malakai wasn't a threat to Shiori's career, he wouldn't fucking hide. No way in hell would he let anyone tell Dariel he couldn't be out and proud. "I get this is all happening fast—"

"Nothing's happening at all yet." Dariel gave him a sideways glance, a devilish smile on his lips. "I got your brother's number. Give me yours too. I'll call one of you tonight."

"Sure." Brave put his number in Dariel's phone as the fangirls started his way. "Not sure why you need both."

Dariel chuckled, leaning close to whisper in Brave's ear. "I've never done brothers before. Shy boy over there might need some convincing."

Well then... Brave laughed and shook his head, turning his attention to the fans. On the cab ride, he repeated Dariel's words, figuring Alder would find them as funny as he did.

The band needed Dariel. Let him believe he might get laid if he showed up to check out the contract. Maybe he'd like Connor. The guy sucked dick like a porn star. They only needed a chance to prove the violinist would be fucking set if he joined Winter's Wrath.

Glaring out the window, Alder let out a sound of disgust. "He's just looking for some action."

Inclining his head, Brave folded his hands behind his head. "Then he'll fit right in."

Chapter Twenty-Three

A nice big fancy room. New clothes from a spontaneous shopping trip. The day had been a Cinderella story, Fairy Godmother and all. Shiori still couldn't believe Sophie had come all the way to New York just to congratulate her on hitting ten thousand likes on her fanpage.

The gift Sophie had given her to celebrate—while they were at a restaurant so expensive Shiori was afraid to order water—was still in the elegant, dark brown gift bag, surrounded by tissue paper. Where it would be safe.

As soon as Shiori saw the purse, she fell in love. The blue and green checkered design with the black and red diagonal stripes giving it an edgy racecar style. The leather was soft and sleek and the sporty look would fit with all the colorful new clothes she'd gotten.

But she'd heard of the Louis Vuitton brand. The purse had to be expensive. Ducking into the bathroom, she'd Googled the purse on her phone. When she could breathe again, she returned to the table and told Sophie, as politely as possible, that there was no way she could accept the gift.

When Danica let out a heavy sigh, Shiori was confused, but after the following, hour-long lecture Sophie gave about how her appearance reflected on the agency, on how Diverse Faces models deserved the best and she should get used to expensive gifts…

Yeah, Danica had probably gotten the same talk a time or two. The passion and dedication Sophie showed made Shiori feel bad for even *considering* rejecting the gift.

She was forgiven. And given a box of chocolates and a fluffy white teddy bear.

"Now these you shouldn't expect often, but I'm so proud of how you handled the press. Besides, I thought you'd like him." Sophie leaned in close, as though sharing a secret, but spoke loud enough for Danica to hear. *"I have one just like this. He travels everywhere with me."*

Making her way to her bed, Shiori picked up the teddy bear and hugged it tight. The bear didn't scare her like the purse did. His pudgy little face, tiny blue nose, and soft white fur were exactly what she needed.

She'd never felt so alone.

After the whirlwind of a day with Danica, she'd been eager for some quiet, but before long she was missing the bus. Sure, she'd been bored on the trip at first, but then she'd gotten used to being around the band. To squeezing in next to Brave in the morning, teasing him about being grumpy while grabbing an apple from the fruit basket. Being gifted with a sleepy smile as he poured them both some coffee. He'd get up early just to spend time with her and she loved every minute.

Yesterday morning they'd taken their coffee outside and he'd put his arm around her as they looked over the snow dusted trees surrounding the small pit stop on all sides. The temperature outside had dropped considerably, but she didn't feel the chill misting her breath.

Then she'd spent a few hours curled up next to Malakai while he watched crime dramas. Which had never been her thing, but his reaction to her not having seen *Pulp Fiction* peaked her curiosity. He hadn't gotten upset when she'd fallen asleep, with her head on his lap, halfway through the movie. Instead, he asked what she wanted to watch and grinned when she told him she wanted to try another of his favorites.

He put on *Training Day*, which she absolutely loved. After that, he seemed to know exactly what she'd enjoy. The time flew by with her finding a whole new kind of film genre to get into while he answered all her silly questions—without making her feel silly for asking. She learned about different directors, movies based on books, and Malakai's passion for both.

Like with Brave, there was some tenderness, but both men seemed to be taking her lead. Which was sweet. But frustrating. Not that she'd expected more while they were stuck on the bus with the band.

Thankfully, she'd had plenty of other distractions.

Tate had tried to teach her how to play *Call of Duty*. Alder explained how the messy scribbles on his notepad would become music, laughing when she commented on him being so patient and telling her he'd considered becoming a teacher.

Connor showed her how to exercise on the bus and got her to take a run with him a few times when they stopped to get some air or fill up on gas. Jesse told her funny tour stories and gave her tips on how to get a good night's sleep in a moving vehicle.

And Danica? Danica was a godsend. She helped Shiori interact with her new fans online. Showed her how to take a good selfie, explaining angles and lighting and how to decide if the photo would interest her followers. She suggested cute captions and ways Shiori could share the experience of touring so her fan base would feel closer to her.

Just that morning, when they'd been getting dressed, ready for her to make her first appearance, beside Danica, in New York, Danica had done her makeup, smiling at her as she told Shiori she had such beautiful eyes. Tears had ruined all her work, but she'd hugged Shiori, dried her tears, and let a few fall herself when Shiori said Danica reminded her of her sister.

Kyoko had always made Shiori feel beautiful. Special.

"She sounds like she was an amazing young woman." Danica dabbed Shiori's eyes with a tissue, then did the same to her own. *"I can't replace her, but I've never had a sister. And I feel like I've been given one now."*

Damn it, she almost wished she'd accepted Danica's offer to stay with her tonight. This room was huge. And too quiet. Like a great big reminder that she'd chosen to keep doing things the way she always had. By herself.

Danica wasn't the only one who'd offered to keep her company. They'd met Tate on the elevator and he'd told her to hang out in his room. He and Connor were trying out a new game on a live vid. Tempting, but she really sucked at video games. She didn't need public humiliation to prove it.

The two people she really wanted to spend time with hadn't offered. No surprise, she'd made it clear she wasn't ready for them. That she needed time to think.

Fifty-four minutes alone in her room and she was tired of thinking. Tired of looking at the clock and wondering if she should sleep until someone gave her something to do.

She pulled out her phone and sat on the edge of her bed. Should she text Brave or Malakai?

Opening a new message, she added them both.

SHIORI: HEY! BUSY?

Within seconds, both replied.

MALAKAI: I DO BELIEVE YOU JUST SAVED BRAVE'S LIFE.

BRAVE: NOT AT ALL, SWEETIE. ... HELP!

Snickering, she rested against the mountain of pillows.

SHIORI: ARE YOU TWO FIGHTING?

BRAVE: NOT EXACTLY... ALL RIGHT, SO MAYBE I'M A HYPOCRITE. I GAVE YOU SHIT ABOUT GIVING OUT YOUR NUMBER. BUT WE HAVE A NEW VIOLINIST! NOT MY FAULT HE WANTS TO HIT THIS.

MALAKAI: YOU ARE SITTING NEXT TO ME. I WILL HURT YOU.

SHIORI: LOL! YOU'RE BOTH TOO CUTE. I'LL LEAVE YOU ALONE TO WORK THIS OUT.

BRAVE: NO!

MALAKAI: NO!

BRAVE: ALL JOKES ASIDE, YOU DOING OKAY?

She licked her bottom lip, not sure how to answer that without sounding needy. Maybe she should focus on the new info.

SHIORI: A VIOLINIST? IS HE HOT?
MALAKAI: :/ NOT YOU TOO.
SHIORI: WHAT?
BRAVE: HE'S SOOOO HOT. THE FANS WILL LOVE HIM. THE FANS. I'VE TRIED TO EXPLAIN TO MALAKAI THAT'S ALL I CARE ABOUT. THAT AND WE WILL MAKE SWEET, SWEET MUSIC TOGETHER.
SHIORI: I'M WITH MALAKAI. ARE YOU TRYING TO RECRUIT HIM OR...
MALAKAI: YES. OR...
BRAVE: OR FUCK HIM?

Blunt. As always. But Shiori couldn't be mad at him. He loved the band and his focus was on the music. There also seemed to be some flirting going on. Her stomach tightened at the idea of Brave casting both her and Malakai aside.

She didn't see him doing that, though. Maybe she was naïve, but what they were exploring felt real. Real enough for her to take a chance.

A small one. One that wouldn't destroy her career.

While her thoughts drifted, the conversation kept going.

MALAKAI: I HAVEN'T MET THE GUY AND I ALREADY HATE HIM.
BRAVE: YOU WON'T. HE'S A PROFESSIONAL. BESIDES, I THINK HE WANTED ALDER FIRST.
MALAKAI: ARE YOU SERIOUSLY PIMPING YOUR BROTHER?
BRAVE: NO! DUDE, THAT'S NOT COOL. I WOULDN'T DO THAT. I'M JUST...HOLDING OUT A CARROT.

Shiori laughed and hid the chat so she could find a Bugs Bunny gif. She posted it as her reply.

MALAKAI: *GROAN*
BRAVE: ROTFL
SHIORI: OK, I HAVE NO IDEA WHAT'S GOING ON. IS IT WEIRD TO SAY I WISH YOU GUYS WERE

HERE? THIS ROOM IS INSANE. AND DANICA LEFT ME A BOTTLE OF RUM I CAN'T POSSIBLY DRINK BY MYSELF.

Neither answered. She bit her bottom lip, wondering if she'd been too forward. Maybe she should have just asked them if they wanted to hang out.

A soft knock sounded at her door. Swallowing hard, she set the teddy bear down and went to answer.

Malakai stepped in first, holding his arms out to pull her in for a hug. He was wearing black jogging pants and a white tank top, which left his arms bare so she could feel the wiry muscles flex beneath his smooth skin. Her outfit wasn't that different—except her pajama pants were pink—so at least she didn't have to worry about being underdressed.

One arm still around her, Malakai moved away from the door so Brave could pass. "For future notice, all you have to do is ask and we'll be here."

"Good to know." She rested her head on his shoulder and grinned at Brave. "Nice bathrobe."

Brave's lips quirked as he smoothed his hands over the front of the white bathrobe with the dark blue hotel logo on the chest. "Thank you. I think I'm gonna get me one for the bus. Only black and red."

"I fucking knew it!" Malakai snorted. "You're going for the Hugh Hefner look. Damn it, can't you wait a few years before hitting your midlife crisis?"

"What the hell are you talking about?" Brave arched a brow, turning toward the small wet bar tucked in the alcove by the entryway. "I plan to live to at least a hundred and twenty. I'm nowhere near midlife."

Shiori let out a light laugh, but her chest tightened at the way Brave had walked by her so casually. He'd been affectionate on the bus. What changed?

Not moving away from Malakai, she frowned at Brave. "Don't I even get a hug?"

He shook his head, setting three glasses on the gray marble countertop. "I've been told I'm greedy. You're tempting, little moon. If I want to redeem myself, I need to keep my distance."

"Why?"

He sighed, one hand on the bottle of white rum he still hadn't opened. "I want to be a good man for you. A good man who's patient and gentle. You deserve all that and more. But if I touch you, I'll want to kiss you. I remember how you taste and the memory tempts me every fucking day. The man I was would seduce you, not caring if you'd regret it tomorrow." His throat worked as he swallowed. "I don't ever want you to regret us, Shiori."

"Us?" Shiori looked from Brave to Malakai, who had gone still beside her. His expression was impossible to read, but he'd made it clear where he stood. Both men were waiting for her to decide what she wanted. She pressed the tip of her tongue into her bottom lip. "You're not the only one who's supposed to be good, Brave. I'm trying really, *really,* hard."

"There's no pressure. I need you to know that." Malakai moved away from her, as though to prove his words by keeping his distance as well. "We can watch a movie and not have this conversation again."

With a nervous laugh, she tipped her head back to meet his eyes. "I *don't* want to have this conversation. Not now."

He nodded slowly. "Then what do you want?"

She didn't know how to answer. Besides, words were overrated. Reaching out, she latched her fingers behind his neck and pressed her lips to his.

At first, he didn't move. Her pulse pounded, and she started to pull away. But then he raked his fingers through her hair, slanting his mouth over hers as he took control of the kiss.

Unrestrained passion erased all uncertainty. Lifting her up against him, Malakai tasted her lips and the whole universe tilted, whirling like comets caught in a dizzying dance. This man, always so contained, always letting her lead the way, stepped through the door she'd swung open without hesitation.

Exactly what she needed from him.

What she needed from them both.

A hand curved around her side. Not Malakai's, he was using both to hold her up. Lips brushed along her throat, the barest touch waking all her nerve ending, sending shivers up her spine. She moaned into Malakai's mouth as Brave sucked lightly on her neck.

His lips trailed up to her ear and she trembled as he whispered. "One hit of him won't be enough."

"I know." She gasped as Malakai kissed down the other side of her throat. "It won't be enough of either of you."

Brave released a low sound of pleasure. "Welcome to my addiction."

Talking was done. Malakai drew her away from Brave and carried her to the bedroom. Laying her on the bed as he kissed her, slowly, leaning over her as his tongue dipped into her mouth, slipping and sliding with a smooth pressure that made her whole body writhe. He hooked his thumbs at the base of her tank top without breaking the kiss, drawing the soft material up over her breasts.

The bed shifted as Brave sat by her head, bending to claim her lips as Malakai lowered his mouth to the curve of one breast. Malakai's tongue circled her nipple, getting closer and closer until she was tempted to grab him and guide his mouth to where she needed it most.

She groaned when he shot her a lazy smile, easing back. "Up, beautiful."

"Up?" She stared at him.

Hand at the small of her back, Brave eased her off the mattress just enough to help her remove her shirt completely. "I should probably warn you. Our man's evil."

"Ya think?" She frowned at Brave's chuckle, but he slid behind her, settling her between his thighs as he rested against the bedframe.

His hands curved under her breasts and he brushed his thumbs over her nipples, soothing the needy ache. Resting her head against his chest, she watched Malakai through half closed lids as he yanked off his own shirt and tossed it aside.

Damn, the man was fine. She licked her lips as he crawled over her, the tight muscles of his broad shoulders rippling as he braced his hands by her hips. His lips slanted into a playful smile as he dipped down to give her another long kiss.

Between his lips and Brave's hands, her body was reaching a fever pitch of longing. Her core throbbed, clenching as heat spilled slick between her thighs. She appreciated them wanting to take it slow, but…

All right, maybe she didn't. She wanted them everywhere. Not carefully teasing her until they drove her insane. She needed them to take her with all the wild passion she felt. Needed to know she wasn't the only one ready to lose control.

"Please." She cupped Malakai's cheek as he grazed his teeth down her throat. Her breath caught as he bit down lightly. Shards of pleasure dug in deep, testing her ability to say a single word. But somehow, she managed. "I want you."

Malakai rested his lips against her throat and went still. "And I *need* you."

"Then take me." An erotic shiver slithered down her spine as Malakai rose to meet her eyes. The deep blue of his irises almost vanished into black as his pupils dilated.

She wasn't drowning in desire alone. With that one look, she could see restraint slipping from his grasp. He held back for her.

"I'm ready, Malakai." She curved her hand around the back of his neck. "I've never been *more* ready."

Behind her, Brave let out a rough sound of amusement. "Should I be insulted?"

"Shut up." Malakai's tone took on a rough edge. He buried one hand in Shiori's hair. "We go at your pace, Shiori. Whatever that is."

Biting hard on her bottom lip, Shiori wrapped her legs around Malakai's thighs, tugging him close. "My pace is much faster."

Malakai's lips quirked. "Is that so?" He slid his hand between them, slipping it under the waistband of her pajama pants. His fingers touched her and a low growl sounded deep in his chest. "Mmm, so fucking hot and wet. I can already taste you."

All strength abandoned her as Malakai's finger dipped inside her. Her back arched as he pressed in, then drew out to glide his finger over her clit. He moved down her body, laying light kisses on her stomach as Brave massaged her breasts, his thumbs passing over her nipples in a gentle caress that kept them hard. Stimulated so they pulsed in time with her clit.

Moving away just long enough to pull off her pajama pants, Malakai hooked his arms under her knees, lifting her to his mouth. His tongue pressed into her and her lips parted. The slick pressure triggered a white-hot wave, edging on the brink of everything she'd been craving. She tipped her head back, crying out as Brave pinched her nipples and covered her mouth with his.

She shuddered, and the world seemed to drop beneath her, catching her seconds later as Malakai lowered her thighs and eased two fingers inside, drawing out the mind-numbing pleasure as it reached another peak. Her core clenched around him and she lifted her hips in time with each steady thrust.

"So close. Let go, love." Malakai's breath teased her clit as he lowered his lips once again. "I want to feel you come around my fingers. I need to see you completely lose control."

"I need more." She whimpered as he filled her with another finger. The stretch felt so good, but it wasn't enough. She needed him inside her. Above her. Needed to share all she was feeling.

Malakai flicked his tongue over her clit, moaning as if the taste of her was everything. As he pulled her closer, Brave slid out from under her, piling pillows under her head to take his place. He reached into the pocket of his bathrobe, then shoved it off his shoulders, letting it fall to the floor.

At the end of the bed, he pulled Malakai off her, latching onto the back of the other man's neck as he kissed him, a smile on his lips.

"Thankfully, one of us came prepared." Brave kissed down Malakai's chest, shoving his pants off his hips and taking a firm grip at the base of his dick. "I should be jealous. I should be fighting to make her mine. But I won't. Because she already is."

His words wrapped around Shiori's heart, binding her close, without constricting her at all. She knew exactly what he meant and she loved him for it. They'd been going back and forth, so cautious, but never drifting too far apart. Without needing to define their relationship, they'd accepted where they would end up.

The missing link had always been Malakai. A man they both fell in love with in a way neither could have predicted, but made sense. Without him, they might have found a starting point, but it wouldn't have been solid. Brave wouldn't have trusted himself. And Shiori had no clue how she would have shown him he could.

Malakai was reality. He was all she could have ever wanted. A man who could be her friend, her lover, shielding her when she needed, by her side when she didn't, taking a step back to let her face the world if she asked. He did the same for Brave, but even with all that, he was more.

He was...

She pulled her bottom lip between her teeth, watching Brave as he slid his lips over Malakai's dick, taking him in deep as words became meaningless. They couldn't explain why the three of them fit so perfectly. And they didn't have to.

Seeing the men together kept her on that sweet edge, as though they were all hovering there together. Impatience dwindled away as she watched Malakai bury his hands in Brave's hair, moving with each glide over his dick. When Brave slipped away, the muscles in her stomach tensed even as Malakai cursed.

Every pause was painful. But when she saw the condom in Brave's hand her whole body lit up. Her feet shifted restlessly on the bed when he rolled the thin latex over Malakai's dick.

Kicking his pants aside, Malakai eased away from Brave and climbed onto the bed, covering her with his body and taking her mouth in a deep, hungry kiss. She dug her nails into his shoulders, her breath catching as his hard length pressed against her stomach. Thick and hot, just feeling him against her turned up the volume of arousal until her brain couldn't process anything else.

Shameless, she reached down in the small space between them and wrapped her hand around his dick. He sucked in a breath as she gripped him loosely, sliding her hand from the base of his cock, up over the firm crown. She took her time there, exploring the indent with her thumb, eyes on his face as he inhaled sharply.

His lips curved slightly. "Payback?"

"No, I just wanted to feel you." She grinned, enjoying his reaction to her fingers and thumb tightening around him. A fine sheen of sweat had formed on his skin and she leaned up to kiss his jaw. "I didn't get a chance to do this with Brave. Tate was—"

"Move your hand faster, little moon. He fucking loves it." Brave knelt on the edge of the bed, smoothing his hand down Malakai's back when he tensed. "This is a conversation for another time."

"But one we *will* be having." Malakai's jaw tensed, then relaxed as Shiori followed Brave's advice and stroked him faster. He shook his head and chuckled. "I'm not sure how I feel about you two ganging up on me."

"Hmm, maybe this will help." Brave nudged Malakai up and bent between him and Shiori. His lips wrapped around the head of Malakai's dick and he moved with the motion of Shiori's hand.

Pulling her hand away, Brave turned his head and slipped his tongue over her clit. He kissed her pussy like he kissed her lips, so thorough he woke nerves beneath her slick flesh she didn't know she had. Just before she was about to beg for…for hell, she wasn't even sure anymore…he stopped.

And took Malakai in deep one last time before shifting so he could guide Malakai's dick to her.

"Oh fuck." Malakai looked down, breathing hard as Brave stroked her with his cock. "You're driving me insane."

Shiori licked her lips, the sensation of Brave rubbing that hard length over her not helping her sanity much either. Would it be pathetic to beg again?

"Take her, Malakai." Brave positioned Malakai against her so the head of Malakai's dick pressed in slightly with each breath. "She's ready. I want to see that beautiful pussy wrapped around you."

Lowering one hand to the bed by her hip, Malakai pressed in. The stretch was uncomfortable at first, but he glided easily in the slickness of her body. She moaned as more of him filled her until Brave's fist covered her, adding to the stimulation. Her tender clit throbbed under his first knuckle and the way he moved his hand increased the pleasure. She couldn't help moving with him, which made the thick length inside her slip in and out, but only enough to make her want more.

Almost as though he'd read her mind, Brave drew his hand away. And Malakai sank in deeper. He hesitated as the stretch became uncomfortable and brushed his fingers through her hair, his eyes searching hers.

"I don't want to hurt you." He rocked his hips carefully, frowning when she winced at the growing ache. "If it's too much, don't be afraid to tell me."

Even if she'd had the slightest bit of uncertainty—which she didn't—his concern would have drowned it out. Losing her virginity hadn't seemed like a huge deal, just something she hadn't done yet.

Now, she couldn't imagine losing it any other way. Lips parted, she inhaled slowly, glancing over at Brave who was gently stroking her thigh. They both treated her like she was precious. Whether they could have forever or not, they could have this. Something she could share with them, without regrets.

"I'd tell you anything, Malakai. I'm okay, I promise." She whimpered as he pressed in. The ache sharpened. Then he settled between her thighs, filling her completely. Her eyes teared as her body tightened around him. "Oww."

He kissed her again. "Do you want me to move?"

"Damn it, give her a fucking minute." Brave shifted up the bed, brushing a strand of sweat dampened her from her cheek. "You could have warned her."

"I did."

"'I'm okay' isn't a fucking green light."

"Then what would you call it?"

I am going to slap them both. She rolled her eyes, bringing her hands up to cover both their mouths. "Nope. We're not doing this now. You two can hate-fuck and make up later."

The men exchanged a look and the hostility between them vanished.

"What do you need, love?" Malakai's tongue traced her bottom lip. He drew out, then slid back in, shifting the ache into liquid pleasure so quickly she gasped. "Does that feel good?"

"Mmmhmm." Her eyes drifted shut as he moved again, slowly, carefully, at a steady pace that renewed her arousal so quickly the pain did nothing but give a sharp edge to the exquisite sensation. The languid drag of his dick passed over a spot within that sent a white-hot current through her core. Her whole body tensed, gripping him tight.

He gave her a lazy smile, bringing his lips close to her ear. "Baby, we're just getting started."

Rising up, he angled his hips, curved his hands under her ass, and targeted that same euphoric spot like she'd revealed the secret to her every desire. Brave relaxed on his side, sliding his hand down her stomach, kissing her as his fingers parted at either side of her clit.

He stroked the tiny, overstimulated nub lightly, which lit all the nerves like a spark had been set off from one to the other, shooting inward to gather with the building pressure in her core. She panted against his lips, whimpering as her skin tingled and her nipples tightened. She brought one hand up, squeezing one breast.

Brave lowered his lips to the other, sucking her nipple, his tongue circling it over and over until the sensation pulsed down to her clit, to her core.

Everything wound together, inside and out, and she bit back a cry as reality fragmented, electric surges of white flashing through her, blinding her as she came apart. Lips shaking, her back bowed and she writhed as all the shattered pieces snapped into place, melting together like blazing bits of steel.

All the muscles within convulsed, keeping time with the rapid beat of her heart. Her bones liquefied as the aftershock drew another shudder from her. The air she sucked into her lungs became damp. Hot. The scent of sweat, a musky masculine aroma surrounded her. She soaked it in, letting it steady her as the world righted itself.

Her vision cleared and she looked up at Malakai, who'd gone perfectly still. By her side, Brave murmured softly, stroking her hair.

She smiled, turning her cheek into Brave's hand. "Wow."

All right, that didn't cover how amazing that had been, but she didn't have the strength for more.

Brave grinned and kissed her cheek. "You're happy. Good. I don't have to kill him."

Malakai chuckled and began easing out of her. "That's good to kn—"

"Not yet...please..." She clenched her thighs against his hips as her core throbbed with pain. "Wait."

Eyes narrowed, Brave glared at Malakai. "Maybe I spoke too soon."

Shiori weakly smacked her hand into his bare chest. "Stop it. It felt so good I wasn't expecting that to change."

Brave's expression softened. "Take your time. He's not still hard, is he?"

"I don't know..." She frowned as she realized Malakai still felt huge inside her. Had he enjoyed himself at all? Bad enough Brave had been mostly left out.

Malakai wrapped his arms around her waist, turning so she lay on top of him, his length still inside her. "I came with you, Shiori. I couldn't hold back." He glanced over at Brave. "And I'm usually quite good at that."

Jaw ticking, Brave stood. "I'll go get a warm wash cloth. Try not to rush her."

"I won't." Malakai watched him leave, his eyes hard.

Shiori rested her head on Malakai's shoulder and sighed. Fine, she hadn't expected the bad blood between the men to disappear overnight, but they'd gotten together before she'd even considered being with either of them. Was she making things worse?

A deep sound rumbled through Malakai's chest. "I can practically hear you worrying, my love. This isn't your fault. Brave and I return to default when we don't have control. We both want to protect you. It's easier to get mad at each other than admit we couldn't make this perfect for you."

She wrinkled her nose, pressing her hands against his chest and easing up. His dick slipped free and she tensed, but it wasn't that bad. Sore, but she could deal. "It *was* perfect. I don't regret a thing. I wanted to share this with you. But now I want to know you're as happy as I am. Tomorrow might be rough. There's so much we have to figure out. Tonight... Tonight is ours."

Halfway across the room with a washcloth in his hand, Brave stopped and groaned. "Fuck, I'm an idiot. I'm sorry. I kept wondering if I'd done the right thing. If I should have... I couldn't have been as gentle as he was. I would have tried, but..." He rubbed a hand over his face and shrugged. "I trust him more than I trust myself."

Malakai's lips curved. He met Brave's eyes. "Thank you. But I would have trusted you too. And she trusts us both. In the end, that's all that matters."

"You're right." Brave approached the bed, a crooked smile on his lips. "Truce?"

"Truce."

Yep, I'm gonna have to hurt them. "Better be more than a truce. I may need a few days."

"We can wait." Brave glanced over at Malakai, who inclined his head. "Seriously, Shiori. Men don't die if they don't get off. That's fake news."

Shiori snickered, not sure what to make of that comment. 'Fake news' was often facts people didn't like. Did that mean she could condemn both her men to a slow death if she agreed?

No need to risk it. Besides, she had absolutely no problem with them satisfying one another, so long as she got to watch sometimes. She arched a brow at Brave as he perched on the edge of the bed, cleaning her thigh with the washcloth.

Better to tease him than focus on the mess she'd made. Her cheeks heated, but she had a feeling he didn't want her to be ashamed of it. "I don't want you to wait. I need visuals for when I touch myself."

"Now *that* we can do." Malakai lifted up, pulling the sheet out from under him and folding it over a dark patch of blood. He continued without pause. "I plan to save our man shortly. We wouldn't want to test his theory."

"True." Her lips slid into a mischievous smile. "Besides, I can't take…someone else up on their offer to teach me how to give a blowjob."

Brave's eyes widened. He gave her inner thigh a playful smack. "You're bad. Stop that. He doesn't joke about Tate."

Slapping a hand over his eyes, Malakai cursed. "She didn't say it was Tate. *You* did."

"I…" Brave pressed his eyes shut and tipped his head back. "Damn. Sorry."

"Uh huh." Malakai shook his head and placed his hand on her back. "I can pour you a bath if you want. Help you clean up while Brave calls for clean sheets?"

Her throat tightened. Tamping down an unexpected rush of panic, she shook her head. "No, I'll take a quick shower." She eyed the sheets. She couldn't see the blood anymore, but she knew it was there. She didn't like the idea of some poor maid having to deal with it. "Maybe I can rinse the sheets a little? Call for new ones, but I can't—"

"I can do it." Brave's brow furrowed when she shook her head again. "Shiori, it's okay. You shouldn't be embarrassed."

"I'm not." She had to cut this conversation short. Climbing off Malakai, she slipped off the bed. "It would make me feel better. Like, if I had my period—"

"Got it." Brave's cheeks reddened. He stepped back as Malakai got up and stripped the bed. "But when the bed is fixed, will you let us stay?"

Gathering the sheets in her arms, she smiled at him. "I hoped you would."

He inclined his head. "Then we aren't going anywhere."

Chapter Twenty-Four

Long after the morning sun crept through the small slit in the curtains of the hotel room, Brave lay awake, head rested on a folded pillow, watching Shiori and Malakai sleep. The night had gone well—he thought so anyway. After the bed was freshly made, and Shiori finished her shower, Malakai had cleaned up quickly and they'd all curled up together, murmuring goodnight as they closed their eyes.

Halfway through the night. Malakai woke him with a long, slow blowjob, torturing him while Shiori sleepily watched, nodding as Malakai gave her a few tips. She'd set Brave off the second she'd suggested joining in. Even though she'd fallen asleep seconds after her offer, he'd been laid out by Malakai's attention and her eagerness.

He wasn't sure he'd ever had a more restful night. Been more excited about the future. And not because of all the wicked, erotic fantasies he imagined playing out. Being with Shiori and Malakai was like laying the foundation to the first home he could truly call his own. He couldn't wait to see what they'd build together.

But first, he needed to know where Shiori's panicked look had come from. Remembering the brief instant of fear in her eyes cast a shadow over her glow of happiness. Malakai suggesting a bath scared her. And not like she was scared of *him*. Thinking back on his time with Jesse, Brave recognized a trigger. One he'd ignored with the man his brother loved. Which had been fucked up, but he had to live with his actions.

He wouldn't make the same mistake again, but he had to figure out what exactly had happened to make the suggestion so horrible for Shiori.

And he didn't have the first clue how.

A faint *buzz* came from the side of the bed where he'd dropped his robe. Easing his arm out from under Shiori's head, he held still, watching her press closer to Malakai, her deep breaths steady.

Reaching down, he plucked his phone from the pocket of his robe and headed to the living room, shutting the bedroom door softly behind him as he answered.

"Hello?"

"Brave? It's Dariel." The cocky violinist sounded relaxed, as though he hadn't let the phone ring a dozen times. "It's almost noon, so I figured it was a good time to call, but you sound like you just woke up."

"I did, but it's fine. One good thing about this lifestyle is you don't usually do nine to five."

"I haven't had a regular schedule since I was in the military, so I'm good with that." Dariel chuckled. "You awake enough to talk business?"

"Always." Brave headed to the wet bar to put on the coffee maker. "What's up?"

"The offer to meet the band still on the table?" Dariel cleared his throat. "I'm not making any promises, but I'd like to swing by. Maybe talk to your manager. Hear the offer."

"Cool, but let's do one better. I can have Reese send you a copy of the contract to look over within the hour. You'll get the same offer we all have. I'm working on a song and I want the guys to hear it with you playing along. Come for rehearsal. See what we can be together." Brave took a deep breath, knowing he was pushing the man, but he needed Dariel to commit. He would do whatever it took to convince him he belonged with

Winter's Wrath. "We're going to Europe in a month. I want you with us."

"Fuck." Dariel sighed. "It's fucking tempting, Brave. I want to say yes, but—"

"Sometimes opportunities come at you fast. I get this is crazy. You've had other offers and you turned them down. You were waiting for the right one." Brave's jaw tensed. Hell, this wasn't his thing. Reese would have Dariel on board in a minute. But he didn't want to have to convince them both. She might be hesitant if Dariel started playing hardball. Drama was her kryptonite. "This is the right one"

"You're damn convincing. And you managed without sucking my dick. I'm impressed." Dariel let out a soft laugh. "This is me being professional."

"I can tell." Brave snorted. "I ain't gonna suck your dick. But I am giving you a chance to use your talent to get all the dick—or pussy—you could ever want."

"I get that without you."

"Can you get a music video? An album? A future with a band no one will ever forget?"

"No. And I didn't believe I'd have that with the other offers." A long pause. "I believe I can have it with you."

"Good. Come in with that attitude and your only concern will be packing your shit to hit the road." Brave looked up as soft footsteps approached. He smiled as Shiori slid up to his side. "Hang up and I'll text you the address where we're rehearsing. The music we'll make together is gonna be fucking *intense*, man."

Dariel chuckled. "No doubt about that. See you in a bit."

Hanging up, Brave pulled Shiori into his arms and bent down to kiss her, savoring the sweet mint on her breath and the soft warmth of her lips. He'd never get tired of having her close.

Wrapping her hands around the back of his neck, she peered up at him, all cute and sleepy. "You're in a good mood."

"I really am. Dariel's agreed to come meet the band. I think I can convince him to join. Coffee?" He grinned at her nod, eased away to send the text, then fill two mugs. "I wish you could've heard him on the violin. You will today. He's absolutely perfect."

Shiori waited while he added sugar and cream to her coffee. Her brow creased when he passed her the mug. "Malakai doesn't share your enthusiasm."

"Malakai's being paranoid and overprotective." Brave rested his hip against the counter and took a gulp of the rich, sweet brew. "I told him Dariel has a thing for Alder. He doesn't want tension in the band."

"Neither do you." Shiori cocked her head. "So Malakai's not jealous?"

"He's definitely jealous." Brave shrugged, not sure what she was getting at. "He'll get over it when he sees what Dariel can do for the band. The music is everything."

Sighing, Shiori turned and headed for the small round table set close to the picture window across the room. He placed his coffee and the coffee pot on a tray with the cream, sugar, and an extra mug for Malakai and brought it to the table, setting it down before taking a seat beside her.

Cupping her mug in her hands, Shiori met his eyes. "Malakai is just as invested in the band as you are. The only way he'll have a problem with Dariel is if you give him a reason."

"I love Malakai. He knows that." But was that enough? Malakai's concern for Alder made sense, worrying about people was the man's MO. But jealousy? Hell, what was Brave supposed to do with that besides prove he wasn't gonna mess around?

Shiori shrugged. "Maybe he does. I don't know how things will work between the three of us, but I get sometimes I'll have to step back and let you deal with your issues. Like you'll have to step back if it's me and Malakai having trouble."

Inclining his head, he reached out to put his hand over hers. "You still get to have an opinion."

"I better!" She grinned and brought her coffee to her lips, not moving her hand from his. "Talk to him. That's all I ask."

"Consider it done." Brave gave her hand a light squeeze. "Now, let's talk about you. How are you feeling?"

Her cheeks flushed and she ducked her head. "Umm…a little sore. Good, though. It won't affect my dancing tonight."

Fuck, why hadn't I thought of that? His jaw hardened as he considered how their night together could have spoiled Shiori's chance to make an impression on a huge stage. All their secrets wouldn't mean shit if she couldn't perform in front of the crowd.

"Don't." Shiori frowned at him. "You don't get to take the blame."

"Take the blame for what?" Malakai crossed the room, his tone sharp. He shot Brave a cold look before pulling out the chair at Shiori's other side. "Are you all right?"

"Yes!" Shiori slammed her mug on the table and shoved her chair back as she stood. "But I saw that. You're ready to be mad at him. You're both incredible. I think we have something good and then…" She motioned from Brave to Malakai. "This."

"Already breaking your own rules, babe? I thought you were gonna let us work out our own issues?" Brave grinned, trying to lighten the mood, but the second Shiori's eyes narrowed, he knew he'd fucked up.

Before he could take it back, she snatched the creamer off the table and splashed the liquid over his face. "Get out!"

Cool cream dripped down his chin, joining the puddle soaking his boxers. He wiped his face with his hand. Stared at her. "Shiori—"

"*Now.*" She pointed to the door, then spun on her heel and stormed into the bedroom.

All right, what just happened? He moved to follow her, but Malakai latched onto his arm. "Give her some space. Let's go to our room. We've got to meet the guys soon."

"I'm not leaving with her pissed."

"Because you're an idiot. Whatever." Malakai made a dismissive motion, cutting across the room in long strides and disappearing into the hall, shutting the door softly behind him.

Damn. That got fucked up fast. Brave raked his fingers through his hair, looking from the closed bedroom door to the front door, completely lost. He'd never done relationships before—barring the reprehensible exception with Jesse, which didn't count—and now he was in one with two people. And making a mess of it.

He picked up his phone, doing the only thing he could think of to make things better.

One message to Shiori. One to Malakai.

With two words.

I'm sorry.

Halfway down the hall, Malakai's phone buzzed and he pulled it out, cursing softly as he read the message from Brave. The anger that had flashed so hot within died a quick death. Damn it, he didn't even know why he was mad.

Fine, Brave hadn't been too bright with his comment, and Shiori definitely needed time to cool down, but the man hadn't really done anything wrong. He was being...well, *Brave*.

Not the old Brave either. Simply a man who'd only truly cared about one other person in his life. His little brother. And their relationship had almost been fucked up beyond repair.

Malakai could get on his high horse all he wanted, because he cared about a lot of people. Tate and Alder. Shiori. Anyone he thought needed him.

But he never let them too close. He was trying with Shiori, but then he'd gone back to default mode and tried to find something to protect her from, rather than admit he was fucking terrified he'd hurt her. That he couldn't be the man she needed after what she'd shared with him last night.

Brave had been the easy target. Malakai lashed out without a second thought because that's what he'd always done. And he'd usually been justified.

Not today, though.

Today, he'd taken away the one thing Shiori needed with a look. One that proved the three of them weren't as solid as she'd believed when she gave herself to them. Two people in a relationship was complicated. Three? Almost impossible without trust and communication.

Both issues they could work on, but not if he walked away the second things got rough.

Heading back to Shiori's room, he rapped his knuckles firmly on the door.

Brave opened the door right away, which meant he'd probably been about to leave. He swallowed as Malakai backed him into the room.

"Malakai, I'm—"

"Don't say it. Not again." Malakai took a firm grip of Brave's shoulders. "This was my fault. I assumed you'd upset Shiori. It was easier than facing my own guilt."

Brave frowned and shook his head as Malakai nudged the door shut with his foot. "Guilt? But she's fine."

"I needed to hear it from her." Malakai pressed his eyes shut and groaned. "All I had to do was ask."

"Then why didn't you?" Shiori spoke up, standing just outside the bedroom door. She pressed her tongue into her bottom lip. "Wait. Don't answer that. I'm guessing it's for the same reason I kicked you out rather than telling you my fantasy of a sweet, cuddly morning together was ruined."

Brave dropped his gaze. "I wanted to let you both sleep. I had to take the call from Dariel. Otherwise, I'd have stayed in bed."

Malakai ground his teeth at the mention of their potential band member. He did his best to keep his voice level. "What did *he* want?"

"He's coming to rehearsal." Brave held up his hands as Malakai took a step back. "I was a dick for joking about how hot he is. About him wanting Alder when he should want me. Yes, he's a flirt. But more importantly, he's smart and talented. And I believe he'll respect my brother's relationship. And ours."

Somewhat reassuring? Malakai relaxed, pressing his lips together as he eyed Brave. He'd never known Brave to pass up a possible conquest. "What if he doesn't?"

Shoulders lifting, Brave held his gaze. "That's his problem. I'm with you and Shiori. I don't want anyone else."

Sounded perfect, but he'd have to trust Brave and he was still working on that. They had history that hadn't suddenly gone away just because they'd started fucking. Saying 'I love you' didn't erase the past.

But they had to start somewhere.

"Fine. I'll try not to worry about Dariel." Malakai chuckled at Brave's heavy exhale. He held out his hand to Shiori, the tightness in his chest easing as she laid her hand in his. "As for the cuddling, we don't have much time, but we can get back in bed and chill for a bit."

"I'd like that." Shiori started toward the bedroom, then stopped. She glanced over at Brave. "I'm sorry I threw cream in your face."

"It's all right." Brave closed the distance between them, curving his hand behind her neck as he pressed their foreheads together. "I was trying to break the tension, but it was stupid of me to toss your words back in your face, even as a joke."

"It really was." Shiori laughed as she continued into the room, still holding Malakai's hand. "We're so messed up. But this was good, right? We figured it out."

"We did. And we'll keep doing that." Brave swooped her up into his arms, carrying her to the bed without pulling her hand from Malakai's. "I was prepared to do a lot more groveling. If you'd both cut me out for any longer, there would have been begging."

"You're making a good case for us to hold grudges. I wouldn't mind seeing you beg." Malakai smirked when Brave stopped at the edge of the bed and scowled at him. "Hey, don't get all moody. I'm just saying you're hot on your knees."

Shiori let out a soft sigh as Brave lowered her to the bed. "He really is."

Brave knelt on the edge of the bed. "You two are driving me nuts. I'm getting hard and I have a feeling that makes me the bad guy. *Again.*"

"Nope." Shiori giggled as Brave lifted her shirt over her ribs and bent down to nibble at her ribs. "Stop it! You can be the bad guy if you want. But I think it's hot."

"Me getting hard?"

"Oh, *definitely.*" Shiori sprawled back on the pile of pillows. "Isn't that the fun of the three of us being together? We can all torture one another. And when I'm not up to playing, I can sic Malakai on you."

Lust surged down low as Malakai considered her words. He loved how easily she flowed from one emotion to the next. It wasn't complicated. She'd been angry, but they'd resolved the issue as much as they could right now. And she was in the mood for fun.

He hadn't missed her mention of not playing. Sex would be too painful for her for a few days. He'd expected as much.

What he hadn't expected was for her to suggest he and Brave carry on without her.

"You enjoyed your lesson last night." He loved the way she blushed every time he or Brave casually brought up anything sexual. But she never backed down.

She gave him a quick nod, scooting closer to Brave and he reclined against the headboard. "I did, even though I didn't do much. I love the way he tastes, but…seeing you take him over the edge?" She ran her fingers over Brave's bare chest, down the neatly trimmed dark hair trailing between his abs, inhaling roughly when he shuddered. "No sure I can do that. But I love watching you."

This triad definitely had perks he hadn't considered. He'd been so torn between wanting to please both his lovers, he hadn't considered pleasure could come from watching. But it made sense. Seeing Shiori lying there, next to Brave, touching him as though she had every right to his body, turned Malakai on. The idea of her getting off seeing him and Brave together made his dick swell.

Neither she or Brave were bound by the pointless limits he'd put in place. It didn't have to be all or nothing.

"You like torturing him." Malakai slid closer to the bed, his lips quirking as Brave eyed him warily. "Would you enjoy watching me fuck him?"

The deep red on Shiori's cheeks spread down her throat. "Yes."

Malakai jerked Brave off the bed, positioning him bent over with one hand around his throat, nuzzling the curve of his shoulder when Brave stiffened. "I won't be as gentle with him as I was with you."

"I know." Shiori turned on her side, elbow bent, her head in her hand. "But you love him as much as I do."

Brave's muscles tensed. He lifted his head. "I love you. And him. It happened fast and it's fucked up. But it's true."

Shiori reached out to place her hand over Brave's. "If I didn't know that, this would hurt. But it doesn't. I want you to be as happy as I am."

"I'm already there, Shiori." Brave bowed his head as Malakai stroked along his spine. "I don't need proof."

"This isn't proof. It's me being greedy." Shiori cocked her head, glancing up at Malakai. "Please tell me he brought enough condoms?"

Knowing Brave? Malakai bent down, reaching into the pocket of Brave's abandoned bathrobe. He found two more condoms and a package of lube. "He never disappoints."

Dropping the packets on the nightstand, Malakai leaned against Brave's back. He wasn't sure if his pulse or Brave's pounded harder, but he could sense the rhythm coming together, as it did so effortlessly on stage.

He slid his hand over Brave's chest, laying open mouth kisses on his neck as he held him, knowing they didn't have much time, and yet, he needed this. One peaceful moment without the world fucking things up.

Here, with Shiori sharing their pleasure, with Brave not putting on the arrogant rock star mask that slipped more and more every day, Malakai didn't have to wonder if they were strong enough to face tonight. And tomorrow. And all the tomorrows after that.

"I want to stay here. Like this." Malakai's brow furrowed. Why had he opened his damn mouth?

If Brave fucking laughs—

Brave turned his head, bringing one hand to the side of Malakai's face as he kissed him. Rough with emotion, fingers digging into Malakai's jaw, the kiss showed a longing that wouldn't make sense if all Brave wanted was sex.

Or if he didn't share the uncertainty.

He tugged Malakai's bottom lip with his teeth and held his gaze as he released him. "So do I. Things won't get easier. But I want to feel you when we're back out there." Brave inhaled roughly. "The spotlight isn't my whole world anymore. The music is one of my passions, but this…" He smiled. "This right here is my reality."

Rising on her knees in front of Brave, Shiori put a hand on each of their shoulders. "This is ours. No one can take it away."

Malakai loved their confidence, but sharing their optimism was hard. He brushed his knuckles down Shiori's cheek. "They'll try."

"Let them. I'm tougher than I look." She leaned back and held up her fist playfully. Then she bit her bottom lip. "Did I ruin the moment?"

Brave huffed out a laugh. "No, I think I did."

Shaking his head, Malakai rubbed his still fully erect length against Brave's ass. He gave Shiori a hooded look. "I don't pass up opportunities."

Eyes wide, Shiori's sat back, bracing her hands on the bed behind her. Pink shaded her cheeks, but she didn't look away as he hooked his thumbs to the waist of Brave's boxers and worked them over his hips. Brave's dick was only semi-hard, so Malakai palmed it, stroking until it lengthened and firmed in his hand.

Groaning, Brave shifted back, spreading his thighs. Impatient as always. Malakai wouldn't torture him now.

They were running out of time.

"Can you help me, Shiori?" Malakai grinned when she blinked at him. "Open the lube. I don't want to stop."

Nodding, Shiori snatched the package from the nightstand, tearing one end, then squeezing half the liquid into his palm. He inclined his head to tell her it was enough and brought his hand between Brave's ass cheeks, letting the lube trickle down to his fingers. He circled them around Brave's hole, pressing in and slicking him up just enough for an easy glide.

Without him having to ask, Shiori passed him the condom, already open. He rolled it over himself, releasing Brave to use the rest of the lube on his own length. One hand on Brave's hip, he positioned against him, filling him in one smooth thrust. The tight grip around his dick pitched an erotic, pulsing ache up into his balls. He sucked in air, willing his pulse to slow.

A rough growl escaped Brave as he fisted his hands in the comforter. "Oh fuck."

Malakai grazed his teeth over Brave's bowed shoulder. "You good?"

"Fuck yes." Brave shifted restlessly against him. "Don't stop."

Fisting Brave's dick in his hand, Malakai stroked him as he moved his hips, thigh muscles clenching as he picked up the pace. The sound of flesh slapping flesh filled the room and he looked to Shiori to see her reaction. She might say she was fine with him being rough, but she'd never seen them like this.

Reclined on the pillows, Shiori rubbed her nipples through her shirt, bottom lip held tight between her teeth. Her legs pressed tight together and she seemed close to the edge.

Sex might be too much for her, but maybe she could still find some pleasure.

"Let him use his mouth on you, love." Malakai changed his pace, drawing out slow, then driving in hard. "He'll be gentle."

Shiori drew in a sharp breath. Uncertainty filled her eyes, but vanished as she lifted up to wiggle out of her pajama pants. She eased closer to Brave, gasping as he grabbed her ankles and tugged her beneath him.

"I won't last long with my mouth on her while you're fucking me." Brave let out a low growl, flicking his tongue over Shiori's clit. "Tell me you're close."

Malakai choked out a laugh. "More than close."

"Good." Brave cupped his hands under Shiori, lifting her pussy to his mouth. "Mmm, so fucking good."

A small whimper escaped Shiori's parted lips and Malakai tightened his grip on Brave's hip in warning, but the way her back bowed and her eyes squeezed shut showed only pleasure. Brave was being careful.

Angling his hips, Malakai focused on hitting Brave's prostate, grinding in deep at a steady pace as his breaths grew ragged. He could feel Brave holding back. Hear Shiori's whimpers turn to moans she couldn't contain.

He took a firm grip of Brave's dick as Shiori cried out, trembling with her release. The hot length was swollen at the crown and with each rapid stroke Brave's movements back against him became more erratic.

Barring his arm across Brave's throat, Malakai drew him up straight, slamming in hard one last time as the building pressure within fragmented, sending shards of ecstasy from the base of his spine, bursting through his balls and his cock with pure white-hot pleasure.

Warm liquid spilled over his fist as he stroked Brave to the end of his climax, not letting him go even when Brave shifted as though he wanted to collapse on the bed.

Just a few minutes. Or even seconds.

Brave sighed, patting Malakai's thigh lightly. "We have to go. None of us are dressed."

Malakai chuckled, even though his chest tightened as he pulled away. He knew Brave was right, but he didn't have to like it. "You noticed that, did you?"

From the bed, Shiori let out a happy sigh. "I am not seeing a problem with staying naked."

Glancing at his stomach as he turned, Brave bent down to grab an abandoned towel and quickly cleaned himself. He passed the towel to Malakai, shaking his head. "Don't make me be the reasonable one again. It feels weird."

"But the grown-up look is sexy on you." Malakai wiped off his hand, smirking when Brave made a face. "Fine, I'll do it. Quick showers then we get dressed."

"Separate showers." Shiori added, a sweet smile on her lips as she looked from him to Brave. "I don't need one—besides, if I get my hair wet I'll definitely be late. Brave can use my shower."

Made sense. He wouldn't question the 'separate showers' comment. He'd have suggested the same for her and Brave. Or himself and either of them. Even now he had to fight not to recalculate the bit of time they had left to crawl back in that bed.

Still, he hesitated before grabbing his clothes. "Why have Brave use your shower? I'm more likely to behave myself."

Brave scowled at him.

Shiori snickered. "Because he's the one who's all sticky."

"Good point." Malakai shot Shiori a sheepish look, pulling on his sleeping pants before bending over to kiss her. He grabbed her keycard from the night stand. "I won't be long."

And he wasn't, but by the time he returned to the room with a change of clothes for Brave, Shiori was already dressed, doing her makeup in the mirror over the desk in the lounge while Brave brushed her hair with a wide, soft-bristled wood brush.

They were both sensual and sweet, domestic in a way he'd never found appealing before. Brave in his boxers, a soft smile on his lips as he ran the brush over her hair, nodding to whatever she'd said. In a transparent, dark green shirt, black bra, and faux leather leggings, Shiori visibly fought to keep her lips still as she applied a pale peach colored gloss. When she finished she grinned at Brave in the mirror.

Chemistry—hell even hot, wild sex—didn't guarantee they'd last. But moments like this proved they had a chance. He held his breath, not wanting to move at first. He loved seeing them happy and relaxed. His presence would remind them that they were running out of time.

Shiori cleared her throat. "I can see you, Malakai. Don't stand so far away. I'm about to lose you too."

Malakai's jaw hardened. He crossed the room and took a knee at Shiori's side, passing the clothes and boots in his arms to Brave before sliding his hand around the back of her neck.

"Not fucking happening, love. I'm not going anywhere."

"But it won't be like this." Shiori sighed and shook her head. "You wouldn't have come in quietly if you didn't know it too. We'll have to pretend—"

"'*Pretend*' being the key word." He shoved aside his own misgivings, searching for a way to assure her she wasn't losing a thing. "The band knows. There's no way they've missed the way Brave and I look at you."

Her cheeks reddened. She dropped her gaze, but he tipped her chin up.

"In public, we'll be careful. But it doesn't have to be awkward. You and Danica claimed you're so comfortable on the bus you change in front of us. It would be weird if we were cold toward one another."

"Yes, but—"

Brave dropped his clothes on the desk, set his boots on the floor, and grinned at Shiori as he pulled on his tight black jeans. "Sneaking around will be fun too."

Biting her bottom lip, Shiori watched Brave dress. "Why are you doing this?"

"Because you're worth it." Brave leaned over and kissed Shiori's forehead. He groaned when his phone buzzed. Grabbing it from the desk by Shiori's purse, he glanced at it with a heavy sigh, typing in a quick reply. "We're being summoned."

Before Shiori could move, Malakai cupped her face in his hands. And kissed her, ruining her lipstick, but hoping she could remember what they'd had, and what they would have again, even when the cameras were flashing around them and she felt completely alone.

She was strong. She was building an amazing career for herself. And he'd do whatever it took not to get in her way.

He still needed to make sure she never forgot all she had to do was reach out and she'd find him, right there.

Her smile reached her eyes when he let her go. She took a deep breath. "I love you."

He smiled back at her, using his thumb to wipe away a smear of lipstick below her bottom lip. "I love you too."

Brave's phone buzzed again.

"Have I ever mentioned Jesse is a pain in the ass?" Brave shoved his phone in his back pocket. He jerked his boots on, audibly grinding his teeth. "We're on our way is clear, no?"

"He's doing his job." Malakai chuckled at Brave's muttered curse. "Come on, we're gonna be all right. Tell me you believe that."

Pressing his eyes shut, Brave nodded.

Slipping up against him, Shiori tucked her thumbs into the front pocket of his jeans, rising up on her tiptoes to kiss him. "No sulking. I love you too."

"And I love you." He let out a rough laugh. "I didn't realize how hard this would be."

"We're coming back here tonight, right?" Shiori waited for them both to nod. "Then let's not think any further. Nothing will change today."

"I hope you're right." Brave smoothed his hand over her hair. "Damn it, I never knew being crazy about someone could be so literal."

Another text from Jesse got them moving, but every time they got close to one another they had to kiss or touch again. They ended up running to meet the band in the lobby.

Thankfully, there was no media or crowd of fans.

But standing beside Jesse was Reese. Which was worse. One look and Malakai could tell she knew everything.

Their first real chance to pretend they were no more than friends.

And they'd failed.

Chapter Twenty-Five

Shiori's pulse wouldn't stop racing. She paced the greenroom, rubbing her hands on her leggings, which didn't help dry them since the material was slick. Damn it, she wanted a drink. Or a pillow to scream into. A pillow would probably be better. No need to get tipsy and have Reese think even less of her.

"Please sit down, you're making me dizzy." Danica took a long drink from the water bottle in her hand, grabbing Shiori's wrist the next time she passed. "Reese isn't mad."

"How do you know?" Shiori dropped down on the hard cushion of the sleek, slate-blue sofa. She brought her knees up to her chest and hugged them with one arm. "She didn't say *anything*. She just looked so...so disappointed."

Danica nodded slowly. "I think she's worried." Her brow creased slightly. "Should she be?"

"No! I can still perform. I won't distract Brave. Or Malakai." Heat crawled up the back of her neck when Danica's lips quirked. "I didn't mean to make them late."

"They're big boys, no one's blaming you. Besides, no one was late. We got here on schedule." Danica relaxed back against the sofa. "Honestly, I wouldn't worry too much. Reese always puts the band first. She's focused on business, but she cares about the guys."

"So do I." Her mouth went dry as she considered exactly how this would look to Reese. Shiori had promised not to act like a groupie, but she was sleeping with two members of the band. And doing a horrible job hiding it. "She'll get rid of me. That's her only option."

"She hasn't gotten rid of me."

"*You're* a proven asset. I'm expendable."

"I doubt the guys will agree." Danica held up a hand. "Stop thinking the worst. The way I see it, Reese will come here and give you one of two options. One, do better at keeping your relationship private. Two, bring it out in the open so she can play some naughty angle in the media. Give the band some publicity when your unconventional relationship goes viral online."

Is there a third option?

Even with the little Shiori knew of Reese, she doubted it.

She met Danica's eyes. "What would you do?"

"In your position? I'd keep it private." Danica's eyes darkened with sympathy. "And I feel like such a bitch saying that. People have speculated about Alder, Jesse, and I for a long time. Sometimes I tease with vague suggestive comments during interviews, and sometimes I tell the media absolutely nothing. It doesn't affect my career either way."

"I've discussed this with Brave and Malakai. We're all fine being discrete." She ducked her head when Danica's brow lifted. "We have to do better."

"Just a bit." Danica let out a soft laugh. "Don't leave together, wherever we are. That should help. So far you're pretty good keeping your distance when we're with the crew. On the bus, it doesn't matter, but anywhere else, just make sure you're not alone with them. Which will suck."

"I can do it." Shiori inhaled deep, letting the air out slowly to calm her frayed nerves. "Do you think Reese will let me try?"

Before Danica could answer, the door opened and Reese stepped into the greenroom. She didn't look upset, but she'd had time to compose herself. That flawless, professional persona was back. No different than when Reese had given her the first contract to sign.

"Please have a seat, Shiori." Reese pulled up a chair from the table in the center of the greenroom and sat facing Shiori and Danica. "And stop looking so scared. I have a proposal for you that might work for us all."

One of two options. Danica was right.

Shiori inclined her head. "Okay…"

Reese's lips curved slightly. "You're better on social media than I expected. You were told not to read comments, but I've been paying close attention to what people are saying."

Wincing, Shiori glanced over at Danica, whose brow furrowed. She hadn't been reading them either.

"That one blurry photo didn't get much attention—though the photographer tried hard, your making light of it with Danica took the steam out of the scandal. The majority want two things. More of your random, excited take of being on tour, and to see an unknown succeed." Reese paused for a moment, smiling when Shiori blinked at her. "You've brought them on this exciting journey. Without drama, without any expectations. Every post gives a fresh look at the lifestyle people haven't seen before."

"And…that's a good thing?" Shiori always felt silly when she posted comments above pictures of her with Danica, or with any of the guys. She wasn't funny. Wasn't cool or sarcastic.

She *was* excited to be with the band. Honesty was the best she could do.

"Absolutely! Shiori, you've made your journey into a reality show without all the demand for attention most have. You're sweet and almost shy and young girls can relate to you." Reese leaned forward, placing her hands over Shiori's. "You're living a modern-day Cinderella story. Coming from nowhere and appreciating everything you're given. You're beautiful, but you take pictures with your hair a mess, your eyes wide like you can't believe this is happening. A pair of shoes is a big deal. A purse has you acting like you're handling something precious.

You take nothing for granted and that's clear in every picture, in every word you say."

"But…" Shiori considered the angle Reese focused on and shook her head. "You make it sound like I'm doing a good job. But you were upset when you saw me with Brave and Malakai."

Nodding slowly, Reese met her eyes, expression grim. "I was. You could lose all the support you've gained in an instant. Those who are jealous of your success could warp this little affair as you being a groupie faking it all to get attention. I know you're not. And I understand how appealing those men are. But that sweet innocence, that untouched appeal, will be ruined with the wrong twist."

"So what should I do?"

"What you're already doing. Show clips of you with the band, simply amazed that you've gotten this opportunity. As you tour, show you a little more with Brave. Spending time together. Talking and having fun. Let people see how close you've become." Reese sat back, her lips curving slightly. "Let the media make you a thing before you've said a word. Let them ask for more. Tell you how cute you are together. Some will tell Brave he's a fool if he doesn't see what he can have with you."

That made sense, and could work, but Shiori stared at the floor as she considered the one flaw in Reese's plan. "What about Malakai?"

"Shiori… What you do with the men is none of my business. My job is to give them—and you—the best opportunities. Danica is riding the wave of controversy. But she's never really come out and said she's with two men. It's a huge risk." Reese folded her hands in her lap. "I wouldn't suggest you test public appeal at this point. Let them fall in love with you. Let them cheer for you. And once you're a top pick for every commercial, for every magazine…if this relationship is meant to last you'll have a story to tell."

"So we have to be careful." Shiori glanced over at Danica, who inclined her head. "We can do that."

"Excellent." Reese stood, her countenance much more relaxed. She'd been expecting resistance, which explained her initial approach. Motioning for Shiori and Danica to stand, she looked them over with a satisfied smile. "You're both perfect. We have a huge stage, so go with the more elaborate routines. You'll both be on for four of the ten songs. Sound good?"

Inhaling slowly, Shiori nodded. She'd only practiced two of the songs with the band, but she knew Danica's choreography for all of them. This would be the true test to prove she belonged here.

No way am I gonna mess this up.

"All right, let's go join the guys. There's time before sound check and they're going over a few numbers with some musician Brave insists I meet." She lowered her voice as they followed her to the door. "Back me up if I have to show the man the door."

Danica chuckled softly as they made their way down the hallway, which was slowly becoming crowded with the crew from both Winter's Wrath and the top headlining band. "Brave or the new guy?"

Reese smirked. "There are days... To be fair, Brave has been on his best behavior lately, so I can't complain."

"You can thank Shiori for that." Danica looped her arm around Shiori's shoulders, grinning at her. "She's a very good influence."

"I've noticed." Reese slowed as they approached the side stage door. Cocking her head, she hesitated with her hand on the doorknob.

Even through the door, the sound of a wailing guitar could be heard, clashing, then coming together with the long, pure tones of a violin. The combination was powerful. Eerie as the violin hit a minor key that made all the hairs on the back of Shiori's neck stand on end.

"Iron Maiden." Shiori tongued her bottom lip, searching for the name of the song. The chorus came and she shivered. "Hallowed Be Thy Name."

"Very good." Reese arched a brow at Danica. "You didn't know that, did you."

Gracefully, using her middle finger to flick a nonexistent strand of hair from her cheek, Danica nudged Reese aside to open the door herself.

Since the instruments weren't hooked up to the sound system, the music echoed in the huge concert hall, but being this close, the effect wasn't lost. Standing center stage, Alder ripped out the chords with the same enthusiasm he showed when playing for thousands. His long hair spilled over his shoulders, slicked back with sweat as he attacked the strings of his guitar like he was challenging them to do more.

Facing him, black skin glistening under the harsh lights, the violinist—Dariel, the man Brave had put all his faith in—slashed a long bow across the violin strings, moving with the same emotion pouring through the music. But he didn't play like he had something to prove. He, like every member of the band, knew exactly what he had to offer.

With his sound, with how good he looked on stage next to Alder, Shiori could understand why Brave wanted him to join them. He would be a perfect fit.

Hopefully, Reese agreed.

From the other side of the stage, Brave stepped out, followed by Tate, Connor, and lastly, Malakai. She frowned, not liking the distance between her men, but then she remembered she wasn't the only one who had a part to play.

They were in this together. She'd have to get used to being no more than friends again. At least in public.

On stage, with other bands coming in and out carrying equipment, fit the bill.

"Our audience has arrived." Brave stepped up to the mic, shooting Shiori a wink.

Reese let out a heavy sigh beside her.

"Reese, baby, you're gonna love this!" Brave looked over at Connor and Malakai as they took their places on stage. "Let's do *Subsist*. Once Reese hears how fucking awesome it sounds with Dariel playing, she'll join me in begging him to sign the contract."

Letting out a rough laugh, Reese shook her head. "I don't beg. And if you call me 'baby' again, your next sponsor will be the local greasy spoon."

"I'm sorry." Brave's cheeks reddened as all the guys stared at him—except for Dariel, who had a slanted smile on his lips. "What? It pisses her off. I gotta stop that shit."

Connor nudged Alder with his elbow. "Your big brother is growing up. Should we be afraid?"

Alder laughed and shook his head, as though to clear it. "Nope. I was hoping he'd smarten up before she handed him his balls. I'd like nieces and nephews some day!"

Cheeks blazing hot, Shiori glanced at Malakai, whose lips parted. Then quickly slammed shut. When his eyes met hers, there was heat in them, which sent a sweet spill of pleasure deep into her core.

She couldn't imagine him thinking of babies. Not this soon.

But practice making them? Yeah, his mind had definitely gone there.

Thankfully, Tate started the opening beat for the song, bringing the band's attention to the music.

Subsist was one of her favorites by Winter's Wrath, already perfect as far as she was concerned, but she couldn't deny the intensity Dariel added as he joined in. He didn't drown out the guitars, or Brave's intense vocals. Instead, he brought another layer to an already captivating arrangement. The band didn't seem to need to adjust to the addition. The violin simply filled a void they hadn't realized was there.

As the last note trailed off, Shiori clapped, too moved to show restraint. They'd done an amazing job. Who cared if she looked silly?

Only, she wasn't alone. Roadies had stopped to watch and cheered as they clapped as well. Beside her, Danica bounced in place, throwing Alder a kiss before slapping her hands together.

Reese hadn't moved. Hadn't reacted at all.

Brave shot her a nervous glance.

She smiled and strode across the stage, clapping slowly. "You won't hear me say this often, Brave, but you were right. Dariel, I won't beg, but I do want a few moments of your time while they're on stage to convince you to join. I brought a copy of the contract. I think you'll like what we have to offer."

Dariel placed his violin carefully in its case, shutting it securely before grabbing the handle and crossing the stage, holding his free hand out to Reese, a charming smile on his lips.

"I have a feeling I will too."

While the band cleared the stage, Dariel and Reese disappeared into the hall, Reese already giving her pitch. Danica walked over to Alder, hugging him and laughing when he grumbled something to her Shiori couldn't quite hear.

Shiori considered going to Brave, but she didn't trust her acting abilities. Her body was still tender from his lips on her. Ignoring Malakai when the sensual ache reminded her of him inside her was impossible.

The two men hadn't exchanged a word, so they weren't having an easy time of playing it cool either. Her only option was to keep herself busy until it was time for the show.

Stepping through the side stage door, she caught sight of a few roadies and trailed after them, hoping they were going out a private exit. Luckily, they were. She slipped out the door labeled 'employees only' and fished her phone from her purse.

There were texts from both Brave and Malakai.

BRAVE: I FUCKING MISS YOU ALREADY. I DON'T THINK I'VE EVER WANTED TO GET BACK ON THE ROAD MORE.

BRAVE: THAT WAS SELFISH TO SAY. I'M SORRY. IGNORE ME. I LOVE YOU.

BRAVE: I MAY GO INSANE IF I DON'T SEE YOU SOON.

BRAVE: IGNORE THAT TOO.

MALAKAI'S ONE TEXT WASN'T AS RAW, BUT ALSO MADE HER FEEL LIKE SHE WASN'T ALONE IN BEING SO TORN BETWEEN DOING WHAT SHE HAD TO DO, AND WANTING TO THROW CAUTION ASIDE.

MALAKAI: I'VE BEEN THINKING ABOUT YOU. CAN'T WAIT TO SEE YOU ON STAGE BECAUSE YOU'RE GOING TO PROVE TO EVERYONE HOW INCREDIBLE YOU ARE. WHICH I ALREADY KNOW. <3

How in the world did she reply? She didn't want to distract them. Didn't want to sound needy. Didn't want them to worry.

But this was all they had right now.

So she did her best.

To Brave, she kept things light.

SHIORI: I MISS YOU, BUT I'M SO PROUD OF WHAT YOU DID OUT THERE. THERE'S NO DOUBT DARIEL IS MEANT TO BE PART OF WINTER'S WRATH. YOU WERE ALREADY KILLING IT WITH YOUR MUSIC, BUT WITH HIM? HOLY SHIT! \m/ SO MUCH LOVE, BABY.

With Malakai, she had to thank him, because he'd managed to put her head back in the game.

SHIORI: I WASN'T SURE I COULD DO ANYTHING BUT THINK OF YOU. NOW I WANT TO BE THE WOMAN YOU THINK I AM. I ALWAYS DOUBT THAT I'M HALF OF WHO I NEED TO BE, BUT YOU MAKE ME BELIEVE I CAN BE EVEN MORE. I LOVE YOU.

She still had time to kill before Winter's Wrath hit the stage. Danica would be expecting her in the dressing room soon for last minute touch ups and to go over their routine.

But she had a couple of calls to make while things were somewhat quiet. It wasn't too cold outside, so a few roadies and band members were hanging out, smoking and chatting. Walking to the edge of the building, out of the wind, she called home to talk to Hiro.

No answer.

Maybe Elizabeth had taken him out for dinner? Shiori tried her cell, but there was still no answer.

She pulled up Wendy's number, then shook her head. Wendy would be at work now. No need to bother her. Fine, it was a little weird that she couldn't get ahold of Elizabeth, but there could be many reasons. She could be taking a shower. Be at a movie with Hiro. In the middle of driving—which usually meant Hiro would answer, unless he was playing a game on her phone.

It hit her, suddenly, that while she was here, trying to build a future for herself and Hiro, life back home had gone on without her.

Everything routine and familiar was gone. Which would be good in the long run. She needed to change things to provide Hiro with all he'd need when she took over as his guardian. She'd promised her sister she would do whatever it took.

And she was keeping that promise.

Chapter Twenty-Six

The music blared as Shiori slid onstage, thrusting her chest forward and her shoulders back. All around her, the pounding beat urged her on, and she drank in the fervor of the crowd as she punched her fist up in the air.

Uncertainty melted away in the moist, smoke-filled air as the music took over. She saluted sharply as Brave gave a shout out to all the service men and women in the crowd. This song was dedicated to them, honoring their sacrifice. Yes, it also protested needless death, but the lyrics expressed the power of intent. The need to protect against all adversary, even when facing hate, they stood for what they loved.

When she'd danced to *S.L.U.T*, the dance had been sexual. The new routine took on more of a burlesque feel, playfully sensual. But for this song, both she and Danica were truly backup dancers, their every move bringing attention back to the band. To the lyrics. To the core meaning beneath it all.

Marching in place, she kept her eyes forward, her movements crisp, hardly blinking even though the light blinded her. When Malakai stepped up to her side, leaning down as he strummed out a deep, powerful note, she didn't react. This dance wasn't integrated with the band in the same way the others were. The choreography was as strict as any march until it switched drastically at the chorus so they moved with the crowd, egging on their shouts while punching their fists up.

A final, patriotic drumbeat and Shiori stood at attention, counting in her head for her exit. She caught the eye of a man close to the stage, who she'd noticed singing along the whole time.

He was an older man, maybe in his fifties, which might seem strange to some at a metal concert, but she'd noticed the appeal of Winter's Wrath didn't have an age limit. His black t-shirt read "Crawl, Walk, Run" in a large army font. And he had tears in his eyes.

Not thinking, she went to the edge of the stage, took a knee, and held out her hand. He smiled at her and reached past the barrier, squeezing her fingers and mouthing "Thank you."

She didn't know his story. Didn't know if he was really a vet—but she had a feeling he was. This song had touched him on another level.

There were flashes of cameras all around. Jesse—who'd joined security behind the partition—moved closer, but didn't intervene.

Someone approached her side. She caught Brave's smile from the corner of her eye.

"What's your name, sir?" Brave held out the mic.

Jesse passed it to the man.

"George Harris." The man's voice was strong and clear. "I was a Wolfhound for thirty years. Not sure you kids know what that means, but I have to say, I fell in love with your music when I heard this song. *Nec Aspera Terrent.*"

"*Nec Aspera Terrent.*" Brave slipped off the stage and gave the man a hug. "Thank you for your service."

More camera flashes. This would bring good publicity to the band, but Shiori knew, like her, Brave hadn't considered that at all. He patted the man's shoulder as Tate came to the edge of the stage, offering his drumsticks. Alder, Malakai, and Connor each gave the man guitar picks. Small gestures, but the man's smile grew wider with every one.

He still had the microphone and spoke into it with a laugh. "I've heard your cover of Megadeth *A Tout le Monde*. Be awesome if you could play it."

"Consider it done." Brave took the mic back and looked over the crowd. "You all good with that? This man deserves all the thanks we can give."

The crowd went wild. Then they started singing. Shiori half expected the American anthem, but instead, the people sang *America the Beautiful*. Not everyone knew all the words. But they did their best and those who did sang loud and clear.

Pulling himself back onstage, Brave joined in, with the band quickly adding their instruments, albeit softly, without drowning out all the voices.

Blinking back tears, Shiori sang along, hand over her heart, not sure why the crowd singing was so emotional. She'd always loved hearing this song, or the anthem, at events, but this was different. This held a unity she hadn't realized she missed.

The show had been paused to give the people this moment. The war veteran had fresh tears running down his cheeks. He knew what this meant, far better than she did.

She didn't think about politics much. They could be confusing and a little terrifying. But in moments like this, all she saw was so many amazing people, honoring another's sacrifices.

As the song ended, Alder began the opening notes for *A Tout le Monde*. And it was perfect, because that unity didn't fade. Everyone sang along with Brave and got lost in the escape he'd given them. Music had a power to unite. And Brave wielded that power effortlessly.

She took Danica's cue to retreat from the stage after the first verse and met her backstage. They hugged and didn't say much. So far the night had been amazing, for so many reasons.

Two more songs and it was time to hit the stage again. This song was light, defiant and sexy. There was a wardrobe change and Shiori was a little nervous about dancing in a short skirt and tiny silver tube top, but with a few tips from Danica, she managed not to humiliate herself.

They finished their closing number to an insane round of applause. The fans were happy. The show had gone off without a hitch.

And Shiori had been part of it.

She was high on what she'd accomplished as she left the stage. Her whole body hummed with excitement. Nothing could go wrong now. All she had to do was *this*. Again for every crowd. A performance of a lifetime. A dream she never had to wake up from.

Maybe she was still in that dream when she saw Wendy. Nothing could make this moment better than having her best friend here to share it with.

But she definitely wasn't dreaming when she saw her stepfather, struggling with security a few feet away from the side entrance.

Her 'dream' had just turned into a nightmare.

Chapter Twenty-Seven

He can't be here.

Shiori closed her eyes and backed up a step. She wasn't afraid of him. Not really. Not anymore. He'd become an abstract menace. The person who controlled Hiro's life, and by extension, controlled hers.

But he was gone so often, she'd gotten comfortable. She always had time to prepare before seeing him at home.

He shouldn't *be here.*

Her chest tightened as Wendy took her hand and leaned close to her, forcing her to open her eyes and face that he *was* here and wouldn't simply go away, no matter how much she wanted him to.

"Tell security to get rid of him. We need to talk." Wendy kept her voice low, putting her body between Shiori and her stepfather protectively.

Which made Shiori nervous. Sure, Wendy didn't like him, but she had no reason to consider him a threat.

Did she?

"Shiori, tell these assholes I'm your father." He let out an irritated sound as security loosened their grip, but didn't release him, looking to her for confirmation. "Damn it, let me go to my daughter."

She shook her head, backing up a little more. She'd never seen him this angry. No way in hell was she letting him get closer. "You've made a point of telling me you're *not* my father. And you've never been one. Kyoko and I earned everything you ever gave us. I owe you *nothing*."

"That's fucking *bullshit!*" He growled as the bigger guard blocked him from lunging at her. "You little slut, I might end up in jail because of you! If you ever want to see Hiro again, you'll testify on my behalf. You tell them I never hurt you. Tell them those pictures were innocent."

Her stomach dropped. Her blood ran cold. Darkness swam in her vision and she had to hold on to Wendy to keep from dropping to her knees.

This can't be happening.

"Shiori, tell them you don't want to see him. I need to explain what happened." Wendy gave her a little shake, holding her gaze with a determined stare when she looked up. "Honey, just tell them. I've got you."

Swallowing hard, Shiori nodded. She glanced over at the big guard. "He shouldn't be here. Please see him out."

Eyes filled with sympathy, the big guard inclined his head. "My pleasure."

A tug at her arm got her to turn. Danica slid her hands over Shiori's ears as her stepfather shouted. It didn't block out everything, but Shiori could hardly hear past her heart pounding in her skull. The world seemed ready to collapse around her.

When Danica moved her hands, the only sound was the final act of the band. She took Shiori's arm, holding her close, while Wendy pressed against her other side.

Then they were in the greenroom.

Shiori was sitting on the hard sofa.

And Danica was pressing a glass of water into her hand.

"Drink." Danica crouched in front of her, smiling as she took a sip. "Good. Now, it's up to you if you want me to stay. I recognize Wendy from your video chats. If you're more comfortable speaking to her alone, I'll leave. I'm sure she knows more than I—"

"She doesn't." Shiori could hardly hold the glass. She handed it to Danica and leaned back against the sofa, pressing her hands over her eyes. "I never told anyone. I just wanted to forget. But you should stay. This could affect the band, and you'll know how to handle... Or...or maybe I should quit. They don't need me bringing them down."

Wendy hugged her. Kissed her temple. Then pulled her hands away from her face. "You're not quitting. Tell us what you're dealing with. Or I can just go kick his ass. Up to you."

Laughing, tears blinding her, Shiori shook her head. "I need you here." Her whole body shook as she thought back on all she'd believed she could leave in the past.

But she'd been wrong.

"Af-after my mother died, my stepfather struggled to support us for a while, but then, suddenly, things were okay. He'd been threatening to send me and Kyoko to a foster home for months. We never had enough food. He complained that we ate too much, that we were lazy..." She folded her hands on her lap and stared at them. "Out of nowhere, he stopped. He didn't have a better job, but he had lots of money. He got a new car and started buying me and my sister new clothes. I was only seven, so I didn't ask any questions. Kyoko had somehow made him happy. She told me not to worry."

She inhaled roughly, squeezing her hands together until her knuckles hurt.

"For almost two years, things were good. But then the phone and cable got cut. Our stepfather couldn't pay the bills. He was angry all the time again." She pressed her lips together. Now both Wendy and Danica would be disgusted with her. But they had to know the truth. "He came home one day—Kyoko was at school, but I'd been sick. He said he wanted to bring me to a doctor, but he couldn't afford to. So he needed me to do something for him. Let him take some pictures."

Neither Wendy or Danica seemed to be breathing.

Shiori kept going.

"It wasn't a big deal. Just pictures of me in my PJs. He asked me to lift my top a little. Lay on my side and hook my thumb to my bottoms." She unclenched her hands and rubbed her thighs. "He brought me to the doctor. Got my medicine. And he was happy with me. Told me I was 'earning my keep'."

Wendy rubbed her shoulder. "But it didn't stop there."

"No. There were more pictures. Always when Kyoko wasn't home. They didn't seem like a big deal until...until he wanted to do a video. With me in the bath." Goosebumps spread over her skin as she remembered that day. He hadn't really touched her, but still made her uncomfortable. Being naked in front of the camera while he washed her crossed some invisible line she hadn't understood. "I...I felt weird after. Kyoko noticed my behavior changed. She asked me what happened and wouldn't leave me alone until I told her."

Both Danica and Wendy nodded, leaning forward slightly.

Shiori smiled and took a deep breath. "She told me I would never have to do that again. She talked to our stepfather. And that was it. He never asked me again."

"So your sister saved you." Danica spoke softly, taking Shiori's hands in hers. "She knew what he was doing was wrong."

"Yes, but...she told me not to talk about it. That we would be separated if we told on him. That it wasn't a big deal." She knew that wasn't true. She'd heard things, read things...but those horror stories weren't her life. What had happened to her had been brief. And she'd made a promise to her sister. "Our stepfather ended up getting a great job. He bought a new house and it was over."

It wasn't. You know it wasn't.

She ground her teeth. "Long story short, Kyoko started going out a lot. Disappearing for days. Our stepfather never said anything. He was busy. I worried about her, but all she would ask when she came home was if he was leaving me alone. And he was."

Both women nodded.

"And…she got pregnant. And she talked about Valor all the time. The doctor told her having a baby could kill her, but she didn't believe him. She told me over and over again their child would make Valor love her. Love her as much as she loved him." Her eyes burned and a single tear trailed down her cheek. "She started asking me how old I was when our stepfather took the pictures. Then she said, if anything happened to her, I had to get her baby away before he reached that age. I promised I would."

"She thought he'd be safe until then." Wendy held her hands and sighed. "I wish you'd told me about all this. I understand why you didn't, but… Elizabeth found the pictures on his hard drive. She sent them to the police. She called your stepfather and told him there was an emergency so he'd fly back early. He was arrested yesterday. And let out on bail this morning."

"And he wants me to defend him." Shiori shook her head. "If he has Hiro somewhere, I *have* to."

"He doesn't. And no bloody way in hell are you taking the stand at all." Wendy's tone sharpened. "Elizabeth provided the police with all the evidence they need. She found the website he was selling the pictures on. She didn't find many of you, but Kyoko…" Wendy's bottom lip trembled. "He used her for years. The things Elizabeth saw, when she told me…" Tears filled Wendy's eyes, dripping down her chin as she tipped her head back. "This wasn't a small thing he did. The job he has now? It looks like he got it because of connections with people involved in…in the black market. He's made a sickening amount of money off you and your sister. Of off exploiting and abusing you both."

"No." Shiori pulled away from Wendy. Hugged herself. Clung to Kyoko's words.

"I don't want you doing that again. But, Shiori, you can't tell anyone. He shouldn't have taken that video, but it wasn't so bad, right?" Kyoko smiled when she shrugged. "Sure, it's weird. But now he can't tell you that you don't help him. You did. And it's over. Try to forget about it."

She'd tried. Damn it, she'd tried so hard. But the idea of Kyoko doing it for years? To protect her?

She said it was over.

The focus had to be on Hiro. Not on something that happened so long ago. She met Wendy's eyes. "Where is he?"

"Elizabeth took him to your grandparents." Wendy made a face. "When I talked to her she was ranting about you not appreciating the support they gave you for years. That you refused to see them. That you'd put Hiro at risk because you were too lazy to grow up and move out."

"I wasn't... I..." Her grandparents had been supporting her? *When? How?* From everything her mother and her stepfather had told her, her grandparents didn't even acknowledge her existence. "I thought they hated me like they hated my mother. They liked my father, but when he died they wanted my mother to marry a man like him. Not a white American man she'd met online. My stepfather told me they'd be disgusted by how I was raised."

"Elizabeth said they don't care about any of that. They've sent you letters for years." Wendy made a rough sound of frustration. "I knew what you thought about them, so I told Elizabeth there's no way you knew about the letters."

"I didn't."

"Exactly. But Elizabeth wants to 'save' Hiro from you." Wendy sighed. 'Talking to her is pointless. She's freaked out. But from the sounds of it, your grandparents are awesome people. They paid to fly her and Hiro to California. They already have a lawyer on retainer, looking at the whole case so they can legally gain custody of him."

Custody? Shiori's whole body shook. She drew her knees up to her chest. "I can't afford to fight them if they have the money for a lawyer already."

"You might not need to." Wendy pulled Shiori against her side. "Give them a chance. Meet them at least. The point is, Hiro is safe. And he's not alone with strangers. Elizabeth won't leave him and he loves her."

True. Whatever Elizabeth thought of Shiori, she treated Hiro like a little prince. Spoiled him, played with him, and even stood up to Shiori's stepfather when he was cold to the little boy.

She had taken Hiro away because she believed he was in danger.

Shiori had to find a way to prove she would never have let anything happen to him.

Even though she *had* stayed there, knowing what her stepfather could do.

Even though she'd let herself believe she had time.

Even though her plans to give Hiro a better life had been part of a dream that was all about her. Sure, she'd planned to make enough money to get him away from her stepfather, but what if she'd failed?

"Elizabeth has no reason to trust me. I was stupid. I wanted…" She pressed her fingers over her eyes. "I saw what Danica was doing and I wanted to follow in her footsteps. I knew it was a long shot, but I did it anyway. I was selfish—"

"No, you had a goal and you fought for it. Shiori, there's no fucking way I'm letting you put this on yourself." Wendy gave her another shake when she didn't reply. "This situation isn't normal. You should be able to have dreams. To want something for yourself. But I can't help but wonder, after what he did to you, how being in front of a camera sounded like a good idea."

Selfish *and* stupid. If she wasn't pretty, would any of this have happened? Her stepfather always focused on how she looked. And then she did the same.

How fucked up was she?

But…wanting to be like Danica hadn't felt wrong.

Frowning, she tried to put her thoughts into words. "When I went to the interview I wondered what it would be like. Sophie made me so comfortable. Asked me what I wanted to wear for the first few shots. Got me to take funny poses to relax."

Danica smiled and inclined her head. "She's amazing. I've seen her work with girls from all different backgrounds. She makes sure they know they're in control. God help any photographer that tries to push them beyond what they've agreed to."

Shiori nodded, knowing exactly what she meant. "I think that's what I needed. Some control. I had pushed what happened to the back of my mind, but I guess some of it still got to me. I wanted to see myself like I saw beautiful women between the covers of my favorite magazines. Graceful. Powerful. Giving interviews that show how smart and talented they are."

"But you wanted to be with the band, instead of in the magazines." Danica headed to the mini-fridge to grab a can of diet 7UP. She held up another, putting in back when both Wendy and Shiori shook their heads. Then she pulled up a chair and settled down, her relaxed posture breaking the tension in the room. "Was it only because you wanted to know Hiro's family?"

"No. I love the music. I wanted to be close to it." Shiori rolled her shoulder. "But the Trousseau brothers were a big part of it. I'm so happy he'll have a chance to get to know them."

"They're happy too." Danica took a sip of her drink. "Alder won't stop talking about Hiro. Despite how bad things look right now, you accomplished everything you wanted to. Hiro is safe. He has family to take care of him. He still has you—I don't see your grandparents keeping him from you."

"I hope not." Shiori's throat squeezed like a huge fist had tightened around it. "I can't lose him. He's the only family I have left."

"You won't lose him." Wendy kissed her cheek noisily, then laid her head on Shiori's shoulder. "Besides, *we're* family. Right?"

"Right." Shiori pressed her lips to Wendy's bushy red hair. She couldn't have asked for a better best friend. Even with her crazy schedule, Wendy had dropped everything to make sure Shiori's stepfather couldn't catch her off-guard.

But how in the world had they gotten here at the same time? If her stepfather was out on bail, could he still fly?

Silly question, but she asked anyway.

Wendy snorted. "I jumped on a bus early this morning. He got on the same one. I may have had homicidal thoughts the whole way here, but I let him live."

"Generous of you. I'm not sure I would have shown that kind of restraint." Danica's eyes narrowed until her smooth, golden features took on a feral edge. The door opened, but she didn't notice. "Then again, men can live without their balls, right?"

No one entered the room, but Tate's voice could be heard from the hall. "I am *not* going in there."

A heavy sigh, then Jesse strode in, followed closely by Alder. He immediately focused on Danica. "If you're gonna kill someone, love, give me some notice. There are no shovels on the bus."

Warmth filled Danica's eyes. She shot to her feet and threw her arms around Jesse's neck. "Damn, I love you so much!"

"Ha! How much you want to bet he'd make the rest of us dig the hole?" Alder stepped up to Jesse and Danica, folding his arms over his chest, even as a broad smile lit his face.

Danica brought her finger to her lips. "Shh. He's being awesome. Don't ruin it."

Jesse shot Alder a smug look. "I am so getting laid tonight."

"*Annnd* he ruins it." Alder snorted when Danica smacked Jesse's chest. Then his expression turned grim. He waited until the band filled the room, then turned his attention to Shiori. "Security told us some guy came in, following a few band members, acting like he belonged here. They stopped him when they didn't see his pass. He claimed to be your father."

This is it. Shiori stood even as Malakai and Brave moved towards her. She couldn't lean on them while she relived the past again. She couldn't lean on Wendy either. The band had dealt with more than enough drama as they struggled to succeed in the music industry. They'd come so far, and she refused to let her problems taint their accomplishments.

But as she went over all she'd just told Danica and Wendy, she didn't see a single member of the band ready to pull away from her. Their expressions ranged from shock, to anger. Brave cursed once and looked ready to storm out. Said something about wanting to meet her stepfather.

Malakai stopped him. Told Shiori to go on as he kept a firm grip on Brave's wrist. As she finished giving them all the details they could possibly need about her stepfather's presence, a weight lifted from her chest.

They knew everything, and they didn't seem to think less of her. The way Brave and Malakai looked at her hadn't changed.

But no one seemed to know what to say.

Finally, Alder spoke up. "Shiori, you're one of us. Don't *ever* doubt that." He reached out and squeezed Brave's shoulder, taking a deep breath when Brave nodded. "The question is, how do you want to handle this?"

Good question. And she gave the only answer she could.

"I have no idea."

Chapter Twenty-Eight

Brave gnashed his teeth together as he led the way to the private parking where the van was parked. His mind raced as he tried to absorb what Shiori had just told them. He couldn't wait to be away from all the other bands, from security and staff, so he could hold her.

Not that he gave a fuck about what people thought, but the way Shiori hung back with Danica and Wendy, shoulders squared as she smiled for the press, he figured she was clinging to the little bit of normal she had left.

And for them, normal meant keeping the masks in place. Be happy. Agree it had been a great show. Express how awesome it was to be back in New York.

Give the media absolutely nothing to twist into a story.

Usually, he had no trouble playing his part of the aloof, smooth-talking bad boy, but tonight, the best he could manage was not to growl at reporters and bloggers.

The woman he loved had been abused as a child and the disgusting bastard who'd victimized her was here. Somewhere. Way too fucking close.

He'd threatened *Hiro.*

My nephew.

And now, Hiro was with strangers.

Fine, Shiori's grandparents were her family, but even she didn't know them. What if they were mean to that sweet little boy who wanted someone to play ball with and give him ice cream for breakfast? A little boy who'd been yanked from his home suddenly to protect him from his sick fuck of a guardian.

Shiori had jumped on an opportunity to give Hiro and herself a better life. She'd hoped Brave and Alder could help her. That their parents might be able to fight for custody when she couldn't.

He was tempted to call his parents, even though he hated the idea of Hiro spending a day in their dubious care. They'd be better than Shiori's stepfather. Which was pretty fucked up.

Once they got back to the hotel, they could help Shiori plan her next move. Get in touch with her grandparents. Hire a lawyer. A *dozen* lawyers. He'd sell the bus if they couldn't come up with the money. No way was Shiori dealing with this alone. He didn't care how rich her grandparents might be. If they tried to keep Hiro away from her, they'd have a fight on their hands.

The small lot behind the arena was packed with roadies and opening bands still hanging out. Smoke filled the air, a strong mix of cigarettes and weed. He swallowed hard, not sure which he craved more. Either would calm his frayed nerves.

Pull it together, asshole. Shiori needs you.

Right. No drugs. No alcohol.

Just a clear head. And hopefully, a solution.

"Shiori!"

Brave glanced over at the shout and frowned. A man came running toward them, his eyes hard.

Behind him, Shiori inhaled sharply. Without looking at her, Brave stepped forward, cutting between her and the stranger.

No. Not a stranger. This must be her stepfather.

"Back the fuck off, man." Brave braced himself as the man tried to shove him aside. He grabbed the man's jacket. "If you don't leave, I'm calling the cops."

Laughing, the man grabbed him by the throat, leaning close to hiss in his face. "Go ahead. I've got nothing to lose."

Before Brave could react, Alder ripped the man away from him. Lifted him straight off his feet and slammed him on the pavement.

Letting out a feral sound, Alder cracked his fist into the man's jaw. Then hit him again. And again.

Alder's going to kill the bastard.

For a split second, Brave considered letting him.

Shouts sounded around them like white noise. His pulse pounded in his skull. He watched blood spray up into his younger brother's face.

He is going to kill this man.

And it would ruin his life.

No one had moved. Time passed in a blur. Brave thought he told Alder to stop, but he couldn't be sure that the word left his lips.

Because Alder didn't hesitate. Didn't even flinch.

So Brave did the only thing he could. He tackled Alder, grabbing for his wrists.

Alder's head cracked into the pavement.

He stopped fighting.

Stopped moving.

A sharp cry sounded. Ripped from Brave's own throat.

What have I done?

Chapter Twenty-Nine

Alder's blood ran cold as the man grabbed Brave. The past and the present rushed together. His vision flashed red.

Not again! Never fucking again!

This time he'd strike first. He wouldn't be the one taken down. Wouldn't be useless while his brother was still in danger. Wouldn't let anyone take the life he loved away.

The man hit the ground. Struggling, eyes crazed, like those staring at Alder when the knife pierced his chest onstage that night. One punch didn't stop him. Alder shifted his weight on the man, hammering down with his fists. Hot blood sprayed his face.

He had to keep fighting. Had to survive.

A solid weight struck him. He hit the ground hard.

Pain radiated through his skull.

Darkness stole him away.

But not for long.

Opening his eyes, he winced at the commotion all around. His head throbbed and he squinted at the form leaning over him. Brave. All blurry, but definitely Brave.

Alder tried to sit up.

"Don't you fucking move." Brave pressed down on his shoulder. "An ambulance is on the way."

"Ambulance?" Alder shoved Brave's hand off him and sat up. *Too fast.* He searched his surroundings even as his stomach turned and bile filled his throat. "Where's Danica? Jesse?"

"We're here." Jesse sat beside him and put an arm around his shoulders. "Try to relax. You cracked your head pretty hard."

Soft fingers brushed over his hair. Danica let out a sigh of relief as she knelt beside Brave. "You're not bleeding. But you still need to get checked."

"No. We need to make sure that man..." Alder blinked and looked around again. Blue and red lights flashed. As his vision cleared he made out Tate and Connor speaking to the police. Malakai and Shiori were off to the side with two more cops. "That man. Where is he?"

"First cop that got here took him to the hospital. The fucker's banged up a bit, but he was able to resist arrest before whining that he needed medical care." Brave let out a low growl. "He didn't say if he was pressing charges, but I wouldn't be surprised."

Alder snorted, which sent a stab of pain through his skull. "Let him. It was worth it. No one fucks with my brother."

"We agreed the next time someone attacked us, I would deal with them." Brave's tone wasn't as playful as his words. He sounded scared. "I didn't mean to hurt you."

Hurt me? Alder frowned. Then he remembered being knocked to the ground. "You're the one who rammed into me?"

Brave's lips parted. He swallowed hard.

Jesse squeezed Alder's shoulder. "If he hadn't, I would have. You weren't going to stop."

"No. I wasn't." Alder took a deep breath. "And as much as I want the bastard to pay for what he did to Shiori, what he could have done to Hiro, and...and for putting his hands on Brave..." He reached over, pulling Danica's hand to his lips. "He's done enough damage. If Brave hadn't stopped me, he would have done more."

"But it's over. And you are going to the hospital." Danica's lips drew into a firm line. "It's not up for discussion."

"Fine. But I'm not going in an ambulance." He wouldn't bother arguing with her, but no need to make this into a huge deal. Already he could see reporters pressing against the edge of the police barrier. Along with some fans. "I want to get up and show them I'm okay. Prove to *you* that I am."

Danica and Jesse exchanged a look. Both nodded.

But it was Brave who stood and held out his hand. "Let's show everyone how tough my little brother is."

Holding tightly to his brother's hand, Alder stood. His head spun, and his stomach lurched. He sucked in air through his teeth. Then met Brave's eyes.

The guilt hadn't faded, but there was something more. Protectiveness, as though Brave wanted to shield him from the world, but knew he couldn't. Then the warm glow of pride. Like he'd realized he didn't have to.

"I love you, you crazy little shit." Brave laughed and pulled him close, hugging him tight. "I don't deserve you."

"Shut up." Alder cupped the back of Brave's head in his palm and pressed their foreheads together. "I'm a fucking mess. And this might not be over. I need you."

Brave nodded slowly, then lifted his head to kiss Alder's brow. "I'm right here. And I'm not going anywhere."

Exactly what Alder needed to hear. And he held on to his brother's words as the cops questioned him. As the media tried to stop the van from leaving before they headed to the hospital. As the doctor examined him and diagnosed him with a mild concussion.

This wasn't over, but one huge thing had changed.

His brother was an ally.

The band stood together as one strong unit.

Danica and Jesse were on the same page.

With that, he could face whatever the world threw at him from this point on.

Chapter Thirty

Shiori stared at her phone. Turned it off. Turned it back on and dialed the number again. The number Wendy had given her.

The number to her grandmother's cell phone.

Sitting in her hotel room, on the fancy, crisp white sofa that seemed carved out of thinly padded stone, she sensed Brave's and Malakai's eyes on her from across the room. Could tell Wendy was holding her breath beside her.

But Shiori couldn't make the call. Not until she was sure she'd say the right thing. Because, if she didn't, she might never see Hiro again.

"Honey, listen to me." Wendy locked her hands around Shiori's wrists. "Your grandparents really do seem like great people. They're just in a bad situation. I don't know what Elizabeth told them. But they need to hear from you."

Inclining her head, Shiori stared at her phone. "But what do they need to hear? My stepfather is in jail. They know what he did. If I say the wrong thing, they might think—"

"Shiori, stop. *None* of this is your fault."

"But it *is*. I could have reported him. Maybe I should have..." The messages on her phone from her stepfather's lawyer shook her to the core. He'd said since she'd waited so long she clearly didn't think he'd done anything wrong. She was a model, so she liked having pictures taken. He'd subpoena her and she'd be obligated to appear and respond to the allegations.

Which didn't make sense to her. Taking the pictures hadn't been what started all this. They had evidence he'd sold them. Wendy had explained how Elizabeth found evidence on his computer to prove he was involved in child pornography. The strongest evidence involved her sister. Even if she wanted to testify on his behalf—no way in hell, not now that she knew Hiro was safe—it wouldn't matter.

He was guilty. The prosecutor would deal with him. The attorney had everything he needed.

And he'd told Shiori as much when he called her.

The call had been frightening, but the man was very nice. He answered her questions and told her she could come in if she wanted to, but he didn't see any need to put her on the stand.

Relief made her feel guilty.

Which brought her back to the call she had to make now.

What if her grandparents were disgusted with her? What if they looked at Hiro and imagined the danger she'd put him in? It was hard enough to look in the mirror without condemning herself.

Kyoko had told her the pictures weren't a big deal. Kyoko had told her to keep quiet.

But Kyoko had been the real victim.

A victim who'd believed what she said to survive.

I miss her so much. I wish we'd had someone to protect us. Someone who saw we were little girls without our mother. Without anyone besides each other.

The more she thought about it, the more she realized Kyoko hadn't been allowed to be an innocent little girl. Their stepfather had taken that away from her.

But he hadn't taken that from Hiro.

Maybe Hiro had someone else now. Someone who'd make sure he could be a kid. That he never wondered if he deserved the love he was given.

I can't let him go. He still needs me.

Or…was it just that she needed him? Maybe she was being selfish again.

"Call them." Wendy dialed the number, without pressing send. "You need to know them too."

A firm nod and Shiori called. Even if Wendy was wrong, she had to know these people her little boy was with. To know that he wasn't afraid. That he understood she'd be with him when she could.

"Hello?" The woman had a nice voice. Calm.

That Shiori got all that from one word showed how desperate she was. She cleared her throat. "Is this Misaki Sato?"

"Yes. May I ask who's calling?" Her grandmother had a thick accent, which reminded her so much of her mother. It had been a long time since she'd heard someone speak in a way that brought back those memories.

"My name is Shiori. I'm…I'm your granddaughter."

Misaki released a sharp breath. "I've been hoping to hear from you. And Hiro has been asking about you."

Shiori's throat locked and she swallowed hard as tears filled her eyes. "How is he?"

"He was confused at first, but Elizabeth told us the games he likes. He thinks he's on vacation. Being given so many treats. I admit, I'm spoiling him." Misaki laughed, but the sound faded quickly. "She told me you never read my letters."

Shiori nodded, ready for that after Wendy's warning. "I never got them."

"I expected as much. I wish I'd tried harder to reach you. Your grandfather would grumble now and then that *the man* our daughter chose wouldn't do right by you. But Himari had so much faith in him. She was angry when we questioned her marrying so soon after your father died. The distance between us grew and we didn't know how to make her believe we still loved her. I think your stepfather convinced her we didn't. She stopped taking our calls."

Was anything I believed true?

Could she trust this stranger over her mother?

Damn it, she had no idea. But with how manipulative her stepfather was?

Maybe I should. She inhaled slowly. "She told me you disowned her. That you wanted nothing to do with me and Kyoko."

Misaki cursed under her breath. "It hurts that she thought I would... Shiori, you were a baby when she married him, so you can't possibly remember how it was before. I was still living in Japan, but I was with Himari when Kyoko was born, and within days of your birth—only because a storm delayed the flight. You took your first step when I visited again. You used to coo at me on the phone..."

Shiori blinked fast as Misaki's voice broke. She could hear the pain in her tone.

"I held you at their wedding. Fixed Kyoko's hair and played with her when she fussed. That was the last time they let me see you. I called when I returned home and things became tense. Your mother was so distant. Weeks later, we spoke again. I asked if she was getting enough help. If her friends visited often. She said your stepfather didn't like them, so she'd cut ties. With women she'd known for years—who'd always been there for her. I was shocked. He didn't like a single one? Wasn't she lonely? Her answer was no. She had him and he was all she needed. I disagreed. That conversation convinced her I would never accept the man she loved."

"He isolated her. She never spent time with anyone when I was little." Shiori hugged her knees to her chest. "I thought she was lonely too, but she said her little family made her happy when she'd lost hope of ever finding happiness again. I felt special, but I was sad for her."

Misaki sighed. "After the love she shared with your father, I think she was desperate to fill that void. I should have seen it. I should have been more careful."

"You couldn't have known. I just wish things had been different." Shiori pressed her head back against the sofa. "I want better for Hiro."

"He will have it. And so will you. You have a family I hope you'll want to be part of." Misaki's tone grew so soft, Shiori could hardly hear her. "You have five uncles you've never met. Twelve cousins. Six of them live in California, close to me and your grandfather. They're so excited to meet Hiro. To finally meet you."

"But…" Shiori couldn't imagine a big family. Her mother hadn't said anything about brothers. As far back as Shiori could remember, she'd thought her mother was an only child. She shook her head, afraid to hope she'd be accepted by these strangers. "Has Elizabeth told them…told them how I put Hiro in danger?"

"Elizabeth is a fierce woman, and I can tell she loves our boy, but she's in shock from what she learned. She thought your stepfather was cheating on her. That's why she went through his files." Misaki went quiet. "Shiori, what happened to you…I wish I could take it away. I can't fix the past, but there's much I can do now. For Hiro. And for you, if you'll let me."

"I can see him?" Shiori blinked, tears spilling down her cheeks. That was all she wanted, but her grandmother was offering so much more. "I was afraid you wouldn't let me."

"My sweet girl, that hadn't even crossed my mind." Her grandmother's voice was a soothing balm on all her fears. "I know you're working, but when you're ready, I'll buy you a plane ticket. There's a room in the main house. Or the guest house. Whatever you're comfortable with. But I expect you'll want to be close to your nephew."

"Yes! I would love that!" Shiori didn't hesitate. "You don't have to buy the ticket. I've been saving money. I can come tomorrow."

"You will not use the money you saved. Let me give you this." Her grandmother laughed. "I plan to spoil you too."

They spoke for a little longer, her grandmother catching her up on all the family drama as if they'd known one another forever. Giving her a play by play of Hiro's day.

In return, she told her grandmother about the tour. About dancing on stage and laughed when her grandmother found her on Facebook and twitter, exclaiming about how much she looked like her mother in the pictures.

The sneaky woman asked where she was staying and had a car coming in the morning to take her to the airport. Had her flight booked. *First class.* Then asked her favorite color and told her she'd have a surprise when she and Shiori's grandfather picked her up at the airport.

When they finally said goodnight and hung up, Shiori couldn't stop smiling. One call and the world didn't look so hopeless anymore. Fine, her grandmother was still a stranger, but the old woman had kicked Hiro's butt on Madden. Had gotten him a new Black Panther plush the second he mentioned he loved the superhero. Had managed to make the trip a fun experience for him when it could have been so traumatic.

Setting her phone aside, Shiori smiled up at Malakai. Then Brave.

And they were smiling back.

Happy for her.

By her side, Wendy flashed her 'I told you so' grin. Then hopped up to her feet. "I'm gonna go raid the snack machine. Want anything?"

"No, thank you." Shiori reached out to squeeze Wendy's hand. "You're the best, you know that?"

"Damn right I do!" Wendy laughed, backing behind Brave and Malakai before wiggling her brows and mouthing. "Lucky bitch."

Shiori snickered as Wendy slipped out into the hall.

Brave came over to sit on the edge of the coffee table. "Hiro is where he needs to be. That was good to hear. I was worried."

"I was too, but now..." She tugged her bottom lip between her teeth, reality hitting her like a block of ice in the center of her chest. "He's okay. And I'm leaving."

"I wouldn't expect you to do anything else." Brave held up a hand when her lips parted. "This is me being selfish. I can't go with you, but knowing you're there...I'll feel better."

"You *can* come..." Damn it, she wanted him to. But she also knew he shouldn't. If Sophie and Reese wouldn't give her a break in her contract to see Hiro, they'd have to sue her. She didn't see that happening, but she didn't care. The choice was obvious.

For Brave, it was much more complicated. Reese might be sympathetic, but the record label? The fans who'd bought out tickets for his next few shows?

Without making the whole thing public, he'd be risking his career.

"We're booked solid for three weeks. Then we have a week off before we head to Europe." Brave lowered his gaze. "If it was just me, I'd say fuck it. Alder would agree. None of the guys would blame us."

"You're in charge, Brave." Malakai stepped up behind him. "Say the word and the tour is canceled. I'll stand by you."

Brave's lips curved slightly. "That means more than I can say. But...I'm not sure the band would recover from this. We've canceled shows in the past. We've got a good momentum going."

She pressed her hand to his cheek. "Look at you, being all responsible."

He laughed. "It fucking sucks. I want to go with you."

"But you need to stay." Her chest hurt, thinking about leaving both him and Malakai so soon after they'd found a way to be together. But life wasn't always fair. "Hiro looks up to you. He'll be watching all your shows on YouTube. Make sure he can find them."

"I can do that."

"Good. I think…this will work. He'll love knowing you're visiting in a few weeks. I'll be there to help him adjust to his new life. To see if it's really what's best for him."

"You think it will be?"

"I really do." She didn't have much to go on, but she never had. Now, at least there was a family who seemed to want to give Hiro everything any of them could want for him. And she had a chance to find out if that was true. "This is hard. But I have to go. We both know it. Tell me again I should."

"You should." Brave delved his fingers into her hair. "Little moon, go. And call me every day. Show me how you've accomplished everything you fought so hard for. Because it's what I want too. For that little boy to have what we never did."

"That's what really matters, isn't it?" Her fingers curled against his cheek. "Kyoko's baby. Valor's son. It's up to us to make sure he never goes through what they did."

Brave's brow furrowed. "Valor was—"

"Your brother. And you hate him and I get it." She probably shouldn't bring this up, but time was closing in on her. "One of the songs you sang to me, the one you didn't finish. It was about him. About the brother you loved. The one Kyoko probably fell in love with. And…and I think it's okay to be angry with him for what he did to you. But that song is one you needed to write for a reason. He was someone else to you once."

His jaw hardened. He nodded slowly. "Maybe."

Malakai placed his hand on Brave's shoulder. "We'll finish that song together. With Alder. And one day, Hiro will hear it and know what it means."

"But it's fucking…cold." Brave rubbed his face with one hand, leaving the other tangled in Shiori's hair. "Hiro doesn't need to hear that."

"That's not what I heard." Shiori wrapped her arms around his neck. "The song can mean so many things, to so many people. I heard pain. Regret. It's…*real.* I don't know what other word to use. Even when Hiro's old enough to be told what happened to Valor, I don't believe he'll think of his father when he listens to it."

Brave's brow furrowed. "But the song is about *Valor*."

"No. It's about you." Shiori shook her head when Brave's brow furrowed. "I'm sorry. Forget about it for now. I don't want to ruin the rest of our time together—"

"You're right about the song." Brave eased away from her, crossing the room to open his luggage—which he'd brought to her room earlier—and pulled out his notebook.

Sitting on the floor, he braced it against his knees. He drew a pencil from the spiral binding and began to write. His breath sped up, his skin growing pale. As though each word was stealing the air from the room. Draining him with each stroke of black graphite on the page.

When he was finished, he stood and handed the book to Malakai, without a word.

Malakai read the song, his voice growing tighter with every word. He slowed with the last few lines.

> "Let me pretend,
> Make it a new game.
> You were the man I looked up to,
> So alone.
> Never found,
> But I'll never stop searching.
> For you in my reflection."

He set the notebook aside. Held out his arms. "Come here."

Brave went to him, pressing his face into the crook of Malakai's neck. He didn't cry. Didn't tremble. He didn't move at all.

He simply let Malakai hold him.

After the call with her grandmother, after having everything she'd held on to for so long ripped away like a bandage off a wound that hadn't healed, Shiori could imagine how he felt. Raw and shaken, as if the foundation of reality had splintered.

But maybe that's what they needed. To let the wounds breathe until they faded to nothing but scars.

Her phone buzzed and she glanced down at the text. From Wendy.

WENDY: CAUGHT UP WITH CONNOR IN THE BAR. HE SAID I CAN CRASH IN HIS ROOM.

SHIORI: ISN'T TATE STAYING WITH HIM?

WENDY: OH! I HOPE SO!

SHIORI: YOU'RE NUTS! LOL! ENJOY YOUR NIGHT!

WENDY: RIGHT BACK ATCHA, BABE!

Malakai and Brave had moved to the sofa, speaking softly while Malakai jotted notes on a free page. Shiori wet her lips with her tongue, considering what to do with the last of their time together.

They could spend more time talking. Missing one another before she even left.

But she had a much better idea.

Chapter Thirty-One

Striding across the room, Shiori pressed her hands against Brave's shoulders, straddling his lap and covering his lips with hers. She kissed him until he groaned and wrapped his arms around her.

His dick swelled in his jeans and she ground down on him, ignoring the slight ache within from the other night. The pain had faded enough for longing to set in. She needed to feel Brave against her. Inside her.

Easing away from him, she pulled off her shirt—one borrowed from Malakai to cover her tube top—and tossed it aside. Brave helped her slide off the tube top, his hands covering her breasts the second they were bared.

A brush of his thumbs shot a thread of pleasure from her nipples straight down to her core. He lifted one breast to his mouth and she arched her back, moving restlessly, needing every bit of pressure from his solid length against her pussy.

Still wasn't enough. She groaned as she reached for his belt. Malakai stopped her.

He gave her a heavy-lidded smile. "This time, I came prepared. Let me get him ready for you."

Nodding, Shiori lifted up enough for Malakai to unzip Brave's jeans and pull out his cock, hard and darkened with the swell of blood. He rolled the condom over Brave's dick, stroking him languidly as Brave pressed his eyes shut and tipped his head back against the sofa.

With his other hand, Malakai reached under her skirt, pushing her panties aside to stroke her with two fingers. He slid them into her and she quivered as he drove her to the edge with a few deep thrusts.

He withdrew his fingers and brought them to Brave's lips. "She's so fucking wet for you. And so close. Take her, or I will."

Brave sucked Malakai's fingers into his mouth, opening his eyes as his lips curved. He released Malakai with one last flick of his tongue. "If I didn't love you so much, I'd hurt you."

Malakai smirked. "I can't say the same. I love you. And I'll fucking hurt you." He leaned close to whisper in Brave's ear. "And you'll love it."

"Wait your turn." Brave latched onto Shiori's hip, pulling her down so she could feel his dick rubbing against the thin material still partially covering her. His eyes met hers. "Put me inside you, little moon. You're in control."

Rising up, Shiori fisted her hand around the base of his cock, lowering until the thick head slipped past the pulsing ring of muscle. The pressure made her shudder as her body tightened around him. She rocked her hips, moving her hand to take him deeper.

Lacing her fingers behind his neck, she sank down, lips parted as he filled her. She was still tender, but that only added an edge to the sweet sensations. She kissed him as her body adjusted to the deep penetration.

Then she couldn't keep still.

Sucking on his bottom lip, she lifted her hips, dropping down hard. The shock of pleasure jolted through her core and she gasped into Brave's mouth, digging her nails into his skin.

His fingers dug into her ass as he helped her move, thrusting up into her when she reached the threshold of a violent orgasm that locked all her limbs, strength surrendered to ecstasy.

Brave slammed into her and she cried out as he prolonged the erotic pulse within. His steady movements built up all the wicked heat until she could feel the urgent drive to reach the summit once again.

Malakai moved behind her, kissing her shoulder as she tried to quicken her pace, faltering every time Brave lifted and her core clenched. He whispered in her ear. "Do you want more?"

"More?" Her voice was scratchy and breathless. A fine sheen of sweat broke out over her skin. She turned her head, groaning as Malakai's lips covered hers in a slow, lazy kiss. "I need you."

Drawing away, Malakai knelt behind her. His breath brushed the base of her spine. Beneath her, Brave released a soft curse. He shifted forward and she could feel Malakai's hand where their bodies joined, stroking Brave.

His fingers slid up over her back hole and she shivered. The sensation was strange, but a little pressure triggered nerves that intensified the pleasure of every slow glide of Brave's dick inside her.

Malakai's fingers left her, then returned, slick with lube. He slid the tip of one into her and she tensed at the slight burn.

He kissed her hip. "Relax. Press back against me, love."

Brave stopped moving, claiming her lips as Malakai eased in deeper. With the lube, and her body relaxed, the stretch didn't hurt. She braced her hands on the sofa above Brave's shoulders as the penetration stirred the growing need to keep moving.

"Oh fuck." She jerked as Malakai's finger drew out, then thrust back in. "That feels good."

"Mmmhmm." Malakai let out a soft laugh. "Let's see how much you can take, sweetheart."

She wasn't sure what he meant until he added more lube and a second finger slid into her. Her core clenched at the heat gathering down low, building as he fucked his fingers into her ass, one hand on her hip encouraging her to rise up until only the head of Brave's cock was still inside her.

"Move with me, baby." Malakai wrapped his arm around her, his chest against her back, his hand on her breast. "Let's drive him out of his mind."

Since she was already there? Seemed fair enough. She rose and fell to Malakai's rhythm, taking Brave harder, tipping her hips back to feel more from Malakai. A whisper of protest escaped her lips when he pulled his fingers free, but they returned, slick again, with a third that tested her limits as they sank in deeper. Having him finger her ass seemed so naughty, and she would have been shy to discuss going there, but good god, she understood why Brave loved being fucked so hard by this man.

Malakai's every touch skillfully silenced any objections, tempting her with her own body's response. She lost herself to him, wanting nothing more than to let him have his way. With him, all she had to do was surrender and enjoy the ride.

"That's it. Fuck, you're beautiful. I want this sweet little ass." Malakai slid his lips across her shoulder, setting his teeth lightly into her skin. "Do you think you can take me, baby?"

She shivered, looking down at Brave, who reached up to brush her sweat dampened hair off her cheek. His eyes searched her face, as if to judge whether or not she was ready.

Then his lips slanted. "You want to say yes."

She nodded, her eyes fluttering shut as Malakai pressed his fingers in deep. Opening her eyes again, she saw her pleasure reflected on Brave's face. "You can feel him too."

"Yes. And every time he plays with you, your pussy squeezes my dick and it's driving me fucking crazy." His lips parted as Malakai repeated the action and she jerked, clenching down. "I won't last long if he keeps that up."

Behind her, Malakai chuckled. "Oh yes, you will." He withdrew his fingers and patted her ass. "Don't move, pet."

Easier said than done. She leaned down over Brave, giving him open mouthed kisses and struggling against the drive to reach the climax that she'd been denied.

Returning quickly, Malakai took hold of her waist and lifted her off Brave. She gasped at the sudden, agonizing emptiness. The man was fucking *evil.*

"Trust me." Malakai kissed her nose when she scowled at him. "I'll make sure he stays with us for a long, *long* time."

Her brow furrowed as Malakai knelt between Brave's thighs. He had a strange leather thing in his hand.

Brave grabbed his wrist when he attached one strap around the base of his cock. "What is that?"

Malakai arched a brow, staring at Brave's restraining hand until he moved it. He attached the second strap under Brave's balls. "Discipline. You clearly need some help with it."

"Discipline? What the…" Brave rolled his eyes. "Whatever, you kinky fucker." He looped an arm around Shiori's waist, pulling her over him. "Get back here."

Shiori snickered, tangling her fingers in his hair, teasing him with shallow dips of her hips when he pressed into her. *These two are nuts. And I fucking love it!*

Grabbing her ass, Brave pulled her down, flicking his tongue over her bottom lip when she gasped. "Brat. Careful, our man is into spanking. He might pull you over his knee rather than let you fuck me."

She wrinkled her nose. "He wouldn't dare."

"Don't tempt me." Malakai pulled off his shirt, twisting it in his hands as he watched them. "I plan to show you exactly how fucking hot that can be. But not tonight." He locked his eyes on Brave. "Lift your hands over your head."

Brave blinked at him. "What?"

"What was unclear?" Malakai gave Brave a hard look, which was fucking hot.

Shiori felt as though her whole body had gone liquid in response. She swallowed hard and gently pulled Brave's hands off her waist. "Do what he says. He's being scary sexy."

"He really is, isn't he?" Brave inhaled roughly, lifting his hands the rest of the way on his own. His jaw tightened as Malakai used his shirt to tightly bind his wrists. "Aren't we supposed to negotiate *before* you tie me up?"

"Sure." Malakai straightened, folding his arms over his chest. Still wearing his black jeans, while she and Brave were fully exposed, gave him the essence of complete control. His every word held an edge of power. "We can stop everything and talk. Print out a contract. Go over each and every section until we come to an agreement. *Or...*" Malakai's stance relaxed. He reached out, brushing Shiori's hair over one shoulder and bending down to kiss along the side of her neck. "Or we can improvise and deal with the details later. I promise, no spanking tonight."

Sounded like a very good plan. Shiori gave Brave her sweetest smile.

He sighed, tugging at his wrists. "I'm a little worried at how well you 'improvise', but fine. So long as there's no spanking. Or nipple clamps."

Malakai's brow arched. "Anything else?"

"*Jesus.* Should I worry about what else you've got in that bag?"

"No. I don't believe I'll need anything else." Malakai wrapped Shiori's hair around his hand, tugging slightly until she was bowed on Brave's lap, gazing up at him, eyes widening at the intensity in his. "I am giving her a night she'll never forget."

Malakai brought his lips down over Shiori's, loving the way she gave in, eager to experience everything he offered. After living so long for someone else, she was using her freedom to savor the forbidden without regrets.

Tonight wasn't the end of their time together, but he and Brave were losing her for weeks. They'd have one another, but he needed her to know all they'd be missing without her.

He'd explored different levels of kink for years, but mostly with strangers. Finding a local club to play in wasn't difficult, but being with Brave and Shiori showed him how shallow every scene had been. Shiori was still too innocent for more than light play, but Brave?

Brave could take it. And as much as he resisted, Malakai could tell giving up control turned him on. They had a long way to go before he'd admit he enjoyed everything Malakai did to him, but the journey would be fun for them both.

While Shiori was gone, delving a little deeper into a power exchange might distract Brave enough to keep him going. Malakai could easily see Brave sliding back into old habits when missing her became too much to bear.

I won't let that happen.

So tonight, while making sure Shiori was satisfied in every way possible, Malakai would lay the groundwork between himself and Brave. The man would be easier to play with while they were focused on Shiori's pleasure.

And she was loving her little intro to kink. Seeing a strong man like Brave tormented fascinated her.

And Malakai was just getting started.

"Does he feel bigger inside you? Harder?" Malakai ran his hand down Shiori's chest, between her breasts, kissing her again as she shuddered. "The harness I put on him will keep him like that for you. He won't come until I release him."

Brave snorted. "Malakai, I love you. And I'm into you being all freaky, but with Shiori's sweet, wet pussy milking my cock, nothing you can do will stop me from losing it."

Shiori's cheeks reddened. Absolutely adorable. Even with Brave's dick deep in her body, dirty talk still embarrassed her. A reaction that would be fun to play on while it lasted.

"He talks big." Malakai whispered against Shiori's lips. "Should we prove him wrong until he's begging for relief?"

Her lips parted. Her throat worked as she swallowed. Then she nodded.

"Good girl." He loosened his grip on her hair and bent down to nip her earlobe. "I'm going to corrupt you, pet. I hope you don't mind."

A naughty smile on her lips, she shook her head. "Not at all. I'll have fun being bad while the focus isn't on me."

Sexy and smart. Malakai took Shiori's hands in his and brought them to Brave's bound wrists. "Hold him for me. If he struggles too much, we'll make him pay."

Grinding down on Brave, Shiori latched onto the restraint and smirked when Brave hissed through his teeth. "Mmm, I like that idea."

Brave let out a low growl. "I'm feeling outnumbered."

"Good." Malakai undid his jeans, stroking himself as he watched Shiori playfully torture their man. "You are."

He had one last toy that he'd hesitated to use, but Brave's arrogance made the decision for him. He went to his bag, pulling out a bottle of lube and a nice sized butt plug. He returned to the sofa, enjoying the way Brave's eyes widened when he saw the plug.

"She can't…" Brave jerked at his wrist. "Malakai, what the fuck?"

"It's not for her." Malakai put the plug and the lube on the sofa by Brave's hips. He latched onto Brave's legs, making sure Shiori was with him as he pulled Brave's hips off the edge of the couch. Shiori leaned over, still holding Brave's cock tight in her pussy. Her ass was bared perfectly to Malakai. And Brave was completely off balance, his thighs spreading hers, his ass exposed. He couldn't close his legs without tipping Shiori off him. Couldn't use his hands to pull himself back.

Perfect.

Malakai grabbed the lube and spread a generous amount on his palm. He slicked up one finger and pressed it into Brave, smiling when the man jerked and Shiori moaned. With her thighs spread so far, Shiori couldn't move much, but Brave's engorged dick pulsing in her tight pussy must feel nice.

And Malakai was about to make it feel even better.

After making sure Brave was nice and prepped, he covered the plug with the rest of the lube. He pushed the tip into Brave, watching his face as the widened part stretched him.

Panting, Brave tugged at his wrists. They were high above him, and without leverage, Shiori didn't have much trouble holding them with both hands. The plug widened even more and Brave tried to pull away.

"Fuck. It's too big, Malakai." Brave's thighs tensed as he realized he was trapped. "Stop."

"Are you sure?" Malakai tapped Shiori's side. "Help him. I think he needs some distraction."

Undulating her hips, Shiori curved her hand under Brave's jaw, giving him a long, deep kiss.

Malakai eased the pressure on the plug, then pressed forward again as Brave's body relaxed.

"Fuck!" Brave turned his head. "I'm not sure how I feel about this, man. It almost hurts, but...but almost feels good."

Good boy. Malakai inclined his head, knowing better than to voice the praise. Brave wasn't there yet. He wouldn't take it as a compliment, but as a challenge to his manhood.

"You called me kinky. Well 'Stop' can be vague." Malakai grinned as Brave huffed out a laugh. "Choose a safeword."

"How about 'I'll kick your ass if you *don't* stop'?" Brave pressed his head back against the sofa. "Not saying that now, though."

"Good. But we'll choose something shorter for next time." Malakai flattened his palm against the base of the plug, pushing it in until the widest part stretched Brave to the limit. A little more and it sank into place, only the circular bit visible. He glanced up at Brave, who'd gone still. "Are you okay?"

"Not sure." Brave tugged at his wrists. His thighs clenched. And his breaths went shallow. "Oh fuck. I can't do anything."

"Anything?" Malakai looked over Brave, then Shiori, who was moving against Brave while the man held perfectly still. "Fuck her, Brave. She needs you."

Brave lifted his hips, then dropped back down, his ass so full he likely regretted the effort. "You're an evil fuck, you know that?"

"Still love me?" Malakai rolled on a condom, holding Brave's gaze as he covered his dick with lube.

The man's answer didn't surprise him. "You don't want to know how I'm feeling right now."

Pressing his dick against Shiori's spread cheeks, Malakai grinned. "Do you really want me to stop?"

As his dick breached that tight ring of muscle, Shiori gripped hard on Brave's restraints, lowering her head to Brave's chest. She was so fucking tight with Brave filling her, but the lube and her pressing back, letting him in, made taking her easy. Still, he was careful. One bad experience could ruin being claimed this way.

He hesitated when Shiori clenched around him.

"Wait...oh, fuck, this is..." Shiori pressed harder against Brave. "This is so wrong. And it feels good. But...but almost too much."

His hips settled against her ass and she wiggled back against him as if she wanted more. Brave's whole body was shaking. He was pulling so hard at his restraints Malakai put his hand over Shiori's to keep him from wrenching free.

"I won't move until you're ready, Shiori." Malakai slid his free hand down her side. "But I love feeling you both. I want to see you come apart. You're almost there."

"Yes, but..." Shiori eased her hips closer to Brave, then back against him. "When I'm close I can't move at all. I don't know why. I can hardly breathe and it just takes over."

"Sweetie, you don't have to do anything. Just take what I give you." Malakai curved his hands around her hips. With her knees on the edge of the sofa, she couldn't take Brave in fully.

He slid his hands down her thighs, guiding her feet to the floor. In this position, both her and Brave were powerless.

By moving into Shiori, he controlled all their pleasure. A position he relished.

But he was careful not to make that too obvious. "I've got you, love. Move with me."

As he drove into her, he pulled her down so she took Brave in deep. When he drew back, he lifted her away from Brave, ensuring she always had them inside her together. As she adjusted to the rhythm he moved faster. Then he tipped her back so he could bring his hand down to her pussy, his fingers pressing down on her clit.

After that, she did exactly as he'd told her. She went slack, letting him move her over Brave, fucking into her ass harder and harder until the three of them were grinding into one another mindlessly. She cried out, shaking and arching back against him. Her muscles convulsing around him tipped him beyond his cool restraint.

He grunted as he slammed into her, his hands splayed on the sofa so he wouldn't bruise her with his grip.

Beneath them both, Brave panted and let out a low moan. "I was wrong. Please fucking take this thing off. I can't...fuck, please!"

How amazing would it be to leave Brave this desperate? Pull away, rest, then use him again. Malakai considered the option, then tossed it aside. Not tonight. Maybe, one day, when they weren't about to say goodbye to the woman they both loved.

Easing away from Shiori, Malakai unsnapped the leather cock and ball rings. He watched Brave come apart, bring Shiori to another orgasm before he slumped on the sofa, completely drained.

Shiori recovered before Brave did, lifting off him and curling against his side, her head on his chest.

Malakai removed the butt plug, smirking a little when Brave called him some creative names. After disinfecting it with the supplies in his bag, he stashed the toy. Then he went to the bathroom to toss his condom and fetch a warm cloth for each of them. When he returned, the sight of them holding one another broke his heart.

Pleasure could only do so much. Reality hit fast and hard. In the morning, Shiori would leave. And the way Brave held her, kissing her and whispering soft promises that nothing would ever change, brought what they faced to focus.

That sweet, beautiful woman Malakai loved more than anyone he'd ever loved before had opportunities he couldn't compete with. And didn't want to. If he didn't love her so much, he might try. She'd always be part of Winter's Wrath. Have the family they'd built.

But he had to let her find the family she'd been denied. One that might make her see him and Brave as nothing more than a pleasant experience. Two men she'd enjoyed before deciding what she really wanted.

And...so long as she was happy, he'd accept that.

He didn't want tonight to be the end, but part of him braced for the possibility that it would be. Because he wouldn't have Brave if not for her.

And he might lose the man once she was gone.

Chapter Thirty-Two

Brave set his notepad aside, rolling his shoulders to stretch the stiffness from his back. Lifting his coffee cup, he frowned, finding it empty. He couldn't remember taking that last sip, but damn it, he needed more.

Damn, when was the last time he'd pulled an all-nighter like this? Keeping his eyes open was getting difficult, but he wasn't ready to turn in yet. A few little touch ups and he'd be finished the last song for the new album. And several potentials for the next one. His muse had been very active lately, and having the music come to him so easily gave him an awesome high.

Didn't lead to much sleep, but who needed rest?

He stood, holding on to the edge of the table as the bus jolted, then made his way to the kitchenette to put on another pot of coffee.

Malakai stepped out of the bunk area, folding his arms over his chest and leaning against the door frame. "You haven't been to bed."

Not a question, but Brave answered anyway. "No, but I made those changes you suggested to *Demon Doll* and *Vapid Games*. Also…" He tried to stifle a yawn, but it overpowered him. He covered his mouth with his hand and shook his head. "*Fucking Gaston…*"

Blinking at him, Malakai leaned forward. "Fucking *who?*"

"Gaston…" Brave rubbed his eyes. All right, maybe the song needed another name. "Remember, the Beauty and The Beast one?"

"Ah…" Malakai chuckled, but the sound was hollow. "Might wanna rethink the title. After you spend a few hours in bed. We'll be in Austin around five and sound check is at six. You're gonna be burnt out if you don't sleep."

"I know, but I'm almost done." Brave yawned again. "Don't worry about me."

Lips drawn in a hard line, Malakai inclined his head sharply. "Fine. I won't."

Stepping past him, Malakai strode over to the sofa, dropping down and flicking on the TV. He put on CSI and glared at the agents like they'd pissed him off.

Brave stared at him, not sure what had just happened. Was Malakai really that mad that he hadn't slept?

Thinking back over the past two weeks, Brave realized Malakai had become more and more distant. With their crazy schedule, and every spare minute going to writing the songs that were way past due, Brave hadn't had much time to delve into the reasons behind his behavior. He should have noticed something was wrong.

It could be that Malakai missed Shiori. Brave did too. Even though they spoke to her every day, brief video calls weren't the same. They'd had some chances for longer, erotic calls when they'd spent a few days in Boston, then again in Louisville, and he loved how into getting naughty long-distance Shiori had been.

He was still counting down the days until they could be with her again.

He sighed and walked over to the sofa, standing between Malakai and the TV. "Listen, man. I get how much this sucks, but next week, we'll be in San Diego. And Shiori's thinking about coming with us to Europe. It's going to be okay."

"Is it?" Malakai let out a cold laugh. "We'll see."

"Fuck, what's your problem?" Brave stumbled as the bus swayed. Frustrated with his fuzzy brain and the moving vehicle testing his already messed up equilibrium, he plunked down on the sofa. "You miss her. I do too. But—"

"This isn't about her. Even over the phone, she makes me feel like things won't change." Malakai pressed his eyes shut and shook his head. "Look. Forget it."

"Not happening. Talk to me."

"It's stupid."

"Who fucking cares? I love you and you're pissed at me and I want to know what the hell I did." Brave relaxed as Malakai's lips curved slightly. "We both know I suck at relationships, but I want you to be happy."

Malakai groaned and latched his fingers behind his neck. "Damn it, now you're being sweet and I feel like an ass. I just…it seems like you're killing time until you can be with her again. And I understand."

That clarified absolutely nothing. "But…?"

"But I'm right here." Malakai shrugged, looking uncomfortable. "We're always working. Or hanging with the guys. I think we spent more time together when we fucking hated each other."

Aw hell. He's right. Brave reached over, pulling Malakai's hands from behind his neck. Then he fisted his hand in Malakai's shirt and drew him forward, kissing him slowly, lips parting as Malakai's mouth slanted against his.

The kiss was passionate, but not one that would lead to sex. He wasn't sure how to tell Malakai how much he meant to him. That if he wasn't here, Brave would be going completely insane.

But he'd try to do better at showing him.

He let out a soft sigh as Malakai eased away. "I'm sorry I'm a shitty boyfriend. How can I make it up to you?"

Pulling Brave to his side, Malakai shrugged again. Then snorted. "Flowers? Seriously, it's no big deal. I'm preparing myself for when you get sick of me. Guess I've got nothing to worry about yet."

Yet? Okay, time for some serious damage control. Malakai had accepted Shiori leaving, but it had probably hurt him as much as it had hurt Brave. He hid it well. A little too well.

Recently, Brave had been forced to face the impact Valor had on his life. And not only when he died. Brave had ruined relationships because he'd been so fucked up. Almost destroyed the band he'd helped form.

Shiori had faced her demons as well, but healing would take time for her. He wasn't sure what damage had been done by her stepfather's abuse, but her grandmother had already talked her into therapy. She'd stopped being so afraid that she'd ruin Hiro's life. She was happier. Didn't have the shadow of the past holding her back.

While they'd been moving forward, Malakai had supported them. He'd been strong and steady, giving them everything they needed, from a shoulder to cry on, to space when they wanted to be alone. Or, like Shiori, had to take steps without him.

Malakai's own pain hadn't really been explored besides the counseling he did with Ballz. He'd lost his parents. Lost his younger brother, and everyone he'd ever been close to.

He'd have a hard time trusting what he had with Shiori or Brave would last. And there was no easy way to fix that. But Brave could make sure his man didn't feel like an afterthought.

Or like his opinion didn't matter.

"I changed my mind. Scoot over." Brave shot Malakai a sleepy smile once he'd moved to the other side of the sofa. Stretching out, he rested his head on Malakai's lap. "I'm gonna take a little nap."

"Here?" Malakai laid his hand over Brave's hair, idly stroking it as Brave's eyes drifted shut. "You'd be more comfortable in your bunk."

"Mm, maybe. But you won't be there."

"I could lie down with you…" Malakai hesitated, clearly not loving the idea.

Which Brave understood. Their first night in the cramped bunk had been fine, but a few more and they were both sore and exhausted. And not from anything fun. There just wasn't enough room.

Shaking his head without opening his eyes, Brave brought his hand to Malakai's knee. "Here's good. Now *shhh*. I'm fucking beat."

The tension surrounding Malakai dissolved as he continued petting Brave's hair. Sleeping next to him wasn't a grand gesture, but Brave sensed he needed more of the little things. Acting like they always had as bandmates was easy. Days could go by on the bus with the other guys where they'd hardly exchange a word. Brave hadn't seen his brother at all yesterday, because he'd been in the back room with Danica, then taken off with Jesse and her during rest stops.

He hadn't noticed how much effort Alder put into his relationships. The three were together all the time, so it seemed simple, but Brave had clearly been missing something.

He let sleep take him, deciding he'd have a chat with his little brother when he woke up.

Hours later, when they reached Austin, Brave joined Alder in the van to make a quick stop at a local pharmacy. While in New York, Alder had seen a doctor—after a long talk with Ballz and Reese—and was now on Zoloft. It didn't seem to be doing much yet, but the doctor had said it could take a few weeks. Dariel, who'd joined them and made his debut on stage on their last night in New York, said he'd been on Zoloft himself for about a year after leaving the service, and told Alder about his experience, which seemed to help.

Still, Alder had been a little moody about taking meds. And the rules that went along with them. He couldn't drink alcohol anymore.

To show him support, the rest of the band had stopped drinking on the bus. Which had gone better than Brave expected. The guys had been freaked out when Shiori's stepfather lodged a complaint against Alder for assault, even though no charges were filed. Every single one of them knew the result of Alder losing control could have gone so much worse.

That he was accepting help, however reluctantly, was a relief.

After handing over his prescription to the pharmacist, Alder stepped back to wait, eyeing Brave curiously. "Did you come along to make sure I actually got my meds, or is something up?"

Brave shoved his hands in his pockets. "Something's up. I need your advice."

Alder's brows lifted. "This oughta be interesting. About what?"

He better not fucking laugh. "Relationships."

"Ah…" Alder bit into his bottom lip hard, his shoulders shaking. He burst out laughing when Brave smacked his shoulder. "Sorry, I just wasn't expecting that! Damn, my big brother, all in love and shit." He backed up when Brave swung at him again. "All right, all right, I'm done. Who you having trouble with? Shiori or Malakai?"

Dropping his gaze, Brave took a deep breath. "Malakai. Even I can't fuck things up from across the country."

"Could happen, so don't get too comfortable. Besides, if Shiori comes with us to Europe, you could have the same issues with her." Alder rubbed his jaw. "I noticed Malakai seemed off. But you two don't do anything together. Today was the first time I'd seen you in the same room actually in contact. Maybe neither of you are that affectionate, but it would drive me nuts if Danica sat far away from me all the time and Jesse never touched me."

"Jesse spends most of his time on the road either driving or sleeping." Brave shook his head, still not sure how the three managed. "It's not like you can sit on his lap while he's behind the wheel."

Cheeks reddening, Alder folded his arms over his chest. "No, but I hang out with him. We talk. I rub his neck sometimes. I don't fucking ignore him and neither does Danica."

"Got it." Brave raked his fingers through his hair. "So I should do more with Malakai. What else?"

"Fuck, I don't know. Be spontaneous. Bring him coffee or make him his favorite snack. He does that shit for you and you don't seem to notice." Alder's tone softened. "It's good that you're trying, but part of your problem is you aren't paying attention. He's making all the effort in the relationship."

"So I've got some major work to do."

Alder inclined his head. "Tons. But the crazy bastard loves you even though you're a lazy, spoiled fucker." He smirked. "Probably worked out better when he was getting *some* benefits."

"You mean when he got to fuck my brains out more often." Brave smiled sweetly at an old lady who gaped at him as she passed. "My apologies, ma'am. I have no manners."

Surprisingly, the woman laughed, glancing back without slowing. "You tell your man he's lucky to have you."

Grinning, Brave turned back to Alder.

Who rolled his eyes and shook his head. "Do *not* tell him that."

"I won't. But she's right."

"God, you're hopeless." Alder tipped his head back, mumbling a prayer. The pharmacist called his name and he went over to pay for his meds, leading the way out once he had them in hand. "Not sure what else to tell you. When Jesse fucks up, he surprises Danica with silly little presents. Then sucks up for a while. Try that."

Near the exit, the gift section caught Brave's attention. He walked over, grabbing a couple things, ignoring Alder's incredulous laugh.

Hey, *he'd* suggested presents. Brave had to start somewhere.

About twenty minutes later, they returned to the bus and Alder went in to see if everyone was ready to head to the venue. Brave got out of the van and walked around to the back of the bus, sitting on the bumper and inhaling the cool, dry air as he waited.

He wasn't sure Malakai would think to come look for him here, but he hoped so. This bumper was where they'd taken those first steps to building what they now had. Most people had nicer spots they called theirs, and maybe he and Malakai would find a better one someday. Until then, this was as good a place as any to reconnect.

If it didn't work, he'd figure out another way. He might not be a great boyfriend, but he'd damn well fight to keep his man.

"Hey, what's going on?" Malakai strode up to his side, his eyes dark with concern. "Everyone's waiting for you."

"I know, I just needed a minute alone with you." Brave put his hand behind him, touching the gifts. They'd seemed good choices at the time, but maybe they were stupid.

Malakai shook his head, kicking Brave's feet apart and stepping forward to stand between Brave's thighs. He curved his hand around the side of Brave's neck. "You need time with me, you might wanna let me know."

"I'll try to remember that." Brave rested his forehead against the other man's. "Listen, I know I fucked up. I want to do better. I *will* do better. But...call me on my shit, okay? You used to be real good at that."

"You want me to start being a dick to you again?" Malakai shifted back, his brow furrowed. "I don't—"

"That's not what I mean. I'm saying…" Brave groaned, not sure how to explain what he meant. "I'm with you, Malakai. I won't be the one who leaves."

With a sharp inhale, Malakai's eyes locked on his. He swallowed hard. "I guess it's hard for me to believe that."

The pain in Malakai's eyes made Brave's neglect so much worse. He couldn't kiss this away. Couldn't earn his trust with words. But maybe he could show the man he had been paying some attention to what he was going through.

"You've lost so much. I wish I'd realized how fucking hard it would be for you to believe you wouldn't lose me too. I got so comfortable because you've always been there." Brave slid his hands down Malakai's sides, resting them on his hips. "I figured you always would be."

Lips slanting, Malakai nodded. "So nothing's really changed. We just fuck now and don't fight all the time."

"No. *Everything's* changed. You deserve better." Brave leaned forward, brushing his lips over Malakai's. "Give me a chance to give it to you."

A horn honked, breaking the moment. But there was something different in Malakai's eyes.

Hope.

"We better go." Malakai smiled, kissing him quick before backing away. "But you have your chance. Don't make me regret it."

"Wouldn't fucking dream of it." Brave yanked out one of the gifts, shoving it at Malakai before he could walk away. "Here. I got you this."

Taking the devil plush, Malakai arched a brow at him, then stared down at the cute little thing. With big eyes, a huge, round head, and little black horns, the stuffy had been irresistible. Not that Malakai had any stuffed animals, but devils were metal, right?

Brave shrugged when Malakai didn't say a word. "Thought it would look cool in your bunk."

"It will." Malakai blinked fast, shaking his head. "Fuck, this was really cool of you. I think I was four the last time someone gave me a gift like this."

Four? Holy fuck. "Damn it, I'm sorry."

"Don't be."

"Seriously, I'm gonna buy you all kinds of gifts. Got like twenty years to make up for and I love you and I get to fucking spoil you, all right?" That no one had before made Brave angry.

Hugging Brave tight, Malakai chuckled. "All right. Just keep in mind, the bunks aren't big."

"I will."

Another honk. They had to go.

But first…

He pulled out the last gift. "And I got you flowers."

Malakai burst out laughing, but Brave didn't mind.

His man looked happy.

Mission fucking accomplished.

Chapter Thirty-Three

"It's today, it's today!"

Shiori smiled, then leaped forward as Hiro bounced off the sofa and almost sailed into the coffee table. Swinging him around, she tickled him until he was screaming with laughter, then set him on his feet.

"You excited to see your uncles?" She knew the answer, but she loved how enthusiastic he was. From the way he'd been acting all morning, it might as well be Christmas.

Hiro jumped up and down, his cute little face going red as he shouted. "Yes! Uncle Brave said he might get me a puppy! And Uncle Alder is bringing me a guitar. And he's gonna play baseball and bring me fishing and teach me how to drive!"

Coming in from the kitchen, her grandmother chuckled. "Really? All that today?"

"Uncle Alder can do lots and lots of things. He's really cool." Hiro ran over, giving Misaki his most adorable smile as he eyed the plate of cookies she'd come in with. "Can I have one, please?"

"Yes, you may." Misaki handed him a cookie. "Now why don't you go outside and play on your swings. Maybe *Jiji* will give you a push."

"Okay! Thank you, *Baba!*" Hiro took off running out the front door of the guest house.

Shiori watched him leave, still uncomfortable with him going outside by himself. She kept having to remind herself they were surrounded by family, on gated property. From the first day, she'd felt like she'd stepped into a whole different world.

Her grandparents lived in a huge house they refused to let her call a mansion. To her, the grand, French Chateau style home was like a castle straight out of a fairytale. The gray stone structure had spires and pinnacles and all kinds of fancy features that made it a true work of art. The estate itself was huge and even after three weeks, she still hadn't explored all of it.

Two of her uncles lived here, with their families, and yet she'd been given her own suite, not far from Hiro's room. Misaki hadn't been joking about spoiling her. The first week she'd insisted on bringing Shiori shopping for all new clothes. Asked her what changes could be made so the suite felt more like it belonged to her.

Shiori hadn't known what to say. So far, she hadn't changed a thing. She was still waiting to wake up from this dream.

For Brave and Malakai's visit, she'd be taking over the guest house. Which she hadn't bothered arguing about. Misaki was a savvy businesswoman who knew how to negotiate. She'd said the men would be more comfortable with a bit of privacy. Shiori had a feeling Misaki had told her grandfather Brave and Malakai were just her friends and was trying to keep up appearances.

Which was fair. *Jiji* treated her like she wasn't much older than Hiro. While Misaki was trying to provide Shiori with everything she could possibly want, he'd taken a more protective approach. He asked if she ate enough. Wanted to look at her contract, then speak to Sophie to make sure she was being treated well. When her uncles had friends over, he watched them like a hawk if they spent too much time near her.

Strangely enough, neither Misaki's pampering, or *Jiji's* overprotectiveness bothered her. Sure, it might be too much after a while, but for now, she could tell they were trying to make up for the years they'd lost with her.

Besides, her uncles weren't like the rich kids she'd always heard about. They were hard working men, who pulled their weight in the family business. Once her grandparents got used to having her around, she'd be treated with the same expectations they had for their sons.

That is *if* she stayed.

She still wasn't sure what she wanted to do. Her life here was amazing. Hiro was happy, and she could have a job tomorrow if she wanted one.

But...

Stepping up to her side, her grandmother set the plate of cookies on the coffee table and turned to face her, taking her hands. She pulled gently until Shiori sat with her on the cushy, beige leather sofa.

"You've been very quiet. Are you worried things will be different with your men?" Misaki grinned as Shiori's cheeks heated. "Don't be shy. I may be old, but I've been around the world and know love comes in many different forms. All I care is that they treat you well."

"They do." It was still weird, talking about stuff like this so openly, but she was as comfortable with Misaki as she was with Wendy. And she'd already talked this subject to death with her best friend. "Honestly, it's not really about them. I have no idea what to do with my life."

"Anything. *Everything.*" Misaki smiled and shrugged. "You're young, Shiori. I think you've been responsible for so long, you're seeing your future as something that needs to be carefully planned out. And if that makes you feel more secure, then that's what you should do."

That made sense. Shiori nodded.

Her grandmother wasn't finished. "But you also told me being with the band gave you the freedom you needed. Was it enough after such a short time?"

"I don't know." Shiori groaned, even more confused than she'd been before. "Can't you just tell me what I should do?"

Misaki let out a soft laugh. "That I can't do. But I'll support whatever decision you make." She lifted her head at the sound of Hiro's joyful shouts. "I think our visitors are here. Come, I can't wait to meet them."

Pulse quickening, Shiori stood, rubbing her sweaty palms on her jeans and straightening her snug black T-shirt. She was pretty sure everything was ready, but maybe she should check again? And her hair must be a mess from playing with Hiro. Maybe she should—

Her grandmother grabbed her hand and towed her out the front door.

The second Shiori saw Brave and Malakai, all her nervousness disappeared. Her heart swelled as she watched them shake hands with her grandfather. Brave swooped Hiro up in his arms, laughing as Hiro laid sloppy kisses all over his face.

She hadn't been sure how they'd feel, being here, but all that really mattered was that they were.

Breaking into a run, she skidded to a stop right in front of Malakai, then threw her arms around his neck. He lifted her up against him, his broad smile lighting up his whole face.

"Damn, it's good to see you." He kissed her, lowering her slowly, cutting it short as he seemed to recall her grandparents were watching. Clearing his throat, he inclined his head to her grandmother. "Mrs. Sato, it's a pleasure to meet you."

"Please, call me Misaki." Her grandmother turned to Brave. "That goes for both of you."

"Thank you for inviting us, Misaki." Brave's eyes shone as Shiori slipped up to his side. He put his arm around her, balancing Hiro against his side and leaning over to kiss her. "How are you doing, little moon?"

"Incredible. Have you seen this place?" Shiori laughed when he nodded, looking around like he couldn't believe it himself. She reached out to take Malakai's hand, then Brave's, leading them both inside. "You'll be staying in the guest house. There's a room for Alder too, if he wants. I'm surprised he didn't come with you."

Brave grinned. "He'll be stopping by later. He promised this little one a present and is being very picky about it." He kissed Hiro's cheek, grin widening when the little boy giggled. "If your great-grandparents say it's okay, we'll go find a puppy for you at the shelter."

"And then go fishing!" Hiro threw his arms up in the air, and Brave released her hand to secure him when the boy almost tipped backward.

Laughing, Brave bent down, setting Hiro on his feet and staying at his level. "Not sure we have time to do both today, buddy, but while I'm here, we'll definitely go fishing."

Cheering, Hiro scurried across the room, helping himself to another cookie.

"Hiro, don't you eat all those, they're for our guests." *Jiji* shook his head, standing next to his wife just inside the living room. "Please, make yourselves feel at home. We'll leave you in a moment, but I believe Misaki has a gift for you."

"Oh! We brought flowers." Brave glanced back toward the door. "I left them in the car."

Malakai chuckled, bending down to whisper in Shiori's ear. "He has a new thing for flowers. Expect to get a lot of them."

She snickered, recalling the story of Brave getting flowers for Malakai. Them telling her had been sweet and funny. Only Brave would make such a tender gesture by awkwardly shoving a gift at the man he loved.

Misaki's full attention was on Brave. "I absolutely love flowers. I hope you'll enjoy my gifts as much!" She pulled two black gift bags from behind the sofa. "If they don't fit, please let me know right away and I'll have them replaced."

The men took the bags, looking stunned. Brave traced his finger over the sleek, silver raised B with horns on the bag. "Black Diablo? Fu—I mean, wow. This brand is expensive. I'm not sure we can accept this."

Jiji's smile faded. "It's expensive because it's of the finest quality. All custom made."

"Yes, but—"

"Is it not worth the price?"

"Absolutely!" The back of Brave's neck reddened.

Shiori stepped forward before the situation got out of control. "*Jiji*, Brave's overwhelmed by the gift, he's not trying to offend you." She glanced over at Brave, feeling bad that he hadn't been warned in advance. She should have mentioned this earlier. "Black Diablo is my grandparents' company."

Brave's jaw nearly hit the floor.

Her grandmother patted his hand, then shot her husband a dirty look. "We *know* Brave wasn't trying to offend us." She smiled up at Brave. "Please, take it. I'm eager to see what you think."

Without hesitation, Brave reached into the bag. He pulled out the boots, holding them almost as carefully as he'd held his nephew. His gaze took in the sleek Italian leather, black with flames reaching up the sides, with seven straps and studded detailing.

Shiori was happy Brave had looked at her with more love than he showed those boots. Otherwise, she might be jealous.

"These are magnificent." Brave licked his lips, never taking his eyes off the boots. "Thank you. Damn, I can't wait to show these off on stage."

Meanwhile, Malakai was trying on his leather jacket, which looked just as good on him as Shiori had imagined. It had an Assassin's Creed style, black with blood red straps on the arms and a large hood. And it fit him perfectly.

While he complimented the design, her grandmother fussed and made sure it wasn't too snug anywhere.

Moving closer to Shiori, *Jiji* spoke softly. "I'm not sure if I like them yet, but they aren't as bad as I expected. They may stay."

"Thank you." She bit back a smile. "And you'll be nice to them?"

"If you're still smiling so much tomorrow?" He tilted his head to one side. "I'll consider it."

The rest of the day passed in a blur, with Hiro running in and out of the house, Alder coming over, then all of them going out to eat before finding Hiro's puppy. They dropped Alder off at the hotel where he was staying, then returned to the estate, parting at the end of the split drive.

Hiro seemed to have forgotten all about his uncle, and Shiori, now that the puppy had his full attention. Her little boy had found the cutest, scruffiest little mutt and fallen in love. The Yorkshire Terrier mix had patches of fur missing— growing back from a recent surgery—and was blind in one eye. The shelter attendant had warned Hiro the puppy would need special care. Had tried to talk him into a dog that might be easier for him to handle.

Misaki had taken the man aside and assured him the puppy would have a loving family to look after him. Hiro wouldn't be caring for him alone. After that, the attendant eagerly told them everything they needed to know about the dog as he packed up 'Captain Hook's'—Captain for short—favorite toys.

Captain slept in Hiro's arms the whole way home. Once out of the car, both dog and boy went exploring, with *Jiji* trailing close behind. She sat outside for hours with her men, just watching the little boy play with his puppy. He'd never been this happy.

His excited shouts, his laughter, were the most beautiful sounds in the world.

That night Shiori lazed around the house with Brave and Malakai, catching up, making love, and falling asleep tangled together in the huge bed. If Shiori had been living a dream before, she was in absolute heaven now that her men were with her.

Only, she couldn't stay there indefinitely. Every day she realized she'd have to make a choice at some point, but she didn't want to ruin a single moment

By the end of the week, neither Brave nor Malakai had asked her what she planned. Her grandmother never brought it up either.

For the first time, she wasn't able to hide in her happy bubble. Tomorrow the band would be leaving. Taking their flight across the ocean for a tour that would last for almost two months.

In the middle of the night, Malakai came down to the kitchen where she was drinking tea and staring out the window. He slipped up behind her silently, wrapping his arms around her.

She closed her eyes and rested her head back against his chest. "Why haven't you asked me about Europe?"

Malakai sighed and pressed his lips to her hair. "Did you want me to?"

"No. Not really." She stared out at the view of the ocean bathed in moonlight stretching out into the distance. "What should I do?"

She'd asked her grandmother that question. And Wendy. Both had given her the same answer. The one she needed.

That she had to decide for herself.

Her choice was already made. Nothing anyone said could change that. But she wished…she wished there was someone who truly understood why this was so damn hard.

Turning her in his arms, Malakai delved his fingers into her hair, bending down until his lips touched hers. "Come with us."

"Damn it, Malakai." Brave cut across the kitchen, glaring at the other man. "Don't do that to her. You were the one who always insisted on no pressure? She's just found her family."

"I know." Malakai backed away from her, letting his arms fall to his sides. "And even if she stays, I'll still love her." He looked at her again. "I'll still love you and I'll always come back to you. If you stay, you won't lose me."

"You won't lose either of us." Brave's expression softened. "Fuck, I know this is hard. I'm sorry."

"Don't apologize." Malakai's lips quirked slightly. "I don't need more flowers. The bus is full of them."

Shiori giggled, grateful that the tension had broken. She shook her head, shoving past all her uncertainty. "I'm coming with you."

Eyes wide, Malakai put his hands on her shoulders. "Brave's right. Don't decide because you feel pressured. I just wanted you to know, I want you to come."

"Perfect. Because I am." Damn, that felt good. And no less crazy than the first time she'd decided to leave home to join a metal band on tour. Only, this time, she knew exactly what she was in for. "I'm excited. And terrified. And a little homesick already. This has become my home in a way no place ever was."

"But you're still ready to leave?" Brave wrapped an arm around her side, his eyes searching her face. "Are you sure?"

"Yes. I loved the career I started building and I still want to do that. The music videos, the photo shoots, the endless days of traveling. I want to experience it all." She hugged Malakai, then Brave. "Being in love with you both made the decision a little easier. But then I'd get caught in a loop of choosing between you and Hiro and my grandparents. So I decided to be a little selfish. To consider what I want to do with my life."

"That's not selfish. That's what you should have been able to do all along." Brave picked her up abruptly, wrapping her legs around his waist. "I tried to enjoy this week and not think too hard about losing you, even for a little while. I gotta admit, Europe would have sucked without you."

"I second that." Malakai moved up behind her, lifting her hair over one shoulder and kissing along the side of her neck. "Now it's going to be fucking awesome."

Shiori moaned as Brave held her against him with one arm and somehow managed to undo her bra. "We've got a long flight tomorrow. Shouldn't we all get some sleep?"

"We can sleep on the plane." Brave sat her on the kitchen island and pulled her shirt over her head. "I need the woman and the man I love all to myself before I share you with the world."

Put that way, she didn't mind at all. Tonight, they would enjoy the last time they'd have alone for who knew how long. Winter's Wrath was still clawing its way to the top. The road would be rough, with challenges they hadn't even considered yet. But they were stronger than they'd ever been before.

The experiences she'd had with them already were incredible. She'd found her passion. Fallen in love.

And their journey had just begun.

The End

About the Author

Tell you about me? Hmm, well, there's not much to say. I love hockey and cars and my kids…not in that order, of course! Lol! When I'm not writing—which isn't often—I'm usually watching a game or a car show while networking. Going out with my kids is my only downtime. I get to clear my head and forget everything.

As for when and why I first started writing, I guess I thought I'd get extra cookies if I was quiet for a while—that's how young I was. I used to bring my grandmother barely legible pages filled with tales of evil unicorns. She told me then that I would be a famous author.

I hope one day to prove her right.

For more of my work, please visit:
www.Im-No-Angel.com

You can also find me on Facebook, and Twitter

Made in the USA
San Bernardino, CA
22 November 2017